What Goes Around

SYLVESTER YOUNG was born in the West Midlands, England of Jamaican parents and he trained as an engineer. After several trips back and forth to Canada for his employers, he now lives and works in Ontario.

What Goes Around is his stunning debut novel.

WHAT GOES AROUND

Sylvester Young

BLACKAMBER BOOKS

BLACKAMBER BOOKS

First published in 1999 by BlackAmber Books
PO Box 10812
London SW7 4ZG, England

Copyright © 1999 Sylvester Young
All rights reserved

The moral right of the author has been asserted.

All characters in this publication are fictitious,
and any resemblance to real persons, living or dead,
is purely coincidental.

A CIP Catalogue record for this book is available in The British Library
ISBN 1 901969 02 9

No part of this publication may be reproduced, stored in a retrieval system
or transmitted, in any form, or by any means, electrical, mechanical,
photocopying, recording or otherwise without prior permission
of the publishers.

Designed by Judith Gordon
Typeset in 10/13 Times
Printed and bound in Great Britain by Antony Rowe Ltd,
Chippenham, Wiltshire

This book is dedicated to the memories of
Oliver Pryce, Joy Gardener, Clinton McCurbin,
Richard O'Brien, Shiji Lapite,
Brian and Wayne Douglas, Leon Patterson,
Ibrahima Sey and many others.

Many thanks to Nana Yaa Mensah and Georgia de Chamberet for their encouragement. To Bernie Davis, Ken Gulak, Sandra Robb and Colum Hegarty.

A large dept of gratitude is owing to my friends in Ireland for their advice, support and help with the dialect and Gaelic, especially to Ger and Colum.

Prologue

LONG FINGERS COMBED the wispy fair hair. A pair of hard, deep-set eyes turned to the crumpled figure that was tethered to a chair in the middle of a bare room. Three men nonchalantly propped themselves against the crumbling wall and looked on, sometimes drawing on a shared cigarette. An interrogation was nearing its inevitable and bloody end.

Conrad 'Shaka' Williams was still unaware of his fate but the moment of terrible realisation was fast approaching. He had only a short time left before his face would finally come to rest on a strip of damp and grimy cobblestone, before a bullet to the back of his head would cease the rapid pounding of his heart.

Spasms of pain and the smell of his own fear had intermittently brought Shaka back to a dreadful reality. He did not know the men who growled at him from the surrounding darkness, nor what they wanted from him.

Precise gritty footsteps measured the perimeter of the dusty wooden floor as a voice hissed repeatedly that Shaka's crumbs of information were not enough. At first Shaka had roared defiantly as fists hammered at his flesh, but when the glowing end of a cigarette burrowed its way into the back of his neck he bawled out like a branded steer while the men laughed and told him to pray for deliverance.

Fear had turned the air into choking treacle; the ramshackle building creaked and groaned; the slow rhythmic paces on the bare boards were now the only measurements of time that Shaka cared about.

'Jesus Christ,' he groaned through bloodied lips. 'Please, man, please, I've told you everythin.'

'Oh no, you haven't. I want to hear all of it.'

Shaka swallowed. 'Please, man. I don't know what else to say.' He heard the footsteps quicken, come closer, and the man snarl, 'You stupid black bastard! You will tell me - you will beg for me to listen!'

A fist struck Shaka's face and blood filled his mouth. He fell back and the suffocating darkness enveloped him.

Two days after Christmas, in the dark hours of early morning, Shaka had tottered from a party, his bladder full and his senses dulled by rum and ganja smoke. He had intended to call on a woman who had borne him a son some years before, confident that she would be alone and able to provide what he wanted - but first he badly needed a piss. Rounding the corner of an alleyway, he was fumbling for his zip when he felt the presence of others close behind. He looked over his shoulder to see four white men and immediately knew that he was in danger. The tallest one stepped forward. 'Mr Williams?' he said. 'Or should I call you Shaka?'

Shaka's eyes widened with alarm. He thought they must be cops and was about to ask what they wanted when a blow from a short wooden club thudded against the side of his head. Shaka's legs gave way and he collapsed slowly like a crumbling chimney-stack amongst cartons and plastic bags full of rotting kitchen refuse. He looked for a means of escape but the tall man moved quickly and pinned him with a foot.

In the half-light, Shaka could see the man's thin lips curl with a cruel smile. He tried to shout for help but the party's thumping bass beat swamped his desperate cries. The shouting stopped with a second blow of the baton.

Shaka was jolted back into consciousness as he felt himself being thrust onto the back seat of a car. A man got in behind him. A door slammed, another one opened and a blast of cold air hit Shaka in the face as a hand grabbed at his short locks and raised his head. A second man sat in and thrust Shaka's face into a lap that smelt of stale urine and lightly scented soap. Cold metal stroked the back of Shaka's neck and the man said, 'Keep quiet.'

That had been the beginning of the nightmare, thought Shaka.

And was brought back by a jolt of pain as his chair was hauled into an upright position. A hand rested on his bowed head and a new voice came out from the darkness. 'Conrad - Shaka - can you hear me?'

The new voice was sharp, cultured and impatient. When he made no response, a finger lifted Shaka's chin. 'We need to talk about your friends Errol Morgan and Gilbert Peters - I think you called him "Animal".'

'Hanimal, we call him Hanimal.'

'Quite. Now, the only way I can stop these gentlemen from doing terrible things to you is if you answer three very straightforward questions. All they require is a simple yes or no. Do you understand?'

'Yeah.'

'You were involved in what they were doing, weren't you?'

'You're not gonna hurt me…'

'Answer my questions and I give you my word that no one will hurt you. You were involved with them, weren't you?'

'A lickle bit. I didn't hardly do nothin.'

'Yes or no I said.'

'Yeah, but–'

'Was anyone else involved? Yes or no, Conrad.'

'Nah, it jus them two.'

'Gilbert told us that you were the one who showed them how to make things. Where did you get that information? Was it while you were in prison?'

'Yeah, yeah, Jesus Christ, yeah. I'm hurt bad, man, can you get me to a doctor?'

'In a while.'

Shaka heard the man move away from him and whisper before two pairs of booted feet came close. His bound wrists were released from the back of the chair and for a brief moment Shaka thought his agonies were at an end. He tried to focus on the shapes in front of him and said, 'Which station are you tekin me to? I ain't mekin no statement widdout a brief.'

The new voice said, 'My, my, you have perked up all of a sudden.

Whatever gave you the idea that we were members of Her Majesty's Constabulary? Surely we weren't *that* rough.'

Shaka's throat tightened. 'Then who the fuck - what's this all about?' he squeaked. 'Wha happen to Errol an' Hanimal?'

The man answered, 'What I can tell you is that you will be joining them very soon and all your troubles will be over.'

Shaka struggled to free his arms but he was easily subdued by the fist that was driven into his unprepared midriff. The voice became excited. 'The last time I saw Errol Morgan he was lying in a country lane looking up at the stars. Peters was still in the car as it burst into flames. I heard him scream. Two victims of what will look like a tragic accident.'

Powerful fingers gripped Shaka and pulled him outside. The light shone through his swollen lids and it dawned on Shaka what was about to happen. He felt his bowels loosen. 'Hey! Hey!' he panted. 'Me jus remember. Please, me–'

A gag turned Shaka's pleading into muffled screams moments before he was thrown into the boot of a car. The slamming of the lid echoed in the crisp morning air.

Terror became fluid and warmed his legs as he heard the cultivated voice say, 'Take the black piece of filth back to the alleyway where you found him and do it there. One more dead nigger around those parts will not count for much.'

Belfast, 28 February 1994
A month after the killings of Shaka, Errol and Hanimal, an unseasonably warm sun cheered the women who made their way along a Belfast street. They chatted and laughed as they flitted between shops while their children played around them. On drawing level with a pub that had seen much better days, a car slowed down and allowed a rusty blue van to pull out and provide a parking space. A casual thumbs-up from the departing driver signalled that a deadly countdown was in motion.

A young black-haired man swaggered along the pavement with a rolled-up newspaper in his hand. He let the glowing remains of a cigarette fall to the ground and went into the bar. A man on the back seat of the car said, 'That's McGrady. Let's make this a tidy one.'

Hardly a head turned as the door of the bar swung open and two strangers entered. Most eyes were fixed on the television that was spewing out the hysterics of a final furlong. McGrady was in a corner talking to a taller man of around his own age. Hughie Maguire, an old man, short and rotund, moved away from the counter with a glass in his hand and looked out towards the open door. Instinctive bravery made him shuffle sideways to put himself between the man who was talking to Anthony McGrady and the AK-47 which was pointing in his direction.

A final thumping heartbeat. A thunderous and terrible noise. Within an instant four bullets had torn into the aged body. The old man cried out, squawked, as he spun to the floor. Blood and slivers of shredded tissue splashed against the counter. More bullets from the Kalashnikov found McGrady before the old man had completed his descent.

The AK-47 then turned rapidly towards the television and the men who had thrown themselves to the floor. Those who were not hit lay amongst the dying, their shaking limbs soaked in the blood of their friends, their quivering lips mouthing a prayer.

The gunman made his way across the red and sopping linoleum to the body of Anthony McGrady. In different circumstances he would have taken his Browning pistol from his waistband and put a 9mm bullet between the vacant eyes just to make sure, to make things tidy. He bent down for a closer look, and prising a betting slip from the dead man's fingers he murmured, 'All bets are off.'

Belfast, twenty months later
Turlough stroked the silver stubble on his chin and said, 'You can make the break - that way you're assured of at least one shot. I think everybody is entitled to one shot.'

Danny Maguire bent his tall frame over the billiards table and let out a dry snorting laugh. He spent the following ten minutes sipping at a glass of stout and chalking his cue as he watched the old man make most of the red balls disappear into the pockets. 'That's a pint you owe me,' said Turlough as the pink rattled in the jaws of a corner pocket.

Danny Maguire chuckled. 'You still have the touch,' he said, putting his cue back into the rack.

'Hah, I'm not a patch on the player your da was, God rest his soul.' On seeing Danny's hand tighten around the cue Turlough added, 'I'm sorry, son, I know it still hurts.'

'And why shouldn't it hurt? He was my da for nearly thirty years; he's been dead two - that only leaves another twenty-eight.'

'You mightn't have to wait that long for it to stop hurting.'

'You reckon?'

'If the bastards who did it were brought to account it might ease the pain for you and your family.'

'Ach, there's no chance of that happening, now is there?'

'There might be a chance, right enough. That's why I asked you here.' Turlough walked over to a small round table and then beckoned for Danny to join him with a brusque waft of a leathered hand. As Danny sat down, a bearded round-faced man appeared and settled into the third chair. He unzipped his jacket and stretching out a leg he said, 'Danny.'

'Martin. 'Bout ye.'

'I have some news that might be of interest to you, Danny. Turlough, how about if you go and find us some liquid refreshment?'

Danny Maguire watched the old man make his way to the bar through layers of wavy blue smoke. He looked back to Martin. 'So, what's the score?' he asked.

'The score remains six-nil. Your da, my brother, young Barry Smyth, Peter Ryan, Seamus Mulholland, wee Mickey McKenna. I make that six-fucking-nil.' Martin McGrady picked up a beer mat and began to turn it between his thumb and forefinger; each quarter revolution was signalled by a tap on the tabletop. 'But I'm after coming by some information that could help to even up the score.'

'I'm listening.'

'As you had suspected, they were not killed by any of the usual death squads; it was a band of Brit agents who carried out the slaughter. They wanted my brother Anthony. I can't go into the whys and hows here, but what I can tell you is that we have a strong notion about their identities and where they are. Still listening?'

'Aye. Get on with it, will ye.'

'They happen to be in a part of Britland that you know well. I believe you still have friends there - wasn't one of them with you during a rare trip home a few years ago? See, Danny, I cannot rest while that slime, and I mean slime, is still breathing. I want them stiffed. I want them left riddled with bullets, the way they left your da and my brother. I was wondering, Danny, wondering if you were feeling in a similar way.'

'And how did you find all this out, all of a sudden - their identities and that?'

'You know me, Danny. You know my comrades. And you know we're not dealing in shite. Since the ceasefire was called the Brits haven't stopped waging their dirty war and they are the ones behind a plan to flood this town with the drugs that could destabilise our community. We have good reason to believe that the bastards who killed your da and my brother are involved in some of the dirty deeds that are going on at the minute. That's some of the story. Straight to the point, if we are to take them out we will need someone who knows their territory. Now, are you in or are you out?'

'In.'

'Then you'll know where to come tomorrow night, eight o'clock.'

'Eight o'clock.'

Turlough returned with a round metal tray and three glasses swimming in spilt beer. 'Where's Martin?'

'He had to go.'

The old man smiled at the third glass and said, 'Would be a pity to waste it.' He took a drink. With his eyes scanning the younger man he began to talk of his pride in having Martin McGrady as a son-in-law; he was a good husband to Siobhan and a good father to the twins. 'But I see the hurt in him, Danny, I see the poison too. It will have to come out before it destroys him and those around him. He's after telling me of a way to get rid of that poison. Are you interested?'

'I could be.'

'Then you take it, son. Me and your da were the best of friends, and I have known you since the day you were born. I can see the same poison in you and I hate what it's doing to you young fellas. You have to cleanse it from your system. If you can't forgive and forget then you get even.'

Danny Maguire took a sip of his drink and pulled a face as though he did not enjoy the taste. 'I intend to. Like you say, everybody is entitled to at least one shot.'

1

THE MUD SQUELCHED beneath my frozen feet; I had never felt so cold or miserable. The mud squelched beneath my frozen feet, the minister droned on, and an icy wind scattered the amens of those of us who stood around the coffin like the dead leaves which tumbled over the green grass.

To the whimpering women behind me the Errol Morgan who had died at the age of twenty-nine would forever remain a cute, if mischievous, little brother. On the other side of the coffin the mother of two of Errol's children wailed hysterically. The little girls looked up at Beverley with dry and uncomprehending eyes. Within Beverley's tormented shrieks I could hear her pleas for answers: what would she do, now so many hopes for her future had abruptly turned into a pile of rotting flesh in a shiny wooden box? A short but discreet distance away stood Carmen Swaby and her son Tim. She was silent and dignified, tall and beautiful; while the boy, who reminded me so much of his father, acted bored with the whole proceedings.

I blew into my cupped hands and cast a resentful eye over those who were huddled farthest away. Why had they bothered to come out in such foul weather? To most of them Errol was only a deejay who played nice music, a local celebrity, a man with a reputation. But there was more to Errol Morgan than that. So much more than they could ever know.

The smell of damp earth drew my gaze back to the grave. It was not only the cutting wind that made me shiver; within a few minutes the broken body of my friend would be devoured by the earth and I would be left all alone to face the consequences of our actions.

Like Beverley, I too had been left with many unanswered questions. What were Errol and Hanimal doing in a dark and twisting country lane miles from home? Had it really been nothing more than a simple road accident, or was the shooting of Shaka Williams - that had followed only hours later - linked to their deaths? It was something like a mathematical problem: I knew the result - three dead men - but I knew only a part of the equation.

Shaka was the one who had supplied Errol with the telephone number of the man called the Field Marshal. I had never trusted Shaka and when I heard that he had been found face-down with his brains splattered all over a grimy alleyway a perverse sense of relief came over me. He had known too much about what Errol and I had done.

The coffin came to its final resting place with a gentle thud that made me turn my eyes away and catch sight of Danny Maguire. He stood head and shoulders over those gathered close to him; his normally thick and wavy black hair was wet and plastered to his scalp. Our eyes met and I wondered for a moment if he had been reading my thoughts. His expression gave nothing away. In all the time I had known him I was never sure which of his utterances were down to his Belfast brand of cynicism and which were professions of cherished principles. He was the one person who really knew of what I, Robbie Walker, had done with Errol; I had needed to tell someone.

Cold rain started to fall again. The minister's droning halted abruptly. Someone nudged my elbow. A man thrust the handle of a spade into my hand while another peeled away a piece of green nylon carpet to expose a mound of sodden orange clay. 'If you would be kind enough to make a start,' said the minister.

I pushed the spade into the clay and my face grew warm as I stamped on the blade. I was angry with Errol, angry that he had died, angry that he had left me. I cursed him viciously from under my breath and hurled a clump of earth onto the coffin's lid. There was a look of bewilderment on the minister's face as he reclaimed the spade, while some of the mourners craned their necks to see if the coffin's lid had remained intact. I turned for the cemetery gates and glanced over at Danny; there had not been even the slightest flicker in his stony expression and I flashed a grim smile at him.

Leaning against a wall I tried to come to terms with never seeing Errol again. I looked out to the traffic and people passing by and resented their movement, their indifference.

I had known Errol since we were both eight years old, and although he had been fifteen days older than me I had often thought of him as a troublesome younger brother. The last time I had seen him alive was as we sat in his car which was parked outside my house. His head in his hands he moaned, 'We're in shit, Robbie, big shit.'

I dug my thumb deep into his shoulder in the hope that the pain would distract him from any thought which might weaken his resolve. It was the first time in the twenty-one years I had known Errol that he had allowed his mask of bravado to slip. I shook him and he looked up at me. I said, 'Get your mind right, E. You see Shaka tonight. Cuss him, pretend to be vexed, an' say there was no answer on that number he gave you. Make out we never got to arrange any meetin. Right?'

His eyes began to clear and then he said, 'Yeah. Hey yeah, that way he'll think we never reached that guy.'

'Exactly. Keep to that story an' everythin is cool. Remember what Bubby used to tell us when we were trainin: discipline is everythin. Stay disciplined, guy, an' we're safe.'

Three days later Errol, Hanimal and Shaka were dead.

A hand rested on my shoulder. I turned and said, 'Danny, we need to talk.'

'Do you fancy coming for a wee gargle then?'

'No, I've got things to do.'

'Are we still on for decorating your place tomorrow?'

'Yeah, I've got everythin but the paste.'

'Right, I'll bring my brushes around tomorrow morning and we'll make a start on giving that wee boy of yours a house to be proud of. We'll have time enough to talk then. Just you make sure to have plenty of spuds and cabbage and a nice piece of bacon. I don't want you feeding me any ackee and saltfish shite.'

A laugh escaped from my taut lips and he turned and walked away. After a short distance he stopped and shouted back to me but the wind was buffeting my ears and I did not catch what he had said. He waved and I saw him laugh. I raised a hand and called, 'Tomorrow.'

Two years later
The recent redundancies made by the management had cast a dark cloud over the factory where I worked as a maintenance fitter. During midmorning tea break, I dropped into the canteen and felt relieved to see Fidel sat playing a game of chess with Mr Robinson at the table known to most of us as 'Little Cuba'.

An unfamiliar face in a navy-blue suit watched me as I sat down. I did not know the tall man with thinning blond hair but he had a vulturine look about him. I let my expression show him that I did not appreciate his stare until Fidel, his thoughts elsewhere, asked me, 'So how was your weekend?'

'Not bad,' I said.

Mr Robinson laughed dirtily as he repeated what I had said and moved a pawn. 'Oi, Fidel, man,' he said, 'I think you were right - Robbie has found 'imself a woman.'

Ignoring their knowing smiles I hungrily devoured a sandwich. I let a mouthful of tea wash it down and thought about changing the subject. 'It doesn't seem the same without Greg,' I said in a manner I knew would irritate Fidel.

'Silly bugger,' he said sharply, looking up after taking a pawn with a bishop. 'What the hell did he expect would happen when a woman of twenty stones or more is squatting on top of a glass coffee table? I heard the one piece of glass went straight through his jugular.'

Mr Robinson lifted his old leather cap and clawed at his head of silver hair. 'Mi ras,' he grumbled as if profoundly troubled by either the loss of his pawn or the vision his old friend's words had conjured. 'What a way to go, killed by a dutty great battyhole.'

The three of us laughed loudly above the clatter of cutlery and immediately drew admonishing glances from the surrounding tables. It was not that our fellow diners were grieving for Greg, the derisory amount collected for his widow was an indicator of how quickly the shop floor's loosely-woven camaraderie was unravelling. For weeks the talk in the factory had been of the impending 'downsizing' of the workforce by the new management. 'What the fuck they lookin at?' I hissed from between my teeth. 'You warned them what would happen if they voted for this so-called workers' council instead of a proper union.'

Mr Robinson nodded in agreement.

'It's not as simple as that, Robbie,' Fidel sighed. 'The new crowd had made it plain that there would have to be lay-offs when they bought this place. I doubt if the union could have made a much better deal in the circumstances.'

'But you could see what was goin on and got people organised before it happened,' I protested.

He leaned back in his chair. 'And I'll tell you what would've happened if me or Cecil here had asked them to hit the gate. Most of them would've turned around and told us that we were two sad old gits looking for one last scrap with the management before we retired. They would've called us trouble-making bastards who had nothing to lose. It would've been like leading the Charge of the bloody Light Brigade. And that unctuous git Ken Barker wouldn't have been the only one doing his best to undermine any action.'

Mr Robinson moved a rook. Fidel frowned, leaned forward and muttered to himself. I wanted to continue to press my point that the new owners should not have been allowed to put so many men out of work without a fight, but it was unwise to interrupt their daily game, even though it rarely ended in either victory or defeat.

I looked around for the tall man in the suit but he had disappeared and so my gaze returned to the board and I thought about how weary both men had sounded. And then, for the first time, I noticed a fragility about their gnarled hands. It was at that moment it registered with me how much they had changed since the day I had entered the factory as an innocent fresh-faced kid. It was a strange and unsettling moment. They had been two of my constant points in a fast-changing world for almost sixteen years. But now I saw how the lines on Fidel's long lean face had deepened, how the tired flesh hung loosely around his throat.

I had thought I would not last a day, the factory complex seemed so vast, so much bigger than school. The incessant sound of crashing metal set my young nerves jangling; the language of the older men sounded so aggressive and threatening. In those first few weeks in the big bad world Fidel and Mr Robinson adopted me, made me their son for eight hours a day, five days of the week and the occasional weekend fishing trip.

I did not understand everything that Jack Reardon had said to me back then because of his strange accent. I thought he was called Fidel because he really was from Cuba and not because of his political disposition. My face still warmed when I recalled his puzzled expression as I asked him about Cuba. 'Sorry, kid,' he said, 'I haven't got a clue. I'm from Sunderland, me.'

At least I didn't make a mistake about Mr Robinson's origins. He was from Jamaica and sounded like it despite living in England for almost forty years. His waist and the lenses of his spectacles had got a little thicker over the years but he still had the look of a raffish dandy with his silk cravat, carefully trimmed moustache and a wedge of hair under his lower lip.

A sadness touched my heart as I thought about their approaching retirement and how my time with them was running out like grains of sand through my grasping fingers.

Mr Robinson abruptly turned my mind to other matters when he asked me, 'Who do you think will win the fight at the Town Hall tonight?'

'Aye,' said Fidel, 'what do you think of this Palmer kid?'

The siren sounded and the thunder of chairs moving across the floor gave me a few moments to consider a reply. As the three of us made our way out of the canteen I said, 'I think Burley will be too much for Palmer right now. If they were fightin in another twelve months it might turn out different but Burley should stop him in seven or eight.'

'Right,' said Mr Robinson, 'so are we gonna see you up at the Town Hall later on?'

'Er, nah,' I said hesitantly.

He laughed that dirty laugh again. 'Wha we seh, Jack? We said he find imself another woman at last. Only a woman could stop him goin to a fight. It's as simple as that.'

It wasn't that simple, it wasn't simple at all. As I walked to her front door I still wasn't sure if I was doing the right thing. The seed of doubt which normally resided in the back of my mind felt as though it had descended to my stomach and was beginning to germinate. Of all the women in the world, why did I have to start a relationship with Carmen Swaby?

'Hi,' I said and moved awkwardly to kiss her.

Carmen stepped back into her hallway and raising her hands, which were dusted with flour, she said, 'Watch these!' Then softening her voice she added, 'The lounge.'

She had me confused again. It was not the first time she had reacted so coolly towards me. I followed her to the L-shaped room and thought about the last night we had spent together. As I had drifted into a contented sleep she had asked me how many women I had slept with. Drowsily I raised a hand and said, 'Less than the fingers on this hand.' She turned and put a space between us. I knew my reply had not made her happy but I did not know why.

I caught her scent and knew then that I did want her - but just her and not all the complication. As I entered the lounge I saw my son Nathan sitting next to Duane on the threadbare sofa. The two seven-year-olds looked distressed and at first I thought they had been fighting but then I saw Tim slouching in an armchair and Carmen's brother Tyrone standing over him. 'What's goin on?' I asked.

Tyrone, broad and brooding, didn't bother to turn to look at me. 'Arks Tim,' he snarled.

'Duane got all upset in the park,' explained Carmen. 'Him an' Nathan thought that somebody pulled a knife on them.'

All eyes turned to Tim. The boy, only twelve years old, coolly put a piece of gum into his mouth and chewed noisily while gazing at me with eyes full of disdain. 'Tim!' barked Carmen. 'Tell us everythin that happen. Now!'

Throwing a leg over an armrest, Tim explained how he had taken the two younger boys to play on the swings. They hadn't been long in the park when an older youth on a bike tried to sell him the knife; Duane must have thought it had been produced as some sort of threat. 'Nex ting me know, Duane an' Nathan start to run 'way bawlin them heads off. That's all that happen, right. I was just tellin the guy that I don't deal with them sort-a tings when them two start screamin. Didn't I do right, Mom?'

'Well yeah,' said Carmen.

Tyrone bristled. 'I can't believe you're swallowin this shit! We all know what kind-a business goes on in the park. Carmen, don't you hear how him lie?'

'Oi, don't come round my yard callin my son a liar,' she warned her brother. She turned and asked me, 'Do you think Tim could lie about somethin serious like that?'

Tyrone, or Tariq as he now called himself, hated my guts and I doubted if he wanted me backing him up; Carmen was already on the defensive and didn't look ready to hear a truthful answer. I had seen enough of Tim to know that he had inherited two of his father's traits: deceitfulness and a talent to manipulate.

I thought it better to say nothing and Tyrone muttered something in my direction through his untidy beard before he gestured for Duane to stand up. He put an arm around his son and said to Carmen, 'Don't seh no one never warn you.' He shot a sideways glance at me and continued, 'Sis, you should find yuhself a man who will speak up for the truth, a man who can give the boy some discipline, some guidance. I wonder what Errol would-a said if he was still around. Don't you ever wonder 'bout the same sort-a tings, Robbie?'

A contemptuous chuckle funnelled through his nose as he brushed past me. The front door slammed and Carmen turned her eyes to the ceiling. Without looking at him, she said to Tim, 'Go tidy your room, an' take Nathan with you.'

He slowly rolled out of the armchair and Nathan gaped at me open-mouthed until I tersely ordered him out. Once we were alone she said to me, 'I'm sorry about all that. I'm sure Tim wouldn't –'

'No one got hurt - maybe the kids just took things the wrong way an' got frightened,' I said impatiently. An uneasy silence followed for we both knew that Tyrone had obliterated any concern about what had happened in the park when he had conjured up and put a name to the unspoken anxiety we shared. She moved to come close but stopped. She tried to speak but only grimaced. Finally she said, 'I've got to cancel tonight, I have to go to the "Justice for Mark Finn" meetin. It's a last-minute ting, the police are tryna pull some skank with the inquest.'

'That's fine with me,' I said.

She flinched on hearing the sourness in my voice. 'Why don't you come with me?' she asked.

'I've got better things to do with my time. The fact that there's gotta be a campaign should tell you that there ain't no justice for guys like him.'

She stepped closer and briefly touched my arm. I brushed specks of flour from my coat and she smiled as if she had guessed what my reaction would be. 'You got good intention, Carmen,' I said, 'but you ain't dealin with reality.'

Her small smile made me want to kiss her lips but she turned her face away with the sound of a door opening. Nathan was in the doorway pleading with his eyes for me to take him to my mother's. 'Okay,' I said, 'we're goin now.'

Carmen laughed quietly to herself and dabbed a finger onto my nose. 'I'm sorry I have to go to this meetin,' she said. 'Give me a call tomorrow, all right?'

I said, 'Maybe.'

She crinkled her still smiling lips. I took Nathan by the hand and she said, 'Stop tryin to be so macho, it doesn't suit you. Call me tomorrow, okay?'

As I drove to my mother's house I stopped at a red light and turned to ask Nathan if he was all right; I still wasn't sure what to make of Tim's story of what happened in the park. Nathan nodded and frowned quizzically as if he had already forgotten his frightening experience. 'Dad,' he called from the back seat, 'you got white on your nose.'

I wiped away the flour as the lights turned green and I felt confident that nothing of lasting harm had occurred. It was a sign of what was happening on the Blackmore estate that the less dangerous sort of youths now often carried knives.

Further along the road I caught sight of Tyrone marching towards the park with Duane reluctantly in tow. I could almost hear Tyrone barking questions at his child about the youth who had produced a knife.

As I had found out over the years, Tyrone was one for retribution. He had once worked at the factory but after failing to get promoted he got himself fired because of an altercation with the new supervisor. Tyrone no longer considered me a friend because I did not share either his anger regarding his dismissal or his conviction that he had been right to smear the man's nose all over his face.

I wasn't surprised when Carmen told me that he had joined the Brothers of Islam - they seemed well suited. From what I had heard they were angry young men who were also convinced of the right to use physical force when confronting what they perceived as injustice.

That night I dreamt of walking along a dark and twisting country lane. A scraping noise drew me to a field of grey grass where I saw Tyrone frantically hacking at the earth with a shovel. I wanted to run away but my feet were stuck to the ground and I looked on helplessly as Errol's face began to slowly emerge from the loosened soil. I called out for him to stop but Tyrone took no notice and he lifted Errol's hollow corpse to show me the rotting remains of the three men that lay beneath a churning mass of bloated black beetles.

Tyrone laughed maniacally as he pointed an accusing finger at me. 'Robbie,' he roared, 'I know that you put them there!'

2

BARELY ABLE TO lift my hot and leaden feet I traipsed over to Little Cuba and flopped onto a chair. 'The very man,' said Fidel. 'We've some news for you, my son.'

'Is that right?' I replied without interest.

'Are you okay, Robbie? You look bloody knackered.'

'I didn't get much sleep last night, that's all.'

Mr Robinson took my reply as a cue to let out a deep gravelly laugh. 'I don't know who or what was keepin you awake,' he teased me, 'but you missed a great fight last night. An' you wasn't too far wrong. No, not far wrong at all. Palmer knocked Burley down in the third but he couldn't answer the bell for the seventh. You did say Burley would win in the seventh or eighth, didn't you?'

'I think you'll find that will go down in the record books as a TKO in round six, but you know that already,' I said.

Fidel wriggled on his seat and said sternly, 'Never mind the fight, I might've told you wrong yesterday about there being no action around here. Last week they laid off fifty men and now it looks like they've just employed as many security guards. There's more blokes in uniforms in here than in a bloody army barracks.'

I had already seen them. Previously there had only been two kind souls to take dockets from lorry drivers arriving at the main gate but the new security personnel were quite different. The newcomers were younger and looked much fitter; their straight backs and the way they pulled the peaks of their caps over their eyes bestowed on them a stern military demeanour. 'And I've just been told there are sparkies running cables for CCTV all over the place,' Fidel continued. 'CCTV, for

Christ's sake! Something dodgy is going on but that slimy toad Barker isn't letting on a thing. He's still giving the blokes this old bollocks about how it was all in the new work practices agreement.'

The lack of concern in my tired eyes brought a sigh from his lips which then curled sagely into a smile. He gestured for me to look to a far corner of the canteen with a tilt of his head and whispered, 'And I see your mates have honoured us with their presence once again.'

Sitting at a table were six sullen-looking men who were not regular visitors to the canteen. 'Go on,' chuckled Mr Robinson, 'give Kyle a wave. Better still, blow im a kiss.'

'Not now,' I said. 'He told me he wants to keep our love affair a secret.'

Fidel laughed loudly and confused me: nothing I had said was that funny. Mr Robinson slapped the table and joined in with the uproarious laughter. Despite the suspicion that the joke was on me I laughed too. 'You've just been givin me crap about the cameras, right?' I said to Fidel.

His happy bellowing faded to a rueful chuckle. ''Fraid not, Robbie, you'll see it all for yourself soon enough.'

'Guess where you is headin after the break,' wheezed Mr Robinson. 'Me hear them have annoda breakdown in that lickle hideout out the back an' you is just the man to fix it.'

The 'hideout' was a small workshop at the rear of the main factory building. The six men had appeared not long after the factory had changed hands and it was rumoured that they were working on a range of prototype hydraulic valves away from prying eyes.

Fidel leant forward and murmured, 'Robbie, see if you can find out any info about what those fuckers are doing when you're in there. I've a hunch that whatever they're up to is linked with all this new security business that's going on.'

I caught the smell of strong tea off his stained teeth before I looked again to the corner table and the heavy man with the permanent scowl. Even though he had never introduced himself, we called him Kyle because that was the name etched on his thick arm under a tattoo of the

Red Hand of Ulster. As if by some sixth sense, he lifted his broad bald head and pierced the rows of hunched shoulders between us with a withering stare. Trying to show that I was not intimidated I took my time turning my head back towards Fidel. 'You mean like last time?' I said, referring to my one and only previous encounter with Kyle some six weeks before.

A drive belt had needed replacing. 'Shouldn't take long,' Kyle had growled impatiently. Normally someone telling me how to do my job is the one thing that gets me pissed off but I ignored him and got on with my work in my own sweet time. 'Will you be much longer?' he asked as I knelt down to put the machine's cover back on.

I told him I was nearly finished and thinking that I had detected an accent, and just to make conversation, I asked him if he was Irish. An answer wasn't forthcoming so I got on with what I had to do while figuring he hadn't heard me. Once the cover was on I stood up and turned to see his darkening face coming close to mine. 'So there's no misunderstanding,' he spat, 'if you ever call me Irish again I will rip off your balls and stuff them in that stupid black mouth of yours.'

My back against the machine, I arched my spine and pulled my head away while trying to catch my breath. Eyes full of spite bore into me as he shuffled closer. It was then I noticed the scar tissue around his left eye and the bridge of his nose. In that instant I concluded he was the sort of man who wore such marks of battle proudly. One of his colleagues, an athletic type who wore tinted spectacles, called to Kyle to back off. He stepped away but continued to threaten. 'Listen, jungle boy, I'm an Ulsterman, a British Ulsterman and if you want to keep houl of your bollocks make sure you don't forget it.'

Later on, after telling Mr Robinson of what had happened, I began to angrily curse my legs that were still twitching nervously. And then I asked myself, Who was this guy and what sort of man was I to let him get away with threatening me like that?

I picked up a wrench with the intention of re-entering the small workshop to give Kyle a smack when Mr Robinson barred my way and reminded me of what had happened to Tyrone. I snarled at him that there were more important things than a weekly pay packet. The man had abused and humiliated me and I was going to reclaim my dignity. Mr Robinson grabbed hold of me as I tried to pass him. 'Go in there an' you hurt more than him. Do you unnerstan how many of us you will hurt as well?'

Mr Robinson was a man too proud to beg but that was the nearest I had known him come to pleading - not for himself, or me, but for the 'us' he referred to. A message shone through the thick lenses of his spectacles and suddenly I felt like a foolish schoolboy who had been asked to explain why he had not paid attention in class. I handed him the wrench and he said, 'Thank you.'

Rather than let my wounded pride fester, Fidel and Mr Robinson leached the poison from my system by continually immersing the affair in a constant flow of banter. Within a week I was finding my solitary interaction with the Ulsterman a source of amusement, but I sometimes imagined that if I had made the same sort of innocent remark in another time and place Kyle would have gladly tried to do me serious harm.

His belligerence had caught me offguard. Up until that moment - with the notable exception of the incident which had led to Tyrone's dismissal - I had allowed myself to be lulled into thinking of the factory, parochial and insulated as it was, as a pocket of tolerance in an otherwise noxious environment. It was Kyle's disregard for that unwritten rule of tolerance which I had found most startling. I couldn't put a number to the various nationalities and races within the factory walls but, if only to ensure the smooth and safe running of the plant, it was normal practice for the workers to exercise at least a modicum of tolerance towards their colleagues.

After break I pushed open the door of the small workshop and took a deep breath before entering what I felt certain would be a miasma of hot machine oil and simmering contempt. Kyle was not among the four men who had gathered around a lathe and I breathed a little easier until I caught the sharp odour of cutting fluid. One of the men squinted at me as he took a last draw of a cigarette. He let the glowing remains fall to the floor and wandered over to show me the machine that had malfunctioned. The man was not unfriendly and I was pleasantly surprised to find that someone had taken the trouble to sweep away the sharp metal cuttings from around the area in which I had to work.

I got down to make the repair but I remained uneasy and mindful of the likelihood of Kyle coming through the door at any moment. It was only when I started whistling that I realized what was also putting me on edge. It was the silence: they had switched off all the machines.

Once I had finished I stood up and wiped my hands with a rag. I looked over at the four men and, thinking they must have witnessed what had happened the last time I had fixed one of their machines, I felt the need to reassert my machismo. 'Don't stop what you're doin on my account,' I called out sarcastically.

One of them blew smoke from a dented nose. 'No problem, mate,' he said, 'we've been having a smoke and taking it in turns to go and have a shit while you were busy.'

The man did not sound like a local and, heedful of Fidel's request for information, I took a chance. 'Yeah, you might as well have a shit when the gaffers are payin for it. Have you guys been transferred from another factory or somethin?'

He crinkled his lips and made a half-smile as if to say: Don't push it. I've given you a few friendly words, now hurry up and piss off.

Two of his colleagues continued to look over at me with harsh impatient eyes but I took my time, wiping my tools clean before putting them back into the box. As discreetly as I could, I scanned the workshop for any clue about what they were making. All I saw was steel in various shapes and sizes but there were no signs of a finished product.

'All done?' a voice from behind asked me. I turned to see the tall man in the navy-blue suit who I had noticed in the canteen the day before. Kyle was with him.

'Hello, Paddy,' I said. 'You must be working these machines too hard.'

He lurched towards me but this time I did not flinch. 'So, you're after forgetting what I told you, you stupid black cunt, you.'

The tall man spun around and jabbed a finger towards Kyle's face. 'You!' he shouted. 'Shut it!'

The burly Ulsterman bared his teeth but thought better of making any reply. A whip had been cracked and Kyle reluctantly retreated in the manner a hungry lion would back away from its tamer, biding its time. I watched him join the other men and said, 'I can fight my own battles.'

The tall man replied, 'I'm sure you can.' He laughed quietly. 'But I feel I should warn you that where he comes from they call him "Kyle the Killer". It wouldn't be wise to provoke him.' He stared down at my toolbox and murmured, 'Tidy, very tidy. It's a sign of discipline, the sign of a man who's good at his job.' He looked into my face and without shifting his gaze he called out to the man with the dented nose, 'Chopper, go and open the door for this man. He has a heavy toolbox to carry. He's finished here now.'

Carmen stretched and breathed softly. 'Are you all right, love?' she asked as she rolled over towards me.

I was staring up at the light from the street which had cast strange shadows onto her bedroom ceiling. 'Yeah,' I said.

'You're not very talkative. I like how you talk to me in bed. I was...'

'Talkative compared to who?' I asked coolly.

Carmen stiffened. I sensed her alarm before she shifted the leg which had rested on mine and moved away from me. 'I don't make comparisons,' she said sharply.

She got out of bed and a draught of cold air pressed against my damp skin. 'I'm gettin myself a drink, do you want one?' she asked, wrapping a dressing gown around her nakedness. 'No,' I answered as I watched her tall slender shape move through the light and into the darkness of the landing.

The skin on my leg tingled. I pulled at the bedclothes and covered myself while thinking that I *did* make comparisons - and no one I had lain next to compared to Carmen, not even Sharon, the mother of my child. And although I felt warm and safe when I was with Carmen I sometimes thought that our love would be transient and fleeting; that someone, or something, would spring from the shadows to bring our happiness to an abrupt halt.

I knew that there were occasions when Carmen felt the same way, that she had often drawn a breath as if she were about to voice the fear we shared. But I had never made it easy for her and she had always stopped herself before smiling sadly or kissing me tenderly. I figured that some things are best left unsaid, that a trouble shared is sometimes a trouble doubled.

What I had said had provoked Carmen and I pictured her downstairs trying to compose herself. She would come back with a drink in her hand and a determination to speak the words neither of us wanted to hear.

The door closed with a sharp click. Carmen stood clasping a wine glass close to her chest just as I had imagined she would. She sat down on the corner of the bed nearest the door and bowed her head. For a time she did nothing but run a finger around the rim of her glass. I listened to the sound of her breathing as I knew she was listening to mine. She turned her head; the light from the street caught her eyes. 'We can't go on like this. We need to talk about somethin, Robbie.' There was a catch in her voice which she tried to clear before she added, 'We need to talk about the past, about what Tyrone said.'

'No! We had an agreement. I don't wanna hear who you garn-a bed with an' I ain't gonna talk the same way. That was the agreement, right? Was that the agreement?'

She looked to the glass on her lap. 'Not former lovers, Robbie, *a* former lover. He wasn't even that. Me an' Errol made a baby when we were both kids, before either of us had any sense to know better.'

Without realizing it, Carmen was showing me the exit and I could now pretend that leaving had nothing to do with all the doubts and anxiety inside of me. I got out of bed and hurriedly began to dress myself.

'What are you doin?' she gasped.

'What it look like? We had an agreement an' you brek the agreement so me garn.'

She stood up. Her face expressed her thoughts: disbelief and then anger that I was acting like every other man she had ever known. And I was supposed to have been so different.

'No, Robbie,' she cried out, 'I don't believe you're doin this because I want to talk about Errol. He was your best friend.'

'That's exactly why I'm out of here.'

'But the past is why the two of us are in this room at this very moment. This present is the sum total of every second that's gone before. You can't pretend the past never happen.'

I groped around the floor for my shoes determined not to say another word because in my heart I knew I had no argument with Carmen. When I found my shoes I did not bother to undo my laces, I simply flattened the backs and forced my feet inside. I moved towards the door and she said, 'I'm not beggin you, Robbie, but please stay tonight an' we'll sort things out in the mornin.'

There was no time for even a last goodbye; I knew if I paused for just a moment I would not be able to leave. I hurried down the stairs. Carmen shouted to me but the loud slapping of my loose shoes on the bare timber drowned out her words.

Once in my car I cursed the friend who still influenced my life from beyond the grave. The engine roared into life and I put the car in gear, my mind fixed on getting out of Carmen's life and the Blackmore estate as quickly as I could.

A winter's night began to lash against my windscreen. A dark shape moved in front of me. I hit the brakes and my car slid to a halt on the rain-ribbed tarmac. A man appeared at my window and I immediately recognized him as a member of the Brothers of Islam by his cheap grey suit and red bow tie. Led by someone who called himself Malek Abu Bakr, they had attracted both hostility and a grudging respect because of their patrols which had restricted the trade of the smalltime drug pushers and prostitutes on the estate.

I wound down the glass. 'Yes, my brother,' he said as water dripped from the rim of his hat, 'I have to tell you that a lickle further on some young men are performin some dangerous manoeuvres in a stolen car. I think it would be safer for you if you turned around an' made your way to your destination by another route.'

'Thanks,' I said.

The man smiled and answered the question I had no intention of asking out loud. 'They'll soon get bored when no one is chasin them. Sooner or later they will have to leave the car an' then we will endeavour to show them the error of their ways.'

I returned his mirthless smile; it was common knowledge that the Brotherhood's methods of enlightenment often involved large sticks or hammers on the fingers of those who had stubbornly refused to heed the warnings about their misbehaviour.

'Thanks,' I said again as a polite prompt for the man to remove his elbow from the top of my opened glass.

'Ah,' he laughed gently and rattled a collection tin, 'if you think me an' my brethren over there have provided you with a useful service we would be grateful for any small token of appreciation.'

'You know Tyrone Swaby?' I asked.

'Tariq? Oh yeah, he's patrollin down by the shoppin precinct right now.'

I began to close the window. 'Well, he owes me a fiver an' I'd appreciate it if he puts it in your tin for me.'

The man grumbled loudly to his comrades as I turned the car and headed for home. I knew then I had made a mistake to run out on Carmen in a pathetic attempt to avoid the past. For this was the night it would leap from the shadows of the cemetery as I sped by.

The house was full of the smells of new paint and fresh paste. The changes to my home temporarily uplifted me, it gave me a sense that life had to start anew. And yet an inner voice told me that this was the same house, the same life and only thin layers of wallpaper and paint separated me from the past. Danny Maguire was applying a final coat of gloss to a bedroom door when I called up to him that the food was ready. 'Give me a minute,' he shouted back. 'Just this wee bit and we're all done.'

Not yet, I thought as I returned to the kitchen.

There was still a matter for us to discuss but in the ten days he had stayed in my house I had not summoned the will to raise the subject. As

I put the plates onto the table I heard Danny come down the stairs and make a diversion to the living room. I heard him say, "Bout ye, big man.'

'I'm not big,' replied a small and sulky voice.

'Of course you're big, and you'll be even bigger - like your daddy.'

'I'm not big, I'm only four and three-quarters.'

'Four and three-quarters and reading a book all by yourself. You're one big wee man, Nathan, so you are.'

'You're funny. You talk funny.'

'Funny, am I? If I gave you a clatter on your snotter you'd soon change your cheeky wee tune.'

'And then my dad would get you. He was a boxing champion, so there.'

'And who told you all that?'

'My nanny did.'

'Ach, your nanny is only codding you.'

'My dad's better than yoo-hoo.'

'Sure he is.'

'And he's better than my mommy.'

I winced on hearing that last remark and imagined that Danny was wincing too as he struggled to respond. To help him out I shouted that his food was getting cold. He sat down to his meal wearing an apologetic grin. 'A bright wee boy you have there,' he said.

'Maybe too bright,' I replied.

We ate in an awkward silence for a while and then Danny said, 'Robbie, now we're all done I'll be away home tomorrow.'

I was pushing the food around my plate while rehearsing in my mind how to ask him the questions that tormented me every night before I went to sleep. 'Oh, right,' I said, still distracted. 'Give me a call Tuesday. I meant to tell you that Bubby has got us a couple of tickets for the fight.'

'I mean home to Belfast.'

I sat up. 'Oh, right.'

'Yeah, when I was home for Christmas I thought how the mother and father are getting on. To be honest, the only reason I'm not there now was because of the business with Errol, and then his funeral, God rest his soul. And decorating this place, of course.'

Danny resumed eating and my mind began to race. I blurted out, 'Do you really think it was an accident?'

He was looking down at his plate. 'Was what an accident?'

'Danny! Don't give me shit, you know what I mean.'

'The business with Errol? Of course it was.'

'An' it was a coincidence that Shaka was shot a few hours later? Come on, man, you don't believe that.'

He swallowed a piece of half-chewed meat. 'I didn't know much about the Shaka fella but I know he was dealing with some shady characters. Don't you be getting paranoid now.'

'Shit! You're the one who was tellin us that they would show us no mercy if they caught us. You forget already?'

Danny's face reddened. 'For Christ's sake, get a grip. There's more people killed back home in road accidents than were ever killed in the Troubles. You can't be thinking that someone must have been forced off the road every time their car fails to take a bend.'

'Who mentioned bein forced off the road?'

'Ach, that's what you're thinking and it's silly bollocks. This Shaka fella, you told me he wasn't involved.'

'He wasn't. He once supplied some equipment we never used an' the telephone number of that guy the Field Marshal.'

Danny considered a reply as he plunged his fork into the food scattered over his plate. He said, 'But the Shaka fella had no direct involvement with the other stuff you boys were up to, did he?' I shook my head and he continued, 'Well, listen to me now. The Shaka fella got hisself a nut-job because of the dirty sort of business he was involved in. Errol and Hanimal got killed in a car smash the same night. A coincidence and nothing else. The three of them are dead and gone, what youse boys did is finished and gone. You have yourself a wee boy to be looking after. He's relying on you to give him a good start in life. Life, that's what you should be thinking of.'

I wish I could have been convinced so easily, but I doubted if Danny really believed in what he had said to me. As if to stall any further questioning he added, 'Errol used to tell me how he admired the way you stuck to your principles. They're admirable principles, right enough, but they put youse fellas in conflict with nearly everyone outside these four walls. They even put you in conflict with the woman you lived with. Conflict has its casualties and don't you be making a wee boy of four and three-quarters another one.'

'I keep thinkin that if you hadn't called for me that night, I would have been in that car with Errol.'

Danny pushed his plate to one side and let out an exasperated breath. 'And if your auntie had bollocks she'd be your uncle. I'm away to bed, I've an early start in the morning.'

He walked wearily to the kitchen door and I felt angry that he could be so dismissive. 'Is that fuckrees supposed to be some kind-a answer?' I demanded. 'I know it was a set-up. They got informed on an' then taken out!'

Danny paused and looked over his shoulder. 'And besides me, who else knew what youse boys had done?'

I immediately sensed the anger rising within him. 'Hey, Danny, I ain't accusin you!'

'Informed on, that's what you said.'

I saw how flushed his face had become. 'Look, man, I meant that someone else might have found out. You know Hanimal - Christ Almighty, in the back of my mind I was always hopin that the fear of gettin caught would keep his mouth shut.'

Danny turned and faced me; he looked concerned, not angry.

'Do yourself and your kid a favour,' he said softly. 'Leave this town and all the memories behind. Give yourself a fresh start somewhere else or sooner or later the ghosts will come back to haunt you. Now I'm away to bed.'

Later on I lay on my sofa replaying all the events that Danny and I had avoided talking about. My temples throbbed and my eyes were so sore that I decided to rest them before attempting the journey up the steep flight of stairs.

I must have fallen into a doze when I felt someone standing over me; it was a man holding a gun. My blood ran cold and I opened my mouth to shout but no words would come out. I saw the flash of flame and felt an impact on my chest before I heard the dull thud.

My eyes sprang open. I rolled off the sofa and clambering to my feet I saw that an envelope had fallen from my chest to the floor. Inside was a note from Danny my bleary eyes had difficulty focusing on and some money for Nathan.

I smiled but my appreciation of his generosity was quickly overtaken by the sickening realization that he had already left for Belfast. I hurried on unsteady legs to the front door and peered out at the morning mist. The cold air made me fully awake and I walked out to the pavement. I saw a shape and ran down the street but within a few strides it had vanished.

I called out his name and looked all around me but I saw no trace of Danny Maguire.

3

TIRED FROM WORK, I flopped into my armchair in time to watch the evening news.

They were interviewing Malek Abu Bakr - the man who ran the Brothers of Islam, religious enforcers. There were plenty of people around town who said that Malek Abu Bakr had spent his whole life scheming, praying and then scheming some more.

Some women might have considered the guy handsome.

He was of medium height and build and, despite his constant dour preaching about the virtues of modesty, there was an air of vanity about him. Maybe it was the precise parting in his always perfect hair, or the carefully trimmed eyebrows and beard, or the expensive suits which gave him a rakish quality that made men like me suspicious. I had heard that Malek had a certain softly-spoken charm and that he was always polite, that he smiled readily for friend and foe alike. To me it always looked a thin and steel-cold smile and even on television his eyes looked dark and intense, but most of all they looked hungry for power.

That thin smile remained in place despite the hostile questions that were being fired at him by the pack of reporters in front of the local police station. The louder they yelled the quieter his voice became, and once the reporters fell silent in order to hear his answers he replied, 'Yes, the Brothers of Islam will continue with their patrols. If we were white you'd call us Neighbourhood Watch but because we're black you call us vigilantes.

'And yes, we will do everything within our power to secure the release of the three brethren who continue to be unjustly detained in the police station behind me. They are innocent men who have become political prisoners in a police state that is threatened by Islam and the very notion of disciplined black men coming together in order to help their community. We will remain here until they are released.'

It was the sort of performance regular viewers of the local news bulletins had become used to: whatever the subject, Malek's response would always include a few words which came like a mouthful of venom spat into the face of the godless white society he waged war on. No one really knew too much about Malek Abu Bakr before the day he arrived on the Blackmore estate, but in the following eighteen months he had emerged from that stagnant pool of obscurity to become the media's most quoted black person.

The residents of the Blackmore called him 'Aideed' after he was quoted in the local press praising the prowess of the Somalian warlord who had vanquished the American infidel. Apparently he liked the nickname so much that he dubbed the two large American limousines which carried his men around the estate 'Technicals' - a reference to the battered machine gun-toting vehicles which patrolled the war zones in the Horn of Africa.

The night I left Carmen, the broken body of a man named Earl Johnson was found strewn all over the car park of a tower block on the Blackmore estate. Johnson had been snatched from his bed by hooded men and taken to a flat on the fourteenth floor from where, it was alleged, he was pushed off a balcony by three members of the Brothers of Islam. Johnson had been a smalltime drug dealer and pimp who had previously exchanged angry words with the patrols which had disrupted his business. But regardless of the growing tide of rumour and suspicion, Malek Abu Bakr vehemently denied that any of his men were responsible for the incident in the Franklin House flats.

Malek demanded that those who were in charge of the investigation should look to the shooting of another dealer on the estate which had occurred a month before Johnson's death. David Moncrieff had been a much bigger player in the dirty game. It had been around midnight when, unable to park in his usual place, Moncrieff drove two wheels of a Mercedes Sports onto the kerb. As he locked the car door two men came striding towards him. In the moment of hesitation before he fled for his life, Moncrieff must have sensed the danger in the stiff movements of those legs which were a little too anxious to eat up the ground. He ran but didn't get far as a third man had cut off his escape route. Moncrieff - rumoured to have been a murderer and known to be a member of the gang led by the notorious Campbell brothers - stumbled and fell to the ground and a magazine-load of bullets from a Browning 9 mm pistol ripped his head and body asunder. Several men had met a violent end on the Blackmore estate over the years but it was impossible to recall a murder that had matched Moncrieff's in either its ferocity or clinical execution.

'The police are not interested in any links between the deaths of Moncrieff and Johnson,' Malek was insisting now, 'because the men who shot David Moncrieff were white. But the first chance they get, the white racist police tries to criminalise the black men of the Brothers of Islam.'

People less astute than Malek Abu Bakr would also have levelled the same charges at the members of the media. Since the day Earl Johnson's body was found they had returned to swarm all over the Blackmore estate reporting salacious - and conflicting - details of every depravity they had encountered. As well as reinforcing every negative stereotype, it seemed to me they were also intent on conducting their own murder investigation.

'I'm no community leader,' Carmen corrected a reporter, 'self-appointed like Mr Abu Bakr or otherwise. I can only talk for me.' The sight of her face on the screen brought me out of my chair. As she spoke I found myself closing in on her image. For a moment I was touching her again. She looked hard and defiant but never more beautiful. She asserted that the estate on which she lived had been stigmatized by the media because of the activities of a small number of young men who had become trapped within a cycle of drug and money-crazed violence. 'I arks myself what's the agenda. I mean, when an innocent young black man named Mark Finn was murdered as he made his way home from college his murder didn't attract a fraction of this interest. Yet a pimp an' a pusher falls from a buildin an' none of us can make a move without bein arksed for an interview or somethin.'

When the report came to an end I switched off the TV. I had tried to blank Carmen from my mind but it proved to be much harder than simply pushing a switch. Since the night I left I had talked to her constantly; whatever I was doing it seemed my mind was immersed in conversation with her. One day Fidel gripped my forearm after I did not respond to something he had said and asked, 'Robbie, are you all right?' I made some sort of vague reply and Mr Robinson laughed, 'The man lovesick, to rahteed.'

I didn't know if I was in love or sick of love. If I had ever really loved Carmen there were times when I felt it was of the unrequited variety. I still clung to the memory of just how warm she could be; sometimes I had felt my skin melt into hers. But her mood could change rapidly and without warning and she would become cold and aloof. I tried to understand but I was always aware that there was a small part of herself which she had made unobtainable, that she had put beyond my reach. Though she never said it, I knew there had been too many times when she had given everything of herself to a man only for him to discard it and walk away from her. Just as I had walked away.

When I first met Carmen she was seventeen years old and infatuated with Errol. I really did not pay her that much attention as she was just another girl who was going out with my best friend. I did note her flawless skin and a beautiful smile but she was a bit too gangly and frivolous for my taste. After she fell out with Errol she left their poky flat with Tim and managed to get a council maisonette on the Blackmore estate.

Some time later she took up with a waste-of-space named Wesley and they had a daughter who died when only three months old. After the child was buried Wesley tried to kick his way back into her home once he had discovered that Carmen had changed the locks. She quelled the man's noise by calling out from a bedroom window that a pan of boiling water was about to be poured over his head. Wesley went away and never returned. It was that kind of attitude and action which made her something of a hero to other young women on the estate. Carmen had an inner strength which I quickly grew to admire, and over the years her mind and body filled out until the woman who I had only thought of as an acquaintance became the friend who became a lover.

I heard a rumble through the living-room ceiling and was already at the foot of the stairs as Nathan appeared, rubbing his eyes. 'Daddy,' he called down to me, 'I've had a nasty dream.'

Nathan had regularly complained of 'nasty dreams' for more than two years now, and every time he mentioned them I felt a twinge of guilt. In the back of my mind I thought his nightmares were due to the way I had snatched him back from his mother and her new partner.

On a cold and dark night just after Christmas, Danny Maguire accompanied me to a smart semi-detached in one of the better areas of town. I had needed someone who Sharon's new partner wouldn't recognize, to knock on the door. When it opened, Carl, a man who obviously went to bed with a pair of women's tights on his head, angrily demanded who was calling so late at night. Danny gave his answer by throwing his large shoulder against the slightly opened door and pinning the man against a wall. On hearing the commotion Sharon ran downstairs. She hurriedly covered herself and began screaming as I entered the hallway. It didn't take long for Nathan to appear on the landing. I saw him crying and moved towards the stairs but Sharon gripped my wrist and dug her sharp nails into my skin. She yelled, 'You bastard, you ain't tekin my son!'

I brushed her aside and gathered Nathan into my arms and handed him to Danny who then took him out to the car. Sharon shouted to Carl to phone the police but he only rubbed his throat and slunk away into an adjoining room.

Sharon glowered at me through beautiful but spiteful eyes. She slapped me and ranted that I was not man enough to retrieve Nathan on my own. A cruel smile twisted her lips as she began to call out to her partner a whole list of reasons why I had never satisfied her in the way he was able to. I did not react; nothing Sharon could do or say could hurt me any more. In one final desperate ploy to make me respond she drew mucus to the back of her throat and spat it into my face - the instant before a fist flew over my shoulder and rendered her unconscious. 'What the fuck are you doin?' I yelled at Danny.

He drew his upper lip tight against his teeth as he surveyed his handiwork. 'Fuck it, Robbie,' he said, 'you're after taking enough shite from her to last a lifetime.'

I hauled Sharon into a recovery position before ordering Danny back out to the car and calling for Carl to bring some ice and a towel from the kitchen. I left the house with Sharon still groggy and groaning in pain while Carl berated her for bringing such trouble into his home. As I shut the door behind me I heard him shout, 'Anythin like that ever happen again an' your ras is tru the door!'

It all happened the night that Errol, Hanimal and Shaka were killed.

Once I had Nathan back in bed I sat down next to him and snaked my left arm around the back of his neck and around his shoulder. It wasn't long before his breath slowed, rhythmically whistling from between his dry lips. Rain began to beat against the roof and within seconds it started to spill loudly from the guttering I had never got around to clearing of rotted brown leaves. As I listened to the water hitting the ground I imagined how it would soak into the soil and through rocks before surfacing at a place and time I knew nothing about.

Satisfied that Nathan was fast asleep, I gently eased my arm from underneath him and went downstairs. As I stood in the doorway of my living room I thought of how Errol had stood on this very spot a week before he died. In the two years since his death I had tried to discipline my mind so that any memories of him were no more than fleeting glimpses, as if he were a face on a passing train. But the train had begun to slow. I had tried to convince myself that the past had soaked away into the ground, and yet I knew it was still all around me. Not only had I been unable to tear myself away from the place which would always be a frequent reminder, I had let myself become involved with the mother of Errol's son. I had lain with her, kissed and touched her as he had once done. By the time I sat down in my armchair the train had ground to a halt and Errol's sullen face stared out at me from a window.

That long-ago night, Errol's feet had shuffled noisily on the gritty bare boards of my living room. He was anxious - and I was feeling as dark and empty as my home. Frankly, I did not give a shit about what might have happened to get him so worked up. I had enough troubles of my own: Sharon had left me and had taken our son and most of the furniture with her. I sat in a badly worn armchair which I had bought from a second-hand store staring at the flickering blue haze of an old portable TV. I said impatiently, 'Errol, you'd better not be workin yuhself up to tell me you went an' got them shooters when I already tell you to forget them.'

'Nah, nah,' he mumbled vaguely. 'It's somethin else.'

'Then come to the point, guy,' I said.

My blank stare returned to the television and he began to tell me his story. He had been in Mustafa's Sea Star Fish Bar eating a few chips and talking to Danny Maguire when his son Tim stumbled in. The boy was frightened and sobbed that his mother was lying badly hurt on their sofa; a man known as the Field Marshal had given her a beating. Some people on the estate called the man a Yardie but whatever else he was, Beresford Samuels was a drug dealer who had not taken kindly to the woman who had confronted him in a public place over his use of her ten-year-old to deliver wraps of cocaine. Tim had frozen with fear as he saw his mother fall to the pavement, her slender arms unable to fend off the hail of savage blows. Carmen screamed at him to run and he bolted into a shop, but the only person willing to step outside was an old Polish guy who couldn't do much more than help a barely conscious woman to her feet.

I wasn't sure how long he'd stopped talking; I'd been watching some poor woman making a fool of herself in front of millions of viewers for a paltry jackpot of ten grand. My mind had wandered in and out, I wasn't sure if I had heard everything he said, but I knew why he had come to me and I knew what he wanted to do. It was a mixture of fear and a dented pride, rather than any feelings of compassion for Carmen or Tim that had brought him to my house. He was more concerned how his reputation might suffer if Samuels got away with the very public beating of the mother of one of his kids.

He had called at a bad time. Even TV for the brain-dead could not anaesthetize me and I was in no mood to put up with Errol's macho posturing. Couldn't he see that I had enough trouble of my own? I let out an exaggerated yawn and looked up at him in the doorway; the light from the television made deep hollows of his proud eyes. It was at that moment I made up my mind to humble him: he would have to ask, maybe he would have to beg for my help.

'Yardie, fuckin Yardie,' I said in a voice laced with contempt, 'how much shit you gonna swallow, Errol? He's just another mythical black man the white man create, another urban myth. Cha, man, you watch it now, every two-bit ginnal from JA will become a Yardie accordin to the press.'

He reacted angrily, the way I wanted. 'Oi! I don't give a bloodclart about no myth. What that man do to Carmen an' Tim ain't no myth so don't talk fuckrees.'

'Uh oh, so it's me that's talkin fuckrees?' I replied without trying to disguise my mocking tone. 'Well, yuh know, I can still remember how you an' Hanimal were talkin the other day, goin on about how guys like this so-called Yardie is a symptom an' not a cause of black people's distress. Yeah, I remember how you two were goin on like this guy was some sort-a hero but now him involve one of your pickney in his business him turn into an evil bastard. What would you say if it was someone else's pickney him use, some other woman him beat? Cha, just go talk to the man, E. You were sayin the other day how much fairer-minded black people are. This man will be fair with you, won't he?'

At first he said nothing and I thought it was because he was unable to find an answer. When we were at school he'd used to ask me why did I bother to play chess - it was only a game for softie white kids - and I was just about to call 'checkmate' when he began to speak.

'Is this what this fuckrees you talkin is all about? I come to you as a friend an' you wanna turn it into some kind-a lecture, you wanna prove you're the one who's right all the time, is that it? Right, so I was wrong. Is that wha you wanna hear? Am I so wrong to try an' keep a lickle pride in who we are?'

'We ain't him an' he ain't us.'

'Oh yeah? Ain't you the guy who was mekin noise about how we is all lumped together, how the newspapers an' that degrade an' criminalize all-a we? Right, so not everythin I'm dealin with, about bein a black man, is reality but I call that compensatin. Yuh unnerstan that?'

His response had caught me unawares and the best I could do was to turn my eyes to the television as if he had said nothing of importance. 'A'right,' he said, pressing home his advantage, 'I can see the more you know the more easy it is to get vexed. I can see how you must have got vexed with me. But hol' on, we all only got one pair of ears, one pair of eyes. We all got our different way of dealin with tings. Don't be sittin here in your dark lickle room gettin vexed with everyone who nah see the tings you do 'cause you'll end up goin crazy an' vexed with the whole world.'

Errol had said enough, maybe too much, and I wanted him to leave. He went on, 'Yuh nah talk to me, you're gonna stay here in your dark lickle room for the rest of your life? Yuh wanna know wha all your trouble is? It's this born equal crap you swallow. You think just 'cause you can do a ting so can everyone else. Well, not everyone is as good as you.'

I thought he had left me an opening and I said, 'Yuh mean them legs are bruk?' It was meant as a snide remark about something Errol had said to me some weeks before.

We had been in Errol's flat when Hanimal had marched in clutching a copy of the local evening newspaper and demanding to know why he had not taken any part in the incident which had made front-page news. I had told Errol to keep himself out of it, things were getting serious and the cops were cracking plenty of heads in an attempt to extract any meagre crumb of information. What we had planned was for only the two of us to know. There could be no exceptions, not even for Hanimal.

Errol only managed an embarrassed mumble. Hanimal then looked over to me. ''Cause your mouth is even slacker than your balls!' I yelled. An anger had built up within me and I released it in a tirade of abuse that Hanimal had no answer for. When my rage finally subsided he looked over towards Errol. 'Look,' he said softly, 'me know you guys is unner pressure. Me check you later, yeah?'

After Hanimal had gone Errol angrily paced the room. It wasn't only what I had said to Hanimal, it was the way I had belittled him. 'Let's seh we all born equal,' hissed Errol without a halt in his stride. 'I don't believe it, but let's seh it true. Guys like Hanimal got taken out of them cot an' had them legs bruk, them get crippled early on in life. Yet him is one guy that managed to get up on him two foot when the time came to be counted. But you, Mr Big-shot, wanna knock him back down. Just fuckin buck yuhself up, man!'

'Legs bruk?' Errol snorted from my doorway. He pulled a face as though there was a bad smell in my room and added, 'Maybe people get hurt in other places too.'

He turned to leave and suddenly I did not want him to go. I called out his name and halted him mid-stride.

'Apologies, E,' I said, 'I'm out of order. Let's go find this so-called Yardie an' give im a whackin.'

Errol turned and I saw how his lips twitched as they made a lopsided smile. 'Look, Robbie, this guy's a pistolero. Deal with him the wrong way an' it bam-bam yuh dead!'

I thought I had been too hurt to hurt any more; there were times I had been so scared that I had imagined I could never be scared again. I pushed back into my chair and said, 'Then it had better be a serious wackin, Errol. It had better be serious.'

4

I WAS WATCHING Saturday morning TV with Nathan when the telephone rang. My first reaction on learning of the deaths of Fidel and Mr Robinson was that my mother had made some terrible mistake - that what she had heard on the radio could not be true.

There was a silence and then she asked if I wanted her to come around and look after Nathan in case I needed to go out. The first stirring of the storm about to buffet my mind prevented me from thinking of any place I would want or need to go to. In a determinedly clear voice I said, 'No, but thanks anyway, Mom. Thanks for lettin me know.'

I put down the phone and tried to walk back to the living room but my trembling legs could only get me to the staircase before they gave way. I sat on a step asking myself what was happening to me. I was confused by the high-pitched howls forcing their way through my clenched teeth and the salty tears that ran around the edges of my mouth. I told myself that I could not be crying, that I had too much self-control, that this was just another nightmare and I would wake at any moment.

I heard a child's voice in the distance and tried to stifle the sound of my sobs. 'What's wrong, Daddy? Is something wrong with Nanny?' asked Nathan. He put an arm around my heaving shoulders as I angrily told myself it was not right for a boy of seven to see his father crying.

Shame - and the fear in his voice - forced me to gather myself. 'No, Nathan,' I said, 'Nanny just rang to tell me about two of my friends from the factory.' I had to bite my trembling lip before I could add, 'A bad man stole a car and killed them with it last night.'

Nathan stretched out a hand. 'Here you are, Daddy,' he said bravely. 'Don't cry, have one of my sweets - it might help you feel better.'

Nothing could help me feel better in those long bleak days before the funerals of Fidel and Mr Robinson. But not for the first time, Nathan had saved me from a descent into some sort of madness. He gave me a reason to be grateful for our lives together and, for his sake, to get on with mine.

I don't remember much about what I did or said at the factory during that time; I shouldn't have bothered clocking in for all the work I did. I seemed to spend my hours cursing God and wondering if I'd had some sort of premonition that day I looked at their hands as they played chess in the canteen. At break-times I would patrol their old haunts, still stupefied by grief, half-expecting to see them coming around the next corner.

When their bodies were released for burial I could not bring myself to visit the funeral home. I did not want to see them dead. My last sight of them would ensure that I could only remember them alive. It was as I came out of the washroom just before I clocked out. 'Hey, you sly ol' bastards ain't doin overtime, are you?' I said jokingly.

'One last job to do before we go,' said Fidel, tapping the side of his nose. 'We'll tell you all about it on Monday.'

'Yes, mi son, we see you Monday mornin, bright an' sharp,' said Mr Robinson. And up to his usual mischief he added, ''Ave a good weekend, Robbíe, an' go easy on the gal dem.'

The morning of the funerals I received another telephone call; it was Carmen. 'I didn't know if I should ring,' she said hesitantly, 'but I just wanted to say how sorry I was to read about those two men you used to work with. I know how much you thought of them.'

'I loved them.'

'I know you did.'

'Carmen, can I see you later, after the funerals, at the bistro on King Street?' The words just fell out of my mouth without any forethought and, after my surprise had subsided, I silently cursed myself in the age it took her to answer.

She drew a sharp breath. 'Okay,' she said, 'what time?'

Unsure I was doing the right thing I said, 'One-thirty?'

'Right then,' she said, sounding more positive. 'I'll see you at one-thirty.'

It was a bad time, one-thirty in the bistro. The small restaurant seemed to pulsate with loud chatter and chinking cutlery as office workers shouldered their way in and out. I had managed to find a table for two away from the mêlée thanks to a French waitress named Marie who had remembered me from the days when I had the time and money to regularly visit for an evening meal with Carmen.

As Marie cleared the table of a half-eaten meal I rescued a discarded newspaper from her clutches and turned immediately to the sports section. I had no stomach for the tales of death and destruction in far-flung places which filled the front page.

After laying a clean set of cutlery she asked, 'Would you like to order now?'

I folded the newspaper and put it to one side. 'No, not at the moment. I'm waitin for someone.'

'Ah, the lovely tall woman, yes?'

'Yeah.'

'Very good, I will come back after she arrives.'

A glance at a clock on a wall told me that Carmen was almost ten minutes overdue and I began to fret that she would not turn up. I chastized myself for blurting out such a request over the telephone. She probably could not find it in her heart to reply that she owed me nothing, or ask why I hadn't even found the time to respond to the messages she had left on my answering machine.

Five more minutes went by. Marie smiled sympathetically in my direction on her way out from the kitchen. When the clock crept around to ten to two I stood up and looked for Marie, to wave goodbye to her. She was taking an order and frowned over at me. 'She will come,' she mouthed. The very next minute, Marie was calling out, 'He is over there!'

I looked up, my rear end barely back on the chair, to see Carmen weaving her way towards me through the crowded tables. I saw how

PLEASE DETACH BEFORE SEALING ENVELOPE *DÉTACHEZ AVANT DE CACHETER L'ENVELOPPE*

Account No. in full *Numéro de compte au complet*	DATE OF MOVE *DATE DU DÉMÉNAGEMENT*
4 5 0	MM MM / DJ DJ / YA YA YA YA

LAST NAME (PLEASE PRINT) *NOM DE FAMILLE (EN CARACTÈRES D'IMPRIMERIE)* | FIRST NAME (PLEASE PRINT) *PRÉNOM (EN CARACTÈRES D'IMPRIMERIE)*

NEW HOME ADDRESS *NOUVELLE ADRESSE DU DOMICILE*

HOME ADDRESS LINE 1 (PLEASE PRINT) *ADRESSE DU DOMICILE - LIGNE 1 (EN CARACTÈRES D'IMPRIMERIE)*

HOME ADDRESS LINE 2 (IF NECESSARY) *ADRESSE DU DOMICILE - LIGNE 2 (SI NÉCESSAIRE)*

CITY *VILLE* | PROVINCE | POSTAL CODE *CODE POSTAL*

HOME TELEPHONE NO. *N° DE TÉLÉPHONE (DOMICILE)* | BUSINESS TELEPHONE NO. *N° DE TÉLÉPHONE (TRAVAIL)* | OTHER TELEPHONE NO. *AUTRE N° DE TÉLÉPHONE*

CHANGE OF HOME ADDRESS? PLEASE FILL IN <u>ALL SECTIONS</u> AND RETURN WITH YOUR PAYMENT. *VOUS DÉMÉNAGEZ? VEUILLEZ REMPLIR <u>AU COMPLET</u> ET JOINDRE À VOTRE PAIEMENT.*

ADDITIONAL CARD REQUEST

JUST FILL THIS OUT AND RETURN WITH YOUR PAYMENT
I request an additional CIBC VISA Card, with its renewals and replacements, to be issued:

☐ in the name of the following "Authorized User"*

| FIRST NAME *PRÉNOM* | INITIALS *INITIALES* | LAST NAME (PLEASE PRINT) *NOM (EN CARACTÈRES D'IMPRIMERIE)* |

I acknowledge that I will be liable for all charges resulting from the use of any additional card.

Account No. in full *Numéro de compte au complet*

4 5 0

*I am the Authorized User designated above. I will be bound by the CIBC Cardholder Agreement and authorize you to send it and all other information to the primary cardholder. I will be responsible for charges resulting from the use of the card(s) issued in my name and any other use of the VISA Account by me.

DATE

DEMANDE DE CARTE ADDITIONNELLE

VEUILLEZ REMPLIR LA PRÉSENTE FORMULE ET LA RETOURNER AVEC VOTRE PAIEMENT
Je demande l'émission d'une carte additionnelle CIBC-VISA ainsi que ses renouvellements et remplacements:

☐ au nom de l'«usager autorisé» suivant*

Je reconnais que je serai responsable de tout montant imputé par suite de l'utilisation de toute carte additionnelle.

PRIMARY CARDHOLDER'S SIGNATURE *SIGNATURE DU TITULAIRE PRINCIPAL DE CARTE*

*Je suis l'usager autorisé désigné ci-dessus. Je serai lié par l'Entente avec le titulaire de carte de la CIBC et je vous autorise à l'expédier, ainsi que tous les autres renseignements, au titulaire principal de carte. Je serai responsable de tous les frais résultant de l'utilisation des cartes émises en mon nom ainsi que de toute autre utilisation du compte VISA par moi.

AUTHORIZED USER'S SIGNATURE *SIGNATURE DE L'USAGER AUTORISÉ* men looked up and over the shoulders of their companions in order to catch a glimpse of her. In the weeks since I had last seen her, I had put out of my mind just how beautiful she was.

'Robbie,' she panted as she sat down. 'Please, please forgive me. The bus was late and then the traffic came to a standstill. I arksed the driver to let me off so I could walk, it would've been faster. I thought you might have gone.'

'Nah, I would-a been here till closin time.'

'No, you wouldn't,' she laughed.

Her laughter and my smile preceded a clumsy silence that was only broken when Marie appeared to take our orders.

'What do you recommend?' I asked.

'Well, the chef today is making some lovely stir-fry chicken and broccoli.'

I looked over to Carmen who smiled approvingly. 'Then we'll have two of those and a pot of tea, please,' I said.

I then tried to make small talk and ask her questions about subjects I had no real interest in: her son Tim; the Mark Finn campaign; and the work she was doing with the women of the Blackmore estate. The food was mercifully quick arriving and as we ate I became aware of how difficult it was for Carmen to make conversation. What should we talk about? The way I had walked out on her and never returned her calls were like barriers between us. Once I had made up my mind I said, 'I saw your brother at the funeral.'

'Tyrone?'

'Or Tariq if you prefer.'

'Please, Robbie, I definitely *don't* prefer.' She started to say something else but stopped.

Realizing that I had made her feel uneasy I said, 'Don't worry, the guy was actin very friendly.'

'What do you mean, very friendly?'

The tone of her voice had me regretting my topic of conversation. 'Well, you know that me an' him ain't been gettin on for a while, but he came over an' said that the way Fidel an' Mr Robinson had died made

45

him have a rethink. He said things had been put into perspective an' that he didn't feel no bad way towards me. He even arksed me to go around to his place for a chat tonight.'

'Don't go, Robbie.'

'What's up?'

'Never mind, maybe I'll tell you another time.' She pushed her plate to one side. 'Was there many at the funeral?'

Her wish to change the subject was obvious. I wanted to pursue the thing about Tyrone but thought better of it. 'The church was crammed. I mean, all their kids an' their families were there. They had a lot of grandkids between them.'

'I suppose all of their friends from the factory were there too?' she asked.

'That's a sore point,' I said. 'The management let it be known that they expected everyone to turn in as normal today an' that this fool named Ken Barker, who the ol' guys hated, would represent the workers.'

'Does that mean you'll be in trouble?'

'Carmen, I don't give a damn.'

Her face brightened as if just me saying her name gave her pleasure and a hand reached over and touched mine. 'Your eyes look awful,' she said.

'I couldn't sleep last night.'

'Is your mom pickin Nathan up from school?'

'Yeah, I'm goin to try an' get some rest.'

'Then come home with me. Put your head down at my place an' I'll make you somethin to eat after you've had a sleep.'

Maybe for both our sakes I should have said no and returned to my empty house, but I did not want to be alone. I nodded and she compressed her lips to make a thin fleeting smile as I left a large tip for Marie before we made our way out. Once outside I buttoned my coat and turned my back on a bitter wind. A sudden movement from across the road caught my eye: a tall man with the hood of a tatty parka coat pulled over his head had abruptly spun around and walked away. I watched him until he disappeared around a corner and Carmen asked me did I know him. 'Nah,' I said. 'Come on, let's get to your place before I fall asleep.'

'Use my room,' she said, 'if you remember where it is.'

When I got to her bedroom I stripped and left my clothes in a heap at the foot of her bed and climbed in between the cold sheets. I looked out to the window and said my final farewells. The sudden deaths of Fidel and Mr Robinson had left me with a deep sense of loss. But I was reminded of how selfish grief can be when one of Mr Robinson's sons said that it was a mercy that the two men had died instantly and, more importantly, simultaneously. Neither of the old guys would have had much of a life without the other.

As my eyes closed I thought of all the deaths which had punctuated my life. The first one of any significance was one I did not remember, that of my father when I was three years old, then it seemed no one I knew had died until I reached my late teens. The death of my grandmother was followed by those of an aunt and a cousin, and then a guy I went to school with got stabbed at a party. Into my twenties, the number of deaths accelerated: Errol's mom died of cancer, three guys in a Sound System died in a fire, one more former classmate was murdered and another committed suicide. Then, at twenty-nine, the deaths of Errol, Hanimal, Shaka and Beresford Samuels, all around my own age, finally brought me to an irrevocable awareness of my own mortality.

The bed warmed, my body uncurled and I drifted into sleep with the memories of the dead playing on my mind. But most of all I remembered Errol.

I had no idea of where Errol was driving to. The road ahead was wet, black and shiny. Orange street lights and the occasional Christmas illuminations became blurred by a fog which retreated at speed and kept a small but constant distance from the front of the car.

The engine hummed rhythmically and in a way which would have helped me to relax if it hadn't had to compete with the sound of Errol trying to summon saliva into his chalk-dry mouth.

I was feeling smug. Errol knew plenty of guys who went on as though they were really hard, but now he had business with the man called the Field Marshal they were nowhere to be found; he had needed to come to me. He mixed with a circle of young men, including the likes of Shaka and Hanimal, who only played at being hard. I had told Errol they were only pretenders, and what had happened around town when men were required to stand up and be counted should have shown him that. Pretending was what irritated me most about Errol. He wasn't going to seek out the Field Marshal because of any notion of justice, he was just acting out a role he thought others expected him to play.

Errol swallowed hard again and I glanced at him from the corner of my eye. I knew my silence was only adding to his nervousness but I had no intention of offering him words that would either encourage or reassure him. After all, this was his car, he was the one who was driving, the one who was seeking revenge. All he had to do was to turn the car around if he didn't want to see this thing through.

He broke the silence. 'What's the plan?'

'How far to go?' I asked while thinking: How far are you prepared to go?

He could not disguise the edge in his voice. 'I ain't sure. It can't be far now. So what do we do when we get there?'

From what I had heard about Beresford Samuels he was as dangerous as he was unpredictable. But as Bubby used to tell us in the gym: reputations of toughness are built by weaker men and don't mean shit. Any man at any given time can crumble, it's all a matter of timing. Personally, I doubted if anything would happen: Samuels would either not be there or not let us in. I said, 'Let's find his yard first, an'...'

'An' then?'

'...An' then wait for the chance to arks him a question.'

'Wha fuckin question?'

'The question you should-a arksed yuhself a long time ago,' I answered, still playing a silly game.

Errol did not speak again for quite a while. I could sense that he was gathering himself for what might be ahead of us. I was still relaxed and confident that our journey would come to nothing when Errol said, 'This is the place. Keep a lookout for number twelve.'

He slowed the car to walking pace. I looked out to the litter-strewn street in another anonymous concrete reservation. It reminded me of the Blackmore estate; the same mixture of high-rise flats and maisonettes that were inhabited by a people who sensed that they were surplus to requirements. I saw groups of youths patrolling the walkways, dressed as though they were in New York or LA and not some forgotten post-industrial backwater in England. Young women, not much more than girls, wove their prams through the dog shit and ignored the boys who leered and shouted down to them.

Number twelve, carelessly daubed in white on a door of flaking green abruptly appeared from behind the remains of a rusting ice-cream van. 'There!' I said.

The car stopped and Errol leant across for a better look. My stomach moved - it was as if the fear he had struggled to control had been transferred to me. The time we had spent boxing, from gawky kids to strutting young men, had taught us how to control fear, or at least its outward signs. It was the control of fear, so Bubby told us, which separated the champions from the rest. The hero felt no less fear than the coward, he only ensured that it did not deter him. The two of us had done so many things which separated us from the people we lived amongst and, if Beresford Samuels let us in, what lay ahead of us in number twelve would prove to be a final act of disconnection.

A snot-smeared child ran along a pavement crying for her mother. I turned and looked at Errol. In that instant I allowed the compassion to drain from my heart so it would harden and my mind could shut out the consequences of what I had planned for the man who called himself the Field Marshal.

'Park this car somewhere more quiet,' I said, 'where it won't get seen, an' then we'll go an' knock on that bastard's door.'

5

It was dark when I awoke and it took me a while to bring Carmen's blurry shape into focus. 'I brought you up some tea,' she said, 'an' there's food for you downstairs.'

Still nauseous from my sleep I asked her what was the time.

'Almost nine,' she replied.

'Nine in the mornin?'

'No, evenin,' she chuckled. 'Now sit up an' drink this.'

I propped myself up with an elbow and Carmen sat on the edge of the bed. 'How are you feelin?' she asked.

'A bit groggy. You should've woke me earlier.'

'This is the third time I've been up. You were out for the count, man.'

'I'd better get up an' take Nathan home from my mom's,' I said. Without bothering to drink I put the cup on the bedside table.

Carmen's spine stiffened. 'Oh right, but you are gonna eat somethin.'

'I don't think I'll have time. Sorry.'

She grimaced and then hummed to herself for a moment before she said, 'Robbie, before you get up can I talk to you?'

Her words seemed to hang in the air between us. My heartbeat quickened. I guessed she was going to ask me to stay until the morning. 'Carmen,' I sighed, 'this is...'

'It's not about us, Robbie, if that's what you're thinkin. You made it clear what your feelins are. I'm not sayin I don't wish it was different.'

'Then what do you wanna talk about?' I said sharply, to take her back to her original point.

'It's a bit difficult...'

'Then can it wait until another day? I can give you more time then. Right now I've gotta pick up Nathan from my mom's.'

'Please, I need to talk now. It's somethin I need an opinion on - it won't take long, it's somethin I want to share. It's about somethin you said earlier about Tyrone. Do you think he was actin normal at the funerals?'

I took a deep breath and tried to clear the dullness from my sleepy head. 'Well, he was actin very friendly. I don't suppose that's normal.'

'The night you left here...' she paused briefly and let the thorns in her brittle voice prick my conscience before she went on '... the night you left, a man went off the fourteenth floor of Franklin House.'

I responded sourly. 'I do read the papers, Carmen.'

'An' you know the police arrest an' charge three of the Muslim guys wid im murder.'

'That was in the papers too.'

'Yeah, well, I think that there were four Muslims involved in Earl Johnson's death an' that the fourth guy was Tyrone.'

My head cleared instantly. 'Hey, before you carry on, is that what you think or is that what you know?'

She pulled her long fingers down her face and as they fell from her chin she said softly, 'I know. He was actin kind-a strange, like agitated, when those three guys were arrested. That would be normal - I mean, he knows them - but then he started sayin stuff that didn't add up. One day he was talkin some kind-a nonsense an' I told him so. He blew up an' started rantin that I was only disagreein with him 'cause of the way you got up an' left me at two in the mornin. So I arks him had he been talkin to you about it. When he said no I arksed him how did he know that you had left all of a sudden when he had already told me that he hadn't been on patrol that night.'

I immediately remembered the Muslim guy who had stopped me because of the stolen car doing manoeuvres on the Blackmore's main road. He had told me that Tyrone was patrolling down at the estate's shopping precinct. I caught the last few words of something else Carmen was saying. 'Sorry?' I said.

51

'I said you hadn't been chattin to him before the funerals, had you?'

'Er, no, Carmen, I can't pretend I did.' I saw her shrink away. There was little point in adding to her agony by telling her that a member of a patrol had told me about her brother's whereabouts. 'Maybe he was out somewhere else when he saw my car. I didn't take the usual way home. Some young bastards were doin handbrake-turns on the main road and I had to go home the long way, past the cemetery an' up by Rushbury estate.'

She was too lost in her thoughts to make a reply. I imagined that she was trying to work out if there was any plausible reason that Tyrone might have seen me because of my enforced diversion. While she was distracted I slid out of the bed and made a start on getting dressed. She looked over her shoulder and gave me that small disappointed smile she often used.

'Do you think I've overreacted?' she asked.

'Nah,' I said while tucking in my shirt. 'These have been stressful times for all of us, in lots of different ways. For you, me, Tyrone. We all had more than our fair share. As Danny Maguire once said to me, "Don't let some wee worm start eating away into your brain".'

She nodded and looked away to a dark corner of the room. 'Hey, that's a pretty good impression,' she said, attempting - but failing - to sound cheerful. 'Do you ever hear from him these days?'

'Nah, it's been two years. You know his father was shot dead in a bar in Belfast with five other guys only days after he leave here, don't you? Six innocent men cut down by psychopaths. Christ Almighty, I wished that ceasefire could-a come six months sooner. Knowin Danny made what happens over there so close, like somethin more real to me.'

'Yeah, you told me before.'

'Oh, yeah I did. Well, I ain't heard from him since whenever. I ain't heard from him since he stayed with me after Errol's funeral.'

I sat down on the bed to put on my shoes and she said, 'That must be the first time you ever put those two words in the same sentence in all the time you talk to me.'

'An' what words are they?'

'Errol and funeral.'

The lilt in her voice offended me. 'We all have our own way of dealin with things, right?'

She let the brief flame of my anger die away and said, 'I just don't unnerstan why you guys get so touchy whenever his name gets called. Tyrone's been the same lately. Me an' him got into another argument over Tim an' I told him to stop bringin up Errol's name in front of the boy 'cause he was never that much of a father. So he went crazy, sayin that if I ever knew what Errol did an' how he was set up an' killed that I would never disrespec his memory.'

Cold blood chilled my heart. 'Set up? Set up by who?'

'Cha, it's fantasy, Robbie, that's all. You, me an' the rest of the world knows it was a road accident but Tyrone was tryna convince me that the government killed those guys. It was talk like that got me thinkin he was havin a mental breakdown. I know the sort-a things Errol got up to an' the only piece of government interested in his carry-on would've been the Child Support Agency.'

I was stunned into silence. She said, 'You don't believe any of that conspiracy crap, do you? I mean, what had Errol ever done to draw that sort-a attention on himself?'

'Nah,' I said, 'I don't believe it. Look - I have to go.'

'I know, for Nathan.'

'Yeah, for Nathan.'

She stood up and put on a smile. 'Will you call me sometime, or at least answer my calls?'

'Sure. An' thanks for lettin me get my head down an' havin the chat.'

'That's what friends are for.'

I turned away on hearing how she struggled to keep her voice from cracking and as I walked to the stairs I called back to her, 'Thanks again an' sorry about not eatin the food. Maybe another time. So later, yeah?'

Carmen didn't answer and by the time I got outside it felt as though something was crawling over my hot skin. In a moment of weakness I had wanted her again - or I had wanted to see if she still wanted me. It had only been curiosity, selfish and cruel curiosity. The pain I had endured since the death of my two old friends had reactivated an instinct that made me want to lash out and inflict pain. It was a frailty about the human condition that I had witnessed many times and, disgusted with myself, I made a promise never to be weak like that with Carmen again.

The route to my mother's house took me close to where Tyrone lived. At the funeral this morning, he had asked me around to his place for nine o'clock. It wasn't yet half-past, another ten minutes and I could be at my mother's - or at his flat. Should I go and see Tyrone? I was only pretending that I was debating with myself: from the moment Carmen had told me that he had talked of the circumstances surrounding Errol's death I had made up my mind.

I turned the car and a mixture of anticipation and apprehension shot through my veins. For some reason the cocktail of emotions drew me back again to that other time and I remembered what had happened in the place inhabited by a man named Beresford Samuels, also known as the Field Marshal.

From behind the blistered green door a gruff voice called out, 'Who dat?'

'Me ring earlier,' Errol called back. 'Shaka's spar.' He glanced at me, his tongue dabbing at his dry lips.

Three bolts slid noisily across the back of the door before it opened slightly; a short but thick chain prevented it from opening any further. 'Who dat behine you?' the voice demanded through the gap.

Errol was edgy. 'My pardna, me already tell you him come.'

The door slammed shut and Errol looked at me as if to ask what should we do next. The tight spring within me began to unwind and I was already imagining the journey home, swapping curses and details of what we would have done if the guy had been stupid enough to let us in. It was then the chain rattled and the door opened. Samuels said, 'Okay, one at a time.'

Errol shot a glance my way before he stepped inside and the door slammed shut. The spring halted its uncoiling and began to tighten again as I heard one of the bolts being rammed home.

Time moved so slowly that a pulsing ache spread out from my stomach and only halted once it had reached my gums. Anxious that some passer-by might see my face I pushed my head down into my shoulders and then towards the door. My ears strained to listen to what was going on inside and I caught the smell of rotting wood from under the flakes of green paint. The tension grew. Sinews turned to thick ungainly ropes moving under my skin. The muscles in my shoulders began to stiffen. I tried to relax and deepen my shallow breathing but the sound of a bolt being drawn cut me short. The door swung open and Samuels barked, 'You, inside an' face the wall.'

The door closed behind me and plunged the narrow hallway into darkness. I peered into the gloom for any sign of Errol until a hand shoved me in the back. 'Spread dem!' ordered Samuels. Shaka had warned Errol that it was normal practice for Samuels to frisk everyone who entered any of his business premises. In his line of work there were no friends, no second chances, and no opportunity for any of us to enter with a weapon.

A hand moved over my arms, down my legs, then up again, over my ribs and around my waist. 'Hey!' I yelled as the hand gripped my balls. Samuels laughed harshly and said, 'Heh, me know plenty guys who keep a bebbi Beretta down deh.' He gestured for me to walk ahead of him to a room at the end of the hallway. It was then, despite the gloom, that I saw why I had been frisked with only one hand; a snub-nosed revolver pointed to where I was required to go.

The high-rise towers of the Blackmore estate rose murkily in the distance behind the terrace of once-opulent Edwardian facades. From my car I watched a group of youths gathered on the street corner. I sat for several minutes thinking of what I should say to Tyrone as they stopped any passer-by who did not look entirely sure of themselves and asked them for 'a loan' of a cigarette or some money.

The young heads turned with the sound of my car door slamming. The biggest youth narrowed his eyes and sized me up. As I turned the key in the lock I let them see that I was taking note of each of them -

they were only boys but they would know enough to take it as a warning that on my return I had better find my car intact. They quickly returned to their huddle except for the big youth; he pulled on a cigarette which his hand shielded from the cold drizzle and gave me a curt nod of his head.

I saw a window blind twitch on the first floor as I climbed the well-worn stone steps. The terraced house in which I lived had been built nearly a century ago and I imagined that it had been designed for, and always inhabited by, people sometimes euphemistically referred to as the 'working class'. But the houses on this street, with their high ceilings trimmed with fancy cornices, although now weatherbeaten and divided into bedsit flats were easy to imagine as once grander affairs, for doctors, solicitors and the like.

Ignoring the rows of bell-pushes, I shoved open the heavy door which had long since lost its lock and made my way to the winding stairway across damp and gritty lino.

Tyrone was locking his door as I reached the first-floor landing. A black holdall was at his feet. 'It's late,' he said. 'Me think you nah come.'

When he did not unlock the door I stupidly asked, 'You goin out somewhere?'

'Yeah, man,' he replied, 'me 'ave a lickle delivery to make. Can you give me a lift?' When I did not immediately reply he went on, 'It ain't far. We can chat in the car, yeah? There's somethin me an' you should talk about.'

The hint of that 'somethin' was enough for me to agree to take him where he wanted. As we went downstairs he asked me about Nathan and then told me that his son Duane was with a woman named Lyzette.

'Who's Lyzette?' I asked him.

'She's in one of the flats in the house next door. She a good black woman, yuh know.'

Emerging into the dank air I allowed myself a smile as I wondered if Tyrone's use of 'black' was some sort of qualification of the woman's goodness.

'Oi!' he shouted to the group of youths. 'Unno had better not be givin nobody trouble.' He looked across the road to a man whose shoulders were hunched against the weather. 'Oi, Mr Brown, it's okay, this man is givin me a lift.' The man raised his head and looked bemused, as if he hadn't got a clue what Tyrone was talking about.

The cold wind hurried the man along. Tyrone grinned and put his bag onto the rear seat before he asked me if I knew how to get to the Rose and Crown pub.

'The Rose and Crown?' I asked. 'The one on the Waterloo Road?'

'Yeah, man, that's the one.'

My trip to his flat was not turning out like anything I had imagined. I looked out to the corner for a sign of the youths but they were gone. Tyrone's behaviour was beginning to perplex me and I asked him, 'What the ras you wanna go down there for?'

He laughed and said, 'Hey, ol' man, it ain't what it used to be. Nah, me 'ear black people are runnin it now.' He could see I was having second thoughts and his tone became serious. 'I'm late already, do you think we can get movin?'

I hesitated. The Rose and Crown was once reputed to be the watering-hole for racist nutcases. It was on the other side of town, on a road which marked the boundary between the Lowlands and Rushbury estates. The Rushbury was supposed to be a 'black' area even though barely more than a third of its inhabitants would describe themselves in that way. The Lowlands was 99 per cent white, and when they weren't trying to impregnate their close relatives, the young men of that estate seemed to spend their time making the 1 per cent of black residents the focus of their violent leisure activities. Over the years there had been a number of pitched battles between gangs of youths from the two estates with the police playing pigs-in-the middle, but it was the murder of a young black man named Mark Finn which ensured that the area's notoriety lived on. A stranger to that part of town, he was looking for a friend who had moved to the Rushbury estate when he took a wrong turn and ended up in the Lowlands. They found his body in a builder's skip the following morning.

'Are we goin, or what?' Tyrone grumbled.

The Waterloo Road. Errol and Hanimal had probably passed that way as they drove out to the place where they would meet their deaths. I turned the ignition and put the car in gear. I had no choice; I had to follow that road.

6

ERROL STOOD IN front of a battered and unused gas fire examining the lopsided photograph of a pair of gun-toting youths. 'Dat me an' mi brodda Rawldie,' announced Samuels as he followed me into the dingy room. 'Wherever me go it go too.'

It didn't take more than two seconds to figure out that this was not a room that was regularly used. There were only three pieces of furniture in it: a torn leather armchair and a couple of wooden stools. The carpet was old and threadbare; the air was cold and fusty. There were three doorways: the one I had just walked through from the hallway with a gun at my back; one with its door ajar which led to a bathroom; and a third that accessed a dimly lit kitchen.

Errol turned around and signalled to me with his eyes to take a look into the kitchen. 'What kind-a shooters are they?' he asked to distract Samuels. As Samuels wandered over to the photograph and answered that they were M-16s I glimpsed a kitchen table laden with bottles of ammonia, packets of bicarbonate and a microwave oven.

'Me 'ear the AK-47s is better,' said Errol to keep Samuels talking and make out that he had some sort of expertise.

'Don't tark 'bout wha yuh nah know!' snapped Samuels. 'The bote-a dem can carry tirty rouns but the M-16 is only two-tirds d'weight. Bloodclart. An' it more accurate in bursts. Pop-pop-pop. Henyway, AKs are communist fuckrees. Me an' Rawldie were JLP enforcers, seen? We hate Cuba an' dem tings. Wha unno, JLP or PNP?'

'Er, we don't know nothin 'bout Jamaican politics,' Errol answered lamely, recognizing that he had strayed into an area of potential conflict. The air crackled with animosity and Samuels spun around and saw me looking into the kitchen. He raised his gun and yelled, 'Bote-a unno, si down!'

The two of us moved towards the pair of stools and Errol exchanged a nervous glance with me. In an instant I was back in a headmaster's office. The last time I had been ordered to sit down next to Errol was after a kid, who had been expelled from another school, had turned up and failed to pay due respect to the way we had things ordered. It was left to me to go with Errol to show the boy the error of his ways. After the interloper had been led away by a teacher to get cleaned up, Mr Jenks took the pair of us into his office and ordered us to be seated in front of his imposing desk. He looked truly disappointed to see me with Errol and said that my friendship with him would only ever lead me into trouble.

'Jenksy, bwoy, never a truer word,' I muttered as I sat down on one of the wooden stools.

'Wha dat?' snarled Samuels.

'Just talkin to myself,' I said.

Samuels curled his lip and stroked his chin with the barrel of the revolver. His cold eyes bore into me until I turned my gaze to the floor; there was no way I was going to engage in a staring match with a psychopath, especially one who was waving a gun around the place. I would bide my time.

Once he was satisfied that he had established his superiority, Beresford Samuels sat on an armrest of the torn leather chair and began to talk with Errol. For a reason known only to himself he began to berate 'Hinglan' and its 'sarf' inhabitants.

While the ranting continued I took my chance to have a good look at Beresford Samuels. Wide shoulders, a thick neck that supported a squarish head. His face was flat, his features broad. A small scar divided one eyebrow. Around the muscular neck were two gold chains to match the pair of gold-capped incisors which gleamed on either side of his mouth. A designer T-shirt was stretched over his broad chest; the revolver now rested on one of his heavy thighs.

While Errol mostly nodded like a jackass, Samuels went on to recount tales of violence that had occurred during his youth in Kingston.

He told of how he and his brother had been abandoned by parents, aunts and uncles who had taken turns to go and search for fortune in the Land of Opportunity. It had, apparently, been a life of 'tufness an' pussyclart tribulation'. He spoke in a Jamaican patois which was sprinkled with American movie-speak; when he referred to himself as a 'gunslinga' I nearly burst out laughing. The crazy ras must have thought he was John-rahteed-Wayne.

'But wait,' he said to Errol, 'me know you fram somewhere.'

Errol replied, 'Go-a dance an' see Sir Jabba an' you see me.'

Samuels said, 'Oh yeah, man, yeah. Some nice music unno play, noh man. One time me let off a couple-a lickshot to show mi happreciation.' He leaned forward as if to emphasize that he was studying Errol's reaction. 'You remember dat?'

Errol could hardly have forgotten the incident. I recalled how his voice had shaken as he told me of the shots at a house party which had downed half a ceiling, almost took the manhood off a guy who had just dropped his pants in the bedroom above and had caused a stampede which left five people requiring hospital treatment. Errol sucked at his teeth. 'Cha, man,' he said, 'plenty lickshot go off when we play. Me can't remember them all.'

A thin smile of begrudging admiration spread across the face of Beresford Samuels. He fingered his chains and, as if hypnotized by the glint of gold around his neck, I sat up straight, lost in the thought that we would be doing the world a favour if we made a bit more room for the good people.

Suddenly there was more gold on show as Samuels bared his teeth. 'Deh sumtin me nah like 'bout you,' he growled at me. He said to Errol, 'You me deal wid but yuh pardna will 'ave to go, by imself or wid you. Mek yuh mind up fast.'

'I'm stayin,' Errol said quickly. 'I wanna do business.'

To me Samuels spat, 'You! Move yuh pussyclart!'

I got up very, very slowly and looked at Errol - my eyes trying to communicate that this would be our chance. He turned his head away, as though he was scared that my unspoken message might be inter-

61

cepted. I watched him stiffen as his gaze fell onto the lopsided photograph above the fireplace.

'Okay, E,' I said so he would look at me, 'I'll wait in the car, yeah?'

He glanced up at me, reluctantly, and mumbled, 'Yeah, wait outside.'

Samuels pushed at my shoulder and turned me towards the door. The gun prodded me in the back and I headed into the darkness of the hallway with him close behind. I had made up my mind about what we should do but what happened next would be Errol's decision.

Maybe Carmen had been right, her brother *was* having a mental breakdown. At the funeral Tyrone had been friendly to the point of embarrassment but once we had pulled away from his place and began our journey to the Rose and Crown I sensed his mood was very different. For the first few miles he sat silently, fidgeting with the hair on his chin and saying very little but for a few brusque directions. His silence made me uncomfortable and warded off any attempt at starting small talk. Not that I was so inclined: all I wanted to do was find out if he really knew anything about the deaths of Errol and Hanimal.

'You're an intelligent guy, I always thought that,' he said abruptly. 'But it's a devious kind-a intelligence. Satan is no fool.'

I carried on with the driving, not knowing how to respond to the man. He continued, 'Malek is an intelligent man but it's a good sort-a intelligence. He has insight, a gift from Allah. He knows the way forward for black people, that's why the white man is out to destroy him.'

Again I failed to make any sort of reply and his voice then took on an accusatory tone. 'They can't deal with a black man who uses his intelligence for the betterment of his own people rather than just sellin it out for the white man's money.'

Tyrone then returned to his simmering silence and said nothing else for quite a while. Occasionally, and more worryingly, he would slam his fist against the dashboard and several times I almost stopped the car. I thought I had wasted my time, the man was ill and nothing he might tell me could be relied upon. I should have gone to my mother's and collected Nathan. If only I could have wound back time an hour or two.

His mood changed yet again and he let out a low moaning sound. Sounding close to tears he said, 'Atonement, that is what we black people must make. There are black men an' women who 'ave to make redress for the sins they 'ave committed.'

A light turned red and the car skidded to a halt on the shiny tarmac. Tyrone's erratic behaviour created a pressure which was building up inside of me. 'Atonement mi bumbaclart!' I exploded. 'Look, man, all this hatred you an' Malek have for what's wrong with this world is turnin in on itself. Suddenly everyone, black or white, who don't see things the exact way you do becomes the enemy. I know all about that, guy...'

'Take the nex lef,' Tyrone interrupted calmly. 'Yeah, me seh you know all about it. Long time me think about how much you know. The man with all the answers.'

I was stung by his contempt. 'For your own good, Tyrone, check what this Malek is sayin an' then try an' match his words with how he lives his life. Like Carmen says, for a man that goes on 'bout the evils of white man's capitalism he sure likes big cars an' fancy shoes.'

'Oh yeah? In all the time I know you, I never hear you goin on the same way 'bout the white bishop in im palace preachin 'bout blessed are the poor, or the preacher robbin his congregation so he can dally over to Jamaica whenever him feel like. I know how Malek stay 'cause I see how him operate close up an' not 'cause I read some lie in a white man's newspaper.'

My anger subsided with the realization that any argument I could offer would only bounce off the wall he had built around his mind. 'Maybe you're right,' I said in an attempt to mollify him.

We continued our journey in prickly silence until we neared the Rose and Crown. 'Go past the pub,' he said, 'an' take the lef into the car park. Make sure you don't miss it.'

In the time it took me to swing the car into the car park I sensed that Tyrone's mood had grown even darker. I stopped the car and turned my head to see him glaring at me, his eyes shimmering with hatred. 'Yuh know,' he hissed through clenched teeth, 'I keep rememberin how Errol was a man of principle. Me an' him had a lot in common. But you, I can't see nothin you an' him could-a shared, except for mi sister's cratchies. An' I ain't talkin superficial, I'm talkin 'bout the stuff that makes a man - I'm talkin beliefs. Tell me, Robbie, did you think he was a man of principle?'

I was unsure how to answer. 'I guess so. Look, Tyrone, Carmen was tellin me that you said somethin the other day 'bout Errol gettin killed.'

'I guess so,' he parroted sourly. 'An' that's why you come to my yard, to find out what I know. I knew you would. So you wanna know what I find out?'

'Well...yeah.'

'But of course, you're the one who has to. But first me 'ave a lickle business in the pub deh. Pass me the bag an' we'll talk when I get back.'

The man was toying with me. More angry with myself, I said, 'You put it deh, pick it up yuhself an' g'wan 'bout your business.'

He laughed in a dismissive way and took the black holdall from the back seat. Once out of the car he lowered his head and said, 'Keep the engine runnin. Black men might own the pub but it's still in an area where crazy white men live.'

I cursed us both as I watched him weave his way through lines of parked cars towards the yellow smoky light which shone out through an open door. I turned the car around towards the road and thought about leaving. But I couldn't and Tyrone knew as much: I had to wait to find out what he had learned about the deaths of Errol and Hanimal.

The slow ticking of the engine made me realize how slowly time was passing so I turned it off. What had he found out? What was he doing in the pub? He was never one to visit this sort of place, even before he had uttered the words of the Shahadah and became a member of the Brothers of Islam. Whatever he was doing, he must have planned to see me at the funeral and then persuade me to bring him here. For some twisted reason he had wanted me sitting in this car park.

A sense of foreboding, like icy-cold fingertips on the back of my neck, sent a shiver down my spine. I licked the salt from the corners of my mouth and thought how I should have drunk the tea that Carmen had brought me, I should have eaten the food she had cooked and then I should have gone straight to my mother's to collect Nathan. I should have done anything but visit Tyrone and then drive him to a place like this.

A man appeared in the doorway Tyrone had used to enter the rear of the pub. Furtively, he looked left and right - as if he were acting as a lookout. He was tall with big shoulders and wearing what looked like a parka coat. The light was too poor and he was too far away for me to clearly see his face but there was something vaguely familiar about him.

As I tried to recall where I had seen him before he melted away into the pub's smoky interior. I knew then that something unpleasant was going on. What should I do? I could turn the ignition key and head for home or I could put the tyre lever I kept under my seat up the sleeve of my jacket and go in and find out what had happened to Tyrone.

Without shifting my gaze from the open door across the car park, my fingers groped under my seat until they found the flat steel bar. Shit, I didn't want all this, especially not for a guy like Tyrone. I tried to strike a bargain with God: if I went into that pub and saved Tyrone, if he needed saving, He would make sure I would live to pick up Nathan from my mother's. He didn't answer but a voice in my head told me to start the engine before going into the pub in case there needed to be a very quick getaway. Yeah, that much made sense but it was hardly divine revelation.

I turned the key but the engine only churned reluctantly and then died. This God, I thought, is He helping me out or taking the piss? I turned the key again. This time the engine churned even more slowly before giving up the ghost while making a sound like a dying donkey. I apologized to God and called out, 'Let the car start now an' I'll take it as a message to get mi ras outta here!'

The passenger door flew open and my heart almost stopped.

'Get this ting movin!' yelled Tyrone as he threw himself onto the front seat.

Again the engine failed to fire. 'Come on!' he shouted.

Tyrone's lack of composure made me take a breath; one of us needed to keep a cool head. The headlights - I had left them on and they were draining the battery. I turned them off hoping that my attempts to start the engine had not used up every drop of power. The engine turned slowly and then burbled. I pumped the accelerator until it roared loudly and with a squeal from the tyres we were moving. I whooped with delight and shouted out my thanks to the Almighty as we left the car park. But it was only a fleeting sense of relief; something made me take a nervous backwards glance and I saw the man in the parka coat looking out from the doorway.

It took some time, and some distance travelled, before I could muster the breath to talk. I looked around me but I could see no sign of the black holdall. I then looked up at Tyrone's face and saw that he was staring at me in a manner that did not appear to be totally sane. The feeling of relief I had felt escaping from a situation I did not fully understand had turned to anger. 'What the fuck you lookin at, Tyrone? You'd better start tellin me what's goin on.'

'A dutty pussyclart, that's what me-a look at. A fuckin informer. A dutty bastard who has betrayed his own people.'

'What? Cha, yuh gone fuckin crazy, guy?' I said as my eyes nervously flitted from the road ahead to Tyrone and back to the road again.

There was a flash. Pain. A blow to the side of my head had sent me, and the car, sideways. I hit the brakes and yelled out, 'You fuckin madman!' As I struggled to straighten the car I was struck by another blow and then another. All the time he was screaming at me furiously. My left eye felt as though it had been pierced by hundreds of needles while a heavy hammer had simultaneously crashed onto my skull. I was momentarily blinded, a wheel hit a kerb and narrowly avoided a litter bin before I managed to bring the car to a halt.

If boxing had taught me nothing else, I knew how to cope with pain. The moment the car stopped my only aim was to prevent Tyrone from hitting me, with a few well-placed punches of my own. I turned on my seat but my attempt to retaliate was stalled by the point of a knife at my throat.

Tyrone bared his teeth and snarled, 'Make a move, bat an eyelid an' I'll gladly kill you right here an' now!'

7

SAMUELS PUSHED THE barrel of the gun hard against my spine. 'Pull the bolts dem fast,' he ordered me, 'or me kill you.'

He was the one with the gun and yet I felt as though I was in control and I think he felt that too. That's what had unsettled him; he knew that none of his threats scared me.

Why should they? I did not care if I lived or died; my relationship with Sharon had disintegrated, my son had been taken away from me, and the home I had built for the three of us had been stripped bare. But most of all, I was sick of the life I led, sick of the way I had been tethered and held down by people's low expectations since the day I left my mother and walked through the school gates at the age of five. It seemed nothing I could ever do would change the way I was perceived because there were always guys like Beresford Samuels who were only too happy to play the role of the lowest common denominator. Death, I sometimes thought, would be a merciful release from the frustration that had begun to crush my soul.

I pulled the first of three bolts.

For two years I had stepped out with Errol and dealt with the stuff of death. We were in the business of trying to kill people. Death was no longer an abstract notion, it was what I thought about every waking moment, in bed with Sharon, playing in the garden with Nathan, enjoying a meal in my mother's house, or clocking in at the factory.

I pulled the second bolt.

In those two years I thought about the people we had set out to kill, the grief, the revulsion, the choking tears our actions would cause. I had learnt that before going out to kill someone, those were the matters I had to confront because they were the reality which lay at the end of the path Errol and I had chosen to walk. Not to face up to that reality might lead to a moment's hesitation that would get either, or both, of us killed. In younger days, when I was more resilient, more flexible, killing was not something I had ever imagined myself doing. 'A killer' was not what I envisaged I could be. But I had been drained of the sweet sap that made life worth living, I had been left with no alternative. Someone had to pay.

Samuels prodded me hard between the shoulder blades and I began to draw the third bolt.

I imagined Errol sitting frozen with fear in the room at the end of the hallway. He was courageous, I never doubted that, but there had been one occasion when he had let both of us down. An older kid named Neville Jackson had snatched the Silver Surfer comic we were reading in the playground. Without hesitation I jumped on the big bastard expecting Errol to do the same thing. But Jackson's fearsome reputation robbed Errol of the ability to move his limbs and I took some bitch-licks as he just stood there gawping. Still, I did get the comic back.

'Now the chain,' snarled Samuels. ''Urry it up, bastard.'

My fingers wrestled awkwardly with the chain. 'Errol,' I muttered to myself, 'you've let me down again, guy.'

It was at that moment I heard him coming down the hallway.

The point of the knife was pushed hard against the top of my throat and in those long and excruciating seconds, reason somehow triumphed over bowel-loosening emotion: I had to get him to talk to me.

'What's this all about, Tyrone?' I asked him. 'You could-a killed us both.'

'You think I'm scared of death, pussy? Nah, it don't scare. I can see how it scare you, though.'

He pressed the knife until my head tilted back and became jammed between the headrest and the glass of the car window. I was certain that if I tried to grab his wrist the blade would puncture my skin and exit through the top of my head. 'Are you scared of dyin, pussy?' he growled.

I couldn't speak; the smallest movement in my throat would have me retching and skewering myself on the knife. He eased the pressure enough to allow me to face him. Through clenched teeth I managed to say, 'I swear, Tyrone, I ain't got a clue what this is all about. Why you doin this, man?'

'For three friends of mine, bastard. Three brave guys who were set up an' killed by a shitstem who couldn't afford to let them go to trial. Set up and delivered by an informer.'

'I swear on my son's life...'

'Fuck your son's life. The informer had to be somebody close an' I arks myself what sort-a darg would betray them. What sort-a darg is smellin aroun the mother of Errol's son now im daddy gone.'

'Nothin went on between me an' Carmen until long after...'

'Like a darg aroun a bitch. See, for two years no police could catch them guys; they tried to keep it quiet 'bout the tings they did, they even tried to make out that them nah really exist. In the end the government decided that they couldn't put in court invisible men for somethin them deny had ever happened, so they had them blown away. Them laid a trap. Three guys were supposed to pick up two AK-47s. But only two turned up: Errol an' Hanimal. Maybe they found out it was a trap an' tried to escape, or maybe they were killed an' then it was made to look like an accident. Whatever happen, them still end up dead an' Shaka got hunted down an' shot before them guys were cold.'

Something he said rang true: I had warned Errol not to have any dealings with whoever offered him those guns. Suddenly my mind was filled with all manner of scenarios. 'Who told you all this?' I asked, in between gasps.

It was the wrong question to ask. The point of the knife lifted me from the seat, the lining of my throat went into spasms and made it impossible for me to breathe, and liquid I thought must be blood clouded my vision. I thought I was about to either pass out or feel the blade pierce my windpipe but once again Tyrone let the pressure ease a little. He was not ready to kill me - just yet. There was something else he wanted me to hear before I died.

He laughed crazily for a while and then explained that I had just assisted in the planting of a bomb which would detonate at any minute. 'Those Campbells,' he snarled, 'they think they're untouchable because they have police in their pockets. Since Glenroy an' im brother Alvin got outta prison they ain't wasted no time in recoverin the business those Italian bastards took from them. All the drugs on the Blackmore is comin from the Campbells an' they don't heed no warnin the Brotherhood has give them so far...'

'You mean warnins like wha happen to Earl Johnson?'

'Exactly,' Tyrone said with more than a hint of satisfaction. 'When I was arksed to take the bomb into that pub it crossed my mind that if it went off while I was headin there I wanted you dead with me. Or if it went off while I was settin it down an' I was killed, I wanted you waitin outside like an accomplice who would do a life sentence.' So that was why he shouted to the youths and the man across the street before he got into my car - to make sure I would be recognized. 'But if I got outta there alive,' he was saying now, 'I prayed that Allah would reward me with the pleasure of killin you myself. Whatever was gonna happen, you nah escape punishment for your treachery.'

Then there was silence, a lingering silence while he savoured the moment, and then came a strange noise from outside. A man standing on the pavement was urinating against the front wing of my car. From the corner of my eye I saw him sway and tug at his zip before he bent down and took a look in at us. 'Oi, Dave,' he called to his friend, 'There's two blokes in here.'

The other man tottered over and pressed his face against the glass in front of Tyrone. 'You daft cunt,' he slurred, 'they ain't blokes, it's two coons. Hey, what you doing around here, coons? Want to end up in a skip, do ya?'

The man slammed his hand onto the roof of the car and Tyrone blinked and looked over his shoulder. I took my chance and pulled at his right arm. In less than a second he turned his head back towards me and simultaneously tried to put the knife through me. I gripped his wrist with my two hands. His arm shook with murderous intention as he screamed that I was about to die. He punched me in the face with his free hand

and then fastened it around my throat. The back of my head thudded against the glass of the door. The wild eyes in front of me grew large, his hot stinking breath filled my nostrils. As my left hand continued to prevent the knife running me through, my right pulled at the fingers which were squeezing the life out of me. I couldn't budge them and I felt myself growing weaker, my arms becoming light and my brain catching fire. I knew there were only seconds left before I blacked out.

I gambled; with one final throw of the dice I let go of the hand around my throat and reached back towards the door catch. My little finger, sweaty and quivering, slid under the black plastic lever and I pulled it forward using what feeble strength remained in my body.

A rush of air, a sudden noise and the back of my head was brushing the wet tarmac. Tyrone was falling forward, his chest coming up over my face, his feet brushing my stomach. In the crazy upsidedown world I could hardly make sense of, I saw Tyrone's shape in the headlights on the road above me. Tyres hissed, brakes shrieked and a white van stopped only inches away from him. He clambered to his feet and disappeared from my line of vision.

I was aware that a small crowd had gathered to watch as I tried to pull myself back into the car. After two or three fruitless attempts to lift my shoulders off the tarmac someone put their hands under my armpits and dragged my lower half out onto the road and helped me to my feet.

'Go on then, coon,' called one of the drunks. He made a sweeping gesture towards the Rushbury estate. 'Go on and chase him then. He went that way, you stupid black bastard.'

Tyrone might have gone crazy but his instinct for self-preservation remained intact long enough to ensure that he did not run in the direction of the Lowlands.

I tasted the blood that ran from my nose as I looked around to see the driver of the white van sitting frozen in shock and Tyrone's knife which lay in the middle of the road. I bent down and picked it up, and by the time I had straightened, all the onlookers had vanished.

The adrenalin was already starting to dissipate and pain was rushing to take its place in every fibre of my body as I struggled into my car and started up the engine. Looking back towards the Rushbury estate I thought about where Tyrone might have run to but I had no mind to pursue him; all I wanted to do was to see my son once again.

My mother gasped as she saw me standing on her doorstep, and once she had got her breath back she insisted that I tell her how I had come by my injuries. I sipped a glass of water and told her five guys had jumped me. She asked if I had called the police and I answered her with a wave of my wallet and told her that there was no need.

Despite her protestations that Nathan was fast asleep, I took him home - I needed him with me - though by the state of his groggy eyes I doubted if he remembered much about it.

In bed I could not sleep. I watched the numerals of my clock-radio silently transmute. The pain of my injuries grew along with my anxiety as I waited for the next news bulletin. I had fiddled continually with the tuning button but had heard no report of an explosion at the Rose and Crown. I began to doubt that Tyrone had really planted a bomb, and once I was convinced that there would be no report of one, I turned so I lay flat on my back. With my head and body throbbing in agony I made the mistake of thanking God for being alive. I had found out long ago that nothing about the notion of God comes for free and as I closed my eyes, memories of that other life-or-death struggle began to filter from the deeper recesses of my mind.

Errol called out, 'Me forget to give him mi car keys.' He then made the mistake of alerting Samuels to his real intention by forcing a laugh as cold and as brittle as early winter's ice.

Samuels turned, I felt the gun leave my back and I spun around as he tried to point it in Errol's direction. I took hold of the arm that still carried the scars of a backstreet brawl in Tivoli Gardens and screamed for Errol to take hold of his free hand. Samuels may have been taken by surprise but his strength quickly returned and he almost lifted me off my feet as he tried to raise the gun.

There was not much I could see in the dark. I could smell Samuels' acrid odour, I could hear his heavy breaths and the mucus rattling in his airways. My skin against his skin, I felt his heat, his sweat. Our bodies moved to and fro as if we were engaged in some macabre dance of death.

He roared and pushed Errol and me against a wall. We shoved him back. I heard Errol yelp in pain and breathlessly shout for me to do something. Like me, Errol must have felt the muscles in his arms catch fire, his fingers must have ached as they tried to maintain a grip, and he too must have been scared of the consequences should the wet skin slip from our grasp.

Samuels lashed out with one of his feet. Errol groaned as if he were winded. I drew back a little and planted my feet before throwing the best left hook of my life. My knuckles exploded onto the chin of Beresford Samuels and the neck muscles that had looked so strong instantly turned to jelly. There was a sound like the cracking of an egg as the back of his head hit the wall. Errol stood over him sucking in air. I asked him if he was all right. Still unable to catch his breath, he showed me the gun and how his little finger had jammed the hammer and prevented it from firing.

'You're good, man,' I said, 'but put it down an' give me a hand to tie the bastard.'

I drew the two nylon tie-wraps from my waistband that Samuels had failed to detect when frisking me for a weapon. Without the need for talk, we turned him on his stomach and bound his wrists and ankles.

I wiped the sweat from my eyes and said to Errol, 'Right, now we're gonna drag him back into that room an' arks him that question I was tellin you about.'

Lactic acid had done its worst. In the few hours I had slept, every muscle in my back had turned into blocks of solid oak. I struggled to the bathroom, whimpering like a puppy and yet still toying with the idea that I should carry on with life as though nothing had happened. It only took one look at the strange misshapen face staring back at me from the bathroom mirror to convince me that I was not fit to go to work.

While I took tentative sips from a glass of milk Nathan happily munched his breakfast cereal after he had enquired what had happened to my face. My voice barely more than a whisper, I answered, 'Daddy fell over.' Nathan turned down the corners of his mouth and shrugged his shoulders like a crusty and cynical septuagenarian might do and then got on with cleaning out his bowl.

We reached school with a good few minutes to spare. Usually I took Nathan to my mother's on my way to work and I would have been at the factory for more than an hour by the time she dropped him off at the gates. I wasn't comfortable with the stares from the mothers who were gathered around the entrance. On reflection, the scarf I had put on in the hope of hiding some of my injuries could have given me the appearance of a potential child abductor and I became worried that one of them would call the police if I remained outside the school much longer.

I scanned the playground for Nathan to wave him goodbye and saw that he was standing with Tyrone's son. I looked nervously about to see if Tyrone was anywhere near. My eyes met those of a petite black woman who was among a group that eyed me suspiciously. She smiled politely and approached me.

'Hi,' she said pleasantly. 'Are you Carmen's partner?'

I frowned and shook my head. 'Friend,' I replied hoarsely.

Her smile turned apologetic. 'Sorry,' she said and looked over anxiously into the playground. 'My name's Lyzette, I've known Carmen for years. I was looking after Duane for Tyrone last night but he never came back for him. He's never done that before. If Duane stays with me overnight he's always at my door first thing in the morning. I rang Carmen but she hadn't got a clue where he was.'

She paused as if to allow me to say something. My silence flustered her a little and she went on, 'Only I, er, thought you and him might be friends. He had said someone was taking him out. I thought you might know who it was.'

I shook my head and patted my throat. 'Sorry, I've laryngitis. Try callin the Brothers of Islam.'

She gave me a smile in appreciation of my efforts to talk and said she would give them and Carmen another call when she got home. 'Hope you get better soon,' she said.

The small red light of my answering machine was flashing when I got home. It was a message from Carmen. She sounded distressed and said she needed to talk. I knew that she wanted to talk about her brother. I did not have the voice to return her call - and even if I had, there was nothing I could truthfully say that would lessen her anxiety.

8

IT HAD BEEN a long and painful week. I gave up on God again. He, She or It was not to be relied upon. We had made an agreement, or so I thought. After I had taken Nathan from Sharon I promised God that I would make peace with the world, avert my eyes from all the injustices that might re-ignite my rage and bring up my son to be a good and righteous person. Nathan would grow to be a better man than I would ever be, would never do the things I had done - on condition that I lived a good, if boring, life. All God had to do was to keep trouble and the past from my door.

It seemed to me that God had been distracted by other matters over the last few days.

With the exception of my throat, it did not take long for my body to begin to mend. Aided by a few well-placed ice packs and very hot baths before I went to bed, the swelling on my face went down and my bruises and stiff muscles began to loosen.

It was the emotional hurt that did not heal as quickly. For the first three days I would return home from the school at around nine o'clock and simply sit in my armchair. With a glass of milk in one hand I would think about all the friends who had died until it was time to collect Nathan in the afternoon. More than once I had allowed myself bouts of weeping but the shedding of tears no longer held any fear for me.

In truth, I felt unburdened. For four years I had been so careful with my words or any expression of what I really felt. Finally, I was being honest, at least with myself.

And Tyrone Swaby had unwittingly prevented me from falling into a deep well of depression. None of it was pleasant but he had provided me with something other than the loss of all my old friends to dwell upon.

Firstly, there was the continuing threat to my life. Every morning, before driving my car to the school, I would inspect the road for any sign of brake fluid. I ensured that the front and back doors of my house were kept locked at all times as I often thought about where Tyrone was and what he might be planning for me.

Secondly, he had brought back to the surface all the questions I had once asked myself about Errol's death. For most of the time I had managed to keep them buried under the petty considerations and routine of a humdrum life. Of course, there were times when I did think of him, but not how he had died - rather how he had lived. Those memories mostly occurred when I was out driving past certain places or when I visited Carmen. Little things that Tim did, gestures for instance, brought his father back to life. Now I was back to thinking about his death: not in a grieving way as I did with Fidel and Mr Robinson, but about matters of how and why he had died. They would be harder to bury a second time.

When my voice was strong again I returned one of Carmen's calls. She asked, straight out, if I had taken up Tyrone's invitation and visited his flat the night he disappeared. It was the question I had expected and prepared for. I told her that I had followed her advice and after leaving her place I had gone straight to my mother's and collected Nathan. She sounded as if she believed me but in case she wanted me to elaborate I told her of my 'laryngitis' and kept the rest of my responses to sympathetic grunts.

By Sunday morning I had recovered enough in body and mind to think of returning to work the following day. On Friday a number of bills had tumbled onto the floor of my hallway and reminded me that, whatever else was going on, I still had to earn a living. Returning to the factory was not something that I wanted to do, my insides churned at the thought of it, but I would have to do so until I found another job.

Just the idea of looking for another job helped raise my spirits. I had spent too much time in the one place, I had been too easily seduced by the comforts of the familiar. It was time to make the changes that I had always postponed. I would start by making moves to get out of the factory, out of this house and, maybe, out of this city. For too long I had ignored the advice Danny Maguire once gave me and engaged myself in some sort of self-inflicted endurance test: I set myself the task of forgetting the past and yet I had remained stewing in the same pot. It was time to get out and walk away.

Nathan, without the slightest consideration for my still imperfect physical condition, had talked me into playing football with him until it was time for us to go to my mother's for Sunday dinner. My muscles were still a little tight, as I reminded him when he implored me to chase the ball. He was winning two-nil when the telephone rang and the ball thudded against the back wall in frustration as I went inside.

It was Carmen again.

'Any news?' I asked.

'Yeah, but not about Tyrone exactly,' she replied. 'I've just had Malek Abu Bakr an' two of im heavies push their way in here. He said he was lookin for Tyrone. He said Tyrone had somethin that belonged to him. They made a search, pulled Tim from im bed an' then asked a few questions about the last time we had seen Tyrone an' if we knew who he was with the night he went missin.'

She paused, in case I had something more to add to what I had already told her. 'What did you say?' I asked.

'The same thing I told the police. The first I knew about him missin was when Lyzette ring me. What else could I say?'

'Nothin,' I said in a vague way, as I wondered about the something that belonged to Malek - a bomb in a black holdall perhaps? Then, aware of the impatient silence on the other end of the line I added, 'They didn't hurt you, did they?'

'No,' she said coolly.

'That's good.'

'Robbie...'

'Carmen, can I call you back later? We were just headin to my mom's for dinner.'

'Oh, okay.'

'Call you later, then. 'Bye.'
'Bye.'

She had sounded so fragile, so unlike the strong woman who I had found so attractive. I hated cutting her short but I had to be cold. If I was serious about leaving I had to cut my ties with her - and with the other woman in my life. Both Carmen and my mother were strong people, they would get over it. I had to cut myself off from anything or anyone that might persuade me to stay.

Before I could continue to mull over what Carmen had told me about Malek and his men I was aware of the lack of sound coming from my back garden: the ball no longer thudded against the wall. I ran to the kitchen only for Nathan to collide with my legs as he hurtled through the open door.

'Daddy!' he gasped. 'There's a man out the back watching me!'

I stepped outside but saw no one. 'Where?'

'Behind the hedge,' he sobbed. 'When I went to get the ball I saw him looking at me.'

I ran to the gate and then down the pathway which divided the rear gardens that belonged to houses in my street and the one which ran parallel to it. Still I saw no one and I hurried back to Nathan.

'Are you sure, Nathan?' I asked. I crouched down and looked into his tearful face.

He nodded gravely.

'Was it Tyrone? Could you tell if it was Tyrone?'

'I just saw his eyes, Dad. I saw a man's eyes when I picked up the ball. I shouted like you told me to if a nasty man ever tries to get me and then I heard him run away.'

My immediate feeling was one of guilt: I had put my son at unnecessary risk by insisting he stayed with me. It would have been safer if he had stayed with my mother until I was fit again, as she had suggested.

'You don't have to worry,' I said while putting an arm around his shoulders. 'He wasn't one of those nasty men.' He looked at me with wide eyes, as if he were making himself receptive to every comforting syllable. 'No,' I continued, 'I bet he lives in one of the houses out the back and when he heard the ball bein kicked he looked through the hedge and thought he was lookin at a brilliant footballer.'

'Do you think so, Dad?' he mumbled.

'You were beatin me one-nil, weren't you?'

'Two-nil.'

'Bwoy, there you are then, you have to be brilliant to beat your old man two-nil. Now, Daddy's goin back to work tomorrow an' I think it might be better if you stay at your nan's tonight. So go upstairs an' get your clothes for school an' that. Is that okay with you?'

Nathan didn't bother to reply. He ran upstairs enraptured with the thought of my mother spoiling him. I looked back towards the hedge. The guilt I felt was overtaken by rage. So, Tyrone had come looking for another chance to kill me.

By the time Nathan stood at the foot of the stairs beaming at me with his little travel bag in his hands I had convinced myself that I would not be surprised by Tyrone a second time. He'd had the only chance I was going to give him. I put my arms around Nathan and silently vowed that I would not allow Tyrone to deprive my son of a father. I knew then that I could kill Tyrone, if that's what it would take to stop him.

Once we had dragged him back to the room at the end of the hallway and laid him on his stomach, Beresford Samuels regained consciousness. He began to scream that we did not know who we were dealing with and that he would have us killed and fed to pigs. I laughed and willed him on while examining Errol's expression. I wanted to see a sign that Errol had reached the same conclusion as I had as soon as we had taken the gun from Samuels: there was no way we could leave this man alive.

I put a heel on the back of Samuels' neck and quelled his noise. Errol stared down at him, anxiously rolling his lips. I knew that he had only envisaged handing out a serious beating, maybe a maiming, in response to the savage beating that was meted out to Carmen. He had come looking for Samuels because of some fool notion that he had a reputation to uphold; Carmen's injuries were only a minor detail.

A line had to be crossed before he was ready to kill, justification had to be provided. When we had stepped out to look to kill other people, the justification was all around us, but I knew Errol still thought that guys like Samuels were bucking the system we hated and not playing a part in reinforcing it. I was sure Samuels would provide all the justification Errol required to kill him - as long as he answered the question I put to him.

I said to Errol, 'Come put your foot 'pon im neckback while I go make preparations.'

The instant I moved my heel Samuels rolled onto his back and tried to lash out with his legs that were bound at the ankles. Errol moved before I did and brought the frantic thrashing to a halt by stamping on the man's balls. I knew then that he was ready to do what was necessary.

Heady with the feelings of power, I looked down to Samuels as he groaned in pain. When he had first come to town I heard from Hanimal that Samuels had boasted that 'Hinglish bwoys' only thought they knew what badness was. Badness, I thought, I will show you badness.

When his moaning had subsided, I said to Samuels, 'I'm only gonna arks this once. Who you workin for?'

He replied, 'Man, unno fuckin dead!'

Another threat, even now. I laughed and said, 'Don't seh me nah warn you.'

Errol put a foot on his throat and I turned around and went into the bathroom.

A bell rang out like a ricocheting bullet as the shop door opened. Balbir, also known as Bill to his customers, was stacking a low shelf. He straightened, momentarily startled, and his already owlish eyes grew larger. 'Oh, Robbie, good morning,' he puffed. 'Haven't seen you for a few days. Sick?'

Fingers indicating the trouble, I said, 'Sore throat.'

Dismissive, Bill said, 'Everybody's had that.'

He moved to the rear of the counter and shifted his daughter sideways. The young girl stumbled and shrieked loudly. 'Be careful,' I said as she righted herself. The girl cast her eyes to the floor and moved swiftly to the room at the back. The old woman in a white sari who sat on a rickety old chair close to the stockroom door was a permanent fixture. I did not know what she said to the girl but the tone was one of chastisement. She closed the door and peered over at me through her jam-jar lenses. 'Hello, mister,' she called, 'all right?' In all the years I had bought my newspaper at Bill's before setting off for work, this was the most she had ever said to me.

All right? If I thought the woman really wanted to know, I would have said: 'I'm all right...Except that two of my best friends were buried the day a maniac tried to kill me. I'm all right, except...' But no, she didn't really want to know.

'Just the paper?' asked Bill. He nervously peered around my shoulder.

'An' a packet of lozenges.' He continued to stare out into the street. I glanced back and said, 'Everythin okay, Bill?'

'A nephew, my sister's son, was attacked last night,' he answered. 'He's in hospital, intensive care, very sick.'

'Sorry to hear that. What happened?'

'A gang of skinheads jumped out of a car and beat him. That's all we know.'

'Things are gettin bad,' I said, sorting out my change.

'Bad? My God, even my brother in America doesn't come across violence like this. While we were at the hospital they brought in those three men who had been shot while sitting in their car. Policemen with guns were all over the place. Look, it's here on the front page.' He turned around a newspaper and dabbed a finger on the banner headline. *'Three men die in gangland shooting,'* he read out loud.

I looked at the photograph of the car which was sitting on a low-loader partially covered by a tarpaulin. Below it was a report which identified the victims as Paolo and Giovanni Cervi and a second-hand car dealer named Ronald Felton.

'Fuck them guys,' I muttered, 'they ain't no loss.'

The Cervis had moved from supplying most of the city's nightclubs and bars with doormen to supplying drugs to most of the dealers who had previously done business with the two Campbell brothers before they went to prison. The story went that on his release the eldest brother, Glenroy Campbell, had called at a nightclub to have a word with Giovanni. When two great slabs of steroid-induced muscle barred his way, Glenroy pulled a gun and shot the two doormen in the legs. When the Cervis retaliated by having one of Campbell's younger cousins blasted with a shotgun and confined to a wheelchair for the rest of his life, Glenroy went crazy. To him, the shooting of employees was purely business but the crippling of a family member had made it personal.

'It was once very peaceful around here,' Bill said fearfully, 'but now there are too many shootings, too much violence. If I could, I would sell up and move far away from here. I would take my family away from these bloody thugs. We are almost having nervous breakdowns, my poor nephew is in hospital and there has been a fellow standing across the road watching this place for nearly all of last week.'

'A black guy with a beard, broad, a bit shorter than me?'

'No, no, no. This was a big white man, his hair very short like a skinhead. I watched him, he was out there for five mornings looking in here. Sometimes he was on his own and sometimes he was with another man.'

'What was he dressed like?'

'Scruffy. He wore one of those dirty green army coats. I called the police about him but when they finally turned up they started talking bloody rubbish. They asked how do I know if he wasn't waiting for a lift or only looking in here for something to buy. To them I am just another Paki bastard who will have to end up like my nephew before they take me seriously. I tell you, Robbie, that man was up to no good. In my heart I could feel his evil.'

Straight away I asked myself if this could be the man who had scared Nathan or if he was the big guy I had seen at the rear door of the Rose and Crown. Maybe he had traced me to my home. But why? Was it something to do with what had actually gone on in the pub that night?

'Well?' said Bill, hovering in anticipation of a response from me. I looked up at the clock on the wall; if I didn't get a move on I would be late on my first morning back at the factory. I slapped the money onto the counter and gathered the newspaper and lozenges before hurrying to the door. 'Yeah,' I called back to Bill, 'the police around here ain't big on feelins of evil in the heart.'

9

HER POWDERED FACE was a mask of perfect disdain. Fidel had called Ms Thornton, the manager's secretary, the 'Great Grimalkin'. And if it wasn't for the rings on the finger of her left hand I would have taken her for a prematurely aged and cantankerous old maid. Her demeanour made it obvious that she viewed the presence of my oily overalls in her office as something approaching a violation of her person.

'My card,' I said, 'it's not in the rack.'

Her lips quivered with distaste. 'Obviously, since you were not here last week.'

'Obviously.'

'Then go out and take the second door on the right.'

'And?'

'And the new procedures will be explained to you.'

'Do have a nice day, Ms Thornton,' I said, purposefully failing to close the door behind me.

As directed, I went to the second door on my right and was surprised to see that a new oblong plastic sign had recently been affixed to it. It read: SECURITY. NO UNAUTHORIZED ADMISSION. It crossed my mind to go back to Ms Thornton and really get her day off to a bad start; surely she had sent me to the wrong room.

I hovered for a moment and then knocked on the door. When there was no response I checked the handle to see if it was locked. The door opened and I stepped in. There was no one about, and figuring that my knock had not been heard I made my way to the room behind the empty desk. I walked straight in and found myself gazing disbelievingly at a whole wall of television screens. All areas of the factory complex were on view and I remembered how Fidel had told me how he'd seen electricians running cables for closed circuit cameras.

'What the hell do you think you are doing?' a voice from behind demanded.

I turned around and saw the tall man with the thinning blond hair I had talked to in the small workshop. I stepped back into the office. 'Ms Thorton sent me here,' I said.

The man put a polystyrene cup of black coffee onto the desk and closed the door to the room which contained the monitors. Obviously aggravated, he steered me to the other side of the desk and said, 'I take it that you can read.' He walked back to his chair. 'The sign on the door - it says no unauthorized admission.'

I really wasn't in the mood for all this; it had taken all my willpower just to get through the factory gates and Ms Thornton had already exhausted the meagre reserves I drew on when confronted with bad manners. I sucked my teeth loudly and said, 'If you wanted to make sure that no one would come in here, you should have locked the door when you went out for your cup of coffee. It's called a simple precaution.'

He sat down and his deep-set eyes angrily flashed up at me before he shuffled some papers around his desk. 'You weren't in last week and you are wondering why your clocking-in card is not in its usual place,' he said sharply.

'Got it in one.'

'So I can take it that you do not have the two passport-sized photographs which will enable you to be issued with a security pass.'

I was baffled. 'Excuse me?'

'You were given plenty of notice that the new measures would be introduced from last week. I know for a fact that your rep Ken Barker kept the shopfloor informed about what was happening every step of the way.'

'Sorry, but you're gonna have to run through it one more time for me. I've had a lot more serious things goin on in my life just lately.'

I thought he would at least acknowledge the deaths of Fidel and Mr Robinson, but he merely explained to me that from now on the factory would be divided into colour-coded sectors. Employees without the correct colours on their badge would not be allowed access to certain areas. He said it was a measure designed to enhance security.

'So what the hell we makin now that needs so much enhanced security?' I asked him.

'The Park-Tec Corporation manufactures a vast range of products, Mr Walker. But to return to the reason why you are here; as you are a member of the maintenance team you will require access to almost every part of this complex. Therefore, I will not only require the two photographs from you, I will also need you to fill in this waiver.'

'Waiver? For what?'

'As you will require one of the highest levels of security clearance, the corporation will have to make a few more enquiries to ensure that you are not at risk of being compromised by one of our rivals. We merely need to know a few details about your finances; loans, HP agreements, those sort of things.'

'Now I know you're takin the piss.'

He took a drink from the polystyrene cup and pushed two sheets of paper towards me. 'If you have an objection you should have brought it up with a member of the workers' council during the consultation period. The forms are very simple and I'm sure you have nothing to hide.'

I put my hands into my pockets and gave the forms a cursory examination. My first thoughts were what Fidel and Mr Robinson would have made of them. 'Religion,' I read out loud, 'political affiliation? Are you a member of a trades union, residents association, sports or social club? Nah, man, this is a piss-take. An' as unions have been banned from here ,why would anyone wanna be a member? Who wants to know all this stuff anyway?'

'The corporation. And the new management wants to get to know its workforce so it can create a better environment for its employees. For example, the religion question may help to have certain foodstuffs provided in the canteen. These are questions your representatives agreed should be asked.'

'All this info seems to be goin one way. I mean, I come in here an' you know my name…'

'Robert Alphonsus Walker,' he said.

It irked me that he knew about the Alphonsus. Now I was even more determined for him to impart some information: '...my department, what sort of clearance I'll require,' I went on, 'but I don't see a name on the door, I don't even know who I'm talkin to. All this about my background - what's yours? Bet you're an ex-cop. Private security is where all you guys who were found on the take end up, ain't it?'

He leaned back in his chair doing his best not to look like he was pissed off with me. The way he had talked to Kyle, and the way Kyle had responded, showed me that he was a man used to giving orders and used to commanding the sort of respect I was not about to show him. He locked his fingers together, cracked his knuckles and then yawned as though he had become so terribly bored. 'I suggest you go and see Ken Barker if you have a problem with the forms,' he said with affected weariness. 'I'm sure he'll explain your position in a way you will be able to understand.'

'An' what position is that?'

'Either you fill those forms or you walk.'

'Bwoy, I don't need Ken Barker for that. Nah, man, I've had an English education. It looks as though I had better clear my locker.'

He opened a drawer. 'No need to be hasty. Like the rest of the workforce you will get five days to comply. Should you fail to comply it will be taken as a breach of contract.' He held out a clocking-in card with a sheet of yellow paper folded over it. 'Keep that paper with you, it will give you clearance to work in all zones during this week.'

After a moment's consideration I took the card and paper. One more week's wages would come in handy and I would book my holidays on Friday and then send in my notice. 'I'd better shift,' I said.'I don't wanna be late clockin in.'

As I went to the door the man called out, 'You have forgotten the forms, Mr Walker.'

I looked back and smiled. Now he would have to give me some information. 'I don't think so. If I want them I'll call back. Who should I ask for?'

He took another drink of coffee and grimaced as though he neither enjoyed the taste nor my little game. 'Ask for me, Mr Walker - the name is Urban.' He returned the cup to the desk. 'And that,' he added ominously, 'is a name you would do well to remember.'

It had been a day of grinding tedium. Luckily, the supervisor did not set me anything but the simplest of tasks and when I had them completed he did not come looking for me to do any more. I think he sensed that I would not be around for much longer now that Fidel and Mr Robinson were gone. In the afternoon I tried to pass the time by going for a stroll and counting the number of cameras that had been installed, but found myself continually confronted by security guards who wanted to see my temporary pass. Things got so bad that I returned to the repair shop and volunteered to help with a strip-down.

Instinct, or maybe it was paranoia, told me to go straight home from work and check that everything was all right before picking up Nathan from my mother's. I knew as soon as I opened my front door that something was wrong: a draught of cold air led me to the back door and its shattered pane of glass.

I bitterly cursed Tyrone as I went from room to room to survey the damage until a knock at the front door roused me from my murderous thoughts. It was Carmen. There was a rare hesitancy about her and I found it difficult to speak because of what had been playing on my mind only moments before. She made a small smile and said, 'I thought I'd pay you a visit as I was around this way an' as you ain't been fit enough to return my calls.'

Confused by her unexpected appearance, I still wasn't sure what to say when she said, 'Robbie, are you gonna let me in or what?'

I stepped back and gestured for her to come inside.

Her mouth fell open as she looked around my living room. It took her several moments to recover her power of speech. 'Mi Lord, Jee-sus Christ, when did this happen?'

'Some time today, while I was out at work.'

'Did they take much?'

'Nothin.'

'What do you mean, nothin?'

'Exactly what I say. Look at the TV an' hi-fi, Carmen. Both of them have been smashed to pieces. This was all about trashin mi yard an' nothin to do with nickin.'

Carmen stared down at the shards of glass on the carpet while I ruefully inspected what was left of my record collection. 'Has Nathan seen all this?' she asked.

'Nah, he was sleepin at my mom's last night. I was gonna pick him up later.'

'Thank God,' she breathed softly. 'There's some sick people around.'

'You think this is sick?' I snorted. 'Come upstairs.'

She followed me to my bedroom and retched as the stench of human faeces hit her. She turned and ran out to the landing, a hand clamped over her mouth. I followed her out and shut the door. Anger had my eyes smarting again. I said, 'The bastard shit 'pon mi bed an' then smeared it all over the walls an' all over my clothes in the wardrobe.'

Her hand left her mouth and touched my arm. 'Who would want to do all this to you, Robbie?'

I gritted my teeth, I wouldn't give her an answer.

'What about Nathan's room?'

'Not touched. That's kind-a good, it means all this is directed at me an' not at him.'

'Who's done this, Robbie? You must have some idea.'

She looked at me as if to tell me that she had a notion that I knew more than I was saying. 'Let's go downstairs,' I said.

Carmen sat in an armchair and gripped the armrests as if she were bracing herself for bad news. I paced the room trying to think how I should start to tell her. 'Carmen, I lied to you,' I mumbled. I then drew a breath and with greater determination I continued, 'I lied to you about goin to my mom's after I left your place. I didn't pick up Nathan, I went to Tyrone's yard.' I paused to glimpse her reaction; she did not seem surprised. I went on, 'He talked me into givin him a lift to a pub on the Wellington Road called the Rose and Crown. When he came back to my car he was actin crazy; he told me that he had just planted a bomb. Then he started givin me all that nonsense he gave you about why Errol an' Hanimal were killed. Before I knew what was happenin he had a hand around my throat and he was tryin to kill me. I really didn't want to tell you all this, that's why I made out about the laryngitis an' that. I'm sorry.'

She looked away from me. Her soft voice began to crack with emotion as she asked, 'What happened then?'

'I managed to get him out of the car an' he ran towards the Rushbury estate. I wish I told you before now, Carmen, but I wasn't really sure what the hell was goin on.'

She straightened herself. 'An' do you know why Malek an' his guys are lookin for Tyrone an' what he has that's supposed to belong to them?'

'Truthfully, I ain't got a clue. Maybe it's somethin to do with whatever was in that bag he left in the pub.' She nodded and then in an instant she was on her feet. 'Right, so it's Tyrone who probably did all this,' she said. 'Well, we had better get it cleaned up.'

It was typical of Carmen; she had spent so much of her life dealing with other people's crises that emotion was never allowed to colour her analysis of what she could do to be of practical help. Her voice strong again, she said, 'I've dealt with enough shitty nappies in my time, so I'll take the sheets off the bed an' put them in your washer.'

'Don't bother,' I said, 'I'm gonna burn them.'

'Okay, I'll take them outside. What about your clothes in the wardrobe?'

'Same thing.'

'Are you sure?'

'Positive.'

She shrugged her shoulders. 'It's your stuff. Have you a mop, bucket an' disinfectant?'

'In the kitchen.'

'Right then, come noh, man.'

Gloved up, Carmen tore the soiled sheets and clothes from my bedroom and once she had deposited them in the back garden she got on with cleaning up the mess downstairs while I mopped the smeared walls. Until I moved the bed I had twisted Tyrone's neck with each turn of the mop. Something on the floor, a piece of paper, a wrapper that could not belong to me, made me pause. I knew then it was not Tyrone who had trashed my home.

'That didn't take long,' Carmen said from the doorway.

I felt hot and flustered. 'Right,' I said, pushing the paper deep into a pocket, 'I'll take you home.'

She seemed startled by my abruptness. 'Okay,' she said sadly, 'if that's what you want.'

We did not say much to one another as we drove to the Blackmore estate. When I glanced at her still face I wondered what she was thinking about and if I had done the right thing in telling her the truth about what had happened that night I left her home. 'Carmen,' I said meekly, 'I'm sorry about lyin to you about not seein Tyrone. I wasn't sure about what he was up to, an' you had enough trouble without me addin to it by tellin you how he attacked me.'

'I do unnerstan,' she replied. 'Lies with good intention don't hurt so bad. I know you were only tryin to help me.'

'An' if you're talkin to the cops again I'd be grateful if you didn't mention what I've just told you. There's no sense in gettin the guy into more trouble. He needs help.'

'I unnerstan.'

The lights were still on in Carmen's house as my car pulled up outside. 'That'll be Tim waitin up for me,' she said pensively. 'He ain't on his own - Lorraine an' her daughter are stayin the night. She's havin a few problems with her partner.' She gave me a troubled smile. 'I'm so sorry about what has been done to your place.'

'You ain't got nothin to be sorry for, Carmen. I'm grateful for your help clearin up the mess. The telly wasn't up to much anyway. Don't worry about it.'

She drew a sharp breath and gazed out at the surrounding darkness. 'Robbie, can I share somethin? Somethin that you'll have to swear on Nathan's life that you'll never mention to anyone else?'

I felt my pulse quicken. 'I suppose so.'

'The reason I felt so certain that Tyrone had somethin to do with that guy Earl Johnson goin off the top of Franklin House is because he has killed someone before.'

I blew heavily, not knowing how else to react.

'It was a couple of years ago,' she continued. 'This bastard who made himself out to be a Yardie had Tim runnin wraps for him. When I confronted him about it he beat me up real bad. A few days later Errol an' Tyrone found him an' killed him because of what he had done to me. God forgive me, but I still don't feel no way about what they did. A guy who starts usin pickney for them tings deserves to die.'

'Did Tyrone tell you this?'

'I can't say how I know but I'm tellin you what he's done so you know how seriously you gotta take his threat to your life. Once a person has killed it's easier to kill a second time. Don't stay at your place tonight, Robbie, please.'

Part of me wanted to laugh out loud - if only it had been Tyrone who was with Errol in that small, stinking bathroom.

I said, 'I'll stay at my mom's tonight.' It was another small lie that I hoped would lessen her anxiety.

'You could stay here.'

'Thanks, but I had better see Nathan.'

'Of course,' she said.

She looked so unhappy. Instinctively, I leant over to kiss her on the cheek. Her face turned and she kissed me on my lips, which instantaneously tightened and became unyielding. I had to keep the promise I had made to myself and not weaken. She recoiled, realizing she had mistaken my intention. I could almost taste her horror. Before I knew what was happening she was out of the car and hurrying to her front door. Once she had the key in the lock she turned and waved, as if to say: Don't worry, I'm all right now.

I responded with a brief, guilty waft of my hand and then I drove away.

10

IN HIS PANIC, Errol had twice taken us in the wrong direction but now finally we were heading for home. I wound down the window; cold damp air had never tasted so sweet.

Whatever the truth about the people he had killed in Jamaica, Beresford Samuels had destroyed many lives with the stuff he had peddled in and around the Blackmore. No one knew much about the self-proclaimed Field Marshal before he arrived on the estate, and I had often thought the stories about him were designed to intimidate people who had been reared on tales of the roughness and toughness which prevailed in their parents' homeland.

I couldn't say how long I had spent gazing down at his wet and lifeless body. He still looked strong and yet he would never again stir a muscle; it was hard to believe that his wide reddened eyes could not see me, that his open mouth was not about to scream for mercy once more.

The violent and sordid life of Beresford Samuels had been brought to a halt by three bullets from a snub-nosed revolver as he lay on the grimy, damp floor of a bathroom - but not before he had answered my question.

Once his car had stopped outside my house Errol dropped his face into his hands. His breaths were deep and trembling. 'We're in shit,' he moaned, 'big shit.'

It was the first and only time he had allowed me to see his fear stripped of the macho bullshit he habitually wrapped it in.

Posturing and pretending was something we both had done as kids but Errol carried it off better than anyone I had ever come across. When he was twelve he told the class that his old man had left home because he was on the run from the cops after he had stabbed a National Fronter. He never mentioned the bottle-blonde with an Afro perm from Merthyr Tydfil who tried to talk Jamaican patois. I never said anything about her either.

At the age of eighteen or nineteen he went to Jamaica and stayed with an aunt for a month. On his return we gathered around him at the boxing club as he told us of an earthly paradise and his plans to return and live there one day. Cha, it was more pretending and I was growing too old to be listening to such fuckrees. So I asked him to tell us just one thing that wasn't so good about the place. He bared his teeth with the pretence of a smile and said, 'The gal dem, dem nah shave them foot.'

Later on, in our twenties, I told him I knew that he was smart enough to put away the labels. We weren't proper Jamaican or proper English; our brown skins were not black. Shit, they were just classifications made up by people who had been setting the agenda since the days of slavery. He laughed as though the identical notion had occurred to him but when I repeated the same argument in front of others Errol got angry and told me not to deny our identity.

'We're in shit, Robbie,' he moaned again, almost sobbing. He had finally stopped pretending. It was the bravest thing he had ever done and I wanted to put my arm around him. But I didn't. Instead, I told him that there was nothing to link us with the scene and I had made sure the gun and every door handle had been wiped clean of prints. He did not respond. I dug my thumb deep into the vulnerable flesh of his upper arm; I had to distract him from any thought that might weaken his resolve.

'None-a that!' I growled. 'Get your mind right, E. You make sure you see Shaka tonight an' tell him that there was no answer on that number he gave you.'

His hands fell from his face. I shook him and again told him to see Shaka. His eyes began to clear and he promised that he would do as I had told him. I opened the car door and looked back at him; I needed to be certain. 'Errol, you make sure you see him an' then everythin cool. We've got to be cool.'

He looked to the small plastic representation of the Jamaican flag which was in the corner of his windscreen. 'What flag do we have?' he mumbled to himself.

Doubt about his strength had me taking hold of his arm again. I said, 'Errol, cut this fuckrees 'bout flag an' think 'bout your ras. Remember what Bubby used to tell us: discipline is everythin an' flags are fe arseholes. Stay disciplined, guy, an' we're safe. Discipline, make sure you remember.'

Errol smiled and I could tell that he was back in the gym for an instant. I knew then he would be strong. During all the dangerous times we had shared I had never doubted his courage but in those few moments of weakness I saw how brave he really was. I smiled back at him, knowing that he would not let us down.

What I didn't know then was it would be the last time I saw him alive.

Four days, just four more days. As I took my place in the queue to the clock, I told myself that I would persevere and work until the end of the week. It was small consolation that when I arrived at the rack my clocking-in card was in its usual place. I had not slept well: the disinfectant on my bedroom walls had left a nasty taste in my mouth and filled my mind with thoughts of retribution. By lunchtime my mood had grown even darker.

I sat alone at a table in the canteen, one from which I could not see Little Cuba. Tiredness had blunted my appetite but I chewed reluctantly while I waited for him. When he entered the canteen I spat a piece of gristle onto my plate and called out, 'Hey, Ken, a quick word.'

Ken Barker, member of the workers' council and the man who Fidel and Mr Robinson had dubbed 'The Toad', waddled over.

'Hello, Robert,' he said with his usual sham bonhomie. 'You were seen at the funeral, you naughty boy. Don't worry, I've squared things with the management. There won't be any repercussions - I saw to that for you at the last meeting.'

'I'm not worryin, I couldn't give a pussyclart, if you get my meanin, Kenneth. But what I am doin is gettin vexed with all these security guys who keep hasslin me.'

'All you have to do is get those forms filled in and give me two small photographs and I will take care of the rest.'

'Ken, forget this nonsense about photographs an' forms that wants to know everythin but the size of my ol' bwoy. I'm arksin you to go tell the guy standin by the stores that he has seen my clearance slip four times already an' if he arks for it again he will get somethin he didn't bargain for.'

The pretence of a smile vanished from his face. 'Come now, Robert, I hope this isn't another example of your chip-on-the-shoulder attitude. Once you're wearing a badge like everyone else the security personnel will have no reason to even speak to you, never mind stop and delay you.'

'Yeah, well this chip is about three feet long an' it's gonna lick that guy's headside if he arks me a fifth time. An' while I'm at it, how the fuck did you let them put these cameras all over the place? A man can't even relax havin a shit around here no more.'

Ken Barker took a step back. 'I'm not going through all that again just for you, Mr Walker. Everyone else has accepted they are only there to enhance the safe and efficient practice on the shop floor through better supervision.'

'You know, Mr Barker, I was just thinkin about Fidel an' Mr Robinson.'

'Ah, yes - we had our differences but they were two grand old lads.'

'They always thought that you an' the rest of them on the council were a bunch of arse-lickin bastards.'

Barker's chins wobbled nervously. He attempted a laugh in the hope I would join in but I simply resumed eating my lunch. I looked up at him, my offence at his nearness growing with every belligerent chew, as he tried to work out if I had been joking. 'Don't just stand there, Ken,' I hissed, 'lookin like a sad, slimy toad. Fuck off.'

Time almost ground to a halt in the afternoon. I had one job to do, replacing 'o-rings' in a machine. It wasn't a very challenging task but I made it last a lot longer than usual as I had no intention of breaking sweat. Despite my best efforts I could not make it last until clocking-out time and as I wiped my hands with a rag I decided to duck out to the washroom and read my newspaper.

I emerged from the toilet cubicle once the pins and needles in my feet became unbearable. I had not been able to focus properly on what was in the newspaper. Errol, Fidel and Mr Robinson, Tyrone, Carmen and the person who had damaged my home all took turns to wander into my consciousness to stir up some powerful emotion and demand that I give them priority. The absurdity of going to the toilet for a little solitude only to find myself crowded out by what was running through my mind brought a weary smile to my lips.

'Forget the dead unless you wanna join them an' concentrate on the livin,' I muttered to the reflection in the grease-smeared mirror. Warm soapy water ran over my face and somehow managed to sting my eyes. Blinded by the soap, I fumbled for a paper towel while thinking of Nathan's whingeing during the times I had rubbed a flannel over his face. As the stinging eased I became aware of a blurry shape near the door. It was the man with the tinted spectacles I had spoken to in the small workshop. 'Yeah, all right, man,' I called, squinting over the row of wash-basins.

The man's lips were not much more than a thin line. 'I'm all right,' he replied, 'but then again I'm not a lippy black cunt.'

I straightened myself as two more men joined him; one of them was the man with the dented nose, the other was Kyle. His broad bald head tilted to one side and a threatening grin spread under his thick moustache. 'Well, well, what sort of smart-mouthed monkey have we cornered here, Chopper?'

The man with the misshapen nose said evenly, 'One that thinks he can call you a Paddy and get away with it.'

'You know his trouble, don't you, Kyle?' said the man with the spectacles. 'He doesn't respect the rules. I think we should teach him to respect the rules.'

A warm and weakening tingle ran through me but the weight in the long leg pocket of my overalls gave me some comfort. I watched for the first move and deliberated over which one of them would be the first to feel a blow from my heavy spanner. But the three men remained still and coolly waited for me to react; I would have to get past them if I wanted to get out of the washroom.

On a very few occasions I had come across men such as these. They were not the sort who needed weak-hearts to laud them as hard men. They were the dangerous kind who had no need to work themselves into a rage or for alcohol to fuel their violence. To them violence would have become a matter of routine and sometimes pleasure.

Kyle rolled his powerful-looking shoulders and, barely able to restrain himself, took one step forward. He bared his teeth and spat, 'I hope to fuck you're not going to disappoint us by starting to beg for mercy.'

I pulled the spanner from my leg pocket and let its head smack against the palm of my left hand. The space between the basins and the toilet cubicles meant they could only come for me one at a time. For one delicious moment I visualised the Ulsterman's bald head splitting open. 'Come, man,' I called out to him, 'me owe you one ras-lick already. Come forward an' let me mash up yuh bloodclart.'

The man called Chopper rested a hand on Kyle's shoulder and stopped him moving forward. 'He's not going to beg for mercy but I am disappointed that he's not got the bottle to sort this out man-to-man.' He called over to me, 'You're slipping up, Mr Walker. I thought it was your normal practice to put away your tools nice and tidy after a job.'

'Nah, man,' I said, 'I always carry this thing to the toilet. You never know what you might find in here that needs fixing.'

Kyle's smouldering eyes almost burnt a hole in me but his glare shifted abruptly with the clatter of metal buckets easing their way through the doorway. 'You boys having a party in here?' called Monica.

The small Hungarian woman pushed her way past Kyle and the other two who were looking at a fourth man who stood outside apologetically shrugging his shoulders. Monica turned to the men and said, 'Don't you boys worry about me. I have a husband and six sons. I have seen enough dicks to last me a lifetime. I won't look, I promise.' She let out a laugh only fifty years of smoking could produce as the men filed out. 'Hey, they shy, Mister Robbie,' she said. 'You know why? Small dicks. A man with a big dick is always happy to show it off. You carry on with what you were doing and don't mind me.'

'That's all right, Monica, I've just finished.'

She let out a groan, pretending to be disappointed, as she began to place blocks of scented crystals in the urinals. I moved tentatively towards the door. 'I see you wear no badge,' she said, stepping in front of me, 'me neither.' She continued, 'They think they can make me wear a badge so I can clean their mess. I should cock-a-doodle-do. What can they do if we don't wear badge - sack us? It is only a shitty job and I do not want to work here any longer.'

'I was thinkin the same thing, Monica,' I said as I made to pass her.

'One minute, please. I finish today, now I have seen you.'

Her voice throbbed and made me pause. 'Is everythin okay?' I asked.

In a whisper, she said, 'The night your two friends died they work late. Me too. The security men caught them in the building out the back. They treat them very rough.'

I swallowed hard. 'How rough? Were they hurt bad?'

'I say they treated rough. I did not see everything but I hear them shout. I see your two friends pushed out of the gate at the front with their hands pushed up their backs.' Monica turned her back towards me and pushed one of her hands towards her shoulder-blade. 'Like this,' she explained and turned around again. 'This is the real reason I not work here any more.'

My mind turned blank for a moment. It was as if someone else were talking when I said, 'I'm not workin here much longer myself. Somethin about this place, Monica, has changed, turned bad.'

Her voice grew distant. 'I'm glad you are going too. You're a nice man, your friends were nice men. I will say a prayer that you will find another job. A nice job.'

The loud clanging Monica made when picking up her buckets brought my mind back to her. 'Now I will go and clean their office toilets for the last time. I never liked it. Only very small dicks up there.'

I stepped from the washroom into a tunnel of indistinct shapes and vague sounds which led to the way out. One of the fuzzy shapes turned out to be Ken Barker. I told him that I had a headache and without waiting for his response I clocked out.

While driving home my mind began to clear. The eyes looking back at me from my rearview mirror tried to tell me that I should forget about avenging the dead - wherever they were, nothing could hurt them now - and concentrate on the living.

'The living,' I snarled. My mind was made up: I would find the person who had trashed my home, the focus of my growing rage, before the night was through.

11

THE DOGS OF the Blackmore estate were yapping incessantly. I could hear their echoes in the distance as I walked through the park for a second time. There was no one about. Very few people went into the park after dark; most of those who did were driven there by darker urges they could not suppress. In some respects I was no different.

It was cold and dank. Part of me argued that I should go home and leave things be, but a stronger voice told me to go on and find the person who had defiled my home. If I was to leave this city it had to be on my terms; debts had to be settled first.

Heading towards the high-rise blocks I saw two young prostitutes, their bare white legs pinned together at the knees and frozen by the scouring wind. In this weather they must have been either optimistic or desperate. Their pimp sat in his car, the engine was running to keep him warm - and so they could make a quick getaway if a Muslim patrol turned up. He eyed me warily as I made my way to the littered thoroughfare of the Blackmore's shopping centre where I took shelter in a boarded up doorway. An empty drinks can clattered its way along the ground and I pushed my head into my shoulders and shivered.

There always seemed to be a wind blowing through the Blackmore estate. It was built on high ground and could be seen from miles around, looming like some ancient citadel. I often wondered what archaeologists might make of such a place thousands of years from now. The ten tower blocks, ten despairing fingers rising from a sea of bitumen, might represent a distant constellation; the spiral ramps might evoke visions of a sacrificial altar surrounded by priests and their followers who lived a spartan existence in tiny concrete cells. All of them members of a civilization they thought was so advanced that they, like their god, would never be forgotten. Or maybe those who discovered the ruins would conclude that the Blackmore was just a crude concrete receptacle for those who were judged genetically disadvantaged.

While I waited I read the fly-posters plastered over the shop frontage a dozen times until my stomach began to rumble. After four hours of fruitless searching, my empty belly was demanding that I go around the corner to get some food, warmth and, perhaps, some information.

The fish and chip shop was steamy, warm and welcoming. 'Hey, Robbie,' called Mustafa, the Turkish-Cypriot proprietor of the Sea Star Fish Bar, 'long time no see.'

Still shivering with the cold, I said, 'Well, I ain't been down this way for a week or two. A special kebab an' chips please, Mus.'

Mustafa wiped his black moustache with the back of his hand and told me to wait for a few minutes. His strong short arms bulged as he emptied a large plastic bucket of raw chips into the fryer. Through a cloud of rising steam he smiled at me. 'Better to have them fresh,' he said.

I looked on and admired him as he began to cut ribbons of meat from the sweating cone which rotated in front of two squares of fierce orange heat. Mustafa was the sort of man who did not consider himself either intelligent or educated and maybe he was neither but there was a wisdom about him. I had learnt how wise he was when Danny Maguire had worked for him. It became part of my routine to call into the shop during the evenings to listen as they debated just about every subject under the sun and a few beyond. But without fail, whatever they were talking about, they would refer to their experiences of religion, partition and inter-ethnic strife. I'm not sure if they taught me anything new but they definitely reinforced a few of my theories about the human condition.

'Mus, I was just thinkin that I ain't seen any Brothers of Islam patrolling around the place tonight.'

'They don't farkin come in here. They came in once to tell me that I was selling unclean food. Farkin pork sausages.'

'Tell me, man, do you think these guys are proper Muslim?'

A sharp knife sliced the pitta bread. 'What is proper? You read too many English newspapers where only the extreme is news. I listen to Christians arguing who is following the proper way, Muslims are no farkin different. When those men come in here I tell them I do not fear them, I fear only Allah. I tell them I cook food for everyone; Muslim and Christian, Hindu and Jew. If the Muslim and Jew don't want the sausage they can eat the beefburger the Hindu won't eat. And I told them to keep the Christians Christian; they farkin eat anything. Chilli sauce?'

'No thanks,' I said, 'my tongue still ain't recovered from the last time.' I put some money on the counter but Mustafa only pushed it back towards me and presented me with a pile of golden chips. 'These are good,' I murmured.

'Of course they're farkin good.'

'Mus, have you seen that young guy who rides a bike around the place? He's always in the park, you know the guy I'm talkin about?'

He emptied more raw chips into the fryer. 'Plenty boys ride bikes around here.'

'You know,' I insisted, 'he's got a mobile phone an' too much jewellery on his fingers.'

'Yes, I know who you mean,' Mustafa replied suspiciously. He moved the riddle through the boiling oil and tilting his head towards the door he said, 'Speak of the farkin devil.'

The lanky youth entered the shop with a gaggle of younger boys trailing in behind him. 'Oi,' he called to Mustafa, 'six curry patty an' chips. Come, man, service, we is in a 'urry, yuh know.' The boys behind him laughed as he continued to hurl insults in an assumed Jamaican accent. Mustafa remained completely unaffected and glanced knowingly at me. He dealt with bad-mannered customers all the time but as I watched the youth I became increasingly offended by his behaviour towards a friend of mine.

Suddenly aware that he was being studied from the other end of the counter, the youth stared at me and I turned my face away from him. His instinct to exploit any sign of what he thought was a weakness and the notion that he was the star of the movie playing in his head allowed him to call out to me, 'Hey, wha you look 'pon we fah? You 'ave a problem?'

I straightened up and held out my kebab. 'Yeah,' I said, 'no chilli sauce. You wanna try some?'

He may have had a man's body but his mind had some catching up to do. 'Nah, man,' he said, 'Jamaican patty do fe all-a we.' He then glanced at me edgily as I gathered up my food and strode towards the door. 'Later, Mus,' I said and Mustafa nodded pensively.

The eyes of the youth and his little gang followed me as I opened the door. One boy was looking in another direction.

'Tim,' I said, as if surprised, 'what are you doin out this time of night?'

The boys around him began to laugh loud and mockingly. For an instant the humiliation paralysed his tongue. Eventually Tim blurted, 'Fuck off, you ain't my ol' man or nothin.'

'True,' I said and went outside. The shop continued to reverberate with raucous laughter until the lanky youth looked out through the steamy window to see me deflating a tyre on his bike. The door opened and the youth raced out. 'What the bloodclart?' he yelled. A hand reached under his baggy top. My food fell to the floor. A bone cracked. The young body folded and fell to the ground. I rubbed the knuckles of my left hand before taking the knife from the youth's waistband to deflate the other tyre. It was probably the same knife which had scared Nathan and Duane during their trip to the park with Tim, I thought.

The boys streamed out of the shop and stared down at their hero open-mouthed. 'When he wakes up,' I said to them, 'make sure you tell him if he ever tries to pull a knife on me again I'll bury it in im fuckin chest. Right?'

They nodded silently and then quickly moved aside as I reached over to take Tim by the shoulder. 'Me an' you must have a lickle chat,' I snarled.

I pulled at him so he had to walk on his tiptoes until we reached my car. I roughly pushed him in from the driver's side and sat in beside him. He squirmed his way onto the passenger seat as I said, 'Who put you up to it, Tim?'

The boy sucked his teeth. 'What you talkin about?'

'Don't give me shit, boy. You trashin my yard!'

Tim looked out to the road. 'Cha, I don't know a fuck.'

I pushed his head against the glass of the door. 'Watch what you say, bwoy. I know it was you so you'd better start showin some respec before I batter your headside.'

He tried to open the door but I pulled him back. 'I ain't respectin you, you bastard,' he whined. I ain't respectin you!'

'Who told you to do it - was it Tyrone?'

'Nah!'

'It *was* Tyrone.'

'Nah, it fuckin wasn't.'

'Was it your mom?'

I saw tears of hatred well up in Tim's eyes. 'You mek me do it. It was fuckin you, right? Just you.'

I shook him. 'Cut the shit, Tim, I'm warnin you.'

'You're the one full of shit! Just like the rest, full of shit.' The boy was breathing hard and then his words came rapidly, like bubbles in boiling water rushing to the surface. 'You pretended to be good at first. But then you started stayin over an' you changed like you didn't have to try any more.'

It wasn't what I had expected to hear. My anger abruptly changed into the need to explain. 'Tim, it wasn't like –'

'You're fuckrees, right, you're fuckrees. You think I don't know what you were doin to my mom? When I was lyin in bed I could hear everythin. I heard the night you left when you slammed the door. I heard her cryin. Then when I came home from school she was happy an' said you were upstairs asleep. The nex day she was cryin again. She pretended it was over Tyrone goin missin but she didn't fool me, I ain't no idyat. I heard how she kept ringin you an' leavin messages, like she was beggin. She's a fuckin bitch, right, a fuckin slag, but she nah deserve you.' He looked straight into my eyes. 'So I shit 'pon you.'

I released my grip on him. 'Don't talk about your mom like that, Tim, she's a good person. Look, you're only twelve –'

'Yeah, I'm twelve an' you an' her think I don't know what is goin on or that I don't exist. You're shit to me.'

Tim opened the door and got out and I made no attempt to stop him. He had crept up and put a blade in me far deeper than the lanky youth could ever have managed. And he had been right: if I had considered him at all it was only as a nuisance. Before spending a night with Carmen I left Nathan at my mother's home; I was so careful with my own son's feelings but I had never spared a thought for Tim's.

The blade continued to twist inside of me all the way home. I had done some things in my life that many people would condemn but I didn't care because I could always justify them to my friends and, more importantly, to myself. It had taken the trashing of my home by a surly young kid to demolish my smug assumption that I was one of life's good guys.

Bill's anxiety had not lessened despite not seeing the big white man in a parka coat outside of his shop for the last few days. 'How's the throat?' he asked.

'It's all right, Bill, thanks.'

He tossed the coins into his till. 'Only you don't look too good. I thought you might be sick again.'

'Lack of sleep,' I said, picking up my newspaper.

'There must be a lot of people in this town who are not sleeping very well just lately. You'll see why on the front page - another man shot dead last night. My brother in America will never believe it.'

I looked down to the bottom corner of the page. I recognized the name of the dead man. He was the same age as me and for a while we had attended the same school. Trevor Bisnott was not the worst of the kids I had known. I remembered him as the boy whose trousers and blazer were a bit too short for him - a consequence of him being taller than his older brother. He had fallen in with the Campbells by way of his sister having a kid for Alvin Campbell, the second-in-command to Glenroy. Trevor Bisnott had made his choice and it turned out to be the wrong one: I gave his life and its ending no more consideration than that.

On my way to work I toyed with the idea of this being my last day at the factory. I kept imagining the rough treatment handed out to Fidel and Mr Robinson that Monica had told me about and let ideas of sabotage run through my mind. A hacksaw and a spanner could do a lot of damage, maybe thousands of pounds worth. It would be a smarter course of action than trying to go the whole day without punching one of the new security guards - and one which would not necessarily be detrimental to my future job prospects.

After shuffling forward in the usual queue, I stretched out an arm to collect my card from the rack next to the clock - only for a hand on the end of a long arm to beat me to it. 'Ah, Mr Walker,' said the man with the thinning blond hair, 'we spoke briefly Monday morning.'

'Yeah, my memory ain't that bad. I still ain't got those photos for you, Mr Urban.'

'Not to worry. Can you come with me? You're required in the manager's office.'

'Yeah, well how about if I clock in first.'

In a tone I thought unpromising he said, 'That won't be necessary.'

As I followed Urban into the office I saw Ken Barker standing in front of a large oak desk. The twitch on his lips as he glimpsed me was the first indicator of trouble. Sitting behind the desk were two men. Charles Morton, the factory manager, was slight and sallow-skinned. I had seen him a couple of times and I was surprised to learn of his status as he did not seem to have the confidence that I thought was necessary to handle such an important job. He pawed nervously at his receding mousy hair and avoided any eye contact with me. I did not know the man sitting next to him. He was older, fleshier and pinker in the face. He had great bushy eyebrows and was topped with a thick mane of silver hair. I sensed his confidence and an air of arrogance that only real power can bestow.

The pink one cast a disdainful eye at me. He said to Barker, 'For the benefit of Mr Walker, you were saying that he has changed the o-rings of the solenoid-operated valve many times before.'

Ken Barker replied, 'Yes, Sir Philip. It's a standard sort of job, well within his capabilities.'

I didn't like what I was hearing. 'Is there anyone here with enough manners to tell me what's going on?' I demanded.

The pink one sat back and crossed his arms. The manager glanced at him and then towards me. 'Certainly, Mr Walker,' Charles Morton replied indignantly. 'A machine operative was seriously injured yesterday and Ken Barker is here to present a case on why we should not suspend or dismiss you immediately.'

My mind raced to recall which machines I had worked on but I could not think of anything I had done that could have led to an injury. I sensed a stitch-up and with all the contempt I could muster I said, 'Then don't let me stop you.'

12

THE MAN CALLED Urban watched me from across the office as Ken Barker continued with his explanation of the malfunction which had led to the injury of a machine operator. Every fibre of my being fizzled with loathing for The Toad, for the two men seated behind the desk, and for the tall man who headed the new security department. Give me a chance, I thought, and I will have the whole plant malfunctioning.

Memories of the treatment meted out to Fidel and Mr Robinson by the security guards didn't make it easy but I controlled my anger. Now and again while stretching in my seat I would yawn scornfully and get Barker stuttering. Finally, the pink one said testily, 'Thank you, Ken, you may go now.'

'By the way,' I said, 'who the hell are *you*?'

The pink face turned scarlet as Charles Morton gasped, 'This is Sir Philip Parkinson, chairman and founder of the Park-Tec Corporation.'

Knowing that I had nothing to lose I sneered and said, 'Wha happen, Pee-pee?'

Without taking his eyes off me, Urban opened the door and Barker waddled out; he then made a gesture and two security guards stepped in. The factory manager turned to me. He said nervously, 'Because of the serious breaches in health and safety...'

I thought I knew what was coming next. 'Hold on,' I said. 'I'm sorry to hear about someone bein hurt an' all that, but as I unnerstan it, you're sayin the injury was caused by a piece of work flyin out of the clamps. Right?'

Morton hesitated and then said, 'That is correct.'

'An' you got me in here because I replaced the o-rings on that machine yesterday.'

'Correct,' snapped Parkinson.

'Well, Sir Pee-pee, since you chat to Barker so much, I suppose you must have discussed with him the fail-safe mechanism which keeps the clamps shut in the event of a fault. Like an electric wire to a Solenoid valve becoming disconnected, for instance. Cha, you guys are so inept you can't even stitch me up properly.' I leant back into my seat and stretched out my arms as if I had been roused from a sleep. 'I resign,' I sighed. 'I can't bring miself to work for such a bunch of bumbaholes no more.'

I thought Parkinson was going to choke with rage. 'Get him off these premises!' he called out to the men by the door.

I quickly got to my feet as the two uniformed men stepped towards me. 'Touch me an' at least one of you is goin to hospital,' I said. 'Now which one of you idyat is the hero?'

They paused long enough for Urban to make an intervention. 'No one is going to touch you, Mr Walker, as long as you go quietly to your locker, collect what belongs to you and then leave the premises.'

The guards backed off and I left the office with Urban close behind. At the lockers I asked him if I could say my goodbyes to the rest of the maintenance crew. He shook his head. 'Can't let you do that, Mr Walker. It is not unknown for former employees to vent their sense of grievance on an expensive piece of machinery.'

'Oh, really?' I said. 'It never crossed my mind.'

He picked up the heaviest of my two toolboxes. 'I'm sure it didn't. But I did think when we were back in the office that it was out of character for you to lose your cool.'

We started to walk out towards the gates. I said, 'An' what would you know about my character?'

Urban replied, 'Enough to know that you are thorough and disciplined. Thorough enough not to make sloppy mistakes; for what's it worth, I think you got a raw deal in there. Disciplined enough not to show your feelings, such as when those three men confronted you in the washroom yesterday. It must have been frightening for you and yet you did not let them see the fear you must have felt.'

111

Like when I had first met him in his office, I felt a menacing power about this man and once again he was letting me know how much he knew about me. 'Fear? Nah, man. It was them guys feelin frightened,' I snorted. 'They looked as if they were shittin themselves when they found out it was me in there an' not two frail old guys.'

'Ah, so you heard about the little incident involving your two old friends. It was nothing more than a very vocal disagreement over security clearance. I can assure you that they left these premises unmolested.'

'An' I suppose you can assure me that you didn't send those three guys into the washroom,' I said.

Urban did not answer and we walked the rest of the way to the car park in silence. He effortlessly lifted the heavy box into the boot of my car and said, 'What will you do now?'

'What, Mr Urban, is there somethin you don't know?'

'I do not pretend to be a clairvoyant, Mr Walker. Perhaps you will go searching for Tyrone Swaby. I was reading in the newspaper that he is still missing.'

'Nah, I don't think so.'

'Oh, I assumed that as you have known him for so long, you would show more concern,' he said, following me to the driver's door. 'After all, not only did you work here with him, you also went to the same school.'

'But we weren't in the same class.'

'He is three years younger.'

I unlocked the door and sat in. 'Maybe I'll get a job like yours, Mr Urban, where I'll have fuck all better to do than rummage through old job applications.'

He bent down and put his face close to mine. 'I was thinking,' he said, 'you must have known Errol Morgan and Gilbert "Hanimal" Peters. *They* were your age and went to the same school.'

His eyes searched for a reaction but I did my best not to look surprised. 'I said Monday that you were a cop. Wha happen, man? They chuck you out because you were a Peeping Tom?'

He put his hand onto the steering wheel. 'And what about Conrad

Williams? His friends called him Shaka - surely you remember him. He was found shot dead a couple of years ago - it was in all the newspapers. But what they didn't say in the papers was that there were signs of torture on his body.'

I turned the ignition key. 'So you hang around the Coroner's Court too? You're a sad man, Mr Urban. I'm sorry to disappoint you but I've never heard of the guy.'

He smiled and said, 'You haven't disappointed me, Mr Walker, far from it. Maybe our paths will cross again some day. I do hope so.'

Urban stepped away from the car and I closed the door. I watched him as he marched briskly through the factory gates and as I made my way home I thought that he could have been the most dangerous man I had ever met.

The day after Errol and I had left Beresford Samuels dead in a dingy bathroom I went to my mother's house for Christmas dinner. The meal was an unusually dour affair. In my more zealous and puritanical teens I had decided that the feast of consumerism and Santa Claus was a manifestation of the Anglo-American capitalist culture I detested and frequently told her so. As with many other matters, my opinion was the exact opposite of the one championed by Sharon - who was always quick to point out that she would not allow our son to become a victim of my eccentric beliefs.

Nathan's absence was too great a disappointment for my mother to hide. She asked if Sharon would get in touch so I could see him over the holiday and I truthfully told her that I did not know. She clamped her lips together, as if scared that she might say something we both would regret, and then she gave me a parcel for her only grandchild. 'I didn't bother with one for you, Robert,' she said pointedly, 'as I know you don't believe in this sort of thing.'

'That's okay, Mom, I didn't buy you a present either.'

She laughed quietly. 'Stubborn like your father.'

'I'm just a heathen. Maybe that's why Sharon leave me.'

Her small smile turned into a grimace of disapproval: the break-up of our relationship was not a subject she thought I should make light of. She said sternly, 'Do your best to see Nathan gets that present before Christmas finishes.'

I gave her a hug, but I made no promises.

Back at my empty house I paced the boards as I waited for Errol to contact me and say that he had talked to Shaka. For two days I did not think of much else but what had happened in that small bathroom.

I replayed every moment that we had spent in there and reassured myself that there was not one piece of evidence to link us with the scene. As I had told Errol, I had wiped every conceivable place where a fingerprint might have been left. The gun lay on the Field Marshal's blood-splattered chest. We pulled the hoods of our jackets over our heads and walked, as casually as we could manage, to Errol's car which he had parked some distance away. There had been no report of Beresford Samuels' disappearance and the longer he lay undiscovered the harder it would be for the police to come across any reliable witness who might have glimpsed us leaving the scene. Errol knew all this but what Samuels had told us before he died had scared him. He also knew that from now on we had to be more vigilant than ever.

All Errol had to do was see Shaka before the body was found and convince him that he did not meet with Samuels. Shaka was not the informing kind but he was the sort to try to impress others with talk of the bad men he knew. A little rum and ganja smoke and the guy would be running off his mouth about what he knew of the Field Marshal and the men who wanted him dead. There were plenty of men in prison because of such slack talk.

I imagined that Errol would pretend to be angry with Shaka and say that the number, the personal mobile telephone number given only to a privileged few, he had provided was useless; there hadn't been an answer despite days of ringing. Shaka would dial the number himself in front of Errol to prove he hadn't been bullshitting and there would be no reply. He would be puzzled but not suspicious. Then, days or weeks later, when the body was discovered, Shaka would find out Errol and tell him the obvious: Beresford Samuels must have been already dead when he had tried to ring him. Errol would feign surprise, or irritation that someone had got to Samuels before he did. Weeks or months after that the police might fit-up another drug dealer and take him out of circulation by charging him with the murder. And as if nothing more traumatic than scraping dog shit from our shoes had occurred, Errol and I would carry on with the rest of our lives.

The day after Boxing Day, seventy-two hours after Samuels had breathed his last, there was a knock on my door. But the person on my doorstep was not Errol, as I had anticipated, but Danny Maguire.

Deflated, and too tired not to show it, I returned to my solitary armchair. He stood in the same place Errol had stood a week before as I watched the Christmas 'Celebrity Edition' of the same inane quiz show.

He quietly studied me until I looked up at him standing in the doorway and said, 'I thought you were supposed to be back in Belfast until the New Year.'

'I was,' he said, 'but I had to come back and talk to you, Robbie, before yourself or someone else is killed or badly hurt. I was talking to Errol in the shop, he's after asking me a few questions about AK-47s that has me worried about youse boys.'

'We ain't dealin with them things,' I said. I stretched out my legs and yawned. 'Anyway, you're too late, Danny, someone has been killed.' I laughed to myself. 'In fact, he was badly hurt an' then killed.'

'Jesus Christ! Who?'

'Just the guy who beat up Carmen after she complained he had lickle Tim runnin wraps for him. You'll probably guess who the bastard was workin for.'

'The cops.'

'Exactly. An' you know what else he said?'

'Don't play games with me, Robbie. If you have something to tell me then just go on ahead and say it.'

'Just before he died he said that we must be the guys that the cops are lookin for. He said one top man didn't want us arrested, he wanted us dead.'

'And how did you manage to get him to tell you all this?'

'We tracked him down to one of the places he uses from time to time. See, I was suspicious 'bout the guy from when I first heard about him. There's plenty of innocent guys that have been knocked back by immigration an' put on the first plane back to JA, but this man was too high-profile for an illegal. An' when a guy who carries a shooter an' carries on with serious shit, beats a woman in the middle of a street right opposite from where it's known the police occasionally house a surveillance squad, I say to myself somethin funny a-go on.'

'So?' barked Danny.

'So, after a lickle tussle, me an' Errol drag him to a bath full of nice cold water, like how you told us the IRA do when they need to extract information. He was brave at first an' still threatenin but after the second time the guy was beggin for his life. After the third time he answered my question. Cha, like I said to Errol, once a man starts troublin pickney he don't deserve to be considered as human - the man was a fuckin child-abuser.'

Danny stepped into the middle of the room and I returned my gaze to the small television in the corner. Amid the recorded cackling Danny's words were indistinct to me but the tone of his voice still registered. It was fretful, angry, sometimes pleading. I knew that he had guessed the motive which lay behind my mention of an IRA interrogation technique.

Over the years I had known him, Danny had told us many tales of the war going on in his country. He had often explained to Errol and me matters of forensic awareness and counter-surveillance; once, after the only time I had seen him drunk, he had even shown me how to construct a device which could kill someone. His stories had found fertile ground and I was letting him know that he could not shirk his share of the responsibility.

Danny continued to talk but it was only Errol who could say anything of importance to me. On recognizing that his words had become lost in the tinny squawking from my television Danny growled loudly and smashed the screen with a booted foot. There was a bang and a flash of brilliant light and then there was nothing but darkness until he pulled the curtains apart to allow in the dim light from the street.

'You could-a just switched it off,' I said.

'Robbie!' he snarled. 'You catch yourself on a minute and listen to me. Carry on with what you're doing and the fellas that are after you will catch you, you can be sure of it. They will show you no mercy - and have you thought of what will happen to wee Nathan then?'

Danny must have known I had cast aside all considerations of Nathan's future. I had never really admitted as much, but there was no way I could allow myself to think of him while Errol and I had put ourselves in dangerous situations. 'I lost my dad when I was younger than him. Kids are resilient. His mom will look after him, he'll survive.'

He paced the room. I knew he was circling my defences looking for a weak point but the walls around my mind were built of great blocks of self-righteousness cemented by the hatred of the injustices happening all around me. The walls were tall and thick and nothing that Danny could say would breach them.

I took Danny's chuckling as an admission of defeat. 'Aye,' he laughed, 'he'll survive. You know, just before I left for home I was on a bus and I saw your boy being dragged along the street by his mother and some fella, a right arsehole by the cut of him. Nathan was crying and if I could have, I would have got off the bus right there and then. But they went into a house and I stayed on the bus. It really troubled me for a minute and I said to myself, "Ach, Nathan, how many men will you be told to call Daddy?" I really felt sorry for the poor wee black bastard.'

No one could call my lovely son a black bastard in front of me and get away with it, no one! I was out of the chair and rolling around the floor with my hands around Danny's throat until a sharp pain in my groin put me onto the flat of my back. Danny was standing over me gasping for air.

'Christ,' he panted, 'I was only trying to get you out of that fucking chair.'

I lay immobilized by the horror of it all. 'Fuckin hell, Danny, what have I done? Why did it have to be me?'

He looked down and stretched out a hand towards me. 'You did what had to be done, Robbie. I'm just sorry it had to be you. Come on, let's go and get Nathan.

Nathan was asleep in bed. I had told my mother that I wasn't going to work for a few days and I needed him at home. I figured it was relatively safe for him to return. If it had been Tyrone peering at him through the hedge that Sunday morning, somewhere in his twisted mind he had decided not to harm Nathan.

Getting fired was not the traumatic experience I had once imagined. In fact, I felt pleased that in the absence of advice from a friend, Fate had nudged me in the direction I had already thought about taking. What was the direction I was heading in? My mother often talked about cycles and circles. 'What goes around comes around,' she would say. 'Whatever good or bad you do will come back to you, and whatever path we take in life we are bound to end up right back where we started from. Ashes to ashes…'

I went into the kitchen and made myself a late-night snack. I was apprehensive and excited about making a fresh start. It was something I should have done two years ago but, as my mother often reminded me, I had inherited my father's stubborn streak.

Suddenly I was dazzled by the array of choices that were laid out in front of me. I could start out on a whole new career, I could move to any city I wanted, or even emigrate. I was like a man coming to the end of a prison sentence. I could, at last, allow myself the pleasure of anticipating a range of new experiences and people waiting for me. I could finally leave the memories behind for ever.

A loud thud at the front door brought an abrupt halt to my romancing and jolted me back into the real world. With the knife I used for cutting bread still in my hand, I went to the bay window in the front room and peered out. The dark shape of a man was at my door; he was too tall to be Tyrone but I did not recognize him.

While my mind raced, I tried to deliberate for a moment about what I should do but another knock took me into the hallway and a third had me stupidly placing my left foot at the base of the door and opening it slightly.

My fingers tightened around the knife. 'Yeah?' I said.

The man put his head close and looked in through the gap. 'Robbie,' he said, 'long time no see.'

My stomach moved as my dreams for the future instantly vanished. Every fibre of my being screamed out that this was the past making one last attempt to claim me, that a circle was about to be joined if I did not shut the door.

But how could I close the door on a friend?

I moved back and Danny Maguire stepped inside.

13

DANNY LEFT HIS two bags in the hall and followed me into the living room. 'When did you arrive?' I asked, still coming to terms with the shock of seeing him again.

'Just this minute,' he said, forcing a laugh, as if he were trying to put me at ease with his unexpected arrival.

I had heard of friends meeting up after not seeing each other for years and picking up the threads as though they had never been apart; I had imagined that is how it would be between Danny and me, but it wasn't.

The Danny Maguire I had known had never had to force a laugh and he looked so different to how I remembered him. The tousled black hair was now cropped short and sprinkled with silver flecks. Around his eyes were deep lines that did not look like the products of laughter.

There was something else about him which made me look him over in more than a casual, friendly way. He appeared a little heavier but still fit, he wore a black leather jacket that looked brand new. I rubbed the edge of a cuff between my fingers and said, 'Very smart, Danny. Is it off the back of a lorry?'

'To the best of my knowledge it's after coming off the back of a cow,' he said.

Our eyes met fleetingly as I continued to scrutinize him and wonder about what had brought him back to my home. He looked away to scan the room and said, 'I see our bit of decoration has stood the test of time, Robbie. We didn't make such a bad job after all.' There was another short chuckle which faded quickly when I did not join in.

'No,' I said, 'not a bad job. When did you get into town?'

He pawed at his cheek. 'I thought I just said.'

'No, you didn't.'

'I did - I said just this minute.'

'Oh, you mean you've only just got off the train?'

'Bus. Do you mean right this minute?'

'Yeah.'

'Oh, er, no. I've been in town since this evening, checking up on a few places.' Danny looked down to the knife in my hand. 'Rob, have I come at a bad time or something?'

The timing of his arrival had put me thinking about the existence of a vengeful God. 'Nah, man,' I replied. 'You've just pulled me outta the kitchen, that's all.'

'And there's me after thinking you were expecting the rent man.' He smiled sheepishly. 'Would it be all right if I stayed the night?' he asked. 'I've had to get some digs sorted out for myself and a few fellas I work with and it took a bit longer than I reckoned. It's a bit late for travelling back now. I did try to ring but the number was unobtainable.'

The sheepish smile, the forced laughter: the man was making me feel as though I had an impostor in the house.

'I've had it changed,' I said, not bothered if I was sounding inhospitable. Danny responded with a worried expression that made me soften my tone. 'Ah, don't take any notice of me,' I groaned. 'Stay as long as you want, don't worry about gettin digs. You lookin for work?'

'Well, I've been doing a bit with three fellas I know and there's a job starting around this way so I've come on ahead to sort out some accommodation for the four of us. But thanks for the offer, mate.'

I looked at his hands and wished I hadn't. They were soft and pink, his fingernails were square and uniform.

'Plastering, is it?' I asked him.

'Ah, yeah, still plastering.'

With fucking gloves on, I thought. There was an uneasy gap in the conversation, as though we had nothing - or too much - to say; it had been such a long time. I thought he was lying but I was not offended by it. I had grown used to lies.

Since the morning he had left my house all that time ago, I had lived a sort of lie every day.

There were ghosts hovering in the air between us that neither of us wanted to mention. They were temporarily exorcized when Danny asked of Nathan's whereabouts. When I said that he was upstairs fast asleep Danny's face broadened with a genuine wide smile and it was only then I recognized him as the friend I had known.

'Do you want a drink an' somethin to eat?' I asked.

'A cup of tea and whatever you're having yourself would do lovely.'

'Fine,' I said. 'Take your bags upstairs an' I'll put the kettle on.'

'Is it all right if I take a wee peek in at Nathan?' he asked in a hushed voice as though he was already creeping into his bedroom. I nodded and he whispered, 'Great!'

Waiting for the water to boil I remembered the very first time I laid eyes on Danny. Two of the whitest legs I had ever seen were nonchalantly crossed at the ankles as he stood in the opposite corner of the ring. His arms were resting on the top rope and he gave me a look of well-practised hard-man disdain. I was eighteen, very fit, very talented and, like a lot of guys my age, of the opinion that I was immortal and indestructible. I smiled and thought to myself: Just another white guy who fancies himself as a hard case.

The gymnasium was situated in the middle of a red-light district. From time to time, if the weather or business was bad, the working girls would take shelter in the entrance until Bubby started locking the door. Less frequently we had visits from men who wanted to find out how tough they really were. The treatment they received depended on Bubby's inclination. If he was in a good mood he would have them punch the heavy bag until they were exhausted. However, if they were the sort to display an attitude like the three guys on a bus who had unknowingly sat in front of Bubby talking about the inferiority of the African race, a very different treatment was meted out. The heavily padded sparring gloves would be dispensed with in favour of older, much lighter, pairs of match gloves. Bubby had whispered only one instruction that night: 'No mercy.'

The night Danny turned up Bubby had me put on the sparring gloves. 'See what him 'ave,' he said as he rang the bell. Danny was quickly out of his corner and took the centre of the ring so I circled and attempted to draw his lead. After a minute or so I grew bored with these tactics and attacked. A jab, then another that I turned into a hook and he retreated to the ropes. It was so easy. I moved in behind a jab and set myself to throw a straight right that would have put his white ras out through the ropes. I'm not sure what he hit me with - all I knew then was that my brain had been turned into a little dried walnut which rattled around my head and the bones in my legs had suddenly disappeared. Ignoring Bubby's call to break, I held onto Danny to stop a second blow separating me from my senses. Within moments my head had cleared enough for me to throw a fast and hurtful combination to his stomach. The air left his body and he retreated again but this time it was no ruse to draw me onto a punch. I closed in. He leaned on. 'So you want it to the body, eh?' he grunted. He broke from the clinch and punched me below the belt before delivering an uppercut to my jaw with the inside of his glove.

I went berserk. I started throwing punches with the intention to hurt, smash, kill. He had come into my territory, caught me with a sucker punch, committed two blatant fouls and I was going to make him pay. Bubby's loud laughter added to my indignity as Danny swayed and rolled his body as I tried to catch him with the blow which would tear his head from his shoulders. I had him pinned in a corner when the bell rang. It had come too early for me but I was content that I would hand out a severe beating in the next round. 'That's enough for tonight,' Bubby called out to Danny. I glared at Bubby, more than furious, and Danny did little for my humour when he strolled across the ring and said to Bubby, 'The kid's not bad.'

As time went by Danny did little for his popularity with the rest of the black guys in the gym by the way he called us Brits or, even worse, English. I called him to one side one evening and told him that if he really didn't want to rile us or risk twenty guys beating him he should stop referring to us in those terms. 'Put it this way,' I said, 'even "nigger" might be more acceptable.'

His eyes sparkled mischievously. 'Oh, really?' he said.

Despite the inauspicious start, I soon found myself liking Danny. None of us had ever met anyone quite like him. He swaggered around the place with a permanent sneer and a refusal to be impressed by anything he either saw or heard.

It wasn't long before he kept us enthralled in the changing room with tales of gun battles in his native Belfast. He drew pictures with his words, his stories put us right there in the streets of Andersonstown. We walked with him up the Springfield Road, through Turf Lodge and into the Murph. Soldiers were putting their dirty hands up the skirts of our sisters, the RUC were stopping our cars and handing out a beating to our friends, the army's bullets were peppering the walls of our living rooms. To us it seemed quite simple: the Catholics were the black people.

'Rahteed,' breathed one of our number excitedly 'If we was in the same situation we'd be doin the same tings as the IRA, to bluesbeat.'

I never forgot the look on Danny's face, it was contempt that bordered on hatred. For what seemed an age he remained silent, taking it in turns to look each one of us in the eye and then he said, 'No youse fucking wouldn't.' He looked at Errol and me. 'Well, not all of youse, anyhow.'

Back then Danny was staying with an uncle who had lived in England for thirty years. From what he told me they never had got on; the uncle did not seem to understand what was going on in his old home town and steadfastly refused to believe his nephew's version of events. Danny's stay only lasted a few months before he returned to Belfast muttering that he was sadly related to a West Brit.

Less than eighteen months later he was back. The uncle had died and as he had never married his relatives back in Ireland decided that his ramshackle terraced home should be renovated, sold and the proceeds split evenly. Danny was to draw something he called the 'broo' while employing his skills as a plasterer-cum-builder and make all the necessary repairs. But the plan hit a major snag when Danny's mother made the mistake of giving him some of his share in advance. Not a great deal of work was done in the first two years.

He had mellowed considerably since our first encounter. There was less certainty about his swagger, less conviction in his sneer. He talked less about home and the Troubles.

I went with him on one rare trip home to Belfast. The first thing that struck me was how much it was like the place I had grown up in, it could have been a lot of places in England - and then an army foot patrol rounded a corner. It seemed that I was the only one taking any notice as they crouched and looked into the sights of their rifles. I stood there gawking, thinking: This is real, those are real guns with real bullets those guys are walking around with. One of the soldiers was a black guy. I was embarrassed by his presence and but for Danny I would have walked over and demanded to know what he was doing in a white man's army.

'Come on,' laughed Danny, 'before the fecking squaddies start thinking you're a target they can practise on.'

Later on, Danny took me to a local boxing club and I sparred a few gentle rounds with several spindly pale boys. Brendan, a small man with sad brown eyes, ran the club and was obviously held in some sort of reverential affection by the boys and their parents. He took Danny and me to a social club where we sipped at pints of stout and talked about boxing. As the night wore on the discussion became political; it was obvious to me that Brendan and Danny had read the same version of the Bible. Now I was amongst it, the guns and the soldiers, I heard what was said to me with greater clarity.

It was only when Brendan asked me for an analysis of my own situation in England that I felt uncomfortable. The sight of a black man in a British uniform had begun to alter my perceptions of who we were. Up until that moment I was of the opinion that black people were incapable of oppression, that we were immune to the values and mores of the people who I had thought perpetually oppressed us. As Danny used to ask me: Who was this 'we' I used to chat about? We knew nothing about the soldier or his background. I had seen his colour and made assumptions, jumped to all sorts of conclusions - the very thing I said pissed me off about how white people in England looked at me.

Brendan saw how I was struggling to make a reply that made any sense and kindly took the talk back to boxing. On leaving the club he clasped my hand warmly and thanked me for giving his lads a gentle workout. '*Slān abhaile*, safe home,' he said. 'But remember, Robbie, that the people who are doing all these things in our country are the same ones who rule the place where you live. You can see yourself how ruthlessly they act when their interests are threatened. Remember that word ruthless and what you've seen in this part of Ireland.'

While walking back to Danny's home I asked him if Brendan had studied politics or if he was a teacher. Danny laughed at my naivety. 'The only teaching Brendan ever did was to show kids how to look after themselves in the ring and the older fellas how to handle an Armalite. Though he did do a bit of the political studying in the Kesh, right enough.'

I later found out that Brendan had once been a top man in the 2nd Battalion of the IRA's Belfast Brigade. That first visit to Belfast not only filled my head with slogans and rhetoric, it had also stirred something within me. But I left that city without any feeling about the real price of war - I would learn that later.

'Is that tea ready?' Danny called from the living room. I threw two plates of sandwiches and a packet of biscuits onto the tray and hurried in to him.

As he slurped the tea I watched how some of it dribbled onto his shirt and saw the soft roll of flesh above his belt where once there had been a stomach of chiselled white marble. He drew the back of his hand across his mouth and said, 'So, I'm after seeing on the telly that there's been a lot of action around this way, a few shootings and that. What's it all about then?'

'People reckon most of it is to do with drugs,' I replied.

'I read somewhere that some Muslim fellas were involved - do you know anything about that? You wouldn't be knowing much about that crowd, now would you, Robbie?'

They were very strange questions from a friend who hadn't seen me for more than two years. Something I was not sure about was making me angry. 'What sort-a shit you talkin, Danny? Why would I know anythin about those Muslim guys? You should know me better than that.'

'Ach, yes, I do,' he said with that irritating fake laugh, 'I was only thinking it's a wee bit of a coincidence that they are after organizing around here, of all places.'

I had enough going on in my head to care if there was a cryptic message in what he was saying. Before I could ask a question he changed tack and asked how was my life.

Again I had to pause. 'Good,' I said, 'very good.'

'Did herself ever come back?'

'A few times, not for a while though. Just to see Nathan.'

'Is she still with the fella with the stocking on his head?'

'I've no idea.'

'A fucking transvestite, if you ask me. Did you ever take up with anyone yourself?'

'Oh yeah,' I replied, trying to sound like I was annoyed.

'Like serious?'

'Very serious,' I snapped. 'You know Carmen, don't you? We're thinkin about makin things a bit more permanent between us.'

It was another lie to add to the barricade of untruths we were piling up between us.

'I hope it works out for you,' he said flatly. He put two biscuits into his mouth and made a disgusting crunching noise. He swilled some tea around his teeth before belching loudly. 'Sorry about that, Robbie, I'm fucking starving, so I am. The long journey and that. Tell me, how are things at the factory?'

'Will I cook you up somethin?'

'Ah, no, the pieces and the biscuits will do me fine. So, how is it at the factory these days?'

'No idea, guy. Got the sack today.'

Danny's eyes signalled his disbelief as he hissed, 'Today? You're joking me.'

I think it was the first time I had ever seen him at a loss for words.

'Don't worry about it,' I said, 'somethin else will turn up. I mean, there's a lot worse things happenin in the world. It ain't exactly Rwanda, is it?'

He nodded and muttered something that I couldn't quite hear. It was one of the strangest conversations that I had ever had with Danny, and we'd had some strange ones in our time. Unable to put off talking about the ghosts any longer, I said, 'Danny, about your dad. I don't know if you ever got my letter but I still feel it. It's hard for me to say exactly how sorry I was. Lots of people say it, I know, but when somethin like that happens to someone you know, all those innocent guys. Man, I jus kept thinkin - you know. I'm sorry for you an' your mom an' your sisters.'

His response was again not what I expected. He talked about burying the past, looking to the future, the duty everyone had to put aside their private grief for the sake of a lasting peace. Maybe it was because so many people had offered him their condolences that his words sounded so empty and rehearsed. But to me his reply sounded like everything else he had said since he had arrived: nothing but lies, lies and lies.

Suddenly I was offended by this conversation. It was like being back in the ring with him again for the first time. He had come into my territory and then brazenly given me shit and I had too many problems of my own to tolerate it. I stood up and said, 'Danny, I'm goin to bed. I've got to take Nathan to school in the mornin. We'll talk some more tomorrow.'

He looked blankly at me at first. 'Ach, no problem, mate. I'm a wee bit knackered myself from the journey and that. Yeah, we'll have some crack in the morning.'

In bed I thought I had got away with it, I had left Danny before he could summon up my ghosts. But still a nagging doubt kept me restless until my eyes reluctantly closed and I drifted into an uneasy sleep.

I dreamt of Errol and Hanimal standing over me as I lay on a floor that was cold and wet. Hanimal put his hand over my mouth and stopped me breathing while Errol pointed a snub-nosed revolver at my chest. I pulled away Hanimal's hand. 'You can't kill a man twice!' I shouted at Errol. He bared his teeth viciously and a flash of fire erupted from the end of the gun.

I woke with a start, desperate for air. Heart pounding, head throbbing. Drenched with sweat, I felt weak and nauseous. Fumbling for the clock-radio I saw how my hands were shaking.

It was only five in the morning. The stench of acrid perspiration which had rapidly turned cold on my skin was too much to bear. I stumbled to the shower and savoured the warm steam in my mouth, the perfume of the soap and the coarseness of the towel on my back. Like a condemned man I savoured every moment, every sensation.

On the way back to my bedroom I noticed a dull light lying at the foot of the stairs. With a twist of the towel on my hips I crept downstairs and heard a faint noise coming from the kitchen. I pushed the door with the tips of my fingers. 'What's goin on?' I asked him.

Danny was standing by the table, his coat on and a bag at his feet. Pink-faced, he said, 'Ah, Robbie, so you're an early riser too, eh?'

I stared at his bag. 'Off already, Danny?'

'Just leaving you a note, so I was.'

'Is this some sort-a Irish tradition you failed to tell me about, a guest leavin a note with his goodbyes while his host is still asleep?'

He flashed a cheerless smile and then said, 'Ach no. I sometimes have these dreams, these terrible dreams about my da. It must have been the way you mentioned him last night that brought it back. I get the shakes and the sweats, you know? Christ, I wouldn't wish them on my worst enemy.'

For an instant I thought that I had cried out in my sleep and he somehow knew of my own nightmare, or he was trying to create a smokescreen. 'You're tryna tell me that you're diggin up 'cause of a dream?' I sneered.

'No, Jesus, no. I just can't sleep and I have a few things to do, that's all. If it's all right with you I'll be back tomorrow or the day after. It's all in my note, I'm just away to let my comrades know that the digs are sorted out.'

'Are you sure you're comin back?'

'I fecking hope so - I've left one of my bags upstairs. There's no sense in traipsing all over the country with the two of them.'

The mention of dreams had struck a chord and I realised that our reunion had evoked sad and powerful memories for both of us. I pushed away whatever was gnawing at the edges of my mind and asked, 'So when are you back?'

'Well, it's Thursday... let's say some time Friday night.'

'That's cool. Have a good trip.'

He made a feeble smile. 'Right, so *slan*, Robbie. I'll see you and we'll make a great day of it on Saturday for wee Nathan, eh?'

'Sure.'

He picked up his bag and said, 'I might as well go out the back way as I'm here.'

I watched him make his way down the garden path. As his shape melted into the early morning gloom I realized what I had unconsciously noted the instant I saw him on my doorstep: Danny was the man I had seen in the doorway of the Rose and Crown the night Tyrone had tried to kill me.

14

A FORTNIGHT AFTER I had seen him at the rear of the Rose and Crown Danny had come to my house and given me nothing but bullshit.

Unless he had changed in character as much as in appearance, I could not believe that he would have anything to do with the shady business that went on in there. I had known him as a man who was not easily tempted by money and I grew to understand that in his own understated way Danny was a person of principle. And yet he had not been honest with me. Something about him had changed; it was more than the lines of grief that were etched around his eyes. Then again, we had both changed.

As I pondered on the real reason for Danny's reappearance a sense of foreboding began to stir within me. If it were possible, I would have left there and then. I would have got up from the kitchen table, taken Nathan from his bed and gathered all our belongings. If it were practicable we would have got into my car and left all the trouble and danger behind. Gone! We'd be gone.

But I didn't open the wardrobe doors and pull what few clothes I had left from the shelves. Reason overcame instinct and I pulled back the bed covers and lay down, resigned to staying put for a little longer.

When the time came to leave, my mom would understand; she knew all about leaving - after all, she had travelled thousands of miles with my dad in search of a better life. She would not allow herself to voice an argument to make me stay. She was the strongest person I had ever known, strong like a man could never be.

Four years after they had landed, when I was three years old, my dad was killed in an accident in a factory and the shock made her miscarry the baby who should have been my younger brother. There was little for her in England but there was even less in Jamaica and so she stayed. Mom remained single and struggled alone, although I do remember when I was around seven or eight she introduced me to a man she told me to call 'Uncle Claude'. I asked her if he was a brother of hers or my dad's. I never saw him again and I never saw her strength leave her, not for a moment. She persevered, she survived.

Mom was strict but she only beat me if I deserved it. She did not allow any patois in the house under any circumstances - it was the language of 'country people' and she made sure that I learnt to read before I went to school. She did the same with Nathan, but never laid an angry hand on him. My dad had been the teacher in Jamaica he was never allowed to be in England, and she would often tell me that education is the key to all of life's opportunities. She'd say, 'The unknown is given shape by prejudice and a mind without readin is a mind that is easily led.'

Later on in my life, while reading of wars in far-flung places I would remember what she had told me and wondered about the shapes of prejudice in the minds of those who perpetrated genocide and how many of them were illiterate.

I wasn't sad that I grew up without my father, for what I never had I never missed. In the wedding photograph on the mantelpiece he looked like Jamaica's answer to Sugar Ray Robinson. Tall and slim with his straightened hair slicked back, he had a pencil moustache and a complexion lightened by the photographic process that was the tradition in those days. He was the perfect role model, and death had ensured that he would remain that way.

The cover tight around my shoulders, I stared at the clock and I waited for the time I would wake Nathan. My mind began to flit back and forth over what reasons might have lain behind Danny's visit but no idea would stay still long enough to make any sense and the fluorescent numerals of my clock-radio began to blur.

The alarm took longer than usual to switch off. I was so convinced that I would stay awake that I momentarily refused to believe that I had fallen asleep.

Nathan was his usual early morning truculent self after I had roused him. He tottered bleary-eyed to the bathroom reasserting his independence: no, he did not require any assistance to wash himself. I listened at the bathroom door for any sound of activity; it was not unusual to find Nathan put into a trance by the sight of his own reflection or a bar of soap. After ten seconds of complete silence I burst in to find the boy mesmerized by a piece of soap again. 'Nathan!' I yelled. His dull eyes did not register me picking up the flannel. Taking advantage of this lapse I began to scrub his face. He opened his mouth to protest and got a mouthful of soapy face-cloth for his trouble. Squealing angrily, he twisted and turned as I made to get the sleep out of the corners of his eyes and then he got another wipe across his mouth just to keep him quiet.

One of the aspects of parenthood that mystified me was how if I got Nathan out of bed five minutes late we would leave our home five minutes late, but if I got him up five minutes early we would still be five minutes late. This particular morning we were almost seven minutes behind schedule as Nathan finally clambered onto the rear seat of my car. The boy had me cussing myself to a warm spot in hell until I saw something out of the corner of my eye. Making out I was checking up and down the road before moving off, I took a fleeting look at the red car parked a little way along the road. It could have been that a neighbour had visitors or had bought a new car but, for no good reason, I felt that neither was the case.

At the bottom of the road I turned right as usual but at the next junction I took another right instead of a left and took two more right turns until I was heading towards my house again. In the rearview mirror I could see Nathan's puzzled frown.

'Dad, are we going home again?'

There was no sign of a red car. 'No,' I said, 'I thought I'd left the front door open, that's all.'

All the way to school I continued to check the mirror to see if the red car was following. There was no sign of it and in a scolding tone I told myself that Danny's arrival on my doorstep had spooked me and turned me paranoid. Nathan left the car huffing and puffing like an old man. 'Two more days, Natty-Dread, you can have a lie-in Saturday,' I said, trying to make amends for my action with the face-cloth.

He rolled his eyes and groaned, 'See you later, Dad.'

I had once gone to school through the very same gates. Almost twenty-five years ago I had met Errol in that same playground. I was eight years old and I had become the new kid in school after I had moved with my mom to the house she lived in to this day. Sweet Jesus, where had all the time gone? What had I done with it? Suddenly I was thirty-two, an unemployed single parent who had become involved with a woman who had once borne a son for Errol. So much for my childhood dreams.

Before Nathan was born I was going to travel the world. I had already put aside all notions of becoming a boxing world champion but I never imagined I would remain in the same place. I was romancing about touring Europe when Sharon broke the news that she was expecting our baby.

At twenty-four, quite late by local standards, the dreams and ambitions were replaced by hunting for a place to rent, setting up home and living with Sharon for almost five years. Errol called me an idyat for almost every day of it. It was quite obvious to him that Sharon was a gravelitious bitch and 'just like a woman' she had got herself pregnant so she could hook a man and suck him dry of every penny he had. That kind of talk got me well vexed; this was a guy who had three sisters and a mother - as I would remind him every time he started to chat such nonsense. It made me determined to prove him wrong, to show him how a man should take on responsibility instead of walking away from it like he had done with Tim. The way Sharon walked out on me when I failed to persuade her that unaffordable luxuries were not necessities proved Errol partly right about her, but at least he resisted the temptation to tell me so.

The bell rang and the children vanished from the playground. I saw Duane's grandmother deliver him to the gates and watched her traipse away.

Mrs Swaby had old, thick and tired legs. Her light-coloured stockings looked out of place against the darkness of her skin. I wondered how many thousands of miles those legs had walked and what burdens she must have carried. Her weary gait took me back to thinking about leaving. If I didn't start to act right away, something else would crop up and I could imagine myself watching my grandchild walk through the same gates. It was a terrible thought.

I headed for the Blackmore estate. The first step of my escape would be to walk away from Mrs Swaby's daughter. Beautiful Carmen, there was not a day that I didn't think about her. When we first kissed it was so gentle, as if we were aware of each other's pain. In our rawness we were careful and considerate. But as we began to heal each other she moved away from me. For all the beautiful recollections I had of her, I often imagined the tears Tim had told me she had shed after I had left her. Tears must be the most corrosive fluid in the world. I hated the thought of her crying.

I had vowed when Sharon had left me that I would never allow another woman to control my life or dupe me into putting aside my principles. Carmen had made me vulnerable in a different way: thoughts of her tears filled me with guilt. I knew that she still harboured a hope that we could start afresh, but for my own peace of mind I would put an irrevocable end to our relationship before I left and give her the chance to curse me. Like self-flagellation it would both satisfy and hurt me. But I could always endure pain.

A glance at the clock in the dashboard told me it was too early in the morning to face such emotional turmoil and I had yet to work out how I should tell her that I was leaving. Part of me, conscience maybe, didn't want her thinking I was just another man who had trailed in, taken what I could, and then walked out of her life. I turned the car in the direction of home. Fools rushing in and all that. I would make myself some tea and a sandwich. Unemployment hadn't changed the need for a tea break at around ten o'clock and I would see her later on.

Envelopes of various shapes and colours were lying on the doormat. I took them into the kitchen. As the kettle began to boil I opened the brown slender one. It was my P45 and a final pay chit attached to a compliments slip. Unmoved by such bogus politeness, but impressed with my former employer's efficiency, I tore open the second envelope and found that I was in danger of winning one million pounds should I fill in a form and return it in the enclosed postage-paid envelope - no purchase necessary. It all went into the bin with the compliments slip. The third envelope was square and cream-coloured, like one which comes with a greetings card. There was no stamp on the front, just my name in block capitals. I slid the bread knife under its flap. Inside was a single sheet of paper; it was a photocopy of the two local newspaper headlines which announced the deaths of Errol and Hanimal and the discovery of Shaka's body in an alleyway. Written at the bottom of the paper was a message. It read: *Remember, remember those days in December?*

Very poetic.

Tyrone and the red car immediately came to mind. He had probably waited in that car until I took Nathan to school before, like a coward, pushing the envelope through my door. If his twisted mind thought that old newspaper headlines were going to intimidate me, then he was seriously mistaken. I would soon be out of here, taking Nathan with me, and I was no longer scared about what Tyrone might do. Fear had been a regular companion during my youth, I knew its nature and how it could be mastered. Before a fight my stomach would do somersaults, my mouth would dry as my palms became clammy, my heart would put my every vein throbbing. But fear has to release its grip, the body gets tired, the mind cannot retain the dreadful imaginings for long, the heart has to slow. By the time I ducked through the ropes all fear and doubt had vanished. In my mind I had entered an arena prepared for anything Tyrone might try.

The envelope and its contents joined the others in the bin. I made the tea and switched on the radio in time for the news. The lead item made me pause as I opened the fridge. There had been another killing during the night, an Asian businessman named Unadkat had been shot as he arrived home. I took out a block of cheese and listened to the report of how three hooded men had bound and gagged the man's family before waiting for him to return from a Conservative Party fund-raising function. 'Fuck him, he was only a Tory,' I yelled at the radio. The difference in the reporting of this man's death and that of Trevor Bisnott rankled me. Unadkat, obviously a pillar of society, was portrayed as an honest family man undeserving of such a fate. But the report of Trevor's death mentioned that he was a former doorman and well-known in the black community. He did not come over as such an unequivocally innocent victim.

I crammed my mouth with a sandwich and sent crumbs over the table as I continued to hurl disparaging and obscene remarks at the radio. But the policeman who described the slaying of Unadkat had me swallowing hard; he said that the one killer who said anything to Unadkat's family spoke with an Irish accent. Reaching for the mug of tea I told myself to behave: I could vouch for the whereabouts of the one Irishman I knew. I blew scornful cooling air onto the tea. My imagination sure was working overtime.

My eyes drifted out to the garden and the path Danny Maguire had walked a few hours before. Again I saw his shape as he furtively peered out through the rear door of the Rose and Crown. I became temporarily paralyzed in a moment of terrible realization. 'Blouse and skirt! Danny, you bastard!' I snarled as I regained movement in my lips.

Suddenly I was breathing hard and in the spare room searching for his bag. It was under the bed. I paused for a moment, unsure if I really wanted to know what was in the green holdall. My sweating hands put the bag on the bed and I studied it for what seemed an age before tugging feverishly at the zip. My heart thumped loudly and my stomach tried to expel half a cheese sandwich as I sifted through a couple of shirts, pairs of socks and a sweater.

Looking at the items of Danny's clothing that were strewn over the bed it occurred to me that I had lost every ounce of courage I ever had. Courage, so Bubby told me, was the ability not to allow fear to mould one's actions or let it drain the mind of reason. It was the sense of foreboding, the crazy notion that Danny's reappearance was about to wreck all my plans, that had put me running up the stairs to trawl through his belongings.

Sickened with myself, I remembered how Danny had proved himself a true friend in my hours of need and I went to the bathroom to wash my clammy skin.

Drying my hands, I stepped out onto the landing thinking all I needed was a fresh start and then I would be back to the person I once was. Rational once again, my hasty, crazy conclusions about what was in Danny's bag had me throwing back my head and laughing out loud. But my laughter halted abruptly and a coldness ran through me as I saw what looked like a dirty thumbprint on the trap-door which led to the loft.

15

THE COPPICE ESTATE was a monument to media-spawned wealthy white fright, though it was often termed 'white flight' and wealth was rarely mentioned. It stood on the city's edge, a short distance from a small wood. Weathered brick and leaded diamonds on the double-glazed windows were supposed to give the plush dwellings an air of antiquity. The high boundary walls, the brightly coloured alarm boxes which sat under the eaves and the private security guards hired by the residents were all there to protect them from the criminal hordes that were supposed to spill out from the inner city.

The houses were a lot closer to the trees than I had anticipated, but I was not about to spend any more time driving around looking for another place. I had decided to go to the woods because it was only a twenty-five minute drive from my house and I had once run through the area as part of my training regime a long time before The Coppice was built.

A woman in a dark quilted jacket and green wellington boots was with her dog somewhere in amongst the trees. I could hear her shrill warble for the animal to come to heel grow more distant. They wouldn't be in the wood much longer: once the mutt had shit on the carpet of dead leaves they would return to the exclusive estate and I would put the large plastic box into the ground.

My back resting against a broad tree, I gazed up at the bare branches and realized this was the first time I had been still since I had pulled the large black plastic bag from my roof space. The weight, the dull clink of metal as it hit the floor: I instinctively knew the nature of the bag's contents before I opened it to find four handguns swathed in oily cloths and several loaded magazines wrapped in greased brown paper. There were two automatic pistols and a pair of revolvers. I wondered, for just a moment, which one of them had killed the Asian businessman named Unadkat the night before.

A potentially long prison sentence immediately loomed large in my mind. The guns had to go - and go quickly. I wasn't prepared to wait for the cover of darkness before getting them out of my house. The bread was rapidly emptied onto the kitchen table and I ran back upstairs and put the guns into the airtight container. Plastic tape went around the edge of the lid to ensure it stayed on and as an extra precaution to keep out any moisture once it went underground.

I knew exactly where I would put the guns as I hurried out to my car. They could have gone into the canal, or into a dustbin. But they wouldn't. I still didn't know for sure what Danny was involved in but I knew enough to put the guns in a place from where I could retrieve them at a later date. The acquisition of guns usually meant big expense, or a big favour. Sometimes it meant dealing with dangerous characters. Shooters had to be handled with respect.

I guessed that Danny had come to my house in desperation, that something had gone wrong with his getaway and he had headed to my place as the police threw a cordon around the area where the murder had taken place. But I did not have a clue why Danny would be involved with the killing of an Asian businessman in England. I had read about IRA men hiring themselves out to gangsters as assassins and getting themselves involved in the drugs trade since the ceasefire, but I refused to believe any of that fuckrees. It was shit, British government disinformation. Those people I had met in West Belfast were bucking the shitstem big time, they were not dealing with criminality; and it would hurt me to think that any of them had finally sold out. Anyway, Danny Maguire had always made it plain that he was no IRA man, but of course he knew a few of them. Like he said, they weren't reared in a specialist compound, they were the kids at the next row of desks at school or the guy living across the road who earned a few pounds fixing cars.

Although I knew there was a chance that Danny might never return to reclaim the guns, I already imagined myself demanding from him an explanation of why he had put me at so much risk without so much as a word of warning.

Except for the sound of a wind whistling through the higher branches all was quiet. I returned to my digging and prickly beads of sweat began to erupt from my scalp and trickle down the side of my face. Breathing hard, I took in the taste as well as the acrid smell of the soft black soil until a burning sensation shot through my hand as the shovel hit a large root. I guessed that the hole was plenty deep enough; it was maybe twice the depth of the plastic box.

Once the container was safely buried I thought about getting back to my car. It was not straightforward: I would have to be careful that I was not seen by any of the paranoid residents of The Coppice estate. Part of the local folklore was how one of the householders, an enthusiastic member of the 'Neighbourhood Watch' scheme, had once succeeded in having a black postman arrested during his first delivery round. I could imagine their reaction on seeing a black man emerge from the woods with a shovel in his hand: they sure wouldn't think I had been digging for badgers. We lived only a few miles apart but we inhabited irreconcilable worlds, a different consciousness.

I had once walked with Errol through an estate similar to The Coppice; it was sedate, comfortable and almost exclusively white. We had been looking for a man, a local councillor, who during an election had decided to play what was called the 'race card' once too often. Not for the first time he had labelled the local black population as a problem, a threat to the oh-so-civilized British way of life. We had identified his house and car and had decided to knock at his door. Errol would shoot the bastard as he answered.

One night we left Hanimal in my car and jogged a short distance to the quiet avenue. Errol was breathing hard as we rounded the final corner. 'Hol' on, man,' he gasped.

'Okay, we walk from here,' I said.

With our eyes fixed on the neatly clipped hedgerows across the road, we walked stiffly towards the driveway with the white saloon sitting in it. I listened to Errol trying to control his breathing. 'Everythin cool?' I asked.

Errol was pumped and primed for killing. Through his clenched teeth he snarled, 'I jus wanna put a bullet tru im fuckin racist mout' an' blow out im pussyclart.'

He was ready all right.

A shout of, 'Halt! Armed police!' stopped us in our tracks. Fifty or sixty paces ahead of us men poured out from a house. There were sounds of tyres skidding on the road behind us. We leapt over a small wall in front of a school and scampered to the shadows. Pressing our backs into the wall of the school building we watched men in peaked caps look over hedges and the small wall we had vaulted. 'Can't stay here,' Errol whispered harshly in my ear.

We ran to the playground at the rear and to the tall metal gates that were topped with barbed wire. Errol was already analysing what was going on around us. 'Cha,' he hissed at me, 'me tell you twice we'd draw too much attention walkin aroun a white man's area.' He pushed his foot against one of the gates to start his climb. 'No,' I said, 'we gotta go under.' The gap between the bottom of the gates and the ground was no more than the width of a man's head but we got through and ran for my car praying that Hanimal had not heard the commotion, panicked, and left us stranded.

Hanimal was where we had left him. Errol sat in the front and I threw myself into the back as he said, 'Be cool an' get us out of here, H. Babylon is all over the place.'

Although there was nothing in the local press, I later found out that a police trap had been sprung by an anti-racist campaigner who had decided to daub the councillor's car. I doubted if armed police would have been waiting for a lone student found in possession of a paint aerosol, and I had to agree with Errol that we might have drawn attention to ourselves by making one reconnoitre too many. 'Look, guy,' said Errol, 'you know how it go. One black man go inna white area an' imma loiter, two must be muggers or wanna burgle some place, an' t'ree black men is a mob. People like we just can't dally where we want. Blouse an' skirt, you must think this is a free country or somethin.'

Though we never said it, we knew that if there was ever to be a next time, we could no longer discount what could prove to be a final encounter with armed police.

I had just got behind the wheel of my car when an inhabitant of The Coppice appeared with a pair of large dogs. He regarded me with suspicion. I didn't want him making a note of my number-plate so I wound down my window.

'Sorry,' I said, trying to sound like a typical middle-class Englishman, 'I'm hopelessly lost.'

He tugged on the leads. Reassured by a familiar deferential tone and the presence of two ferocious-looking brutes he looked down at me and asked, 'Where are you looking for?'

'Some place called the Blackmore estate, do you know it?'

I saw him try not to grimace. 'Just carry along this road for six miles or so. You'll come to a dual carriageway and take the first exit. You can't miss it.'

'Thank you so much,' I said, turning the ignition key.

'Not at all,' he replied, lurching to one side as the dogs tried to make for the wood.

Glad that the dogs would not allow him to stay still long enough to get a good look at my registration number, I moved off. I would take that first exit. I would see Carmen and say the words I had practised so many times in my mind.

It was around midday as I knocked on her door but as I had secretly hoped - there was no answer. So she would know that I had called, and that I had tried to make contact before leaving, I pushed a note through her door. It read: *Carmen, I called at 12.10. Take care of yourself. Love, R.*

I would not bother going back, I'd duck out. She would find out soon enough that I had left town. Now I could tell myself that I had tried to let her know I was leaving but fate had decreed that our relationship would simply wither away. Maybe it was better it happened that way.

As my belly complained it had only half a cheese sandwich to sustain me all morning, I decided to move the car away from outside

Carmen's house and then walk a short distance to Mustafa's Sea Star Fish Bar. To avoid the mounds of dog shit that were strewn around the place, I strode through the precinct with my eyes fixed firmly on the ground. A hand reached from behind me, grabbed at my forearm and broke my thoughts. Instinctively I pulled away but the hand slid down and took hold of my wrist. A voice called out, 'Bwoy, you slow down!'

In an instant I recognized George and did not throw the right hand which had already formed a fist. It was almost impossible to mistake George for anyone else: the silver strands in the bush that was growing out of his head made him look like a derelict, middle-aged extra from the Car Wash movie.

I had always liked George. He was a decent man who had tried his best to steer the local youth from what he called 'blind an' self-destructive anger'. I admired his inexhaustible ability to empathize but the way I saw it the youths he dealt with were suffering a blind and self-destructive *greed*.

In the seventies George led the fight against the skinhead mobs from the Lowlands who were looking for black boys to beat. In the early eighties he spent time in prison for his part in the Blackmore uprising which came about after a local youth worker had been beaten into a bloody pulp by the police. By the nineties his grey hairs and weariness were starting to show. George seemed unable to admit that the youths of today were of a very different generation; a convenience food, drive-thru instant gratification generation. The youths spoke a language they thought was Jamaican patois, although only a few of the words and even fewer of those who spoke that way were from Jamaica. Most of them were far removed from the culture George had been born into or even people of my age: it was as if they were a generation that had wandered far away from the land of their forebears and had become hopelessly disorientated.

The young guys on the Blackmore didn't want to hear George's talk of discipline or politicization. Their anger was similar to that of previous generations but it was an anger that was often driven by a mixture of envy and greed rather than an urge to confront injustice. George could not understand it; he thought melanin would make them oblivious to the images of materialism which bombarded everyone living in what was termed a consumerist society. I heard that George had finally given up shouting at the tide when the council sold the football pitch his team had used for the home fixtures.

I said, 'Wha happen, George? You caught me with my mind on other things, man. I heard you were movin back to JA.'

George looked on edge. He smiled unconvincingly and said, 'Annoda few weeks, Robbie, an' me garn out this bitch of a country. Mi belly full-a it. You's a guy I never thought would hang aroun this shithole. I thought you would-a got out long time ago.'

'That's exactly what I'm thinkin about, ol' man. I'm outta this place as soon as I can.'

George continued to nervously scan the surroundings. He looked into my eyes briefly and then over my shoulder. 'Then wha' the fuck you doin here, Robbie?'

His tone, so out of character, took me by surprise. He looked into my eyes again. He was concerned, possibly upset, definitely worried. He repeated his question even more forcefully. 'Then wha' the ras you doin here, Robbie? Wha' yah tryin to prove?'

Still confused, I shrugged my shoulders and gave him the only answer I could think of. 'Just gettin myself somethin to eat from Mustafa's,' I said, kind of hopefully.

'But wait, man, you mus know bad man look fe you, eh?'

I hadn't a clue what George was talking about but before I could ask a question he took hold of my arm again and growled, 'Kiss mi neckback! Daddy One-foot lookin to kill you!'

I was thinking either this was the sort of joke George was not renowned for or the excitement of returning home had sent him off his head. Convinced that he must be mistaken I said, 'Cha, man, I don't bisniss with the Campbells.'

'No? Then why you bruk im bwoy's jaw the odda night?'

'Bruk im jaw?' I said, sounding momentarily pleased with my handiwork. There were too many things going on in my life; too much loss, too much grief and too much danger to have dwelt on the implications of teaching the youth some manners. Reassured by the thought that I would soon be leaving town, I tried to put George at ease. 'Look, man, the bwoy start to big up im chest so I showed him a lickle lesson in life. They say the last thing to go is the punch.'

'Cha!' George yelled dismissively. 'Feget yah fist, it's the Campbells who are lookin out for you. Word is Glenroy look fe blood! Robbie, you unnerstan? Get your ras an' your pickney far away right now!'

I was going anyway but some remnant of foolish pride made me want to act as if I was unconcerned by George's warning. I didn't want it to look as though the Campbells had run me out of town.

I had never thought much of the Campbells' reputation; like the reputations of many hard men, it had been piled high by people who were easily impressed, easily scared. In their own small circle they were men to fear but that circle didn't include me. And as my mother used to say: 'Duppy know who to frighten.'

My first encounter with a Campbell was when Alvin arrived at our school. He hadn't been there a week when he started acting in the way that had got him expelled from another school. He had disrupted the way we had ordered things and it was decided that Errol should show him the error of his ways. I walked with Errol to the science department. Alvin was outside the biology lab taking money from a group of smaller kids. 'Wha happen, Alvin,' said Errol. 'Let me show you the way tings stay aroun 'ere.'

Alvin made the mistake of standing still while looking at Errol instead of me. Errol's smiling face was the last thing Alvin saw before he hit the ground. The plan had been for Errol to give Alvin a bit of a lick but there was something about Alvin that made me want to hit him. So I clouted the guy with a nice left hand just as Errol was launching his own punch. Alvin fell to the floor so fast that Errol ended up hitting the wall and damaging his wrist. Old Jenksy gave me and Errol a bit of a talking to and expelled Alvin, his second expulsion in a month. Word soon spread that Glenroy was coming to the school to sort us out for what had happened to his younger brother. Errol just laughed and held up his bandaged wrist and said, 'I'll have to leave him to Robbie.'

Everyone in school knew Glenroy was mad as a ras and losing a leg had made him even more unhinged. I fretted and stayed inside most of the weekend but by Sunday evening I had convinced myself that no one-foot man could beat me. Errol came to school the following day without his bandage and impressed everybody by saying he was recovered enough to face Glenroy if he showed up. When news got around that Glenroy had been arrested during the weekend for killing the ponce who had took off his leg with a machete, Errol simply shrugged his shoulders and swore to us that he hadn't heard about it.

Seventeen years later, Errol's attempt at acting shocked at the news of Glenroy's arrest still brought a smile to my face.

'Robbie!' shouted George. He was looking at two men, one black, one white, striding towards us from the far end of the precinct. Both were casually dressed, nylon padded jackets, denim jeans and training shoes. The white man was huge, six-foot-six or seven. The black guy was smaller in comparison. Something about them looked dangerous.

I could see the big guy's eyes, they were fixed on me. I began running after George shoved me but halted after the first few faltering steps as I told myself that George was mistaken. But the fearful look on his face and the fact the two men were now sprinting towards me put me running again.

All I had on my mind was to get away, nothing else, not even to where I should run. A man, white, clean shaven, similarly dressed to my pursuers, stepped out in front of me, his arms outstretched. I simply ran into him, jumped into him, my forearm crashing into his face. We fell to the ground, me on top of him. I saw blood streaming from his nose. He wrapped his arms around me and pulled me close. I thrust my knee between his legs and I broke from his grip as he yelled out in pain. The other two were close behind as I scrambled to my feet. I didn't look back but I could hear their footsteps pounding on the concrete.

I knew the blurred shapes at the edges of my vision were people who were just standing and staring, like they must have done the night David Moncrieff was run down and shot. I felt the strength in my legs leaking away but a sudden instant of hope spurred me on - a few more yards and across a road was safety: a maze of ramps and walkways in which I could lose the men chasing me. I ran across the road without a pause and I did not see the car until the very last moment. The tyres screeched. I twisted and instinctively thrust out my hands towards the car's bonnet. I saw the ground, the winter's blue sky, the kerb, and then the sky again. It was in slow-motion and all I could think of was getting to my feet as soon as I had stopped rolling.

It felt as though I was running in a tank of water as I got to my feet again. Somehow I reached the pavement but two men grabbed me and pulled me back to the ground. I lashed out at them with my feet. I wasn't going to die easily. I struggled, I roared. A man stood over me and reached into the inner pocket of his jacket. It took what seemed the longest second of my life to recognize that he was thrusting a warrant card and not a gun into my face.

'For fuck's sake, stay still! We're police!' he yelled.

16

IF A BLACK man was pushed into a car by three white guys on the Blackmore estate ten years ago a crowd would have quickly gathered. In a matter of seconds it would have been worked out that the four men were cops and action would have been taken to ensure that their car had a hard time getting away unmarked. All I had to protest on my behalf was one middle-aged community worker who could hardly speak due to a shortage of breath. I put the indifference of the onlookers down to the worst sort of assimilation. George stood in front of the car demanding, in between gasps for air, to know what was going on. The cop behind the wheel wound down his window and responded with a curt threat to arrest George for obstruction. Sandwiched between the man-mountain and the black cop, I shouted from the back seat for George to move away and that everything would be cool. He shuffled onto the pavement and I saw his relief that it was the police, and not the Campbells, who had got hold of me.

Once the driver's window was closed again the car quickly filled with the acrid scent of our exertions. Without a word he reopened the window. The rush of air going by and the intermittent crackling of a radio set were the only sounds I heard until the big cop swore and complained of the cold. Again the window sealed us in. It didn't take long to be enveloped once more by the cloying odour of our still sweating bodies.

Menacing and silent, the cop with the squashed red nose continually glanced back at me from the front passenger seat. With each silent mile, with every turn of a corner, the relief I had shared with George on discovering the men were not a hit-squad sent by Glenroy Campbell gradually gave way to apprehension. All sorts of scenarios began to play in my mind. At best, the man with the two dogs at The Coppice estate had got suspicious, had taken the number of my car and rung the police. At worst, I had been seen burying the guns.

The car turned abruptly into the car park of a roadside café and the driver turned around and asked me did I want tea or coffee. I shook my head. The big cop said he would have tea, with milk and five sugars. The man on the other side of me said he would have a coffee, like himself, black and sweet. The three white guys laughed as though they had never heard that one before. The driver told the front seat passenger to clean himself up in the washroom and then bring back a tea, two black coffees with sugar and whatever he wanted for himself.

The cop got out and the car filled with fresh cold air which made me shiver. The driver let an arm drop nonchalantly over the back of his seat as he introduced himself as Detective Sergeant Ian Hooper. He asked for my name and address. I answered, guessing that he had already run a check on my car's registration number. He nodded as though he was satisfied with my reply before asking, 'Why, Mr Walker, did you run and then assault a police officer?'

Tilting my head to the left I said, 'I see a man his size comin towards me an' I run. I didn't know you guys were cops, I thought you were friends of a woman I used to see.'

Detective Sergeant Hooper looked at me with an expression of well-practised scepticism; he wanted me to believe that he was a man who had heard and seen it all before. I returned his stare, knowing he was probing for any hint of uncertainty. He sniffed and then said, 'Would that woman be Carmen Swaby?'

'No.'

'But you did just call at her house.'

'Yeah, but she ain't the woman I was talkin about.'

'Would you mind telling me why you called at her house?'

'Me an' Carmen have been friends for years. I was just callin to see how she's doin lately.'

Hooper made a sucking noise as though he was attempting to dis-lodge a piece of food that had stuck in his teeth. The cops on either side of me adjusted themselves to face me but I didn't let my eyes move from Hooper. He had said enough to confirm what I had rapidly surmised: the cops must have been watching Carmen's house as I posted the note through her door.

Hooper pushed the nail of his small finger between two of his lower front teeth and said, 'Are you as friendly with Carmen's brother?'

He seemed to have no idea of my visit to the wood but for all I knew he was trying to catch me off-guard. I said, 'You mean Tyrone? Nah.'

'But you do know him.'

'Went to the same school as him, used to work with him but we fell out 'cause he reckoned I should've spoke up for him when he got the sack.'

'How long ago did he get the sack?'

'Can't remember.'

'Can you remember why he was sacked?'

'Givin a white guy a box.'

'And you don't agree with that sort of thing, do you, Mr Walker?'

'Depends on the white guy.'

'Did Tyrone ever discuss the Brothers of Islam with you?'

'I never discuss politics or religion.'

'Did he ever talk to you about the Muslim patrols on the Blackmore estate?'

'Nah.'

'I sense you're reluctant to talk to me, Mr Walker.'

'Nah, man, I love sittin here havin a chat.'

His eyes narrowed. Aggressively, he asked, 'When did you last see Tyrone Swaby?'

'According to what Carmen tell me it was on the day he left his flat. He was at the funeral of two guys we used to work with. They were killed in a hit-and-run on Curzon Street. Has anythin been found out about who killed them?'

'I'll ask the questions, Mr Walker, it keeps things simple that way,' he said, his tone flat but still threatening. 'Does Tyrone Swaby drink alcohol?'

The question was not one I had expected and my heart began to thump in a way I thought must be visible. I looked up to a distant point outside: my first sign of discomfort. I felt certain that Hooper was about to mention the Rose and Crown. I forced my eyes back towards him. 'Well, from what Carmen tell me, he'd given up after becomin a Muslim.'

Picking up my hesitancy, Hooper said, 'You don't seem so sure - why's that?'

'What a man says an' what he do is usually two different tings.'

'I don't believe that Tyrone Swaby is a Muslim any more than that wanker who now calls himself Malek Abu Bakr.'

'Don't know the guy.'

Hooper's upper lip began to curl. 'You must have seen him on television and in the newspapers.'

I rolled my shoulders until the weight of two heavy hands quickly brought a halt to my attempt to get comfortable. 'Sure,' I said, forcing the word out from between my teeth.

'What do you reckon to the things Malek Abu Bakr says?'

'Not much.'

'Do you agree or disagree with most of it?'

'I don't discuss politics or religion.'

'You don't have much of an opinion either way.'

'Whether I do or I don't, I wouldn't discuss it.'

'Are you a Muslim, Mr Walker?'

'I love mi pork too much.'

'Politics aside, do you think the Brothers of Islam are doing good for the black community?'

'I didn't know there was a black community. Is there a white community?'

There was a long-drawn-out silence but I didn't think that Hooper was considering giving me an answer. Restarting the picking of his teeth he said, 'Abu Bakr did some good, didn't he? He got a few prostitutes off the streets, got rid of the kerb crawlers... saw off the odd drug dealer.'

'If you say so. I don't live on the Blackmore.'
'But you visit.'
'Yeah, but...'

'You talk to people who live in the Blackmore. What do they tell you about what the Muslims have done?'

'Nothin. I already told you that I never discuss politics or religion.'

Hooper had obviously decided to play 'good cop - bad cop' all by himself. First it was the offer of a drink but now the arm that had been casually slung over the back of his seat was moving in my direction. He pulled me towards him. 'Don't treat me like a cunt, sunshine, or I'll have big Hamish knock some respect into that smart black face.' He then pushed me back into the seat.

'Don't come this nigger shit!' the black cop shouted into my ear. 'You hear me? Quit this nigger shit and start showing some respect!'

I didn't respond or take my eyes off Hooper.

'Look at me, look at me!' the black cop screamed. His gloved hand gripped my jaw and twisted my head around. His eyes were wide and wild. 'I want you to start showing some respect to the man, answer his questions properly. You think we are the enemy, is that it? You think the police are black people's enemy? Look at my face, look at my black face - it don't rub off, it don't change because of what I do!' His fingers pressed into my flesh but I refused to let him see the pain. He blew through pursed malevolent lips and continued, 'I bet you're the type of shit-for-brains that complains about "Babylon" but the second your house gets burgled or your car gets broken into you're the first to come bawling to the police. We want to know where Tyrone Swaby is and Malek Abu Bakr. *They're* the enemy of black people living in this city, you fucking idiot!'

His fingers went further into my flesh and impaled the inside of my mouth on the sharp edges of my teeth. I continued to stare into the wide brown eyes as I tasted blood. He didn't like me looking at him, he didn't like what he imagined was my opinion of him. He turned my face away and I said to Hooper, 'I don't know where either of those guys are.'

Hooper looked at the blood which had trickled onto my lower lip.

He opened his mouth to speak but was cut short by the cop with the drinks kicking at the door. Hooper leant across and opened the door, inspected one of the mugs, muttered to himself and passed it to the big cop. To the black cop he said, 'Norman, let him out.' He again looked at the blood on my lip and said to me, 'Count yourself lucky we're not doing you for assaulting a police officer.' He pushed a card into my hand. 'You hear anything, anything at all, about the whereabouts of Tyrone Swaby or Malek Abu Bakr and you had better ring me on that number. You owe me one. Now go on and fuck off out my sight.'

I looked out to the road and realized where I was. 'Hey, what about droppin me back to where you found me?' I asked.

Hooper took a sip from his drink and the big cop shoved me sideways. I got out and came face to face with the black cop. I wiped the blood from my lip and smiled as he glared at me. 'Ol' man,' I said, 'you must learn to keep your cool when dealin wi' the breddren.'

'Arsehole,' he snorted as I walked to a bus stop. After a few minutes the car moved off, its engine roaring loudly as if it were snarling a warning at me. I gave them a wave but none of them bothered to respond. Errol would have been proud of my performance. I heard him laugh and say, 'Bwoy, you beat them again, just like ol' times.'

I went to bed Friday night cursing Danny Maguire. It was no great surprise that he had not turned up. It was around midday before I finally got out of bed. Feeling sick with tiredness, I couldn't remember the last time I had slept well. After I had dreamed again of Errol firing bullets into my paralysed body I lay awake for some hours listening to the World Service on the radio while watching for the first rays of light to peek through the curtains.

I shuffled my way downstairs and into the kitchen. With bleary eyes I peered into the fridge. At first I thought I was still dreaming but on closer inspection I found the wrapper of the bread that I had to store in there now my bread box was underground had a ragged hole in it. A trail of white crumbs and small black pellets led to a hole at the back of the fridge. A mouse, or maybe a rat, had gnawed its way through. I found more droppings when I pulled the fridge from the wall and I asked myself if some sort of vengeful spirit was trying to bring me to my knees. Slamming shut the fridge door I refused to buckle. I refused!

I walked to Bill's shop and got more bread and gave him a determinedly jovial performance, as if I did not have a care in the world. But when I got back to the house to find Nathan in the kitchen, grumpy and frowning, I exploded.

Not once in my life had I ever put an angry hand on Nathan but for a moment I came very close to warming his backside with the flat of my hand. It was the way he demanded to know what was going on and what he could have to eat that triggered my rage. I hurled the bread onto the floor and yelled at him to eat it. He ran upstairs, frightened by an anger he had never witnessed before.

His muffled sobs had my own eyes welling with stinging water. I felt guilty and ashamed that I had unloaded all my pent-up feelings onto my seven-year-old son. This was the home I had made for him, his place of sanctuary in a dangerous world. I was supposed to be the one who kept him safe but I had punctured his feelings of security in a moment of madness. My outburst scared me too: perhaps it was a sign that I was starting to cave in.

I went up to his bedroom and told him I was sorry, that I had a headache and was not feeling very well. Nathan cut short my mumbled excuses and, being a special type of kid, dried his tears. He then gave me a hug and said that he had been a bit naughty by not saying please when he had asked for something to eat. The boy came near to breaking my heart at that moment. I held him close to me and lost myself in his embrace until he said, 'Dad, can I have something to eat now, please?'

On our way to the stairs I looked up to the ceiling above the landing and momentarily stiffened. Danny Maguire came to mind as I caught sight of the small dark mark on the trap-door.

Watching Nathan happily eating toast and jam I still felt the need to make amends and promised that I would take him to Miranda's and he could go to the park with her.

Miranda was a petite and pretty English woman with long fair hair

155

and I guessed that she was in her late twenties. Wherever she went she wore the spectacles that looked much too big for her slim oval face, and ungainly thick-soled boots. We had met the previous year, not long after she had moved into a house a few doors away, when the sound of her old car refusing to start irritated me enough to make me leave the comfort of my armchair. 'Hol' on!' I shouted over the noise. 'You'll run down the battery. Open your bonnet.'

All that was wrong was a lead from her distributor cap had come loose. I pushed it back, closed the bonnet, told her to turn the key, and once the engine had fired up I went back into my house.

I often regretted doing that small favour. Miranda was so anxious to let me know of how grateful she was; she was so anxious that we should be friends. And she never failed to remind me of the offer for Nathan to call around and play with her children or to accompany them to the park any Saturday afternoon.

She referred to her children as 'bi-racial' and explained to me that the father of her boy was a Palestinian she had met at university and her daughter had come about due to a later relationship with a Latvian Jew. 'Miranda,' I exclaimed sarcastically, 'you should be working for the United Nations.' She had blushed innocently and said, 'I do my best to foster a greater understanding amongst peoples of different races. I really do find other cultures rather fascinating. We'll have to have a chat some time over a bottle of wine.'

I spoilt my chances of wine, civil conversation and whatever else that might lead to when I indulged in a bit of sneering at her liberal sensitivities. Miranda's face became a picture of angst when I replied, 'As long as you don't think that me an' you have a different culture, Miranda. Any different culture got beat out of the black man as soon as he got put onto the slave ship.'

I recalled her expression with some embarrassment as I walked with Nathan to her house but I was soon chuckling darkly to myself at the thought that some white people liked a metaphorical whipping for the sins of their forefathers.

Miranda seemed a little put out to see us standing on her doorstep, the scarf wrapped untidily around her head suggested that she was having a bad hair day. 'Hi, Miranda,' I said with a broad grin. 'Are you goin to the park today?'

She looked at Nathan wrapped up in his warm coat, doing his best to stretch his smile wider than mine. 'Oh, yes,' she lied.

'Would you mind taking this young rascal with you?'

'Oh, Robbie, not at all. We'd be delighted.'

I left four delighted people to have a delightful time and went back to my house scanning the road for any sign of Danny Maguire.

As soon as I opened my front door I saw a square envelope lying on the floor. Like the one of the previous day it had been hand-delivered. I had only been away for a few minutes and I had not seen anyone hanging around or any red car. Had it arrived when it did because of lucky timing or because I had been watched leaving my house?

I took it into the kitchen, hesitated, and threw it onto the table. I paced the floor for a while as I engaged in some ridiculous contest of wills with the sender of the envelope. 'Fuck you!' I muttered triumphantly, hurling it into the bin.

The victory was short-lived. From the bin the envelope beckoned me, telling me there could be a clue to the identity of the sender contained within. Inside was another photocopy of a newspaper's front page. The headline read: *Fanatics in bomb bid to kill police*. At the bottom of the page were scrawled the words: *No trial for black bombers?*

A knock at the door prevented me from dwelling on the message. I squeezed the paper into a ball and hurried out of the kitchen ready to confront Danny Maguire.

'Oh, Sharon,' I said, sounding displeased.

'Hello, Robbie,' she replied, tossing back her exquisite hair-weave and twisting her painted mouth as though just saying my name was an unpleasant experience. She looked better than I remembered and showed a lot more cleavage than I thought she had ever possessed. I averted my eyes and looked to the man standing behind her. His gold hair and white eyelashes accentuated the pallor of his skin. Tall and gangly with a prominent Adam's apple, he looked around twenty-five years old but dressed a lot older. He had a bookish look about him, like he was a solicitor. 'What do you want?' I asked Sharon.

Her eyes sparkled angrily. 'Is Nathan here?'

'He's out with a neighbour.'

'Maybe it's for the best. Can we come in?'

'The two of you?'

'If you don't mind.'

I did mind. This was the house she had upped and left two and a half years ago with Nathan and almost all the furniture. We had met a couple of times since then but always on neutral ground and I did not want her back spreading discontent in the happy home I had made with Nathan. But I could tell this was not a social call and without a word I showed them into the living room.

I caught a trace of her perfume as she passed me. She looked better than good. But then again, she was too vain a person not to leave home without at least three hours of grooming. When I had lived with her, even a trip to the shops would have been preceded by a meticulous application of make-up and a lengthy deliberation over what outfit to wear.

Not long after we had started to live together I found out that Sharon was a fervent capitalist without much capital and to her disappointment she discovered that I could not provide her with a great deal more. The fine jewellery that was on her fingers and around her slender neck indicated that she had acquired someone who could provide for her expensive tastes.

Sharon was the same age as Carmen and I couldn't help but compare how differently life had treated them and how differently we had treated each other. Sharon had a lighter complexion and what was sometimes referred to as 'European features'; in other words she had a straight nose and thin lips. She had been sought after, the prestige model, a catch. Most of the guys I had known, including Errol, Hanimal and Shaka, had chased her without success. So when Errol told me not to have anything to do with her I put his advice down to jealousy. I thought he was telling me that because he only had girls like Carmen who, though attractive, were dark and African-looking. Later on I learned to appreciate that

Carmen was the one who had real beauty. She was one of life's givers and the giving had taken its toll. Sharon was a taker and superficially she had escaped the rigours of life unscathed.

'You decorated the place,' Sharon said, taking a seat with her companion on the sofa.

I stood by the fireplace and didn't respond. I didn't want to engage in polite talk, small or otherwise, with her. Sharon glanced at the man and with a sardonic smile she said to me, 'No television or record player? You haven't changed, Robbie. Still livin out some pathetic socialist fantasy.'

At least she remained predictable - she had to get in her retaliation first. 'Sharon, let me tell you somethin,' I sighed. 'Don't think you can come inside my yard an' give me shit. So don't bother with the snide comments, tell me why you're here an' then haul your ras back out through the door.'

Trying not to show that I had unsettled her, she coughed quietly like she was clearing her throat, crossed the hands on her lap and straightened her back. 'Robbie, I am aware that you were fired recently and therefore your job prospects are not good,' she said sharply. 'I am also aware that you are in a relationship with a woman who has a son who is associatin with known criminals. I am also aware that Nathan is spendin a lot of time at your mother's house.'

'An' who told you all that shit?'

Her eyes glistened spitefully. 'I have it in writing.'

It immediately occurred to me that she had hired a private detective; probably the person who had sat outside in a red car. It was always in the back of my mind that she would come back for Nathan one day. I looked to the man beside her. 'Wha', so you've hired somebody to spy 'pon me? Him?' I sneered, poking a thumb in his direction.

The man looked at me pleadingly, open-mouthed. Sharon smiled, as if savouring the moment. A hand left her lap and rested on the man's clasped hands while the other was dangled limply in front of her face, despite the weight of the diamond on one of her fingers. 'Certainly not,' she said in a voice which shook with a disdainful laugh. 'This is Richard.

We are to marry next month. Richard runs his own computer company.'

I looked at Richard's Adam's apple moving nervously up and down and laughed out loud. 'Wha happen, Dick? Kiss mi neck, bwoy,' I roared. He took hold of my outstretched hand. 'The best-a luck, ol' man,' I laughed. 'You'll need it.'

Sharon's smile had gone and she glared at Richard. He tried to gently release himself from my grip and said, 'Thank you very much.'

'Hey, Dick,' I said, 'now me know wha you-a come fah.'

'I-It's Richard actually.'

'Yeah, Dick, me know. You come fe mi blessin, isn't it? Nah, nah, you 'ear me is outta work an' you come to offer me job at your computer factory. Thanks, ol' man.'

'You fuckin know we ain't here fe dat!' snarled Sharon.

Richard was dumbstruck to hear such words drop out of her delicately painted mouth. 'But wait, Dick, she chat patois to you too?' I asked him.

She stood up and pulled at Richard's hand. 'We're here fe Nathan. We're here to tell you that I'm gonna apply fe custody an' get my son outta this stinkin shithole. We're gonna give Nathan a betta life than you could ever give him.'

'*Our* son, Sharon.'

I watched as her eyes opened with cruel delight. 'No! Me seh my son,' she crowed. '*My* son, not yours!'

It was a cheap shot. In her desperation to get Nathan, and at the same time hurt me, she would stoop to any level. Shit, it wasn't worthy of a second thought. I turned to Richard. 'Hey, Dick, I hope she ain't been tellin you that Nathan was a virgin birth an' she want a white weddin, 'cause me know the woman in the biblical sense long time. Nathan was conceived flesh 'pon flesh. I was there, man, so I should know.'

Out of the corner of my eye I saw her hand coming towards my face. I grabbed her wrist and said to her, 'You should remember what happen last time you tried that... you know, when you were shacked up with that guy, erm, Carl, was it?' To Richard I said, 'I hope you're watchin all this, Dick. Keep an eye out for her right hand if you get her vexed.'

She pulled her hand away. 'I'm goin to get my son,' she hissed. 'If you weren't so selfish we could come to some agreement about it now, an' save Nathan a whole lotta upset. We will take you to the highest court in the land if we have to. I will have my son. Come, Richard.'

Richard looked upset. 'I'm sorry about this,' he said.

I said nothing until we walked to the front door. Sharon had led the way and was already standing outside when I looked to Richard. 'Bwoy,' I murmured as I rested a sympathetic hand on his shoulder, 'if you're sorry now...'

17

NATHAN WAS RESTLESS. He sat up and asked, 'Will you sit on my bed until I fall asleep, Dad?'

I sighed and tried to sound displeased. 'Yeah, but shut your eyes and try and get to sleep. An' no talkin.'

'And can I have the curtains open a little bit?'

'Oh, I don't know, it might keep you awake.'

'It won't, Dad, I promise.'

'Okay then.'

'Will you open them now, Dad?'

'Why? What difference does it make if you have your eyes closed?'

'Please, Dad.'

'All right, but keep your eyes closed.'

I returned to the foot of his bed where I sat resting with my back against the wall. Danny Maguire was on my mind; I looked out to the darkness and wondered where he was.

Looking back to Nathan in the blue half-light I could see that he had inherited the shape of his mother's eyes.

'Didn't I say to keep your eyes shut?' I whispered harshly.

His smile lit up the room. 'Sorry, Dad.'

The rest of him was me. Maybe he had a mixture of our noses; hers at the top and mine at the bottom. My mother often commented how alike we were in character, that he was a smaller version of me. I shouldn't have been straining my eyes to look, I shouldn't have given Sharon's attempt to hurt me a second thought. But I couldn't help myself.

Sharon and her rich Dick would never have him, I swore that much to myself as I watched Nathan feigning sleep. I gave him my love, some of my ambition, and most of my hopes for the future. I owed him that and more. He had given me another perspective. Nathan had provided an anchor to a world that was not cruel or cynical; he had saved my life - and in doing that he may have saved the lives of others. Because of him, I no longer became transfixed by the injustices which were happening all around me. I could now turn my eyes away from them; I had a son to look after.

It wasn't always like that. When Nathan was a baby I did not feel any strong bond with him. It was not until he was about three years old and talking that I really felt like his father. Perhaps it was because at that time I was vexed with the world outside and dissatisfied with my relationship with Sharon. She had taught me that desire was a weakness.

Once the hormonal urge had dissipated, I found that I had little in common with Sharon; in truth neither she nor her friends were the kind of people I could warm to.

There was an intense rivalry within Sharon's small clique. They were all 'baby-mothers' who dressed their picknies in the most expensive attire; miniature leather jackets and over-priced trainers for kids barely old enough to walk. When one of them got a mobile telephone they all promptly went out and bought one before the month was out. It was the same with cars - they all had to have a sporty hatchback.

Setting up a home proved more expensive than I had imagined. I was like a hamster on a wheel, working all the overtime I could get, trying to get us out of debt and then coming home to find Sharon had bought - on hire purchase - another piece of furniture or electrical gadgetry.

One evening, exhausted, I flopped down onto a chair to eat my dinner only for an unfamiliar shrill ringing tone to put me swallowing hard. Sharon smiled at me from the other side of the kitchen table but avoided eye-contact as she put a mobile phone to her ear. Unable to look at her as she talked to her friend Claudette I turned my head and saw that the telephone was not her only purchase: a new and gleaming microwave oven, the sort that needs a degree in computer programming to operate, sat on one of the work-tops.

When Sharon finished talking on the phone she said to me, 'How do you like the dinner? I warmed it in the new microwave. It's all right, Robbie, don't look at me like that. I made the first payment out of my first pay packet. It was a bargain, right, and interest-free for a year. Look, it's my money!'

'An' the phone?'

'I need it just in case the nursery wants to ring me because of an emergency or somethin.'

'What next, a car like Claudette's?'

'Well, I was thinkin, after Christmas, with the mornins so dark an' cold an' that...'

I didn't hear any more of what she had to say. Sharon had taken a job to supposedly help us out of debt, but her brain seemed to be working in reverse gear. She had resumed eating as I got up to unplug the microwave oven. While holding it in my arms I thought about telling her that things like this were like iron chains around our ankles, that we had gone from one sort of slavery to another. But I didn't say anything. Sharon could have understood, she was an intelligent woman but she chose not to understand. And anyway, I thought I had done too much talking as I sent the microwave crashing through the kitchen window. She nearly choked on a piece of meat and coughed it out onto her plate before she watched the gleaming white box somersault its way down the garden. Then I picked up the phone, threw it to the floor and stamped on it before sending it out to join the microwave oven.

The woman went wild, understandably I suppose, and accused me of being insane.

Sounding more like her mother by the second, she peppered me with a tirade of Jamaican curses. 'Cha,' I said when she had finished, 'me tell you one thing, right. You buy a car while we still in debt an' I'm warnin you now, I will burn it the minute you park it outside.'

Our relationship did not get any better from that point. Sharon did not buy a car but she did set her mind on buying a house like Yvette and her partner had done. I just told her no, to get it out of her mind; our rent was small and was the least of our many financial worries.

'It would be an investment,' she protested, 'for Nathan.'

'More like twenty-five years of fuckin slavery.'

I returned to reading my newspaper as she stormed out of the room. She returned a few minutes later with Nathan holding her hand. According to Sharon our son was becoming confused about his identity because of the Asian children he was playing with. 'Tell Daddy what colour you think you are, Nathan,' she demanded.

The boy squirmed, rolled his hands in the bottom of his pullover but said nothing.

'Go on, tell Daddy,' she insisted.

'Brown,' mumbled Nathan.

'See it deh!' she hissed triumphantly. 'Hear your pickney? He don't even know what he is because he's mixin with so many Coolies. That's why we have to move; get out of this area, for his sake!'

It vexed me the way she was trying to use Nathan and I dismissed her attempt at emotional blackmail. 'Sharon, shut up yuh mout an' give your battyhole a chance.'

She looked ready to explode. 'Nathan!' she snapped. 'Say what I told you the other day. If anyone arks what colour you are, you say... you say...'

Nathan only continued to play with his pullover.

She stilled his shoulders and looked into his face. 'Say it, Nathan, say you're black. Say it, Nathan, say you're black. Say it, Nathan. Nathan! Say you're black, say it, say you're black! C'mon, say you're black. Say it!'

Sharon was so angry that she did not see Nathan's tears. He reached out towards me; I stood up and took him in my arms. 'Quiet yourself, Sharon,' I said. 'Nathan, show me somethin that's black.'

He pointed to the hi-fi and I said to Sharon, 'See, he ain't colour blind. The boy's only three, he's got his whole life for the world to convince him that his brown skin is black so give the boy a break... An' don't try an' use him as an excuse for movin out of here.'

'Now me see it!' she snarled. 'You're the one who's fucked up about his identity an' you confuse your own pickney! Okay, Robbie, let me hear it: tell me you're black.'

Nathan's mouth dropped open. I closed it gently and said to Sharon, 'Whatever you see - I'm whatever you see.'

I then took Nathan for a walk hoping that she would have cooled down by the time we returned. She never really did cool down, superficially maybe, but not at her core.

From that time I knew that we would not remain living together for much longer. I did my best with Sharon but doing what is best and doing what is right is not necessarily the same thing.

Still groggy with sleep I hurried down the stairs as a loud pounding rattled my back door. I had fallen asleep on Nathan's bed and it had seemed to take an age for me to work out where I was and where the sound was coming from. Squinting in the fluorescent light I looked at the clock on the kitchen wall. It was almost one o'clock in the morning.

'Danny?' I called out.

'Ach, who else?'

I drew back the bolts and became fully awake. He stepped inside, grinning broadly. 'Sorry about the time, Rob. The bus broke down and for some reason I lost my way and ended up coming around the back road.'

I grinned too and slapped a hand on his shoulder. Danny was still smiling as my fist crashed against his balls. He made a retching sound and collapsed onto the floor, his face contorted by pain. 'No more lies, Danny! No more of your fuckin lies!' I screamed.

Danny continued to moan as he brought his knees up to his chest and rolled onto his side. It was not how I had imagined it would be. I thought that if he ever returned I would be cool, chat amiably, go to bed and then catch him in the act as he opened the trap-door to retrieve the guns that he had hidden in my loft. Suddenly I couldn't be bothered to be cool any more.

In between gasps he grunted, 'So you found them?'

'Too fuckin right.'

'Robbie,' he panted, 'I swear, it wasn't what I planned or wanted. I swear to God.'

'You put me at risk, man. You put me an' Nathan at risk.'

For a while I stood looking down at Danny as his breathing gradually became less laboured. Still on his side, his head jolted back. 'Robbie,' he said, sounding indignant, 'do you know there's a wee mouse under the fridge?' When I didn't answer he looked up at me and stretched out a hand. 'Ach, sorry for all the trouble. Give me a hand up, eh?'

I wasn't falling for any of his amiable bullshit. I understood why informers were shot in his part of the world. Nothing hurts like betrayal, nothing is so grievous. I had let him into my house, given him my trust, my friendship; I thought we had shared something special only for him to abuse it all. He got to his feet without any help from me.

He could not look me in the face as I said, 'You betrayed me, Danny, you betrayed me. Why didn't you tell me?'

He shook his bowed head. 'I couldn't.'

'Nah, you couldn't,' I sneered, 'but you could implicate me in a murder, have me doin time. Deprive Nathan of his father. How do you know that you weren't seen comin here?'

He looked up, frowning. 'Houl on, Robbie, I was wrong to leave the shooters here, so I was, but I haven't implicated you in nothing.'

'An' you're gonna tell me now you had nothin to do with the shootin of that Asian businessman the night you got here.'

'That's exactly what I'm telling you.'

'It was all a coincidence that he got shot by a group of guys, one of them with an Irish accent, the night you turn up here with a bag full of shooters.'

I saw his lips tighten. 'Yeah, a coincidence. Neither me nor those shooters had anything to do with that man's death.'

Something about his voice made me believe him. 'So, what's goin on, Danny?'

He dropped his head again. 'I want to tell you, and I don't want to tell you. Just give me the guns and I'll fuck off. It'll be better that way.'

'Oh no,' I said mockingly, 'oh no, no, no. You tell me.'

Danny's face reddened. 'Don't let me tell you because then I might have to ask you a question that you mightn't want to be asked.'

'Danny, I can't give you those guns without knowin what's happenin. Now, the IRA have got a ceasefire goin on an' I know you ain't a member so it ain't nothin political. An' criminal business was somethin I didn't think was your scene. But then I saw you, I saw you in the Rose an' Crown.'

'Ach, it's not political or criminal.'

'What is it then?'

'Personal.'

'Nah, man, criminal tings g'wan down the Rose an' Crown an' I know it was you I saw hangin aroun the back door.'

Danny let out a deep breath. 'I'm not the only one around here who isn't totally straight. I thought you told me that you had nothing to do with this black Muslim crowd.'

'Cha! I fuckin don't.'

'But if you saw me, you must have been there when the fella walked in with a bomb in his bag.'

The shock made me laugh stupidly and then sit down at the kitchen table. Danny did likewise. 'He really had a bomb?'

'He most certainly did, the stupid fucker.'

'How did you know?'

'Put it down to experience. The fella walks in with a big black bag, orders a drink which he doesn't touch, sits at a table for a minute, walks out to the toilets with the bag, comes back, sits at the table, takes one sip and then leaves without the bag. You don't have to be Sherlock Holmes to work out he was up to something.'

'What happened to the bomb?'

'It got taken care of. It wouldn't have gone off anyway. Your man didn't have the bollocks for it - he forgot to take off the plastic sleeving from the contact arm on the timer.'

'An' how did you know he was with the Muslims?'

'All I can say is that he was recognized,' Danny said, leaning back on his chair. 'Now, if that's all your questions I'll take those guns and leave so you're not at any more risk.'

'You know that ain't all the questions. So you lied to me about arriving the other night.'

He got to his feet. 'Yeah,' he snapped, as if he had grown bored with my trivial concerns. 'Look, Robbie,' he continued in a dismissive tone, 'I'll just take what I've come for and then go.'

'How long have you been aroun these parts?'

He blew out impatiently and then said, 'A while.'

'There's been quite a few shootins aroun here lately.'

'Robbie, none of those guns have been used to shoot anyone over here. Now for your own sake stop asking questions. Just give me the guns and I'll be away.'

'Are you a friend, Danny, a real friend?'

'Sure I am.'

'Didn't I once trust you so much that I told you how I was there when Errol shot that drug dealin piece-a-shit? Are you the same person I asked for advice? Are you the same man who knew of every move me an' Errol made, because I told you, because I trusted you?'

'I'd want to think we're still friends. But people change, Robbie, life changes people. You're not the same person I first met in the gym all those years ago. Don't you be thinking I'm the same person you knew because I ain't. Ach, I didn't want to come here, not in these circumstances.'

'Then tell me, Danny, tell me what brought you here.'

'What brought me to your place was peelers putting up roadblocks and me sitting in a car with a lap full of shooters. I only later found out that the Asian fella had been shot and they were obviously looking for the men that did it. Yours was the only place I could think of heading for. That's the truth.'

'An' what brought you to England?'

His voice faltered. 'To kill the men who murdered my da.'

There was a long silence before I said, 'You'd better sit down again an' I'll make us some tea.'

We talked, we drank, we talked some more. Danny always had a gift with words. A long time ago, when we were both different people, he had kept us entertained in the gym with his descriptions of the Troubles in Belfast, but the tale he told me at my kitchen table had a dreadful resonance. Until then I had not known that he had been in the bar when his father and five other men were cut down. He began to draw a terrible picture with his words.

His father had been at the counter ordering a drink, while Danny stood in a corner behind him talking to an old school-friend named Anthony McGrady.

Anthony McGrady was an IRA man, there was no fuss or bother about him; he was a gunman pure and simple. According to Danny, Anthony McGrady often said with a wry smile that he was on the 'philistine wing' of the Movement as he was one of a dwindling number who had no literary ambition. Anthony had been a soldier and his role in the struggle was to shoot as many of the enemy as possible; he left the theorizing and debate to others in the Movement who wanted to take such things upon themselves.

At school Anthony was something of an artist. He drew horses, especially racehorses - he called them the ultimate athletes. His ambition as a kid was to own a horse but there wasn't the room to keep one in a two-up two-down terraced red-brick house in the middle of Belfast. So he got himself a greyhound - the next best thing - and whatever street disturbance was going on around him he never once failed to exercise it. A British paratrooper eventually shot the dog but contrary to local myth, which Anthony regularly dismissed as propaganda put about by MI5, it was not the incident that drove him into the IRA. He had been a member for more than three years when his greyhound stopped a bullet. It had finally occurred to the security forces that Anthony was doing a bit more than merely exercising his dog while strolling around the more security-conscious areas of Belfast.

When Danny began to talk of the moments that followed the door of the bar swinging open, his voice began to shake. He had felt someone push at his arm a split second before the deafening sound of gunfire echoed around the small saloon. He threw himself to the floor, the air above his head pulsated as bullets cut through it. His father's body fell across him, Anthony McGrady was down next to him.

Danny talked of a feeling I knew only too well: the terrible guilt of a survivor. Though he didn't know it, he described just how I had felt in the days that followed Errol's funeral.

The screams of the dying remained with him, as did the sight and smell of their blood. It tormented him that in those seconds of mayhem he had only thought of his own survival. When the shooting stopped instinct told him to remain still; he had yet to even think of what might have happened to his father.

He took a drink of tea as if he could once again taste the cordite that had filled the air. He stirred sugar into a second cup of tea and heard the tinkle of spent cartridges colliding as the assassin walked towards him. Danny squeezed his eyes shut and relived the moment he was convinced that he was about to be shot. He heard the killer straining to control his excited breaths, he sensed him bending over to examine his handiwork. He heard him mutter something over the corpse of Anthony McGrady. English, the man was English! He heard him chuckle and then walk away, unhurried by the carnage he had created.

I saw Danny's hand shaking and I reached over to hold it still. 'Danny,' I said, 'I never knew you were there to see it happen.'

He nodded sadly and drew his hand from under mine. 'But what hurts me more, Robbie, is the suffering of my ma and sisters, the suffering I see in the faces of people who lost brothers, sons and husbands. One wee young boy, Colm McKenna, visited his brother's grave every day until he finally shot hisself. At the age of eighteen he couldn't take the grief any more. It can never leave any of us, never. When my da and the others were shot it made all the newspapers for a few days but then the world moves on to the next atrocity or disaster. No one came back for young Colm's funeral, no one would read about that wee boy.'

'An' the men who did it are here?'

'They're close, very close.'

'How did you find this out?'

'I can only tell you more if you're in with us.'

'Us?'

'Me and three comrades who've come to bring these bastards to account. I didn't want to say this to you, but you could be a big help to us, Robbie. I understand your situation but if you want to know more I'll have to ask you if you're in or if you're out.'

Taken aback by the enormity of the question he had posed, I stuttered, 'Danny, man, hey - I've got to think of Nathan. I can't...'

He slowly raised his hand. 'I understand, you don't have to say any more.' It was my turn to look away as he added, 'I didn't really want to ask you or put you on the spot.' He let me stew for a while before he asked, 'Can I have the shooters now?'

'They're not here, man,' I said, the guilt of refusing him making me sound timid. 'They're buried in a wood.'

'I need them and quick, Robbie,' he said anxiously.

I looked at the clock, it was quarter to three. 'We'll go an' get them in a couple of hours,' I said, 'before it gets too light. Let's get some rest first.'

18

THE FOG OF our breath froze as it hit the car's windows. Danny reached across and rubbed his gloved hand against the glass in front of me. He made little difference until I produced an aerosol of de-icer. Two squirts and the frost on my side of the windscreen began to dissolve. Danny pushed back into his seat and tried to clear his nose of the aerosol's sharp odour before he fiddled with the levers which controlled the heater. He shivered and switched on the fan. Even more cold air circulated around us and I switched it off and told him that we had to drive for a while longer before the heater would work.

'Feck it,' he said, 'you probably need a new thermostat.'

Until I returned to the car with the plastic bread-box packed with guns and ammunition, that was all he had said to me. On our way back to town he put the guns and magazines into a canvas bag. He inspected one of the guns, a semi-automatic, for any signs of damage caused by moisture. He pulled the slide back, looked into the breech, grunted and then allowed the slide to spring forward. After rewrapping the gun with the oily strips of cloth he said, 'I don't think they would have lasted much longer down there in this weather.'

I pressed a switch, the fan whirred erratically and two streams of barely warm air crept up the windscreen but failed to eat into the frost in front of me. I gave the glass another squirt of the de-icer. Danny snorted and opened the window next to him and let a raw wind cut into us.

The cold air hurt my ears. 'Bwoy, it's cold out there,' I said. Danny closed the window and continued to stare out at the road in front of us as though he hadn't heard me. I glanced at him from the corner of my eye and thought about how much he had changed. My very first recollections of him was as the young man fresh from Belfast who had kept me laughing until my ribs ached. His tongue was often so sharp I sometimes wondered how come it did not lacerate the inside of his mouth as he delivered one of his withering punch lines. It did not take me long to figure out that behind the eyes which twinkled so mischievously there was a good brain. Once he had shed the initial brashness a deeper, more contemplative man came into view and in times of trouble I had no hesitation in seeking his advice.

There was little traffic about; normal was a word I hardly used any more, but the lack of activity so early on a Sunday morning was about as normal a scene as I could imagine while sitting next to a man who had a bag full of guns on his lap.

Danny's silence increased my feelings of guilt and put countless and confusing pictures flashing through my mind. I said, 'Danny, you said that I could be of some use to you. How did you mean?'

'Forget it, Rob. I shouldn't have mentioned it.'

'But you did. What do you think I could do?'

'Forget it.'

'Just like that?'

'Just like that. Drop me anywhere on the Wellington Road and then forget you ever saw me.'

'Near the pub?'

'Anywhere on the Wellington Road will do.'

I resented the belittling harshness in his voice. And how could I forget? For the first time in my life I was turning away a friend who had asked for my help.

In reuniting me with my son, Danny Maguire had saved my life and I would always be in his debt.

I had grown with Nathan, he had helped me to discover so many things about myself. He had taught me about a different type of love. I had loved my mother for as long as I could remember but it was a reflection of what she felt for me. I had loved Carmen and I had thought, mistakenly, she had mirrored precisely what I felt for her. But I found that love for a young child is so different; nothing comes back at first, it's an investment that might show little or no return. For the first time in my life I began to learn of unselfish love, love for love's sake. I could remember a darker world without Nathan and I became aware of what Mr Robinson used to chuckle about: the miracle of life lost none of its wonder despite being replicated billions of times over. I wanted to savour some of that miracle while I had time.

'Anywhere around here will do,' Danny repeated.

My stomach churned. I pulled the car over to a kerb. I wanted to say something - apologize, explain how I had changed and why I could not help him track down the men who had murdered his father.

Before I could open my mouth he looked me straight in the eyes and said, 'Robbie, I don't want you feeling bad or nothing about saying no. You'll always be a friend of mine.'

'Well, I do feel bad, Danny.'

'It's not your fight, it's not your problem.'

'It shouldn't be like that. You came to me for help and I've turned you down. I owe you, but look, guy - the sort-a things you're plannin ain't in me any more. Bubby used to say there's a time when a fighter goes to the well an' the bucket comes up empty. Suddenly he ain't a fighter no more.'

'Ach, you owe me nothing. And in a way I'm glad. Nathan's a great wee kid and he needs you.'

'He's one reason, not an excuse.'

'Christ, I know that,' snorted Danny. He looked down to his lap and then back at me. His eyes turned blank, as though he was no longer looking at me but rather at someone or somewhere far away. He said, 'I know the difference, I know all about excuses. There was a war going on for more than twenty-five years and I did nothing. I knew of plenty of men who were fathers, and when they were killed, the best I can say is that I kept the fuck out the way and let others get on with the war. But when it was my da that was killed I wanted to go to war just as everyone else was talking about peace. Maybe if people like me, who knew the score, had joined in instead of acting like cheerleaders we might have had peace a bit sooner and my da would be alive today.'

'And if your auntie had bollocks she'd be your uncle.'

For a moment his face creased with a reminiscing smile. 'True.' He sighed and squeezed my arm. 'Robbie, we mightn't meet up again for quite a while and I just want to say that I won't ever lose my respect for you. You're one of the bravest men I've known.'

'Leave it out, Danny,' I groaned. Embarrassed, I turned my face away, unable to take his respect or the idea that this might be a final farewell.

'You're a hard man and I know how hard it was for you to say no to me. It was the right thing to say. The best of luck, Robbie, now go'way home and look after wee Nathan. Carry on making a good life for the both of youse. *Slán.*'

The door was opened and shut before I could turn my head or make any reply. The frost had turned into condensation on the windows which obscured my view, and by the time I reached across to wipe one of them Danny Maguire had disappeared from sight.

I'm not sure how long it took for my gut to untwist. For an instant I thought about getting out the car and searching for Danny to tell him I would help. I moved to open the door but then the thought of Nathan asleep in his bed put my hand back onto the steering wheel. Nothing in life comes for free and I drove away resenting the price love demanded and hoping to get back to the house before he awoke.

Along the route home my thoughts were diverted by memories of the secondary school I used to go to and the corner where a crazy white man had once bumped into Errol and me as we walked home. The man in the long dirty overcoat was big and bald but for a few strands of greasy hair. At first we had thought his wide insane eyes were a result of his shock at colliding with us. He stood stiffly and expressionless as Errol began to cuss him, before he reached into his coat and produced a long and shiny bayonet. The stream of Jamaican bad words suddenly dried up and we ran! After a short distance I didn't hear the panic-stricken footsteps that had matched mine and I turned, lungs burning but still running, half expecting to see that Errol had tripped over. But he wasn't sprawled out on the road, he was squatting in the gutter as the big white man marched towards him. 'Errol!' I screamed. 'What the fuck you doin?'

'Lookin for rakstones to ras that fucker wid!' he yelled back.

That was just like Errol, how he was most of his life. In a way courageous but mostly blind to the consequences of his actions. And it took me, with the aid of a fencing pole, to get him out of the danger he had recklessly jumped into.

Hanimal was reckless - but in a very different way. He got his name when the boy we had called Gil up until then ran naked along a street with a bundle of clothes clasped to his chest. Mr Crookes had arrived home unexpectedly and after hearing noises coming from his fifteen-year-old daughter's bedroom he went upstairs to find her in a state of undress with some 'margre an' dutty bwoy'. Mr Crookes ran downstairs for his machete while Gil jumped from a first-storey window. Not to be denied what little piece of flesh he could get hold of, Mr Crookes then ran into the street with the machete waving above his head. 'Hanimal,' he screamed, 'you hanimal! You hinveigle mi dahtah! You spoil mi dahtah, you hanimal!' Poor old Crooksey. If only he had known that the Hanimal would be back to spoil his daughter at least another three times and give her the babies to prove it.

I had always underestimated Hanimal's intelligence. On one occasion after he had told us of another 'triumph' I responded with some irritation and told him he was the white man's dream: a walking, talking stereotype. He frowned as if truly puzzled and said, 'Nightmare, yah mean. I was throwin some bwoy into this white ting larst week an' she say to me that she can never do anythin with the 'usband again. Black man revenge, to rasclart.'

I didn't laugh along with the rest of the guys. In those days I was so steadfast in my belief that I was right about everything that I could not see how Hanimal had purposely misinterpreted my zealous words to take the piss out of me.

Boys, that's all we were, ordinary kids who had the same sorts of fantastic dreams that every other kid would have. We had yet to step into the real world and have our ambitions whittled away to something small and scrawny. It was a time before we became aware that the society we lived in had stripped us of our real skin and had us put on something of its making, something that would set us apart to be feared and reviled.

There was a squeal of tyres followed by the shattering of glass and explosions of metal striking metal. I was shunted, along with my car, to one side. Dazed and confused, I righted myself, threw open the car door and clambered out.

'What the hell do you think you were doing, you stupid bastard?' A man with a fat red face was yelling at me while half out of his car. 'You could have killed us both, you crazy cunt. Look what you've done to my fucking car.'

Errol and Hanimal were still in the process of dissolving from my mind as I looked down at the crumpled bumper. 'Doesn't look too bad,' I said.

The man's face grew brighter. 'Too bad, too fucking bad? If I hadn't fucking braked when I did you'd be fucking dead. Know the Highway-fucking-Code, do you? You do know you're supposed to give way to fucking traffic coming from the fucking right at a fucking island?'

I was perplexed. I must have changed gear, I must have braked and turned corners from the time Danny had left my car. I had not departed from my route home but I had been so immersed in my memories that I had no recollection of how I had got to the traffic island. A shiver brought me back to the man's words. 'Are you all right?' he was saying. 'You're not on fucking drugs, are you?'

'Just driving all night, mate. I'm sorry, I didn't see you. If you want, you can call the cops or you can take my insurance details. I was in the wrong, no argument about that.'

Satisfied, the man crossed his arms on his ample chest. My conciliatory tone had worked; he looked at the damage to his car and saw that it was not as bad as he first feared. He said he'd settle for the insurance details as long as I had them with me. He inspected my policy and my licence and wrote out my name and address with a small blunt pencil on an old envelope while mumbling that he had been caught out before. 'Some Paki cunt gave me a false name and address but the cops found him in the end. Fucking bus driver, he was.'

'You're happy enough with those?' I asked.

'As long as your name isn't Patel or Singh.'

I thought I had grown immune, that repetition had blunted the poisonous tips of words such as those. But I had been born in a place that had stripped me of my skin. At first everything hurt, even the air that touched my bare sinews. So I had put on the black skin that had been tossed my way. At first it shielded me from some of the pain but I knew it would never be my skin, it would always be someone else's creation. I had reclaimed my own dark brown skin but like every other human hide it was not impenetrable.

The man's words had pierced me and ignited something within me. He had sparked an anger - no, it was a hatred. In an instant I envisaged him going to work on Monday morning and his buddies shaking their heads as he told them it was a stupid black bastard who had caused the damage. One of them would say, 'The fuckers all look alike, that's how they get a licence. One of them who can drive takes the test for another twenty.' Another would say, 'You're fucking right there. You should've phoned the cops and let them take care of the black cunt. With a bit of luck they would have arrested him and killed him. The coons are on a constant piss-take, we're too fucking soft in this country.'

That's how it would be.

What I really hated about racists was the way they hid themselves among decent fair-minded people and in doing so they spread suspicion and paranoia. As all bigots seemed able to bend their little fingers, the only way I could identify them was when they opened their mouths to let the shit fall out. Sometimes there was a certain look in their eyes, it was the look from the other side of a counter when I entered a shop. Sometimes it was the talk I heard when out of sight while sitting on the toilet at work, all the unfinished sentences as I walked past a machine, all the forced smiles, all the times I was told it was never me they were talking about; it was always 'the other sort'.

A sudden explosion of rage had me grabbing the man's sweater at the base of his podgy throat and pushing him over the bonnet of his car. 'Where's your documents?' I yelled.

He was petrified. 'Mate, it was a joke…'

'Where's your documents?'

'I - I didn't mean nothing by it. It wasn't your – '

'Sort? It wasn't my sort?'

'No, mate, I was talking about the Pakis.'

'Where's your fuckin documents?'

'In the glove compartment, mate.'

I hauled him upright. 'Then get them.'

I hated that man. I hated how he took my courtesy as a weakness and a cue to mouth his perverse prejudices. I hated how he had turned so weak and cowardly the instant I challenged him. He went into his car with one knee on the front passenger seat. I glared at him. He looked up at me, trying to size me up. I willed him to come back and fight me. He probably had a weapon, a knife or maybe a screwdriver, in with the documents. He was weighing up his chances. He would have to move quickly; he would have to be certain that he could take me unawares or that I would back down as soon as I saw what he had. He looked back to the glove compartment and bit his lip. A dented bumper and a broken light was not about to become a matter of life or death for him.

'Blues beat!' I sneered.

'W-What's up?'

'Your policy, mate, that's what. It's up since yesterday.'

He gawped at the paper and shook his head. 'Can't be.'

'Don't give me shit, man, you were tryna skank me.'

'Eh?'

'Tryin to pull a fast one. We all get sent reminders so don't give me the line that you forgot all about it. What's today's date? It's the twenty-sixth, ain't it? This is up since the twenty-fifth.'

'You sure?' he whimpered, nervously looking at the policy. He shook his head and frowned with concentration as he tried to clear his frightened mind.

'You were tryna take me for an arsehole,' I growled.

'Mate,' he gasped, 'I swear – '

'Yeah, I noticed. Tell you what, we both got one light broke and one wing bent. Let's call it quits, right?'

I took the envelope with my address from between his plump fingers and sat into my car. 'Bollocks!' he roared before pivoting to put a large dent in his car door with his foot.

I grinned and called out to him, 'Hey, ol' man, don't expec me to do that just so we can stay at quits.'

I watched as he drove off. His angry expression gave me great satisfaction, especially as he had failed to realise it was in fact the nineteenth and not the twenty-sixth as I had told him. Fuck him, it was something else he could chat to his buddies about.

19

NATHAN WAS STILL fast asleep. Not wanting to dwell on what Danny Maguire was planning to do, I left my house again and spent most of the morning looking for a replacement for my broken light in various scrap-yards and making arrangements with a Rasta panel-beater people knew as Artist to make good the damage to my car's wing. Enjoying the acid-drop scent of the paint thinners in his workshop I asked him for a price. As usual, it was impossible to get much of a quote from Artist; he told me the cost of the materials and said I could then add on what I thought the job was worth. I told him that I was out of work but he simply shrugged and said as long as I could give the few pounds for the paint and fillers I could pay him for his labour when I could afford it.

I got back to my house just before midday. Any feelings of satisfaction with my morning's efforts vanished when I saw the cream-coloured envelope lying on the hallway floor. Before I could decide what to do with it Nathan came down the stairs rubbing a sleepy eye. 'What's for breakfast, Dad?' he mumbled.

We went into the kitchen and I slid the envelope into a trouser pocket before making breakfast. With the tension welling up inside of me, I left Nathan at the table and walked to the living room. As with the other two, I found that the envelope contained a single sheet of paper. The contents had me pacing around the room like a large bear in a small cage. The headline read: *Court staff hurt in van bomb blast*.

I remembered again Hanimal marching into Errol's flat clutching a newspaper that had carried that very headline and demanding to know why he had not been allowed to play a part. How had Tyrone found out?

When Nathan finished his breakfast he came into me. I couldn't help myself - when he tried to talk to me I was sharp and cold with him. 'Get dressed an' go out an' play till it's time to go to Nanny's,' I said. 'Go on - just go an' play.'

While he was upstairs putting on his clothes I did not love him. I blamed him, I blamed him for what had gone wrong in my life. Nathan was responsible for the misery living with his mother had caused me, it was his fault that I could not have a lasting relationship with Carmen, and most of all he was to blame for the feelings of cowardice which were gnawing at the edges of my tired mind. I could even find a way to blame him for me not being at home the night Errol and Hanimal were killed.

When he finally wandered outside, he paused to frown back at me before joining up with two kids from down the road. I did not call him back to apologize but I did love him enough again to send a little wave. He waved back at me and smiled before I closed the door.

My mind returned to the envelope. It had again summoned an unseen demon to sit on my shoulder to remind me that the comfortable routine and anonymous little world I had constructed for myself was disintegrating at a startling rate. Like a passenger on an airplane in free fall all I could do was pray to survive the landing.

It had never occurred to me that I would not be a survivor. I would survive the disappointment of finding out that what Carmen and I had felt for one another was no more real than a dream - just as I had survived my relationship with Sharon. I had cried over the loss of Fidel and Mr Robinson but I would get over their deaths just as I had done with many others. I would cope with the loss of a job and the money it provided by simply getting another. I would survive the threats, real or merely potential, posed by Tyrone and Glenroy Campbell. The thought that I was a survivor had always helped me to shut out any feelings of grief or anxiety for what only might happen in the future.

But listening to the carefree shrieks of the kids playing outside, I felt the tears gathering inside of me, tears for the loss of a part of me that I had denied for so long. I wanted to cry for me; I wanted big, warm globulous tears to run down my face for the loss of the person I once was and for the person I had become. I wanted to indulge myself in the sort of self-pity I so despised. I wanted to weep over the fact that I had become the apathetic, self-centred type of person that Errol and I had once hated with a passion.

Since his death I had returned to the herd, or at least its outer edges. There were no longer any issues for me to make my heart ache, no travesties of justice that could ignite a rage within me. My son and I had become the centre of a mundane little universe. I had become enchanted with his gold stars on the wall at school, I swelled with a magnificent pride when he brought home a certificate for 'being kind and helpful'. No degree or diploma he could attain in the future would ever mean as much to me. I wanted to see my son grow, and that single-minded ambition for his development was the excuse for my indifference to what was going on around me. I had not only lied to Danny, I had lied to myself: I had used Nathan as an excuse not to help Danny avenge his father's death. Love for this small life I led with Nathan had turned me into a coward.

Is all true love accompanied by a proportionate fear that one day it must come to an end? Is it a fear no one can ever triumph over?

A different kind of fear had been a constant companion as I moved from childhood to manhood. As a small kid I regularly got chased by a gang of bigger boys. I hated the fear they had put in me, the way they made my legs tremble, the sick feeling they put into my stomach every time I walked around a certain corner. The unpleasantness of being afraid is one of the rare emotions that does not fade with the passing of time.

One day my mom asked me to go to the shops and I rounded that corner to see the group of boys on the other side of the road. It was only the traffic that delayed their chase. My lungs and throat were on fire as I hid in an alleyway behind some dustbins while thinking of what excuse I could give to my mom for not bringing home the bread. I wept at the thought of the humiliation of telling her that I was too scared to carry out a simple errand, and as I cried a discarded golf club standing in one of the bins caught my eye. I was not so angry or so stupid as to wade headlong into the boys, but after skipping over a few garden fences I managed to hide myself behind a hedge a few paces behind them. With a deep breath and a final thought of the degrading alternative, I leapt out and struck one of the boys on the ear. He screamed and fell. Almost blinded by fury, I swung the club again and caught another boy on the shoulder and then another on his back as he turned and ran. I chased the boys a short but exquisite distance before returning to the one lying on the ground with blood spurting from his ear. I wanted him to think I had gone crazy and I struck him on the legs a few times while shouting that if he ever chased me again I would 'kill im bloodclart'. It was the first time I had ever sworn out loud in Jamaican and I paused for a moment to check that none of my mom's friends had heard me. Beating the hell out of a boy on a public highway was something I could find an excuse for, but cussing in Jamaican was a guaranteed good hiding if my mother ever found out.

Through his tears the boy screamed that he and his friends would leave me alone and I strutted my way back home, temporarily forgetting the tears in the alleyway and how my legs had trembled. I had reached my front door before I realized I had also forgotten to buy the bread.

That ability to overcome a fear that could paralyse the mind and body was something that I took with me when I stepped into a ring and then when I stepped out into the night with Errol, looking for someone to kill.

But that capacity had diminished as my knowledge of life's complexities increased. I now realized that most of my courage was down in the ground and rotting away along with Errol. In my daily routine there were many actions I avoided taking, many words I did not say. But when he was alive I had something to live up to, there was a role for me to act out.

The note I put through Carmen's door was an example of my cowardice. I balked at the thought of seeing her tears - the tears that would wash away the memories of every happy moment we had ever shared.

'Are you feelin all right? Robert, are you feelin all right?'

I looked up from the usual Sunday feast of chicken, rice and peas and said, 'I'm okay, Mom. I just don't feel hungry.'

She gave me her disbelieving eye from over the rim of her spectacles and told Nathan he could go and help himself to the ice cream in the freezer. She checked to see that he was out of earshot and said, 'So, have you somethin to tell me about your work?'

There wasn't much that escaped my mom. 'Not much to say,' I replied. 'I got laid off last week - part of restructurin or somethin.'

'Or somethin,' she muttered. 'You get redundancy?'

'Oh yeah, yeah.'

'How much?'

The lies were already starting to snowball - and I still owed her two hundred pounds from the loan she had made so I could buy a car - so I drew a breath and told her the truth about my dismissal.

She shook her head to signal her displeasure. 'So you're leavin it at that? You're not goin to any place, say Citizen's Advice, so you can claim unfair dismissal? Are you tellin me you're goin to walk away without a fight?'

I did not reply: I was already full to the brim with conflict.

'Well, I hope you are not goin to continue to sit on your backside an' do nothin,' she added. 'When your father could not get work as a teacher in this country he walked the streets for more than a month. He called on every factory, every office, until he found work.'

I could not count the times she had told me that story. She had yet again evoked the vision of a man I could hardly remember. My mom had held up my father's shining example during every difficulty, no matter how trivial, throughout my childhood and beyond. All my life I had strived to emulate this paragon of manhood she had conjured up but I thought if I had to listen to one more rendition of my father's triumphs over adversity I would spew out something that could prove to be unforgivable.

There was also something else that I could not tell her: it was what Danny Maguire was planning and the arrival of another envelope that had spoiled my appetite. If it was Tyrone who was sending me the press cuttings, what had happened to make him send them now?

And Danny: how was it that he had returned now - and was it a coincidence that the men who had killed his father were close by? He had once told me that there was no such thing as coincidence. I had already begun to imagine cursing Danny with every hourly news bulletin that failed to report a shooting. He was prolonging the agony for both of us.

Mom said, 'Come, Robert, let me hear what you are goin to do about findin another job. Your father wouldn't have stayed idle for long.'

A prickly heat spread across my face and for a moment I was tempted to tell her to let go of the love she had for the man who had returned to the soil. But age, if nothing else, had taught me about consequences and I was all too aware of the irreparable hurt I could cause. 'Like my dad did, I'm travellin.'

Nathan came in from the kitchen and distracted her. She looked at him as he retook his place at the table and then back to me. 'Travellin where?' she asked, her voice hardly more than a whisper.

'A place outside Manchester,' I said. 'I rang a place that was advertisin an' they gave me an interview for a week tomorrow. I've already rung Bubby's sister - she says we can stay at her place for a while.'

Mom's eyes were back to Nathan happily scoffing his ice cream. 'Oh,' she said. No longer sounding so positive, she asked, 'But don't you think you'll have a problem if they arks for a reference?'

'I'll cross that bridge when I come to it,' I said, pretending that I had not heard her disappointment. 'I'll leave Nathan here tonight, Mom, an' pick him up in time for school. Okay?'

She did not turn to face me as she replied, 'I'll take him to school in the mornin, but you will have to collec him in the afternoon. I have things to do.'

'Okay then,' I said, 'see you both tomorrow.'

I hovered awkwardly. Nathan happily waved a spoon at me but Mom didn't say anything else before I left.

At home I lay on the sofa and closed my eyes while listening to the soft hiss of the gas fire. I woke, my face sweaty, to see the fire glowing angrily in the dark. It was pitch-black outside and I figured it was late but a glance at the clock on the wall seemed to tell me it was only seven-thirty. I got up and made sure the clock was working and half remembered a dream. Carmen was on my mind and I knew then that I would have to go and brave her tears.

The small lamp lit one corner of the room. Carmen stood in front of me, but keeping her distance. Her gaze was icy, her lips were frozen with a disdainful sneer and I asked myself why I had bothered to visit her again. Did I really need all the drama? The day my house was trashed I had thought about telling her it was definitely over between us. I should have gritted my teeth back then and made it a quick and clean break, but her kindness had eroded my resolve. There had been enough trauma in Carmen's life since her brother's disappearance and, even though I had not told her it was Tim who had defiled my home, I did have to add to her trouble by telling her about Tyrone's psychotic delusions and his attempt to kill me. There had hardly been a good time to tell her that our romance was at an end. Maybe it was good intention on my part or maybe it was cowardice, but either way, the path I had chosen had led to a little piece of private hell.

'I got your note to say you called,' she said.

'I got the sack,' I began, looking for sympathy and a means of preparing her for the news that I was leaving town. Her frosty expression remained and I did not finish what I had intended to say. 'The cops saw me pushing it through your door,' I mumbled lamely, 'an' then – '

'I know. They arksed to see it, they arksed who you were an' I told them you were a man I used to think I had a relationship with.'

I opened my mouth to say something that would dull the sharpness of her words but she continued, 'Don't look like that, Robbie, I'm not a fool. This business with Tyrone might have distracted me for a while but it ain't turned me stupid. I know why you haven't wanted to talk to me, an' even if you had given me the chance to arks you where I stood you wouldn't have given me a straight answer. I thought I was owed that at least. So why you here now? You finally plucked up the courage to tell me face to face?'

'I came here to tell you that I'm leavin town, goin to a job outside Manchester,' I answered in a tone just the right side of sarcastic. 'I thought I should let you know.'

Twisting her beautiful lips she said, 'Oh, really?'

No, not really. Suddenly I resented the strength in her that I had once admired. I didn't want her to be hard with me; even her tears would have been better than that. I had imagined that in order to leave with a clear conscience, I would have to face the culmination of all the tears she had shed while she waited for me to call. In an absurd flight of macho fancy I had even imagined her begging that we make love one last time. But she was too strong for that, too magnificent. She stood in front of me radiating defiant beauty: she had swallowed her pride once and I had turned her away and a second chance was more than any man deserved.

'Don't be like this, please, Carmen.'

'Like what? Like hurt, let down, like feelin like a fool for lettin myself trust another man?'

I wanted to go right then but the sense that I deserved to be on the receiving end of her anger kept me rooted to the spot. 'Carmen,' I whined, 'I hate to bring it up but it's your brother who tried to kill me an' I've gotta think about Nathan's safety. I got the sack for no good reason so now I've got nothin but trouble waitin for me if I stay around here. There's too much shit flyin in my direction. I have to go, dig up.'

She rolled her tongue and then said slowly, 'Nothin, you got nothin but trouble around here.'

'I didn't mean it like that. Carmen, I still love you, I'll always love you, but there's too much goin on in my head. If I've hurt you in any way I'm sorry.'

The words I had rehearsed while driving to her home had evaporated. The look in her eyes had me bumbling and begging.

I needed to be absolved but before absolution there has to be penance and I was made to pay with every moment she stayed silent.

'Bwoy,' she sneered at last, 'I thought you was a man but you're just a bwoy. You come here an' tell me 'bout your job, my brother, Nathan. How many more excuses, Robbie? You can't come tell me straight, you have to concoct some foolishness. It's everybody, everythin 'cept you an' me.'

The way she kept coming straight to the point, the way she kept talking the truth, was too painful a penance for me to accept. I didn't want to suffer the pain all by myself.

'Look,' I snapped, 'I've gone through this type of shit before. I make a commitment an' I do my best but sometimes my best ain't good enough. I gave you everythin I could but I know now it wasn't enough, you'd always be lookin for more. Women always do.'

Shaking her head she said, 'Robbie, let me tell you somethin. Of all the people I thought I was in love with, you is the one person that I know for sure has never given everythin. You lock away a small secret piece that you don't give to no one.'

'Me? *Me?* Nah, man, it's you who keep a lickle piece back, it's you who put up all sorts of fences!'

She laughed quietly to herself. 'Just lately I became aware of somethin else about you. At first I thought, what a tender, considerate an' lovin person, lookin after his son the way him do. I was impressed, seriously impressed. But there's somethin else deep down inside of you that's as cold an' as hard as you are warm an' soft on the outside. What is it, Robbie - some guilty secret? Or is it Sharon so messed you up that she mek you too frighten to ever have an honest relationship again?'

My heart raced. Why did she mention a guilty secret? Had I shouted out something in my sleep? 'Cha, yuh crazy!' I sneered.

'No need to shout,' she said. 'Things were so good between us an' I'm only arksin was there somethin you can't tell me, somethin that made you change.'

'Oh yeah? I hope you don't go sayin the same sort-a stuff about guilty secrets to your crazy brother.'

I felt satisfied with my retaliation for an instant.

'Go now. We've said enough,' she said.

I immediately regretted wounding her and I drew a breath so I could apologize but the harsh look in her eyes stopped my words before they could pass my lips.

'Just get out an' leave me alone,' she said.

20

MISS BENNETT LOOKED unusually startled to see me and when I asked her where Nathan was her hazel eyes signalled an even greater loss of composure. It was the school's normal practice to keep a child in a classroom until a parent or designated adult turned up. 'Mr Walker,' she replied nervously, 'young Tim came in just before the final bell with a note from you saying that your mother had been taken ill and that you had trouble with your car and that he would be taking him home.'

I could see her face reddening and I quickly said, 'Oh yeah, my car had a couple of flat tyres but, er, he beat me to it. I mean, I thought I'd get here before Tim did.'

'I only let Nathan go because of your note; and Tim is a former pupil of mine, so I know he can be trusted,' she said, looking for reassurance that she had done the right thing. 'They left about fifteen minutes ago.'

I said, 'I'd better head off or they'll be home before me. See you tomorrow.'

'Er, I'm not so sure,' she called after me. I stopped and I looked over my shoulder to see Miss Bennett patting her chest as she said, 'He was coughing in class today, I think his cold may have gone down to his chest. It might be for the best if Nathan didn't come in tomorrow. I have seven missing already, there's no point in spreading it around any more.'

I nodded gratefully and did my best not to sprint to my car as vivid scenes of the damage Tim had caused to my home flooded into my mind. The engine roared into life and I told myself there was no danger of Tim harming Nathan. In my scavenging for scarce crumbs of comfort I recalled how I had seen Tim playing and enjoying the role of the older brother, as I had once done with his father.

But the note Tim had given to Miss Bennett and the fact that he knew of the two flat tyres I had put down to kids playing pranks disturbed me. Had I discovered the tyres were punctured rather than having broken matchsticks wedged in their valves I would have immediately rung the school to let the headmistress know that I would be very late or that I had arranged for a taxi to collect Nathan. Having to pump up the tyres irritated me but I was not alarmed in the way I would have been if the sidewalls had been slashed. I would have put *that* sort of stuff down to Tyrone's insane antics. The forged note and the use of matches instead of a knife seemed too sophisticated a ploy for Tim; I didn't think he was that smart or devious.

What was going on in the boy's messed-up head I could not imagine but I clung to the belief that there was still an innate goodness in him. The way he wrecked my home was peculiar evidence of that: at least he had not damaged Nathan's room and his actions could be interpreted as some perverted expression of love for his mother. No, I repeated over and over, Tim would not do anything to hurt Nathan.

When I saw that the two boys were not waiting on my doorstep my stomach turned over and I ran inside to telephone Carmen. When there was no answer I rubbed the back of my hand over my dry lips and momentarily thought about ringing the police. But the boys had only left the school less than half an hour ago; it was too early to call the cops and, God forgive me, what the black cop had said to me as his fingers almost put holes in my cheeks was still fresh in my mind. I would not, or could not, put aside my loathing to contact them unless I had exhausted all other options, not even for my own son.

Instead, I began to convince myself that I could read Tim's mind. I told myself the story that he so loved Nathan that he found it unbearable that he did not see him any more. Because of the hatred Tim felt for me he could hardly come to my house and ask if he could take Nathan to the park again. As I strung the story together I knew it was only a desperate fantasy and the few moments of calm gave way to a gut-wrenching turbulence.

I re-dialled Carmen's number while reminding myself that her son was a sick kid who had found himself involved in the business of supplying crack when only ten years old. Tim had been exposed to things that most people three times his age were never likely to see - if they were lucky enough not to live on estates like the Blackmore...

The rhythmic shrill tone called for an answer. Not that Tim was a bad kid through and through, nor was it all his fault; I had yet to meet a person who had chosen the circumstances he or she had been born into. The responsibility for his loss of innocence lay with a dead man named Beresford Samuels but I had seen how the grim life on the Blackmore estate had stunted Tim's imagination and how it was gradually shrinking his brain into a dense collection of malevolent and mercenary cells.

I tried to wait for Nathan to come knocking on the door but a feeling of foreboding would not let me stay still for more than a few unbearable minutes. I needed to do something that would help me feel as though I was not totally powerless. Just in case he turned up while I was out searching, I left Nathan a note on the front door which told him I would be back soon and that he should go to Miranda's house.

My journey to the park took longer than usual; every slim youth or small boy in a dark duffel coat put my pulse racing and my foot onto the brake pedal. I was so distracted by any movement on the pavement that it was only the fierce blaring of horns that prevented me from crashing my car on three occasions. I left the car feeling so hot and fatigued it was as though I had run the three miles to the Blackmore.

A winter's darkness was closing in and except for two frolicking dogs, a woman pushing a pram and a group of girls sharing a cigarette on their way home from school, the park was empty. Something in me collapsed with the weight of disappointment. And guilt.

Maybe I should have rung the cops. While trying desperately to think of where Nathan could be, my mind began to bubble over with panic. I had never had to cope with this sort of fear before; this was the fear that is swept away to small corners of the soul and stored by every parent who has seen television pictures of a weeping mother or father pleading for information about their missing child.

A sharp pain in my gut bent me in two. The effort of clearing my mind to work out what I should do next put my scalp on fire. I found myself whimpering and then growling like a tormented dog as I ran back to my car after a prayer for guidance went unanswered.

I pounded on Carmen's door with my two fists and kicked it in frustration when there wasn't an immediate response. My cursing was abruptly halted as the door opened. 'What the hell do you think you're doin?' she yelled.

My anger was far greater than hers. I pushed my way inside. 'What are you doin?' she screamed.

I yelled back, 'Where's Tim? What's he done with Nathan?'

She squared up to me and snarled, 'Get out! No man pushes im way into my yard. Now piss off!'

She was so full of rage that she could not have heard what I had asked her. In her face there was a look of concentrated venom which cried out that I was raping her, that I was violating her space. Her expression jolted me back into some sort of rationality and I raised my two hands in temporary surrender and asked her again. The hostility in her eyes began to fade and in a voice that was quieter, but no less rancorous, she said, 'What do you mean, what has he done with Nathan?'

'He let down two of my tyres outside my yard so I'd be late an' then forged a note so he could collect Nathan from school.' As I said it I could sense her disbelief. The hurt that I had caused her the night before was too fresh. The gaping wound which was the result of the love I had torn away was too raw; she had probably vowed never to believe me again. When she did not respond I gripped her shoulders and screamed that her son had taken Nathan from school. She contemptuously looked at both of my hands and I stepped back, recognizing that she had withdrawn the right for me to touch her again.

She said, 'I don't know where Tim is or what he's doin.'

I resented her lack of understanding and insisted she told me again and she said, 'He left Saturday sayin he was gonna stay with friends for a few days.'

'What friends?'

'I don't know.'

'You don't fuckin know! When is he supposed to be back?'

'He said a few days.'

'Carmen! You mean you let your boy, who ain't yet thirteen, just go where he wants, do what he wants?'

'There wasn't much I could do to stop him. I mean, what could me do? Lock him in im room?'

'It would be a start. You could-a arksed him who he was stayin with, you could-a arksed him what address he was stayin at.'

'Maybe I didn't want to.'

'What do you mean, you didn't want to? You're the bwoy's mother! Christ Almighty, what's got into you?'

'Maybe I'm sick of it, of him. Maybe I'm just too tired to care any more. Maybe every bastard aroun here has sucked me dry. Maybe he's just like im father, put on this earth to give me a hard time. The older he gets the more I see Errol in him an' like Errol he thinks this world was created fe im benefit alone.'

Her indifference stunned me. 'But you're still his mother.'

'From the time he started dealin with that fuckin Yardie who Errol an' Tyrone end up killin I knew he was slippin away from me. I denied it at first, I told myself that he was straightened out. No mother wants to think others got a bigger claim on their child. But you see, I can't compete - I got no big car, no big gold chains, no gun. An' I ain't sure if I got any love left for him.'

If it is possible to really know how another human being is feeling, at that moment I thought I knew of her sense of loss. It was not just the loss of her son, it was the sudden loss of her strength to endure.

Without any conscious thought I reached over and put my arms around her. She did not pull away but rested her head on my shoulder. Her sobbing began to trickle into my conscience. I thought about all the pain I had added to the night before. The guilt almost overwhelmed me but as I stroked her hair it was Nathan who I was thinking of and I told myself that this was not the right time to make any rash declaration of what I felt stirring within me. I sensed her body move as if the sobbing was tearing her apart and I almost said that I would support her any way I could.

'Carmen,' I said, easing her gently away from me. She looked up, her eyes still brimming over with tears, and my good intention left me as I sensed the weight of her burden. I looked away and instead of telling her we would share whatever troubles lay ahead I let out a breath and told her that it was Tim who had wrecked my house because he thought I was mistreating her. She sniffled, dried her eyes and said that she knew - Tim had told her before he left. I then informed her that he had been hanging around with Glenroy Campbell's eldest boy and she said that one of her friends had told her that too. 'I think he's gone with them, but there's so many of the bastards that he could be anywhere,' she said. 'What can I do? If I make a move to tell anyone in authority he's gone I know Social Services will take him away.' Tears streamed down her cheeks. 'Why did he take Nathan, *why?* It don't make sense. He's such a confused, mixed-up kid. I've let him down so...'

I could not stop myself from bending down and kissing her tears. 'You ain't let him down, it's this place.'

'I hate this place, Robbie, I hate it with all my heart.'

Part of me wanted to tell her to come with us, Tim could come too and together we would find somewhere better. But the cruel reality was that Tim would never allow us to find somewhere better. The Blackmore was like a snare clamped around his young leg; to break free he would either have to leave behind a piece of himself or bring a part of the Blackmore with him. 'Once we find them,' I mumbled, 'we'll work somethin out.'

Her eyes bore into me, searching for sincerity. Truth is, I did not know what I meant, the words seemed to jump from my mouth on their own accord. Carmen must have found at least a glimmer of what she was looking for and her fingertips pressed into the back of my head and her warm lips found mine. 'Oh, my love, my love,' she moaned, 'I thought I'd lost you.'

As we kissed I realized how much she was giving to me: all her fears, all of her vulnerability, and her hopes for the future. And I had never given her any of those things. I pushed her head to my chest so she could not see how my eyes were not mirroring her feelings. 'We'll find Tim and Nathan,' I said, trying to fight the tremor in my voice. 'They're like brothers - they're probably out playin somewhere an' when they turn up we'll tell them we're outta here. We'll put things right between us.'

I immediately wanted to pull the words back in and make out that I never said them but Carmen was already kissing me and murmuring, 'My love.'

I felt myself recoil inside before the trouble in our lives prised our lips apart.

'I'd better get home in case they're there,' I said.

Carmen nodded and made her grimace look like a smile. 'That would be for the best. I've got the network of Sisters lookin out fe Tim so if they're seen aroun, one of them will let me know,' she said, and turned me gently towards the door.

'They might come this way,' I said, just to say something.

She held open the door and kissed me tenderly on the cheek. 'Get home an' I'll give you a ring if I hear anythin. Let's try not to worry. Tim's mixed up but I know he would never let anythin bad happen to Nathan.'

As soon as Miranda opened her door I knew that Nathan was not there but I asked her anyway. Already backing away, in response to her puzzled expression I said, 'It's okay. I had to pop out - I left a note in case he arrived before I did. See you around.'

'Em, see you, Robbie,' she called back. 'Do feel free to call around anytime for a chat and a glass of wine.'

The first ribbons of steam were twisting from the kettle's spout as the telephone rang. As I picked it up I was already hearing Carmen's relieved and happy voice telling me that the boys had just arrived at her house. But a man's laughing voice said, 'Robbie, so wha happen?'

Trying to think who it was, I answered, 'Cool. Who's this?'

There was more laughter and the voice said, 'Yuh nah know?'

'Look, er, I'm waitin on an important call.'

''Bout someting you lose?'

'Yeah, in a kind-a way.'

'Hang on a minute.'

I heard distant whispers and then, 'Hello, Daddy.'

It took me a few moments to get my mouth working. 'Nathan, where are you, Natty Dread?'

'I'm with Tim and some of his friends. I'm having some fried chicken like Nanny does for tea. 'Bye.'

'Nathan! Hold on a minute, where are you?'

There was a banging noise as though the receiver had been dropped and the man said, 'Nice lickle bwoy yuh 'ave, mi fren.' The laughter had gone and now the voice sounded threatening. 'Wha is it d' Bible seh? Oh yeah, now me rememba, eye fe eye, a son fe a son.'

I could feel my throat narrowing. 'Who's this?' I coughed.

The laugh came back dark and sinister. 'The name is Glenroy Campbell, you mus know me, though. So bw-ay, when me 'ear someone lick down my son an' bruk im jaw me seh but wait, this man mus 'ave connections. Then me find out it's the same man who tump down mi brodda Alvin at school. Me seh to Alvin, see wha happen, we let the man tek liberty all them years ago an' now im tek liberty again, to rahteed.'

There was a suffocating silence and I put my hand over the mouthpiece before I used what little air remained in my body to say, 'What has this got to do with my son?'

'So wha happen to my son? You injure my bwoy an' the Good Book seh me is entitled to do the same to your bwoy.' There was more laughter and then he added, 'But nah, me seh Nathan is too cute to have im jaw bruk. Alvin still bear a grudge though - him seh we should let one of these dirty white men rape off im battyhole.'

My blood ran cold. 'You fuckin bastard, if that boy is touched – '

'But wait, you treaten me? An' me was gonna offer a deal.'

The line went dead; he had put down the phone. I fell onto my knees and almost vomited with the horror of it all. I cannot say how long I was on the floor, whether it was seconds or minutes, but all I did was stare up at the ceiling. My mind had turned blank, switched itself off for fear that it might be torn to shreds by the visions that wanted to invade it.

The phone rang out and I remained lying on the floor not wanting to pick it up, but knowing it was Campbell and that I had to haul myself upright to answer his call. 'Jus shut yuh pussyclart an' listen 'cause me nah tell you again!' he yelled. 'So you listenin? Me arks you if you listenin!'

'Yeah.'

'This is how it go. Me ring you tomorra, mornin or night, an' you mek sure yuh dutty ras is by the phone deh. Now me know yuh nah deal with Babylon or nutten stup-pid like dat so yuh 'ave a whole night to tink of wha might happen to cute lickle Nathan if you decide not to do exactly wha me seh. Tomorra you'll get a time an' a place fe me an' you to sort out wha we 'ave to sort out. As soon as you turn up Nathan can go. Fuck about or don't turn up an' bisniss will 'ave to be sorted with yuh lickle pickney. Seen?'

'Let's do it now, let's do it tonight!'

'Cha. Me seh tomorra.'

There was a click and the line went dead again and I gripped the receiver as though it was Campbell's throat. The way he had said Nathan's name with a depraved lilt echoed in my head. I knew exactly what had to be done and I put on my coat; there was someone I had to find.

I had become aware some years ago that the human condition I had perceived was no more real than the skin on water, that its existence is only due to the tension between two elements. When Errol and I had set out to kill people, I was aware that there was an imbalance of pressure and I had sunk into dark and cold water. Yet even when plumbing the deepest depths I was aware of a point of light above me and that I would resurface at some time in the future. Nathan was my light, the one who had guided me back to the air which was warm and loving. Campbell had threatened to take away my light.

Cold hard rain stung my face as I walked from my car; it made me aware that I had let my soul plunge into the dark and cold water again. On a hunch, and in desperation, I walked into the Rose and Crown. My eyes scanned the bar, but the faces were indistinct as my mind had been set to register only one shape. Disappointed, I walked out through the front door and stood looking about. From the corner of my eye I saw the shape of a man hurrying towards me. I turned and said, 'Danny, me an' you have gotta talk. In my car. Now.'

He looked over my shoulder and tilted his head as if communicating to an unseen companion behind me. 'Right, Robbie,' he said, following me to the rear of the pub.

In the car he asked me how I knew where to find him. I ignored his question and said, 'Nathan's been kidnapped. I know who's got him. Danny, they threatened to rape him.' It was all I could do to say such filthy words. After the moment of nausea passed I took my hand from my mouth. 'I want one of them guns, Danny. I'm gonna kill those fuckin bastards, I'm gonna kill them!'

Danny frowned as if he was trying to take in what I had told him. He shook his head. 'Calm down, Robbie, and tell me who has taken Nathan.'

'Give me a gun, Danny, an' I'll do anythin I can to help you get those men who killed your ol' man. I swear.'

'Robbie.' I knew what he was about to say but I could not let him refuse me. I took hold of his arm to plead but he turned his face away from me. 'Robbie, I can't.'

'For Nathan.'

'Robbie!' he cried out, as if in pain. 'Tell me what this is all about. Who's taken Nathan?'

I bit my lip and told him of the incident outside Mustafa's fish and chip shop and how I had broken the jaw of a youth whose name I did not know. 'Tim, who hangs around with this guy, picked Nathan up from school after someone let down my tyres. Then this youth's ol' man rings up an' tells me that he will call me tomorrow. If I don't turn up when an' where he tells me, he's got somethin planned. Well, I told you what he said already.'

'So who's this fella?'

'You wouldn't know him, a sack of evil shit.'

'Who is he, for fuck's sake?'

'A guy named Glenroy Campbell. They call him Daddy One-foot.'

Something changed in Danny's voice. 'Glenroy Campbell?' he said. 'Robbie, just you go on ahead and start your motor. I think I might be able to help you.'

21

THE SMALL FLAT was in the middle tier of a three-storey house. A patch of carpet inside the door had been worn black and shiny by the countless people who had needed temporary accommodation. It was cheap and nasty. It smelled too, mostly of bottled gas and stale cooking fat. I doubted if anyone who had stayed here had ever referred to it as home.

The two men who stood in the middle of the cramped room looked barely out of their teens. Danny kept the introductions brief. Kevin was short but thick-set with muscular legs that strained the seams of his denim jeans. His spiky hair was the blackest I had ever seen on a person with skin so white. He kept his arms folded and nodded curtly in my direction and I could tell that he regarded me with suspicion. Eamon was taller and had wiry ginger hair combed back from a more expansive and pinker face. He stepped forward and put out a hand and said, 'Robbie, I'd say you don't remember me, do you?'

I shrugged my shoulders. 'Sorry, can't say I do.'

'I sparred with you when I was just a wee kid, when Danny brought you home that time.'

The colour of his hair was vaguely familiar. 'You've grown a bit since then.'

He laughed easily. 'Well, I was only nine.'

'Before youse fellas get carried away talking about old times, I'm away to fetch Martin,' Danny interrupted. 'Kevin, go on and make the man a cup of tea. And don't you be spitting in the cups - wash the fucking things out with water this time.'

Eamon, choking with laughter, threw back his head but Kevin only glowered at Danny and growled, 'Just go you out and fuck off, fucking prick, you.'

There was a hint of a mischievous smile on Danny's face as he nodded in my direction. 'I won't be long,' he said.

Raindrops as hard as pebbles rattled against the window.

'Christ, what a night,' said Eamon. He looked down to the pools of water around my wet shoes. 'Put yourself over by the fire, Robbie, and see if you can dry out a wee bit.'

The heat from the portable gas-fire warmed the back of my legs as I wondered how much Danny had told them while he had left me sitting alone in my car. Eamon grinned when he saw the steam rising from my clothes, and rather than stand in awkward silence I asked him if he still boxed.

'Doing other things now,' he said. 'I won a junior Ulster but I got a wee bit distracted. We all thought you had the makings of a world champion, so we did. But Brendan reckoned you too might get yourself distracted with other things.'

'Brendan wasn't far wrong. How is he these days?'

'He's grand, still fighting the good fight.'

'Did your friend do any boxin'?'

'Kevin? He reckons he's a GA man. That boy got hisself distracted after catching a few clatters from a hurley stick. I'll just go and check he's not after spitting in the cups again.'

I smiled, a little anxious that the running joke might have some basis in fact. With my calves almost poached I sat on an old wooden chair when Eamon re-entered the room carrying a mug. 'Milk and sugar?' he asked.

'Just milk will do fine.'

Fatty globules floated on the surface. 'Don't you worry yourself about those,' said Eamon, reading my thoughts. 'That's only the cream in the milk.'

Kevin came back into the room in time to watch me take my first tentative sip. 'Kevin,' called Eamon, 'stop acting the Antichrist and sit you down. You're making me feel uncomfortable.'

Kevin joined Eamon on the tatty settee and continued to scrutinize my reaction to the tea he had made. 'That's nice tea, man,' I said to him.

There wasn't even the merest flicker of acknowledgement from him.

'You're not havin one yourself?' I asked Eamon.

'Er, no,' he said, glancing sideways. 'I'm off the tea.'

Eamon then steered the conversation back towards boxing, it was safer ground. Kevin looked on in complete disinterest while Eamon and I happily swapped big-fight anecdotes.

For the next ten minutes or so we talked of our boxing heroes: Ali, Sugar Ray Robinson, Duran and Hagler. 'You know,' said Eamon, 'I thought that you might have been a second Dick Tiger.'

Flattered, I replied, 'Ah, a great boxer, world champion at middle and light-heavyweight, when a world title meant somethin. I doubt if I was up to that.'

'Christ, he was more than a boxer, Robbie, he was a great human being. I mean, didn't he send half his purses back to his people in Nigeria when they were fighting a civil war. If I'd had his talent I'd have done the same, so I would. Sure, I figured you'd have done the same as Dick Tiger if you'd have reached the top, wouldn't you, Robbie?'

Eamon's grey-blue eyes looked straight into me and I took another drink of tea to hide my embarrassment. I wondered what sort of wrong impression he had of me to be so complimentary. Maybe I was being softened up but he looked and sounded sincere. Perhaps my discomfort was down to me: I always had difficulty with being the focus of someone's admiration, I thought that they often bestowed on me attributes that I did not possess. Carmen, for instance, would make me out kinder and more gentle than how I saw myself; Errol had thought of me as far braver than I ever was. I believed Eamon would have given half of his purses to the community he came from, he had an obvious sense of place and belonging to a people who had been bonded together by conflict. He came from what was one of the most militarized housing estates in the world, and while I often thought of myself as from a people in conflict and within a hostile environment I had no sense of belonging to a place or community. There had been me, Errol and possibly Hanimal; our actions had separated us from the people we had lived amongst.

Nathan, the reason I found myself in a dingy flat drinking a dodgy cup of tea with two Irishmen, put himself back to the forefront of my mind. 'Tell you what, Eamon,' I said more testily than I had intended, 'I have my son and my mom an' that's all the people I have.'

A sharp rap on the door put Eamon on his feet before he could react to what I had said. As he went to open the door I saw what I imagined was a look of disapproval on Kevin's face. A strong-looking man with a round bearded face and heavy bags under his eyes entered ahead of Danny. Eamon stiffened a little, Kevin stopped slouching and his surliness fell away. I stood up and took the hand the stranger offered me. 'Robbie,' he said, 'pleased to meet you. The name's Martin.'

There was a harshness in those baggy eyes and I imagined that there were men around Belfast who would be quick to greet a man like him and be grateful for any response. A man like Martin would nod and respond with a name, if he could remember one, for he would know that a hint of recognition was enough. The men would then gratefully move on. Martin was aware that they would want his friendship but he would keep such weak and deferential men at a distance, for they could never be his friends, they would never be his comrades.

I knew then for certain that Eamon and Kevin were involved with Danny's plan and that their reaction to Martin was not due to any weakness or anxiety but rather a respect bordering on reverence, similar to what I had seen displayed by the people in a Belfast boxing gym when the man I only knew as Brendan had approached them.

'Yeah, same way,' I said, releasing Martin's hand.

Martin shook the rain from the arm of his leather jacket and pulled a folded sheet of paper from a pocket. 'Danny has told me that you are willing to help us out with a little job we have to take care of.'

My eyes darted towards Danny and questioned him: I thought we were going to talk about retrieving my son. Danny knitted his brow and nodded once as if he understood my concern and to signal that everything had been taken care of. 'Robbie,' Martin said sharply, 'would you take a look at this for me?'

I looked down at the paper he had laid out on a table.

'You might recognize this place, it's a rough plan of the factory where you worked. In the not-too-distant future, me and my three comrades here will have to get in there. All I know is that we will be going in at night and that we don't want to be announcing our arrival.'

To my surprise there was a sense of humour lurking behind Kevin's hard face and he chuckled to himself while I examined the sketch of the factory's layout. I straightened and told Martin of the new security guards and the cameras. He said that he knew of the cameras but not of their exact locations. Luckily, I could remember most of Fidel's grumbling about the new security measures and where I had seen the cameras being installed. With a pencil I marked where the outside cameras were situated. Martin hummed pensively. 'Where do you want to get to?' I asked.

His finger stabbing at the drawing he replied, 'The loading bay. But I think the cameras have got every approach covered.'

I looked to the drawing again; there was something not quite right about it. 'Ras,' I snorted on recognizing the error, 'you've missed out the boiler-house.' Martin shot disapproving glances at Eamon and Kevin as I bent down to pencil it in. 'It's right against the factory on the opposite side from the loadin bay. The fuel tanks and one of the small storehouses should give you some cover once you're through the fence,' I explained. 'And if you can get into the boiler-house door, all you have to do is follow the pipes into the factory roof-space. Once you're up the ladder there are walkways which'll take you to the offices overlookin the loading bay.'

'But is there any way down?' asked Martin.

'Yeah. The ceilings above the offices are the suspended sort - just remove a tile and you're in. Most of the doors ain't locked but there's also a ladder which will take you down into the main factory.' I made a mark with the pencil. 'It'll take you down to that corner.'

He drew a sharp breath through his nose and nodded approvingly at Danny before exhaling and gathering up the paper. 'Is that all?' I asked.

'That's plenty. Thanks for your help, Robbie.'

He moved quickly towards the door. I went to call out but Danny raised a hand. Martin looked back and said to me, 'Danny has told me about your difficulty with Mr Campbell. He'll stay over with you tonight and let you know the score. *Slàn.*' And then he was gone. His stay couldn't have lasted more than two brisk minutes.

'It's a fucking risk Martin coming here like that,' snarled Kevin.

Red-faced with anger, Danny hissed, 'And if you two had done your job properly instead of – '

'It's not possible to see the boiler-house from any road,' I said. There could have been a flash of gratitude in Kevin's expression but I wasn't counting on it. 'Let's get home,' I said to Danny. 'I'm feelin tired an' seriously pissed off.'

Danny spoke while we travelled to my house but I could not take anything in. The day was nearing its end and I had become aware that all I had done was drive around frantically and aimlessly since Nathan had been taken away. Precious hours had been wasted, nothing I had done had brought Nathan's return a minute closer. Maybe Martin's reaction, so calm and untroubled, was the straw which finally broke my resolve. There was a sudden and terrible emptiness within me.

Once home, Danny asked me if there was anyone I could trust enough to take with me when the time came to collect Nathan - someone I could rely upon to do exactly what was required and ask no questions. I telephoned Carmen. I told her that I had spoken to Nathan and that he had sounded happy enough and then I asked her if she would come with me tomorrow to pick him up.

She said, 'Yes, of course. What about Tim?'

He hadn't even crossed my mind. 'Uh, he's okay.'

'Was he with Nathan?'

'Yeah. Nathan said he was there.'

'Where are they, exactly?'

'All I know is I will get a call tomorrow tellin me where to go.'

'When I come with you I'm gonna arks someone what the – '

'Carmen, don't. All you have to do is take Nathan to my mom's and take Tim home.'

'Take Nathan to your mom's?'

'Yeah.'

'So why won't you be with Nathan?'

I didn't have the energy to give her an explanation. 'I'll call you tomorrow,' I said. 'Don't make a move, under any circumstances, until you hear from me. Okay?'

I put down the phone and told Danny that I was going to bed. 'Me too,' he said. I struggled upstairs ahead of him and kicked off my shoes intending to simply fall onto the bed, but the dampness clinging to my legs and feet made me think better of it. I stripped myself of my wet trousers and jacket. Such was my feeling of total exhaustion, even the initial coldness of the bedclothes could not prevent me from falling into a deep, if troubled, sleep.

It was five-thirty in the morning when I awoke. I shivered as I got out of bed and went to Nathan's room to check that it had not been just a bad dream. His room was so cold and bare. Danny's snoring in the spare bedroom made it all so real. My stomach heaved and I thought if life is nothing but a dream then I wish someone would wake me from this nightmare.

At nine-fifteen Danny came thundering down the stairs half-dressed and asked me what was happening. 'Ah, Jesus, Mary and Joseph,' he muttered darkly as I put my hand over the mouthpiece and told him it was only my mother who had rung to find out if I wanted her to pick up Nathan from school. I hoped it was true when I told her that I would collect Nathan later on.

Danny's sleepy eyes were still fixed on me as I put down the phone. My confidence in him was evaporating. 'What's the plan?' I asked.

He frowned. 'You don't remember nothing of what I told you last night?'

'Not a thing.'

He blew stale air from his dry lips. 'Any chance of a cup of tea?'

While I made him tea and a bacon sandwich Danny went upstairs and put on the rest of his clothes. He entered the kitchen yawning and showing off a horribly coated tongue. I noticed a broken tooth which had turned into a rotting brown stump. 'You wanna get that tooth seen to,' I said.

'Why?' he replied, swallowing a good third of a sandwich.

I didn't know why. I let him take another bite and a drink of tea before I again asked him what was the plan that would safely return my son to me and make certain that Glenroy Campbell paid the price for his depravity. 'You said Campbell would ring today, didn't you?' replied Danny.

'Yeah.'

'Well, we wait for him to ring and then you go and collect Nathan.'

I almost exploded. 'What the fuck? Is that supposed to be a plan?'

'Christ, Robbie, what else can be done?'

'I want that bastard dead!'

'Me too, but nothing is going to happen until your boy is safe home. I mean, do you think we're going to kick down doors with guns blazing or something? You're watching too many movies, so you are. This Campbell is a fucking nutcase but at the same time he's a smart operator. Nathan's only the insurance that will have you turn up at a certain time and place without any funny business. You clattered his son but I think he'll be wanting to do a bit more to you. When he rings, don't tell him Carmen will be with you - wait until you're wherever you're supposed to go and then say she's out in your car with a mobile phone in her hand ready to call the cops if the boy isn't out in two minutes.'

'Then you guys will come in?'

'I doubt it.'

The telephone rang out and startled me before I could make any response. 'Robbie Walker?'

'Yeah!'

'Jus checkin you're outta bed.'

'Who was that?' asked Danny as I re-entered the kitchen.

'I think it was Campbell. He said he was checkin that I was out of bed.'

'The bastard will keep that up all day. He wants to make sure you're not going anywhere unless he tells you.'

'Are you goin to give me a shooter?'

'No.'

'Shit! Then tell me what you an' your spars are gonna do!'

'Ach, we won't know until he rings with an address for you. We'll have to make it up as we go along.'

Danny's reply gave me little comfort but he was right: nothing could be planned until we knew where I was to go. We did not engage in any lengthy chat after that; we were always aware that the shrill ring of the telephone could bring an abrupt halt to any sentence, any word.

By midday Campbell had rung three times. On each occasion he said my name and that he was 'jus checkin'. Every time I heard the phone ring my anxiety heightened, a cold metal band tightened around my heart another ratchet. And each time the receiver was replaced I struggled to find the strength to walk back to the kitchen.

'How about a bite to eat?' asked Danny. 'You look in need of a bit of grub too.' I was hungry but I resented the way my body, indifferent to my mind's turmoil, could continue to crave sustenance. We agreed on sausages and beans. I had struggled to swallow two mouthfuls when the phone rang again.

'Walker?...Walker?'

'Yeah.'

'Answer quick nex time 'cause me 'ave a man who wants to buy your lickle son's battyhole... unnerstan? Me arks if you unnerstan!'

'Yeah.'

'Nex time me call be ready to travel.'

The line went dead and I turned for the kitchen but I was halted by the sight of another cream-coloured envelope lying in a corner of my hallway. I bent down and had it torn open before I had straightened up again. Inside was a single sheet of folded paper; it was a photocopy of the front page which reported a bomb explosion outside a police station. At the bottom of the paper was a short list. The names of Errol Morgan and Gilbert Hanimal Peters had ticks next to them; the name Conrad Shaka Williams had a cross next to it. The last name on the list was mine; it too had a tick next to it.

'Sad bastard,' I sighed as I walked to the kitchen.

'Was it Campbell?' asked Danny.

I retook my seat at the table. 'Yeah,' I said. 'He says to be ready to travel next time he calls.'

'Right,' said Danny, scooping another forkful of beans into his mouth. He saw the envelope in my hand. 'Post is it?' he asked.

I pushed it over to him. He put down his knife and fork.

'I've had a few of these,' I explained as he read its contents. 'It's Tyrone, Carmen's brother, who's sendin them. The mad ras put a knife to my throat an' tried to kill me the night I drove him to the Rose an' Crown. He was mekin out that I'd set up Errol an' Hanimal, an' ever since he's been pushin stuff like this through the door.'

'You mean the fella who went into the boozer with the bomb?'

'That's him.'

'And he posted you other stuff like this?'

'Nah, he pushes them through the door when I'm out. That's the scary bit - he must be watchin me some of the time.'

'So when did this one arrive?'

'It's got the print of your boot on it so it must have arrived last night.'

'You're telling me this came last night?'

'Yeah, it must have.'

Danny handed me the paper. 'Then it looks as though someone else is after finding out about what youse boys were up to. It's not the Tyrone fella who's sending this stuff.'

'How do you know that?'

'I know because he's dead. Dead like the other Muslim fella.'

'You mean Malek?'

'Yeah. He's dead like the Malek fella.'

22

THERE HAD BEEN no phone calls from Campbell since midday so I took the telephone from downstairs and plugged it into the socket next to my bed and waited for the time to pass. The wait was made even more tortuous by the uncertainty; all I knew for definite was that the call to collect Nathan would come any time before midnight.

I could see by Danny's look of concern that he wanted to talk about the envelopes which had been pushed through my door but I had told him that I wished to be alone with my thoughts. I needed to be prepared for what lay ahead of me.

The news of Tyrone's death had shocked me. I lay down on my bed hoping that the phone would not ring until I was ready. But the two flashing green dots on my clock-radio reminded me that while time might have appeared to slow it would not halt just for me; I had to begin to focus my mind.

The thought of Carmen sitting alone in her home waiting for me to make contact was another distraction. Her brother had been murdered within hours of his attempt to kill me and I couldn't help but think of all her wasted prayers and hopes for Tyrone's safety. And there were all the times I had leapt out of bed on imagining I had heard him breaking into my home. What trouble he had caused us both - even when dead.

According to Danny, Tyrone had been picked up in the early hours of the morning by Campbell's men as he ran through the streets of the Rushbury estate. He had suffered a slow and terrible death as a result of Daddy One-foot's fixation with amputation. Information about who had provided Tyrone with the device that had been put in the pub run by Campbell's organization was cruelly extracted. Tyrone had not held out for long. He had quickly admitted to his interrogators that it was Malek Abu Bakr who had given him the bomb and told him where to plant it. The confession would cost Malek's life as well as his own. Tyrone lost fingers, one hand and a piece of a leg before he died; apparently Malek was not so lucky.

Danny's detailed description made me wonder how he knew all this and how much of what he had told me previously was the truth. He had said that no one had been killed with the guns he had left hidden in my loft but that was not saying that he or his comrades had not killed people with other guns. It was possible that the tale about coming to England to find his father's killer was nothing but bullshit to gain my sympathy and to disguise his real reasons for being here; after all, he had lied to me the night he turned up at my house. What had Danny been doing in a pub he knew to be owned by the Campbells? Were he and his comrades acting as hired guns for them, or was he there for other reasons? People who did business with the Campbells only dealt with two things: murder and drugs which in a lot of cases amounted to the same thing.

There were many other questions I could have asked Danny; for instance, why did his comrades want to raid the factory I had once worked in? I hadn't bothered to ask. As the reason was not volunteered I figured it was best if I did not find out. And besides, I doubted if my mind could successfully cope with any more lurid tales.

I had already worked out that Danny and his friends were not helping me because of a few crosses on a drawing or details about a boilerhouse. Maybe all the stories of drug dealing by Republicans in Belfast I had dismissed as government propaganda were based in fact; maybe Danny and his friends had been planning to kill Glenroy Campbell for some time because of a deal that had turned sour. Such notions could have swamped my mind if I dwelt on them for too long. Whatever his real reason for wanting Campbell dead, Danny didn't have to tell me that I was now the bait for a trap within a trap.

When sitting at my kitchen table trying to take in the news of the deaths of Tyrone and Malek Abu Bakr, I had said, 'So, anybody who's dealin with the Campbells is dealin in shit. This Malek, all his Muslim bisniss was just a front for his dealins.'

'In drugs, you mean?'

'What else?'

'No Robbie, the Muslim thing *was* a front of sorts, a flytrap hung up for these so-called black militants. Christ, Robbie, put your thinking head on. It's a bit too much of a coincidence that they would set up here after what all youse men were up to. But it seems the Malek fella was just a man genuinely concerned about his community. I wouldn't say I agreed with everything he said, but he was genuine enough in his attempts to take on the people who are fucking up society. He just got hisself involved in a fight with characters who were way above his league. He couldn't have realized that the two Campbell fellas weren't still the small-fry that went to prison. Those two bastards used their time on remand to make contacts with some of the really big players. When the case against them collapsed they came out with the potential to become one of the biggest drug-dealing operations in Europe. Now they have cops in their pockets and the arrogant shites think they can get away with murder.'

Danny took a swig of tea and looked at me reflectively.

'It was the Campbells who had the two Italian fellas and their car dealing mate shot in the country lane, so it was. And they've a lot more shooters than the Muslim fellas. There's a moral in that somewhere.'

That Malek did not turn out to be a charlatan and that he and Tyrone had taken on such men without any support from the community they had tried to protect made me feel sick. I could now see what drove Tyrone to the edge of insanity. To those who spent a lifetime impassively looking on at events, Malek and Tyrone's efforts may have seemed crazy and futile but I knew that they would have hoped that their actions would have roused the people around them from their torpor. But no one stirred. Most of those who might have aided them were lying in the ground beyond waking or were, like me, stricken with a malignant cynicism.

How had I allowed myself to change so much? I remembered Errol smarting with frustration. After eighteen months and a special squad of detectives to track us down, the police were still no nearer to us. After they had successfully denied us the oxygen of national publicity, the cops then resorted to telling the local press that the attempts to kill members of the Force could be the work of white extremists pretending to be black as a means of stirring up racial hatred. 'You know wha me hear black people sayin now?' Errol yelled. 'It can't be black people usin bomb, 'cause a black man nah use dem tings, to fuckin ras!'

I laughed bitterly. 'Yeah, but if them hear of a black man stabbin another black man over a white woman or some foolishness like that, them all would believe it. Errol, you gettin vexed is what the cops want. Them seh it could be white guys but them only pickin up black guys. Didn't you tell me them arrest fifteen black guys the last time?'

'Yeah, an' them hassle one lickle yout so much that he's ended up in the mental. Some guys unner serious pressure 'cause of what we do.'

'Fuck them guys, they wouldn't feel so bad if them got off them ras an' did somethin.'

'But they would do somethin if they definitely knew it was black men who are puttin down bomb. Them would follow the good example.'

'Cha, E, you just tell me them seh that black man don't use bomb. What else them say a black man nah do? Let me think, oh yeah, black man nah vote, read books, give blood, sing opera... go fishin. Crise, man, the white man nah have to exclude us any more, we're programmed to do it to ourselves.'

Errol paused.

That a black man does not go fishing was a remark he had made to me when I had told him I was away for the weekend with Fidel and Mr Robinson. I watched as a little piece of him crumbled. In growing up in England we had lived a kind of lie; in some cases we were in denial.

'Then who are we doin this for?' he demanded.

'Errol, I do what I do for me, so I can live with myself. An' all them people you hear talkin 'bout black man not doin this or that ain't never gonna be convinced otherwise. They will believe what they want to believe, that's how they can live with cops killin innocent guys while they do nothin about it.'

And I had believed what I wanted to believe about Malek.

With a jolt, I raised my head from the pillow on hearing the phone ring out. 'Robbie Walker?'

'Yeah.'

'Be at 43 Church Street in half an hour.'

'Where's Church Street?'

'Lef at the lights at the bingo hall on the Wellington Road. Look it up in a *A-to-Z*. It's a house with a red door. Kind-a blood-red. Be there fe seven.'

Danny looked into my bedroom from the doorway. 'Was that him?'

'Yeah. I have to be at 43 Church Street at seven o'clock.'

'Where's Church Street, exactly?'

'On the Rushbury estate.'

Danny paused. 'I'll find it. We'll have to play this one by ear, Robbie. All I can say is that we will do what we can. I doubt if Campbell will be there when you arrive. He'll make sure there's no funny business first. The man is so careful. And then he'll let you go after a while. Like he did with the Tyrone fella, he will want you away from any premises that he has a connection with. He'll want witnesses coming forward to say they saw you walking well away from this house. Campbell got lucky when Tyrone was seen going walkabouts.' He paused as if he expected me to react but my expression told him that I had nothing to say. He continued, 'He'll try to make sure you leave on foot. I'm only guessing but I'd also say it'll be then when he makes his move. It's a convoluted way of killing a man but it's how the twisted bastard gets his kicks.'

'That makes me feel a lot better,' I said, acknowledging the implications of what he was telling me. 'I'll ring Carmen.'

He took stock of me. 'You look okay,' he said approvingly.

I was prepared. In my mind I was already on my way to the ring to meet Campbell and there would be no stepping out until the fight was over. There had been times in the recent past when I had doubted if I could cope, but I had survived. 'I'm more than okay,' I said. 'I'm ready.'

He smiled grimly and threw me an orange cagoule. 'Make sure to wear that and we'll see each other later.'

Part of a superstitious ritual of our youth was to never wish each other good luck before a fight; we'd only say that we would see each other later. I said, 'Yeah, Danny, later.'

The gears crunched for a second time. Carmen said, 'Sorry about that. I don't get a lot of practice drivin.'

'Don't worry,' I said, 'there's a lot worse things happenin in the world.'

She laughed sadly. 'There sure is.'

I again admired her strength as she concentrated on the road ahead. Once I had told her where to go she did not ask me who owned the house or what I would be doing as she took Nathan to my mother's; it was as if she had put her complete trust in me.

For a few moments I reminisced about the love we had shared and again thought about asking her to leave this place with me. It was a moment of romantic insanity. 'You're right,' she said, shattering my contemplations, 'right to get out of here. I might do it myself one day,' she added, 'when Tim is grown up. I do still love him, you know, Robbie. I was very tired the other night, I said some things I didn't mean.'

'We all do that.'

She looked at me, as if to ask when was the last time I had said something I had not meant. Her gaze back on the road she said, 'Tim told me his reasons he messed up your house. He said that he had told you as well.'

'Well, kind of.'

'An' he told me those names he called me. Robbie, there have been times I've called them myself. When he was a baby I was still hurtin from Errol, you know? I let other men in my life because I thought I hated him, but really I was hating myself. I got trapped in a spiral of self-hate. There were a lot of men, Robbie. A lot of foolin myself.'

I did not want to hear this sort of thing from her; I did not want her to dilute what I thought we had shared. I told her it wasn't any of my business but she continued as though she had not heard me. Only some of it registered; it was as painful to listen to as it was to say. 'I realized how selfish I had been when Tim went hysterical when that fuckin idyat Wesley started kickin down my door,' she told me. 'I mean, I saw it then that the man was nothin but a darg an' yet I'd let him give me a baby. I understood then there were worse things than bein lonely. God forgive me but I'm glad that Yvonne died when she was a baby; at least she never knew what sort her father was. An' after Wesley I let nobody through my door for years, not until you, an' I guess there were too many bad memories for Tim. I'm so scared that when he grows up he'll be like some of the men I've come across - always lookin to get even with that bitch they hate.'

I had known men like that: Hanimal was one of them. When he was ten or eleven his father turned up and took him to meet his grandmother who had just arrived from Jamaica. She laughed like it was a joke and told him that he had another sixteen brothers and sisters. He never got over it.

Up until then Hanimal had thought he was his father's only child. He went back to the home which he shared with the four sisters who had four different fathers - and, illogically as it seemed to a lot of the guys who grew up with him, hated his mother from that day. He hated her weakness, he hated her inability to recognize the poison seed dipped in honeyed words. By the time Hanimal was dead he had matched his own father's tally of kids but he had never got even.

With four minutes to spare, the car turned into Church Street. Grateful for the chance to put our agony to an end I told her to stop the car. We were some distance away from number 43. I put on the cagoule.

'Expectin rain?' she asked.

'You never know. Now look, Carmen, the kids should be out within two minutes of me goin in there. You don't leave the car under any circumstance. You keep the engine runnin an' if anyone but me or the kids come out you take off an' ring the cops. Is that clear?'

'It clear-clear.'

'Cool. So let's go find number 43.'

The car drew level with the red door. 'Right,' I said, 'so later.'

'Robbie,' she said, 'if Tim doesn't want to come, don't try an' make him. He'll come back in his own time.'

'Okay, if that's what you want.'

She nodded. 'He has to want to come back,' she said, 'otherwise it won't work.' I began to leave the car. She pulled at my arm, kissed me and whispered, 'Be careful.'

I pounded on the red door while muttering the words I had rehearsed a thousand times over. However it was not the big surly black guy I had imagined who opened the door but a petite young black woman who smiled pleasantly. 'Are you Nathan's dad?' she asked. I growled I was. She stepped back. 'Come on in, he's just finished his dinner.'

She led me along a hallway to a room which smelt of freshly fried fish and dumplings. Nathan looked up from his plate. 'Daddy!' he yelled happily.

He got up and hugged my waist. The young woman appeared with his duffelcoat. 'He's so lovely an' bright. How come he can read so good?'

This wasn't what I had imagined at all. 'Practice,' I said, while trying to figure out what was going on. Tim appeared as Nathan put on his coat and the smile on his face told me not everything was as it seemed. 'Wha happen, Tim.'

His response was a curt suck of his teeth. The woman put on a heavy-looking overcoat which could have belonged to her mother and stepped into the hallway and opened the nearest door. 'Right, I'm off now,' she called to someone who was out of sight. 'See you tomorrow.'

A noise followed and a large man, similar to the one I had given shape to in my imagination, came to the door. 'Okay, Gloria, tomorrow.' He looked at me, then at Nathan and back to me. 'Where you-a go?' he asked.

'He's goin home, like Daddy One-foot seh,' I spat. 'An' there's a woman outside in my car with her finger on a mobile phone who's gonna ring the cops if he ain't out of here in one minute.'

The man bellowed with laughter. 'Hey, me only arks where the pickney go. You stayin, though, isn't it?'

'Yeah,' I said. 'Tim, go take Nathan out to the car.'

Tim sucked at his teeth again and did not move until the laughing man said, 'Tim, tek Nathan out before some woman ring the police.'

I gave Nathan a little hug and said, 'See you later, Natty Dread. Carmen is goin to take you to your nan's, right?'

I looked at the man but his expression did not give anything away when he heard me telling Nathan that I would see him later.

'Ah shit!' Tim hissed loudly.

'Wha happen?' the man asked him.

'That's my ol' lady out deh.'

'So? G'wan an' say 'ello to yuh modda. Quick!'

Tim shuffled out with Nathan ahead of him, rolling his shoulders as if there were a ball and chain on both ankles. The man shook his head and gestured for me to enter the room he had just come from. 'Daddy ain't here yet. But you had better call him Mr Campbell when he gets here.'

I walked into the room comforted by the correctness of Danny's prediction that I would not find Glenroy Campbell waiting for me. Three black men were hunched over a coffee table picking at the remains of the fried fish. One of them straightened and eyed me before dismissively returning to suck at the fish bones. Two men with duppy-white or probably prison-white faces were on a sofa. They turned their heads away from the television. The one with a face like a pock-marked Cabbage Patch doll eyed me and muttered something under his breath. The big guy who showed me in cried out in mock indignation. 'Oi, oi, oi,' he called to the white guy with the pasty skin, 'show some respec, Reg. I was there the night this man knock out a bad boxer from Yard. An' him lick down Alvin at school.' The pasty face turned a very pale pink, his eyes darted back towards me, nervously trying to appraise not the boxer but the man who as a boy had knocked out a man he feared.

A man with a goatee beard looked up from his fish and said to the big man: 'Curtis, this the man that lick down Alvin?'

Curtis nodded while shaking with laughter. The man at the table turned to me. 'Bwoy, yuh stup-pid or fuckin crazy.'

I heard the sound of my car driving away and said, 'Or maybe I'm just hard.'

I returned his stare and could see that he was lost for a moment and unsure of me. The two men who sat next to him straightened up. There had been no glibness in his words, for such men rarely possess that sort of attribute. He had been probing, testing what was underneath my skin while thinking he was safe because of the numbers that were stacked against me. He knew my reponse was a challenge. If he wasn't going to accept my assertion of hardness he would have to get up and prove it wrong. He looked to Curtis for an answer. He had stopped laughing. Every head except mine turned towards the door as Tim rushed in, sounding flustered. I watched in the mirror above the fireplace as he scanned the faces and grimaced with disappointment, as though he might have missed something.

It angered me that he had rejected his mother for the company of men such as these but I forced my mind back to other things. 'Any food?' I asked Curtis.

He pulled down the corners of his mouth. 'Elroy,' he called to the man who had not met my challenge, 'go fetch this man some food. Tim, you go an' fetch him a chair.'

Elroy thrust a plate of fish and dumplings into my hands. He was smouldering and I knew that beneath that large and laughing exterior Curtis was scheming: the manner in which he had purposely amplified Elroy's loss of face would ensure he would be a willing volunteer when Campbell asked for something unpleasant to be done to me. Tim came in with the chair and roughly pushed it in my direction with his foot. 'Bring it to the man,' growled Curtis.

Hardly containing himself, Tim placed the chair behind me with a thud. I sat and thanked him but he winced and turned his head as if my words were assaulting his ears. Unable to bring himself to look at me, he joined the two white men on the sofa. 'So what time is Daddy One-foot gonna be here?' I asked Curtis, who sat on a chair between me and the door.

He opened his mouth to remind me of the correct way in which to address Glenroy Campbell but changed his mind. 'Some time,' he answered sharply.

The fish and dumplings tasted very good. As I ate I looked over to the television. As time had crept by every eye had eventually turned towards the Hollywood images of the Vietnam war. Every slow-motion pretend wound, every spurt of pretend blood brought about howls of laughter. These guys were working themselves into a state of arousal. Curtis dried an eye. 'These guys are fuckin weird,' he wheezed.

A slam of the front door echoed along the hallway. The laughter stopped. 'Turn off the telly,' snapped Curtis. He opened the door and stuck his head out before he looked back to me and whispered, 'Daddy's here.'

23

EXCITEMENT, COLD AND liquid, trickled down my spine as Glenroy 'Daddy One-foot' Campbell entered the room. Sure, I appeared to be cool, I had that part down to a fine art, but as Campbell's posse filed in behind him I was unsure if my demeanour looked sufficiently untroubled. There were now a dozen pairs of hostile eyes bearing down on me. My own eyes were drawn to Tim. I drew strength from his lazy, lopsided malevolent grin: I became grateful for his presence because I would not allow that boy to see me buckle.

As it was with his father before him, it suddenly mattered what Tim thought of me. There had once been a time when the opinions of Errol were of the uppermost importance to me.

The headlines that had once labelled Errol and me as fanatical and dangerous had left us unmoved. Every now and again a so-called radical 'leader of the black community' was given a few column-inches to condemn our actions or to cast doubt on our ethnic identity. The stupid rasholes never understood; we could not be shamed into stopping what we were doing, our beliefs were not so flimsy that we could be swayed by public opinion or the public utterances of the self-opinionated. The only opinions that counted with us were those of people who were committed enough to pick up weapons and put their lives on the line for a cause - and around where we lived there were only three: Errol, Hanimal and me. In the space of one year two young black men had been killed by the police and yet not one cop was ever disciplined, never mind taken to court. Consequences were something the cops had to learn about - and anyone who disagreed with our methods of instruction were only chatting weasel words of appeasement.

Errol's presence had emptied me of doubt and filled me with determination, and I knew I had done the same for him. A shared belief and a common objective produced a courage within us that we could never have mustered as individuals. Tim's smirk was unintentionally having the same effect. In other circumstances I might have been scared, but Tim was helping me to clear my mind of any fear, allowing me to focus on the eradication of Glenroy Campbell.

The snakeskin shoes were the first thing I noticed about Daddy One-foot. He walked to the centre of the room without any discernible limp and I wondered for a moment which one of the shoes was on the end of an artificial leg. Despite growing up in the same city, this was the first time I had ever come face to face with him. The heels on his shoes and his broad-rimmed hat might have brought his height to around six feet. His eyes were so black it looked as though his pupils were massively dilated. The flesh on his face was shrunk back against his cheekbones and winter had put an unevenness about the tone of his yellow-brown skin. I imagined that underneath all those clothes was a bony margre body. He unbuttoned his heavy overcoat and showed off the array of expensive jewellery which was hanging around his neck. His slightly bulbous eyes swivelled left and right before they rested on me. 'Robbie Walker?'

In the moment before I responded I put my faith in Danny Maguire and his prediction that Campbell would allow me to walk away unharmed. Stretching out a leg, as though I was making myself comfortable, I said, 'One-foot. So wha happen?'

Glenroy Campbell looked around the room in order to let his men see that he disapproved of the tone of my reply. A man dressed in a similar manner to Glenroy growled something I didn't hear properly and stepped forward. It was Alvin - I would have recognized those big nose-holes anywhere. They gave him the look of a man perpetually vexed with the world.

'Alvin,' I said, 'I can't say it's nice to see you again.'

He rubbed his jaw as if reliving the moment in a school corridor when my fist had cracked against it. He said to Curtis, 'Has dis pussy-hole been frisked?'

I stood up to deny anyone the chance of being ordered to do so, and stretched out my arms at shoulder height. Curtis frisked me and I returned Glenroy's thin smile as I thought that the last man who had frisked me had ended up dead. I caught a glimpse of Tim; the curl on his lip told me that he remained unimpressed with my performance.

'He's clean,' said Curtis. He stepped away and I sat down.

'If you nah carry somethin you mus be *on* somethin,' snorted Glenroy. It was easy to see why the man was so feared. He exuded violence: I could see him eying me with his frog-eyes as if I were a fly on the water. Savouring the opportunity I had presented, he said, 'Let's get tings straight. You nah here for no bloodclart social gatherin.'

'I came here to find out why you kidnap my pickney.'

Again he looked to his men but this time he laughed as if he were enjoying an unspoken joke. 'Kidnap? You too feisty, man. It me who mek sure the lickle bwoy safe. Nah man, the only bisniss we have is you brukin *my* bwoy's jaw.'

'It didn't sound like that over the phone. I thought I heard you say somethin about sellin my son to some pervert.'

Glenroy laughed loud and darkly. 'That only Alvin's lickle joke, man.'

'Well, I ain't laughin,' I said. Glenroy's smile disappeared as I added, 'But down to bisniss, as you call it. First thing, I didn't know the guy who was so out of order was your son. Second, if the bwoy go on like a man him have to take the licks like a man. I thought you'd have shown him that.'

Glenroy, puzzled by my attitude, frowned suspiciously. He said to Curtis, 'Who was wid him?'

Nodding in the direction of the sofa Curtis answered, 'Tim's modda. She took the pickney.'

I watched as Glenroy pondered, his chin resting on the knuckles of one hand as he tried to weigh me up. Without warning, something exploded on the side of my face. For an instant there was a buzzing noise in my head but I straightened myself and saw Alvin's hand continue its arc. 'Alvin!' Glenroy barked. 'Easy, man, hea-sy.'

The initial sting faded quickly. To Glenroy I said, 'Like me say, take lick like a man.' I turned to Alvin. 'Hey, me live with a woman who could do better than that, to rasclart.'

Alvin looked to his brother, and when he did not receive a signal that gave permission to deal a second blow he stepped back, muttering threats. Still pondering, Glenroy called, 'Oi, Tim, come 'ere.'

Tim stepped forward and Glenroy asked, 'Did Ezekiel seh anythin to this man?'

'Nah.'

'Did this man call Zechie's name?'

'He said that he hated the Campbells an' jus punched Zechie down.'

Glenroy shook his head and said to me, 'The bwoy lied - im modda forward you the tun-tun an' get him vexed. An' I know Zechie, him nah the quiet kind. Curtis, see Mr Walker to the door. Me an' him don't 'ave no bisniss.'

I was out onto the street so fast I barely had time to register Tim's expression of utter bewilderment. I looked up and down the road before making up my mind which way to go. If Danny was right, Campbell was about to let me go a distance before picking me up. I scanned the street for Danny or one of his comrades, expecting that one of them would be standing on a street corner looking out for me.

The laughter of a courting couple who walked with arms entwined along the murky street drew my gaze. There was no one else about.

The Wellington Road was about a twenty-minute walk away. I put my head down and followed the couple. The cold damp air hurt my face where Alvin had hit me and a small part of me hoped that would be the end of it, that I would get to my mom's, collect Nathan and in the morning we would be gone. That small and hopeful part of me tried to reason that it was all a mistake, that Tim had taken Nathan from school on his own initiative and Glenroy Campbell had figured that I did not pose a threat to his business and that I wasn't worth the trouble. It only took seconds for such naive notions to be blown away by a cold wind. Like the man who had been known as the Field Marshal, Glenroy Campbell knew that he could only operate in an atmosphere of terror: it kept his men in line, stifled informers and kept competitors wary. He could not afford to let me go unharmed.

The couple went into a house and a shudder rippled through me with the thought of being alone on the street. Almost scared to look behind me, I again searched for any sign of Danny or his comrades. My breathing and stride quickened when I saw no one. It was a small relief to make it to the much busier neon-lit thoroughfare which would take me to the Wellington Road. Walking amongst the late-night shoppers I was safer; Campbell had missed his chance to pick me up, he might have wanted people to witness me walking about but he wouldn't want so many onlookers around as his men tried to bundle me into a car. My attitude must have made Campbell wary. Danny had said that he was one careful bastard.

I thought that Danny and his friends would kill Campbell anyway, with or without my help, although I still didn't know why. Campbell had hesitated and I was going to take advantage and make a change of plan: as soon as I got to my mother's I would put Nathan in my car and we would leave tonight.

Through the clouds of steam rising from the crowd in front of me I could see the blurred lights in the upper tiers of double-decker buses making their way along the Wellington Road. One of them would get me safely to my mother's home.

I found it hard to believe that I had not caught sight of Danny or any of the others. Something must have happened to them, or maybe they had abandoned me. A frightened laugh rattled around inside of me and barely made it to my lips as I thought of how I had treated Campbell because I supposed there was back-up waiting for me outside. I was looking across the road for any sign of Danny when a man in a woolly hat roughly shouldered me. I turned to apologize for the collision and felt something hard dig into the base of my spine. The man in the hat was Reg, the white guy with the pasty skin. He put his Cabbage Patch face close to mine and said, 'Do anything stupid and your fucking guts are all over this pavement.'

He tilted his head towards an alleyway which ran between a Chinese takeaway and a small pub. The man at my rear moved to my side and put an arm around my shoulders as if he were a long-lost friend and the sharp pain moved from my back to my ribs. 'Wha happen, you fuckin bastard,' said Elroy. We went into the darkness with Reg just behind us. Shaka and the way he died flashed through my mind and stiffened my spine. A palm of a hand belted me in between the shoulder blades and Reg snarled, 'Fuck about and we'll do you here and now.'

The ground was frosty and I had trouble keeping my footing as I was steered around a corner to the left and then to the right. A Mercedes with a paint job which could only belong to a Campbell appeared at the end of the alley. A door opened and I was shoved onto the rear seat. Glenroy Campbell swivelled on the front passenger seat. 'So,' he said, 'you act the bad man, you call me One-foot. Well, bway, I'm gonna show you how one foot is better than no foot. By the way, man, tanks fe wearin somethin nice an' bright so we nah miss you. Fuckin idyat.'

The ugly guy called Reg went into another car in front of us. The car took off at speed and we followed once Elroy had sat in beside me and pressed the gun into my ribs.

Like we were a group of guys out clubbing, Glenroy and the driver swayed their shoulders to the music that thundered from what sounded like a boot full of speakers.

A stream of fearful, if unrelated, thoughts began to appear in my head but I made them disappear by repeating over and over that I would survive. SURVIVE! Even sitting in a car full of psychopaths I could still think that I had a tomorrow and that I wasn't about to let myself be chopped to pieces like Tyrone or Malek Abu Bakr. When we reached wherever we were going I would make a move. The worst that could happen was me getting shot - and getting killed that way didn't seem so bad when compared to what Campbell wanted to do to me.

Glenroy looked back to me as the cars stopped at a red light. 'Hey, Walker,' he chuckled, 'jus check the door is locked fe me. Me nah want you to fall out or somethin.'

I did not move. Campbell then said, 'You vex Alvin good an' proper, yuh know.' He turned down the music and went on, 'Yeah, man, him seh unless you beg, him still gonna 'ave some white man rape off your pickney an' sell the video.'

The laughter of Elroy, the driver and Campbell filled the car and I thought, Fuck it, they can kill me now but at least I will die squeezing that bastard's throat. I must have moved, I didn't know it but I must have. The gun shifted from my side to my temple and tilted my head. 'Ai sah! G'wan an' mek your move an' your fuckin brains are comin out!' growled Elroy.

No, not yet, I thought and pushed myself back into the seat.

Elroy laughed again, but this time he sounded strained and nervous. The driver joined in but Campbell only smiled; he was not like the other two, he did not have to work himself up into a fury so his sensations would be blurred at the moment a trigger would be pulled. He wanted his mind clear so he could revel in the experience.

The driver hit the horn and cursed the delay. Suddenly his head lurched towards Campbell. Glass showered me and I felt something warm and sticky splash onto my face. There was an explosion and a pain pierced my left ear like a stiletto making its way to my brain. I felt searing heat on the tightened flesh of my face. For an instant I thought I had been shot but then I saw a flash in front of me, and then another. More glass showered me. I felt the dead weight of a man fall onto my shoulder. I pushed him away with my right hand and with the other I cupped the ear that was boiling over with a terrible ringing noise. I stared at Elroy who was half lying down with his head propped against a door. There was a stupid look in the eyes that were turned towards a hole in the roof of the car just above me. My gaze fell to the smoking gun in his hand and then I felt a blast of cold air as a door was wrenched open. Another flash of light lit up the car. I saw Elroy's head jerk back and blood splatter against the glass. I was outside. I was out on the road. A hand gripping the hood of my cagoule tried to haul my backside off the tarmac. 'Come on, Robbie, on your feet.'

Suddenly the balaclava did not disguise him. Eamon then looked up and shouted, 'Hey! Get that bastard!'

Somehow Glenroy Campbell had managed to get out of the car. He was limping down the road at a speed I could scarcely believe one good leg could manage. Two loud cracks fractured the night air and Campbell collapsed. I watched as he flapped wildly like a fish on dry land until a stocky figure ran to him and stilled him with a foot on his chest. Daddy One-foot let out a final shriek before three more shots stopped his flapping about.

Eamon pulled me past the other car. Alvin Campbell's shattered head lay propped against the windscreen and the ugly guy in the hat was out on the road, a bullet between his vacant eyes. My brain, addled with pain, was still struggling to take in what had happened around me. I slipped getting into the back of the van which had halted at the lights, and Kevin shoved me as he followed me in. 'Put your foot down and let's go!' he shouted to the driver.

The tyres squealed and the acrid smell of burning rubber filled my nostrils. Through the open doors I looked back to the chaos at the crossroads. I fell onto my side as the van turned a corner and righted myself, only to fall onto my back when the van screeched to a halt. 'Our stop,' said Eamon.

It seemed to me that we had only travelled for a few seconds. 'Come on,' he said and we clambered out. Danny walked from the front of the van with a petrol can in his hand. Kevin and Eamon hurriedly stripped themselves of their boilersuits, balaclavas, gloves and training shoes and tossed them into the van. Danny said, 'Robbie, give me your fucking coat, quick!' My numb fingers managed to unzip it and Danny threw it into the rear of the van. 'Right,' he grunted, 'get yourselves into the car!'

Martin was behind the wheel. ''Bout ye, men,' he said as Eamon and I sat in. We accelerated away as the van burst into flames. Martin passed me a handkerchief. 'Do yourself a favour and wipe your face and don't bother looking at the hankie before you throw it out.'

I wiped my face and neck but I could not feel the handkerchief on my skin. I wound down a window and threw it away. The cold air hurt my ear and I felt sick.

'What's happened to the other two?' I asked.

Martin answered, 'That's them behind us.' I turned to see the single bright light of a motorcycle. 'The van was only a stand-by. We'd have just used the bike to draw alongside them if they had taken only the one car.'

I continued to look at the road behind us. 'I can't see how they could have got me on that bike.'

'No,' Martin said dryly, 'neither can I.'

24

MY EAR THROBBED painfully as I pushed a wad of cotton wool into it. In the grubby communal bathroom I watched the mix of blood and water twist its way down the plug-hole. I talked to myself as I had once talked to Errol: warning against the dangers of a lapse in discipline. When the water finally ran clear and I had put on the clean shirt that Martin had given me I returned to the small flat where I had first met Eamon and Kevin. I sat down on the loosely sprung sofa trying to maintain my focus while I placed all that I had witnessed into a small vault which lay buried deep in my subconscious. I had prepared myself for witnessing death, but not on such a scale or at such a close proximity that the bastards would splatter their blood all over me.

There were times, before I had stepped out with Errol with my mind set on killing a cop, when I had imagined the result of our actions and the lengths they would go to in order to find us. But I had still stepped out and there was little point in doing that if either of us were not prepared to go through with what we had started. I had set my mind and drained my heart of any compassion that could later turn into regret. I had made it hard like a stone and that is exactly what I had done before heading for the house in Church Street. I used to tell Errol that there wasn't any use in going out with a gun and then deliberating over whether he should use it or not; all that had to be sorted out before he left his yard. And then I'd say, 'Anytime you wanna pull out just let me know.' But I knew neither of us wanted to be the first to quit: our principles were sometimes forgotten and it was pride that propelled us to put ourselves at risk.

There had already been a news flash on the local radio: *'There has been a shooting incident at a set of traffic-lights in the city centre. First reports indicate that at least four people have been shot dead and another two were seriously wounded.'*

'Wounded?' said Eamon, indignant. 'They must be Kevin's. Maybe the Campbell fella only copped hisself a flesh wound.' He took one look at the expression on my face and laughed. 'Ach, don't you worry yourself, Robbie, I mean the fleshy part of the brain. I'd say we'll be making *News at Ten.*' When neither Martin nor I responded to his youthful bravado, Eamon seemed a little put out and said quietly, 'I'll make us some tea.'

Martin turned off the radio and sat silently in an armchair, his face blank and unexpressive. He remained silent until Eamon handed him a mug. 'You did well,' he said. 'The both of you did well.'

Eamon nodded and made an awkward smile with compressed lips. I said, 'Ol' man, all I did was sit there an' let the bullets fly by.'

Martin shot me a sideways glance and put the mug to his smiling lips. The three of us sipped at our tea until the silence became oppressive. 'What's happened to Danny and Kevin?' I asked.

'They'll be here any minute,' answered Martin.

More silence followed, sticky and sapping. Martin checked his watch and turned the radio back on. An on-the-spot reporter gave a description of the police cordon at the crossroads and the ambulances which had already left the scene. An eyewitness told the reporter that before he had thrown himself to the ground he had seen half a dozen men leap from the back of a van seconds before they began firing into the two Mercedes cars. Another witness talked of seeing a man abducted from one of the cars. The rest of the report was taken up by a police spokesman refusing to confirm the abduction or the identities of the dead men until the next of kin had been informed. A local MP was halfway through his condemnation of the breakdown of law and order on British streets when Martin turned him off.

'You're abducted,' Eamon chuckled. Before I could make a response there was a sharp rap on the door which sent a jolt through me. Eamon opened it and Danny and Kevin stepped in. Kevin's face was a mask of indifference - a show for Eamon, perhaps. 'I'd say we're after making the prime spot on *News at Ten*,' he said.

Eamon looked over at me and shook his head knowingly.

'Everything taken care of?' Martin asked Danny.

'No problem.'

Martin stood up and said, 'Right. I have some news of my own. Robbie, I'm going to have to ask you to leave us alone for a few minutes.'

I got to my feet. 'I'll wait outside.'

Danny's eyes narrowed. 'If this is about the hit at the factory he should stay. I'd stake my life on this man and he might think of something else to tell us.'

'It's other business.'

Suspicious, Danny frowned up at the ceiling before his eyes slowly lowered to meet Martin's. 'What do you mean, other business? There is no other business besides the hit at the factory, is there?'

Martin glanced at me and then said to Danny, 'It's off.'

'What the fuck are you talking about? Like it's delayed, do you mean?'

'I mean it's off, cancelled.'

'By Christ, Martin, you had better be taking the piss.'

With a practised, understated menace, Martin said, 'Does it look as though I'm taking the piss, Danny?'

Kevin circled and took up a position at Martin's rear. He crossed his arms and stared into Danny's face. Eamon stayed where he was but looked away to a far corner of the room and scratched the back of his head. I sensed Danny's isolation.

'Martin,' he said, almost pleading, 'everything is set for tomorrow night. The wagon will be there to take the stuff to Larne. Christ, everything is set.'

'Well, now it's un-set. The wagon will be followed the minute it's off the boat and then we'll know exactly who is supposed to be getting what.'

'You're giving me shite!' snarled Danny. His face glowed, his lips trembled. 'We already know the black-hearted bastards who are supposed to be taking delivery.'

'It's off,' repeated Martin evenly. 'Off.'

'Then tell me why!'

'Because I say so.'

'Shite! Somebody's after giving you orders, is that it?'

Martin nodded in my direction. 'Not while he's here.'

Danny bit his lip and then he hissed, 'Jesus Christ.'

'Shut your fucking gob,' snapped Martin, his finger stabbing at Danny. 'Not while he's here.'

I didn't want to leave Danny outnumbered but I had to say, 'Look, I'll step outside and let you guys get on with it.'

'It's nothing personal,' said Kevin.

'It never is,' I said.

Martin said, 'Thanks, Robbie, this won't take long.'

I went out onto the landing and rested my backside on the smooth curves of the banister. I expected raised voices but the only noise I heard was the blare of canned laughter from a television in a room on the other side of the landing.

My mind turned to the news bulletin and the report of my 'abduction'. If any of the wounded recovered sufficiently to identify me I would make out that I was a victim of mistaken identity; both the people who had done the shooting and those who had been shot had thought I was someone else. The men who had rescued me believed I was a member of Malek Abu Bakr's organization. At least he wasn't around to contradict me. Being in the wrong place at the wrong time isn't a crime, I was just an innocent victim too scared to come forward because of what I had seen.

It was only after I had rehearsed my alibi a few times that I allowed myself to ponder over what was being said inside the flat. I had heard enough to work out that something was leaving the place where I had worked and heading for Ireland, and that Danny had counted on halting the delivery at source. I had also heard the steel in Martin's voice; whatever his reason for not going through with what they had planned, it was not because of any reaction to the blood that had just been spilt. I began to figure that his query about the locations of security cameras at the factory was a sham for Danny's benefit and that his real interest in me was the help I could give him in locating Glenroy Campbell.

The flat door opened and I straightened myself expecting to be invited back in. Eamon stepped out and dropped a large cylindrical nylon holdall at my feet. 'Robbie,' he said while offering me his hand, 'it's been a pleasure meeting you again. Maybe you'll come back to Belfast one day and we'll have a bit of *craic*.'

I shook his hand. 'What? You leavin now?'

'Yep.'

'Well,' I mumbled, 'yeah, man, we'll catch up one day. Say hello to Brendan for me.'

'No problem.'

As he went downstairs Kevin emerged. Almost coyly he put out his hand. I did not expect him to, I didn't think he had liked me. 'You're dead on, Robbie. If you're ever over home again we might have a drink some time.'

I smiled and saw something about him which reminded me of Errol. 'Thanks for you know what,' I said. 'You did the world a favour. *Slán abhaile.*'

'Oh, so you know a bit of Irish.'

'Only that and kiss my arse.'

He grinned broadly and looked completely different from the surly kid with dubious tea-making abilities. '*Slán leat,*' he said warmly before hurrying after Eamon.

From the doorway Martin called to me, 'Come in a minute, please.' Danny was standing where I had left him but his eyes were fixed firmly on the floor as though he could not bring himself to look at me. Martin said, 'I've a question to ask you, Robbie, a question you have every right to say no to. Me and the two boys have to be away, but Danny here does not want to leave a certain business unfinished. But he can't finish it all by hisself. The question is: are you prepared to give him a hand? It could be risky, as risky as anything you are after doing tonight.'

Danny raised his head and glanced at me briefly before turning his eyes away again as I said, 'Can I ask what's involved?'

Martin shook his head. 'Sorry, Robbie, you can't be told anything unless you are in. Now I don't want to be rushing you, but I need an answer. Are you in or are you out?'

What was it with these guys? It is either you are in or you're out and nothing in between. Danny let his head fall back and he blew a soft trembling breath towards the ceiling. I could go now, I was only a step away from walking towards my son but in doing so I would be walking away from Danny. If I did refuse to help him for a second time I would never have a contented life with Nathan; a friend's need would always cast a shadow over the pair of us. I let out a sigh and said, 'In.'

Such a breath came out of Danny I thought he would shrink to the floor like a deflated balloon. Martin said to him, 'Draw two weapons and don't bother coming home if you change your mind.' To me he said, 'Robbie, maybe another time. I can see why Brendan still talks about you. Take care of yourself, okay?'

He shook my hand.

Danny looked almost tearful. 'Thanks, Martin,' he said.

'Don't thank me,' said Martin sternly, 'just make sure you don't fuck up. And that's a pint you owe me.'

'I thought you gave up the drink.'

Obviously a man unused to spouting pleasantries, Martin said brusquely, 'I might've restarted by the time you're home. Right, you're going to need the car so you'll have to come with me and the lads and drop us off.'

'You'll stay here then, Robbie,' said Danny. 'Make yourself comfortable, we'll be here for the night.'

'Yeah,' I replied lamely, not that he would have noticed.

From the window I watched them leave and then I looked to the door and thought about walking out. Martin's coolness towards Danny and his warning of the danger ahead began to burrow into my mind. If Martin could drop his plans for the factory, why couldn't Danny? But I knew there was a chance that he would carry on alone if I walked out on him, that a fixation might get the better of reason. I told myself I couldn't leave, but before I knew what I was doing I was walking down the stairs and out towards the road.

Without the extra layer of the cagoule the cold air cut into my bones. I hid my hands in my trouser pockets and found two silver coins. I must have lost the rest of my money when Eamon dragged me from the car. The light of a telephone booth beckoned me. I rang for a taxi. A man said I would have to wait five or ten minutes so I decided to use the other coin to ring my mother.

She demanded to know what was going on - Nathan had told her he had slept in his clothes the night before. 'He stayed over at a friend of Tim's,' I said.

'Without pyjamas?'

'Yeah, Mom. Now look, I might not be round until Thursday mornin an' I don't want Nathan goin to school tomorrow.'

'He can't go to school with such a nasty cough. An' anyway, where are you?'

'Outside Manchester.'

'What? How did you get there? Carmen left your car here. Robert, what is goin on?'

'I got a job interview at that place I told you about.'

'I thought you said it wasn't happenin until next Monday.'

'Money's goin, Mom, if I don't see you tomorrow I'll see you Thursday mornin. Okay?'

The rattle of a diesel engine preceded the toot of a horn and I left the shelter of the booth. 'You call a taxi, mate?'

'Nah, not me,' I called back. I thought I had made up my mind but as I talked to my mother my uncertainty had resurfaced and I had left myself the option to be with Danny the following night. The taxi driver uttered a curse or two and drove off after casting a dirty look my way.

I walked, but not back to the flat. My route was aimless, my destination unknown. All my life I had taken the hard route; if I saw people mostly taking a right turn I would go left. I put it down to my mother's influence. She often told me not to follow like a sheep, not to do something just because everyone else was doing it. Dare to be different.

'Oh hello,' said a man, wincing and rocking on his heels as his dog shat into the gutter. 'Nice dog,' I said and the man gritted his teeth.

Further along the street a group of revellers celebrating a birthday made up my mind to take a turn to my right.

As the out-of-key rendition of *Happy Birthday* faded I thought of my birthdays as a kid. The most vivid memory was of my thirteenth birthday when Mom bought me a punchball. It had been Errol's idea to take up boxing, and like most young kids we wanted to be Muhammad Ali. Errol was good but I had been better. I loved the training: the way it had hardened and sculpted my body, the discipline, the respect of my peers and of men much older than me.

The other aspect I loved about boxing back then was the naive notion that I was judged solely as a boxer and the all-consuming adjective 'black' was an irrelevance. To the people who loved the art it was true I was just a boxer. But such men are a minority for they have learned what it is to be a man through their art. Bubby had taught me that a fighter was not to be judged by his race or appearance but by what he did with his fists in the ring and how he conducted himself while out of it. It was a lesson that I briefly forgot only once and it was a young roughneck from Belfast who made me quickly relearn it.

Unfortunately, the fight most people remembered me for was not one of my best and it would prove to be my last; it was against a boxer from Jamaica who had been a medallist in the Pan-American games. He came with a good reputation and it was Errol who had been originally scheduled to meet him but a hand injury - similar to the one he had sustained when hearing Glenroy Campbell might be turning up at our school - meant that I was asked to take his place.

By the time I ducked into the ring I was set on proving a point. For weeks before the fight I had listened to the taunts from people who were born in Jamaica. They told me, with an obvious relish, how hard my opponent was - simply because he was coming from JA. It was that kind of talk which created an inferiority complex in some of my friends who, like me, were born in England: we would never be as good as the true Jamaican, or the true Englishman. But cha, to me it was nonsense talk.

The fight with the Jamaican boxer only lasted into the first minute of the second round. I was tall for my weight but my opponent was a good two inches taller. In my determination to prove most of the spectators wrong I rushed in and was made to pay for my mistakes by my opponent's rapier-like left lead. For the very first time in a fight I was aware of the noise coming from outside the ring. What I really heard was Errol's voice; he was frantically screaming instructions at me. With my concentration shattered I was caught by an uppercut to the ribs. I sagged back onto the ropes and Errol yelled for me to jab and move. I almost turned around to tell him to shut his bloodclart, and that if he knew so much he should have got into the ring instead of turning up with a bandaged hand. A right hand crashed against my jaw and I heard the oohs of the crowd and a panic-stricken Errol shouting for me to keep my hands up.

Back on my stool in the corner I watched Bubby's mouth move as he barked instructions at me but none of his words sunk in. Errol pushed his head through the ropes. 'Look, man,' he said, 'every time him throw that friggin lef hand him drop his right - right? Throw the hook like Don Curry versus Milton McCrory, seen?'

I was about to tell him to fuck off when Bubby pushed my gumshield into my mouth. The bell for the second round rang and I stepped out to try and gain the centre of the ring only to catch a hard jab in my face. I tried a jab of my own but it fell short. He threw another left which jerked back my head. Errol cried, 'Mi ras!' I ducked as my opponent doubled up on his jab and then turned and drove my left hand upwards with such a force that I would have dislocated my shoulder if it had missed. But it didn't miss. There was an audible crack of a bone and my opponent pitched face-first onto the canvas. It was like Don Curry versus Milton McCrory all over again.

Unlike Curry I didn't win an undisputed world title or a million-dollar purse. Errol and Mr Robinson won a few pounds in bets with a few Jamaican guys and I knew from the look that he gave me that I would always have Errol's undying respect and that was enough for me. I told Bubby the following week that I did not want to box any more.

On rounding another corner I went head-first into an icy wind which blew away the warm glow of a far-off victory. I shivered and paused to get my bearings. Less than a mile to my left and I was on the main road for my mother's home; a right turn would take me back towards the flat. I cursed Danny's bloody-mindedness and headed for my mom's. I hadn't gone a dozen steps before I hit a barrier created in my mind and I was forced to turn around.

I had to go back to Danny Maguire.

25

SITTING AT THE top of the stairs in a draught for the best part of an hour had done little for my humour. My ear still ached, the inside of my mouth felt sore again and the side of my face where Alvin Campbell had struck me throbbed every time a blast of cold wind whistled up the staircase. There had been several times when I had changed my mind about helping Danny and walked down towards the door only to climb the stairs again.

He finally arrived with a black holdall in one hand and a white paper carrier bag in his other. I followed him and the trail of delicious steam into the flat.

'What were you doing sitting outside - lock yourself out or something?' asked Danny as I shut the door behind me.

'I was goin home but for some foolish reason I changed my mind.'

'Oh?' he grunted, as he put down the bags. 'Ah, but you came back,' he said happily. 'Thanks, mate, you're the one man I know I can count on.'

'That must be down to the company you keep.'

'The lads, you mean? Not at all, you won't be meeting two finer young fellas.'

'I was thinkin about Martin.'

'Ach, he has his strange little ways but he's consistent.'

'You know he never intended to go through with whatever you have planned for the factory, don't you? You know that bit with the drawing was only bullshit. Crise, Danny, the two young guys had their bags already packed.'

He looked to me for sympathy from under his arching eyebrows before putting the containers of food onto the table. I was too preoccupied with other matters to offer him any understanding. After fetching cutlery and two plates from the kitchen he sat down. I remained standing. 'Are you not having a bit to eat?' he asked.

'How can you eat?'

'Easy. I open me gob, chew a bit and swallow.'

'After all that's gone on today?'

'I got you a special curry and fried rice.' He took the lid off one of the containers and the smell made my belly rumble. 'And I told them to leave out the onions.'

'Danny,' I said harshly, 'I need to know about everything that's been goin on before I can help you out. Now, I don't like layin out conditions...'

'Then sit you down, have a bit to eat first and I'll tell you what you want to know.'

The aroma wafted tantalizingly around my nose. 'There's definitely no onions?' I said grudgingly. ''Cause you know they give me heartburn.'

'I remembered. Would be a sin to waste it with all the starving in the world.'

Touched that he had remembered my problem with onions, I sat down and once the food was in front of me I became ravenous. We didn't bother to speak much except to compliment the cuisine as we cleaned our plates. I was too hungry to chance hearing anything that would ruin my appetite.

Finally Danny leant back in his chair and patted his stomach. 'Thank you, Mr Wu.' He gestured in the direction of the black holdall near his feet. 'Do you recognize that? It's the bag your man brought into the pub.'

'Tyrone? The bag with the bomb?'

'The very same.'

'Shit!'

'Ach, it's all right, Martin made it safe as soon as we found it. Do you think I'm a fucking nutcase or something?'

He picked up the bag and placed it on the table. He opened it, took out two automatic pistols and invited me to take a look. I stood up and peered in and thought that if I had not met Martin I would not have believed that anyone could have disarmed a bomb that was discovered by chance instead of simply running for safety. I recognized the type of clockwork timer which sat with a battery in a small wooden box - I had once constructed similar devices and I could see it would only take the joining of two wires to make it viable again. A shudder passed through me as I relived the moment my hand had entered a bag to arm a bomb outside a court building.

'Commercial explosive, not as powerful as Semtex but enough to blow Campbell's pub to bits,' said Danny. 'Your man Malek picked up a few things when doing his tours of duty back home in Belfast. A bit primitive for nowadays, though.'

'He was a soldier?'

'Yeah, I think his name was Neville Davis back then.'

'You said this Muslim thing was a sort-a fly-trap for black militants. If this Malek had been a soldier, how come he wasn't in on it? I mean, he was the guy at the top.'

'Not quite. I'd say the people who started the organization were probably working for Special Branch, you know, just to get it going, and then they let the most committed work themselves to the top. It seems Neville Davis got carried away with hisself. Certain matters were given the blind-eye treatment to help with the man's credibility, but then he went too far when he had that fella thrown off the flats. He must've thought that because there was no retaliation immediately after the Moncrieff fella was shot down on the Blackmore, that the Campbells were not all what they were cracked up to be. But 'twas the Campbells who got Moncrieff nutted. And it was some cop with the Crime Squad who told the Campbells where they could find the place where the Malek fella was hiding out.'

'And how do you know all this, Danny?'

''Cause it was the two boys who stiffed Moncrieff.'

His words had confirmed my worst fears. 'Fuck you! So this was all because of some deal you had with the Campbells. So you shot One-foot 'cause he pulled a skank across you, eh? The stuff he was supplyin not pure enough or somethin for you guys?'

Danny's face grew crimson. 'Houl your horses, Robbie. You had better hear me out and not be jumping down my throat before I've even told you half of it. Christ, boy, what do you think I am?' He put the guns back into the holdall. 'I think you had better go,' he muttered sourly. 'I know your heart's not in it and I don't want you saying anything that might bring our friendship to an abrupt end.'

He had me back on my heels, half wanting to leave, half wanting to apologize. His glistening eyes met mine for just an instant and rooted me to the spot. 'Go on and fuck off home,' he said softly, 'and no hard feelings.'

'Danny.'

'Don't be bothering yourself. I told you before, it was my da, it's my community, you've got no reason.' He paused to halt the shaking in his throat. 'But before you go I wish all of this was not happening. I wish I could be a big man, I wish I could be big like all those people who say they forgive the ones who've killed members of their family. But they have never had a gun put into their hands and been told where the killers are. Would they still be forgiving and sounding all holy if they were in my shoes? Maybe they would, maybe they wouldn't, but I know I'm not forgiving nothing. And, you know, I wish I was big like Martin. I says to him that the fellas who killed his brother are at the factory waiting to be stiffed. But he says to me that he has to sacrifice what he wants to do because he's aware of the bigger picture, that The Cause is bigger than any individual. See, he's a soldier, he can say those things and mean it. But I amn't. I'm still the wee boy inside who can't bear the tears any more. I'm just a wee boy who's scared to go to bed in the dark because of the nightmares.'

All thoughts of leaving him on his own had vanished. Loyalty kept me with him but curiosity also played its part. 'So Moncrieff was shot by you guys to get close to the Campbells?'

He nodded. 'Something like that. We had tried to make out that we wanted to do business and sell his shit back home but he wanted some proof of our credentials. Moncrieff was getting greedy and if it was white fellas who shot him people would assume it was the Cervis who did it. The night your man brought the bomb into the Rose and Crown was the night we were supposed to meet Glenroy Campbell in person. For some reason he never turned up and so got hisself a wee bit longer to live.'

'But why come all the way over here to kill the Campbells?'

'Back in the eighties the Brits tried to flood Belfast with drugs using a bunch of gangsters who were making out they were a paramilitary group calling themselves the IPLO. The influx of drugs caused so much shite and instability that The Boys had to go and shoot eight or nine of them one night; that's a hell of a risky operation around our way with so much RUC and Army about. Those who escaped were put on a plane to London by MI5, that's a fact. As soon as the last ceasefire was called the Brits were at it again. Because of the political situation it was decided it was better to stop things at source; the message comes across loud and clear that way and it doesn't upset things back home.'

'Sorry, Danny, but I can't see what this has got to do with the guys who killed your ol' man.'

'Well, the men who killed him are using the Campbells for the supplying of the drugs. See, there's an element within the British Establishment who are not prepared for a settlement. They are very influential people, not the sort who would gamble with their positions every five years in an election, if you understand me. They still want an IRA surrender, partition, the Croppies back in the bogs and the whole shebang.'

'So you're sayin there's some sort-a plot to destabilize Northern Ireland?'

'That's exactly what I'm saying. But don't get me wrong, I'm talking about influential people outside of the government. Think of it as a scorched-earth policy. If the six counties are going they want to see the place made ungovernable.'

Danny sighed and fell silent, as if his mind had momentarily travelled back to his homeland. He returned with a deep breath and continued,

'Since the Troubles started there has been an element that's backed the loyalist death squads. These are people slightly right of Adolf Hitler; some of them work for MI5 but they come from all different walks of life. One of them is a fella called Sir Philip Parkinson - you wouldn't have met him but he's the man who used to be your gaffer.'

'I have met the man! He's the guy who sacked me!'

'Well, if you're after meeting the bastard you won't be surprised to learn that not only is he the man who's bankrolling the whole affair but he's also behind a plan to arm a few Prod psychopaths in Portadown. To cut a long story short, for quite a few years Parkinson has had the men who murdered my da working for him, and we know he has some sort of links with the Intelligence Service. Before the ceasefire of '94 even the dogs in the street knew it was going to happen but not exactly when.

'Tony McGrady, Martin's brother, had killed a few people in his time including some highfalutin industrialist who was a friend of Parkinson's. Parkinson wanted Tony dead but he didn't want to draw too much shite on his group by doing anything that could have derailed the negotiations going on between The Movement and the British government. So he arranges for some of his men, most of whom are ex-Special Forces, to do the job and make it look like a loyalist spray-job. The more guys who were killed the better - that way, Tony's death would look like a happy by-product of a sectarian murder. And through his links with British Intelligence, Parkinson had no trouble in persuading a loyalist paramilitary group to claim responsibility. To them it was a win-win situation: plenty of glory for killing six Taigs, including a volunteer, and no risk whatsoever.'

I let him shake the awful visions from his mind before I said, 'Hey, Danny, this is heavy-duty information. I mean, how did all of this get found out by you guys?'

'It got found out,' he replied in a flat, matter-of-fact tone. 'You might've seen the man who killed my da around the factory. He's the one who's in charge of this operation to gather all the drugs to send over home. He's a tall, blondy piece of shite with eyes so far back in his head they look like piss-holes in the snow.'

'Yeah, man,' I breathed excitedly, 'his name's Urban.'

Danny smiled to himself. 'Ach, no one knows his real name. They used to call him the "Urban Commando" when he was in Belfast. He did a bit with the SAS and an even shadier gang known as the Green Slime.'

'I had him down as a cop.'

'A killer, that's all he ever was. Now, will I drop you home, Robbie? It's not a problem, you know.'

'Cha! Don't gimme that fuckrees, how can I go now? So what's the plan?'

'A wagon is to collect some sort of weapon they've been creating, like a rocket launcher, and a load of drugs. It's all hidden in machinery. It should be arriving early tomorrow evening and then leaving the factory at precisely nine o'clock. The Urban fella will be there, a couple of his cronies and maybe Parkinson, with a bit of luck. I hope to catch them gathered in the loading bay after the stuff has been put on the wagon. Then I'll stiff the bastards and blow the lorry to pieces while giving praise to Allah.'

The lack of forethought alarmed me. It seemed obvious to me that the security guards would be placed on a state of high-alert while the lorry was in the factory complex. But Danny was so mesmerized by the potential ecstasy of avenging his father, all he could visualize was the moment he pumped bullets into Urban and whoever else was around him.

'Shit, guy - you turn kamikaze or somethin?' I asked him. 'Man, these guys are professional. They are gonna be set in case somethin happen.'

'You told us of a way in, didn't you? I'll be in and out before any of the guards will know what's happened. We'll be out having a drink when the big bang goes off.'

'Was this what Martin planned?'

'More or less.'

'But that was with four men. At least you'd have cover!'

'Well, there's only two now and that'll have to do.'

'Are you scared of dyin, Danny? You'd better be, otherwise I ain't going no place with you, right? Jesus Peace, guy, all you're tellin me sounds like an elaborate way to commit suicide. *Are* you scared of dyin?'

He rubbed his face with his hands. 'I'm tired of living like this, so I am. The monotony of misery, Robbie, it saps everything positive from you. The only thing that's kept me going is the thought of tomorrow night. A life without joy isn't a life worth having. I might laugh for a split second and then I'll remember my da and how I'll never laugh with him again. Every moment of happiness has been taken from me. What happened that day in the bar has poisoned everything for me. To be honest, I don't think I *am* scared of dying any more. But who can say until the moment comes?'

My scalp began to itch. I paced the floor and scratched my head. I desperately wanted to offer an alternative to his recklessness. 'Tell you what,' I said, harried by the pair of expectant eyes that had followed my every step, 'at 8.45 we go to the factory. Once you're through the fence you'll go to the boiler-house that I showed you on the drawing. Once you're inside I will drive the car to the main gate for 8.50. I'll rub some whisky aroun my mouth an' make out I'm drunk an' pissed off. I might crash the barrier or somethin, I ain't sure what exactly, but whatever I do I'm gonna make sure that I draw plenty of attention to myself. I'm gonna try an' stay there but the guards won't let me stay aroun too long an' let's hope they won't wanna call the cops. I'll then drive off but circle aroun to the road nearest to where you'll have cut the fence. If you ain't out by five past then me garn.'

As I finished speaking I instantly regretted making my suggestion: I secretly hoped that Danny would either attempt to dissuade me from taking on such a role or offer an alternative plan of action. 'Christ, that's brilliant,' he said.

Frustrated, I snapped, 'Danny, it ain't nothin like brilliant, it ain't even common sense, but it gives us a slightly better chance of survival. I'm only gonna go through with this if you promise me that you're gonna do everythin you can to make sure that we both come out of this alive. I want us to see my son again.'

He looked out to some distant point. I realized then that my friend had become riddled with something far more malignant than cancer. The only release from his torment was death: the death of the Campbells, of the men who had killed his father, and then finally his own death. My friend had endured the sort of all-consuming pain which can drive a person into madness; it was only the notion of revenge that had enabled him to maintain a tenuous handhold on sanity. As I waited for an answer I prayed that maybe the mention of my son had strengthened that grip or brightened the faint glimmer of a hope that he too might have a son one day.

Finally he turned to me, eyes focused, and said, 'Robbie, I give you my word, I will do everything so we can both see that young wee rascal again. Let's get our heads down, eh? We have a busy day tomorrow.'

'Are you asleep?' he whispered from the bed on the other side of the room.

I let out a tired laugh. 'Yeah, of course I am.'

'How's your ear?'

'Gettin better; the noise has gone from a buzzin to a hummin. It's gettin in the way of my thinkin.'

'What are you thinking about?'

'Lots of things. The Campbells, Eamon an' Kevin, me an' Errol. Those two young guys - man, it's kind-a scary. Their commitment, the way they don't flinch, the way they feed off each other.'

'They're like the way you and Errol used to be.'

'Yeah, I suppose. I was thinkin about the time when me an' Errol were waitin for the cops to come to this industrial estate. Errol asked me if I was nervous an' I told him I was fuckin terrified. But I wasn't, I wasn't scared at all. I just said it 'cause I could see the shooter shakin in his hands. But I was scared the time we went to shoot that councillor an' all those armed cops ran out of his house. We got back to the car an' a cop car started followin us. We got stopped an' I knew Errol was ready to shoot them an' then a van came along, the driver must have been pissed 'cause it hit a parked car. The cops took off after it an' we got away. What scared me about Errol wantin to shoot the cops then is that it wasn't what we had planned, it wasn't what I had pictured when lyin in my bed. I wasn't in control of the situation an' that's what scared me. It's what's scarin me about what you're doin; I ain't in control, it ain't somethin I've planned.'

'It'll be all right. As long as I can get in it'll be all right. It's a good idea for you to make a diversion.'

'That's an idea but it ain't a plan.'

'Trust me, Robbie, it'll be okay.'

Resigned to playing a bigger part in Danny's scheme to avenge his father than I had envisaged, I allowed my eyes to close. In a half-sleep I pictured what might happen at the factory and felt my heartbeat quicken.

'Robbie!'

I woke with a start. 'What?'

'Can I tell you something about what's scaring *me*?'

I said, 'You're gonna tell me anyway, so get on with it.'

'That stuff that's being pushed through your door, about what youse fellas were up to. Somebody must know something.'

'Cha, Danny, me an' Nathan are outta here. Gone as soon as possible. An' I don't even give a thought about it. All I'm thinkin of is this time tomorrow, it'll all be over an' me an' my son will be outta this shithole.'

'I can get you some gear for another identity.'

'Crise Almighty, man, you tryna turn me into The Fugitive?'

'What about after? What happens when they start looking for the man who was at the gate when the shooting started?'

My eyes started to close again. Drowsily I said, 'Don't worry about my business an' concentrate on what you are gonna do. Whatever comes my way I'll deal with it. I always have.'

26

IT WAS EVENING. A dense swirling fog had descended onto the streets. Our progress in the car had been slow, but at 7.30 we had arrived, as planned, at a pub less than a mile from the factory. We sat at a table in a quiet corner. Up until then I had experienced no symptoms of anxiety but now I felt the beginnings of a flutter in my stomach, and a gentle throbbing in my arms and legs. Danny wandered over with another drink. 'Put that down your neck,' he said.

I had barely touched my first drink and yet I felt bloated; the few sips I had taken were only to stop my mouth from drying out completely. When Danny was at the bar I had looked for, but failed to see, any sign of the gun he carried in his waistband. I told him that I didn't want the second gun - I could see no need for it - so he hid it somewhere in the rear of the car.

A young woman, dark-haired and beautiful, was standing at the bar not far from Danny delicately dragging on a cigarette with exquisitely painted red lips. I had watched her since she had made her entrance, poised and graceful. I let my mind wander in a fanciful, but not lustful, way. I wondered about her name and if she could be waiting for someone like me to arrive for a convivial drink after a hard day at work. The way she stood, tall and confident, reminded me of Carmen.

What was Carmen doing now, and had Tim returned to her yet? She hadn't answered when I had telephoned during the afternoon. I had wanted to thank her for getting Nathan to my mother's and to let her know that I was all right. She would have read the newspapers or heard the news bulletins and I felt sure that she would be worrying about my safety.

'Get that down you,' Danny said to me. 'It's almost half past eight.'

The woman drained her glass of the white wine and soda I had heard her order. She folded her newspaper and then put the strap of a bag over her shoulder. She ran a hand through her long hair and smiled at me. 'Bye,' she sang, walking towards the door. I was so surprised that I couldn't manage a reply.

'Do you know her?' asked Danny.

'Never seen her before.'

'Friendly people around here. Come on and finish up the drink and we'll be away. The fog will get no better.'

I glanced at my watch. 'We've got time yet, no point in going in too early.'

Time was rushing by, as it had done since we had left the flat just before noon, not long after I had woken. I had been vaguely aware that Danny had risen much earlier. When I finally left the bedroom I found him still wiping every place with a yellow duster. 'Don't put your maulers on nothing and hop outside,' he warned me. 'We'll get something to eat at a caf or some place.'

I walked to the landing, my vision still blurry. Despite the late hour I was still tired; we must have talked until four or five in the morning. While I had drifted in and out of sleep Danny had gabbled on like a man who was anxious to talk for the sake of talking. His choice of topics was wide and varied; in brief bouts of alertness I could almost hear his mind ticking over at a frantic pace. The only subject he talked of more than once was the war in Ireland. He repeated several times his assertion that no agreement made by politicians could bring peace into people's hearts. I let him talk without interruption; I had seen enough of Northern Ireland to know that no settlement on a piece of paper could ever mop up the hatred swirling around that place. Some hardened hearts were beyond softening.

I had sensed something about the motivation of Eamon and Kevin, that their daily experience in Belfast was an affront to their dignity. Prejudice can either strip the flesh from a person and expose every nerve-ending or it can make the skin hard, calloused and impenetrable. Those two young guys were red-raw. It set them apart, even from a majority of the people who they lived amongst and who endured a similar existence. Dignity is a rarer commodity than a thick skin. Errol and I were once motivated in a way similar to Eamon and Kevin. It was not of our choosing, we had been put into a situation by the murderous actions of the very force that was supposed to protect society. A few years ago, and in separate incidents, two black men had died at the hands of the local police in the space of twelve months. In order to justify what they had done, the cops lied about the men they had killed. When it was proved they were lying they lied again and conjured up every 'black man' stereotype that was ever created. Despite an inquest jury reaching a verdict that one of the men had been unlawfully killed, no one had ever been brought to account.

'Hey, Robbie,' Errol had said to me, 'they've got us black men rated lower than whale shit.' It was a short time later that we took it upon ourselves to look for justice and make the cops think twice before beating a young black man. We looked for vengeance, we laughed and smacked our lips when we read that the cops had been unwilling to reclaim a stolen squad car until the Army had checked it out for booby-traps. We were satisfied too: their caution was a sign that our actions had made them aware that they were now finally accountable for the treatment they meted out.

'Don't you think this fog will delay us?' asked Danny.

I took a sip from my drink. 'Nah, not much. It's a straight road to the factory from here,' I replied. I watched a young man anxiously circle the bar before making a quick exit. He wore a smart suit, had gelled thick hair and looked nothing like me. 'Bye,' I called out after him.

During the afternoon, before the fog came down, Danny and I had gone to the factory and made a final recce. He parked the car and I leant over and pointed out a route across the large piece of derelict ground at the rear of the factory. Danny's eyes widened excitedly, I could see how he could barely restrain himself. All he had dreamt of was almost within his grasp. He put the car in gear. 'Let's go get some grub,' he said.

We spent a couple of hours in a pizza parlour - as much as you could eat for a fiver a head. I nibbled and he devoured. Danny had bought a copy of a national daily as well as an early edition of the local evening newspaper and we took turns to survey the pages of photographs and reports of the shooting.

'Where's the fucking justice, eh?' snarled Danny. 'A bunch of gangsters get stiffed and it's all over the place like it's some fucking tragedy because it happens in an English city street. And what coverage did my da and those five men in Belfast get? A couple of paragraphs next to some floozie showing off her tits. Where is the fucking justice?'

The media were as one in depicting the shooting as the culmination of the feud between the Campbells and the Brothers of Islam. I could hardly believe it when I read that a detective had said that it was a strong possibility that the man who had been taken from one of the cars was Malek Abu Bakr. I pointed at the paragraph for Danny to read. 'I'm gettin worried,' I whispered. 'I'm startin to think like a cop. I was thinkin if anyone grassed me up I would tell them that I had been mistaken for a Muslim.'

Danny grunted knowingly. 'It's round up the usual suspects time. Ach, we should have known the peelers were too stupid to work out that they were meant to go after the Cervis. They're just looking for an excuse to break up the Muslim business. Who's going to claim harassment now?'

He handed me back the paper and got on with his pizza, as if totally unperturbed by anything he had read. I knew, like me, he had drained every drop of compassion from his heart.

The newspapers made much of the Campbells' long and lurid criminal careers. A policeman confirmed that they had been considered the city's main drugs dealers - but there had never been enough evidence to put them behind bars for long. There was also strong suspicion of Glenroy's involvement in at least four murders. 'Four?' I muttered. 'Cha, those bastards ended a lot more lives than that, an' this guy was runnin around as free as a bird. You're right, where is the fuckin justice?'

'In the barrel of a gun,' Danny replied without hesitation. He pointed with his fork to the stop press on the back page. It read: *Fifth victim of gangland gun attack dies in hospital.* 'Another one bites the dust,' he chuckled darkly.

For an instant I had wanted to ask Danny if he thought we were really the good guys, but I resisted.

Maybe I had only wanted him to spout the justification that I had given to myself a thousand times over. I wanted to be a good guy; I loved my kid, my mom, and I had loved Carmen. That none of my actions had been motivated by personal gain provided me with some vindication. Bad guys like Daddy One-foot had never loved anyone but themselves; life for men like him was just one brutal self-gratification kick. The misery people like the Campbells caused was something I had seen too much of and I detested it. I felt pleased that I had played a small part in putting a stop to them. I knew what I had done was right.

Maybe the way my life had turned out was due to too much empathy. I had once had the overdeveloped sense of community I saw in Eamon and Kevin. Would they retain their idealism? I wondered. Were they already aware that all the people they called 'their people' did not have their virtue or dignity? Blouse an' skirt! If all 'their people' were the good guys then they'd all have a full set of kneecaps. If the people who shared my background were all paragons of virtue there wouldn't be a number of them laid out on mortuary slabs with multiple bullet wounds.

'Come on, Robbie, it's time to go.'

I took a mouthful of drink and followed Danny out of the pub with it dribbling from my lips. He tossed me the keys. 'You drive,' he said.

The light from the factory's bright halogen lamps oozed into the surrounding fog like spots of yellow ink on grey blotting paper. 'Do you think you'll be able to find your way back to the car?' I asked Danny.

'I'll get back all right,' he answered.

A silence followed. I peered out at the derelict ground he was to cross but I could see no further than a few paces.

'Danny, a change of plan,' I said.

'Too fucking late for that now, Robbie.'

'Hang on. We'll keep the car here, with the keys under the seat, just in case you have to get out fast. I'll go aroun to the main gate on foot an' kick up a fuss. If I find the car is gone when I get back here I'll know you had to leave in a hurry an' I'll meet you at the petrol station across the road from the pub.'

'Ach, it's all sounding a wee bit complicated now. If I have to leave a bit sharpish I'd rather you were sitting in the car waiting for me. Forget the diversion business - once I'm in they won't find me.'

My heart missed a beat as I heard the words I had wanted him to say when I first told him of my plan. Conscience made me say, 'Then I'll come with you to the fence an' make sure that you get in.'

'If you want to, but there's no need.'

He got out and put the pistol into his waistband again. I went to the boot and took out the black holdall which contained the bomb and a pair of wire cutters. Danny smiled as he took the bag from me. 'I remember you saying that watching is much harder than doing the fighting.'

Watching Danny walk into the factory alone would be much harder than he could imagine.

We set off across the derelict ground and weaved our way through the rubble towards the blurry spots of light. My pulse began to quicken. It wasn't like walking with Errol, for in those days I had my mind set on only one deadly intention - no other idea or doubt was entertained. But with every step I took with Danny a whole jumble of conflicting emotions tried to crowd in on me.

Sensing Danny's suppressed excitement as he closed in for the kill I remembered the strange look of pleasure I had seen in Errol's eyes as he had pumped three bullets into the prostrate figure of Beresford Samuels, and I had seen evidence of the same twisted delight in those bulbous eyes of Glenroy Campbell as he looked at me. For some the impulse to kill for pleasure is buried deep under layers of morality and civilized culture, for others civilization is only the thinnest of veneers, but the bloodlust is always there. To a lesser extent, I had seen it in the eyes of some of those who gathered at the ringside; they didn't want art or sport - only blood. Real blood and not the Hollywood pretend stuff. And I had wilfully experienced that same lust and taken pleasure in seeing five bad guys dispatched to the morgue. And yet at the same time the sight of their blood had repulsed me.

I had set out to kill, I had witnessed killing and, though I was reluctant to admit it, those experiences had heightened my joy of living. While giving thanks for every day since and noting that my every sense had been sharpened, I had pretended my new perspective had been due to Nathan and that I could now love with a passion. In truth, any love of life I possessed had been tainted; its origins lay in the squalid shedding of blood.

My eyes were firmly fixed to the few feet of ground ahead of us as the curtain of fog withdrew in time with our steps. Not-too-distant voices halted us and then moved us in the direction of a wild scraggly shrub which eked a life from the surrounding debris. We peered into the yellow haze on the other side of the wire fencing and watched as a pair of dark figures slowly emerged. They dissolved within seconds, only for the hoarse panting of a dog straining on its leash to warn us of the impending emergence of other shapes. 'Blouse an' skirt,' I hissed, 'I told you they'd put on extra security. You sure you wanna go through with this?'

'Stop talking bollocks and give me the cutters.'

'Not here,' I whispered. 'We'll get closer to the boiler-house an' put the hole near one of the fuel tanks. It'll be harder for anyone to see that way.'

We scrambled in the direction of the tanks, unsure of their exact location until we were almost next to them. Danny took the cutters and began to snip away at the chain-link fence. Every severed strand rattled with such a loudness I thought the guards were bound to come. But no one did. Danny pushed the bag through the hole. 'You sure you know your way? Do you want me to come in with you?' I asked.

'I'll find the bastards, no sweat.'

'Hey, with all these extra guards I think I'd better go aroun to the front an' make that diversion.'

He nodded and squeezed my arm. 'Okay,' he said, 'if you want to. At five-to I'll make my move. See you later.'

I wanted to snarl: 'No, I don't want to, you crazy ras,' but mindful of our superstitious ritual, I said, 'Yeah, later, Danny.'

Within moments Danny was a misty shape closing in on the boiler-house door. I walked back into the fog. The trouble I had in keeping my footing was mostly due to the warm, pulsing weakness running through my legs rather than the unevenness of the ground. Part of me argued that I should have insisted on going into the factory with him but a cooler, more rational side told me that creating a diversion was about the best thing I could do for Danny - short of not letting him go ahead with what he had planned in the first place.

From experience, I knew how meticulous the planning should be for an action like this. Danny's scheme lacked precision; he had too much reliance on good fortune for my liking, as though the simple justness of his cause would be enough for him to achieve his objectives. His idea that the men he wanted to kill would all be gathered in the loading bay to wave the lorry goodbye bordered on a psychotic delusion. I should have gone in with him, or talked him out of going in. I should have done something more. Or nothing at all.

As I stepped from the derelict ground and onto the pavement I picked up one of the many old weathered bricks that were strewn around the place. A glance at my watch told me there were three long minutes to wait before I would start with my diversion. It also occurred to me that one brick would not create a big enough disturbance to give Danny much time or space. I stepped back onto the rough ground and began a frantic search for something else. At first glance it looked like a stick but on bending down I saw it was a metal rod. I pulled it from the debris and found it was almost as long as me.

I ran the length of the chain-link fence and turned a corner. The bright lights ahead of me illuminated the main entrance. I slowed down and made a vain attempt to control my breathing as the thought of failure and its terrible repercussions loomed large in my mind. But like Danny, I fixed my mind on the one chance in a thousand that this crazy scheme would work and that we would both emerge unscathed. I forced my leaden feet to move again.

My arms and legs were aching as I neared the booth at the factory's gates. A guard in one of the kiosks stared out at me for an instant before he pivoted away with his arms clasped protectively around his head as the brick crashed through the window in front of him. I thrust the metal rod through the glass of the door. I could see the guard crouching on the floor shouting into his radio handset. Reinforcements would soon be arriving. I moved back towards the road and broke another window. My attempt at a diversion had worked better than I had dared to hope. Within seconds at least ten guards, and a dog, were running from the direction of the factory. 'Keep back, you fuckin bastards!' I roared.

I thrashed the road with the metal bar as they lined up in front of me. The dog was up on its hind legs barking at such a pitch it was as though it was beseeching its handler to be let off the leash. I swung the rod in a slow wide arc to keep them at bay. I yelled, 'Those are a bunch of murderin bastards you work for!'

They remained threateningly silent as they edged forward.

I had hung around for long enough; it was only the thought of the dog snapping at my heels which stopped me from running away. 'Keep back!' I shouted.

A thud on the back of my neck sent me face-first to the ground and it took a moment for me to realize what had happened. The hungry growl of the dog had me turning onto my side. I could see nothing but slobbering fangs coming towards my face. I lashed out with a foot and the dog caught hold of the end of my trousers. The Rottweiler snarled and shook its head violently as it pulled me across the slippery tarmac. My other foot crashed against its throat and the dog released its grip. It was back on its hind legs, twisting and turning with a crazed savagery, pleading for another go at me.

The dog was pulled away. A sharp dig to my ribs drove the air out of me. I tried vainly to take in more oxygen as the man with the dented nose, who had once confronted me in the washroom, stared down. There was a pistol in his hand. He kicked me again and said, 'Remember me, Mr Walker? One wrong move and I'll happily blow your head off. Now slowly, on your feet.'

27

LOUD VOICES ECHOED around the factory's outer walls and the sound of trampling feet filled the air. Hard rubber heels cracked against my shins as I ran, jostled and prodded, in the midst of half a dozen security men. Despite the dizziness the blow to my neck had caused me, I was alert enough to realize that a few broken windows at the main gate was not the cause of so much excitement. One of the guards pulled open the door of the boiler-house and two of the others pushed me inside.

The whites of Danny's eyes shining out from a mask of crimson were the first things I saw. He was kneeling on the floor, a man standing over him. Someone kicked at the back of my legs and forced me to my knees. The man, disappointed, asked, 'Is this the only one?'

'The only one we found.'

'Shit!' growled the man as he tugged at Danny's hair. 'Where is he - where's McGrady?'

'I don't know who the fuck youse boys are on about,' answered Danny. A punch smacked against his cheek but he had anticipated the blow and turned his head as it landed; he grunted, with painful surprise, when a second punch struck him to send blood and a broken tooth flying from his torn lips.

A man in bomber jacket and jeans hauled Danny back to his knees and pressed the muzzle of a pistol onto the side of his head. 'Where's McGrady, you arsehole? Where the fuck is he?'

'I don't know the man,' mumbled Danny.

The man looked over to me. 'What you staring at, cunt?' He took a swipe at me with his pistol. I moved my head and he missed but there was nothing I could do to avoid the blows of booted feet that came at me from behind. More frenzied blows thumped against me as I rolled myself into a protective ball. The men were yelling maniacally as kicks and punches rained down on me from every direction. Confused by the shouts and fearful of the blows, I felt my brain rattle in my skull as the feet hit my arms which were wrapped around my head. It took a while for me to realize that the attack had halted as suddenly as it had begun.

Not daring to move, I heard the men's laboured breathing and then the yelling restarted. Dull thuds. Screaming. I peered through the gap between my elbows to see five or six men descending onto Danny like a pack of ravenous hyenas.

'Hold it!' someone shouted. Cold air rolled along the floor from the open door. I didn't move and all I could see of him were shoes and the turn-ups of his trousers. I knew it was Urban. 'Get them on their feet,' he said.

Urban examined Danny's face and then turned round to me. His head jerked back. 'Mr Walker, well, well. I did say we would meet again.' The small smile fell away and his voice turned brittle with anger as he added, 'Why don't you save you and your friend a lot of discomfort and tell us where Martin McGrady is.'

It flashed into my mind that I should deny that I knew Danny or anything to do with him. 'I never heard of any Martin McGrady,' I said.

'Then would you tell me what you are doing here?'

I drew a breath and looked defiantly into Urban's deep-set eyes. 'Payin you bastards back for sackin me but most of all for killin my two friends.'

He frowned. 'Payback for two friends?' The man in the bomber jacket opened the black holdall and showed Urban its contents. 'With this?' he asked me.

I nodded.

The man growled, 'The coon's giving us bullshit.'

'Maybe... maybe not, Clive, but let's listen to what he has to say.' To me he said, 'And who are these two friends we are supposed to have killed?'

'Those two old guys you lot found snoopin around the small workshop - Jack Reardon and Cecil Robinson.'

Urban threw back his head and laughed. 'That,' he chuckled, 'is the funniest thing I've heard in a long time. For a moment I thought you were talking about somebody else. No, Mr Walker, no one here had anything to do with the deaths of those two old men. I'd say it was joyriders.'

'He's giving us bullshit,' snapped the man called Clive. 'What's he doing with this Irish bastard?'

I opened my mouth to reply but Urban beat me to it. 'Oh, I think I know. His name must be Daniel Maguire and he and Mr Walker have been acquainted since 1983. Maguire even took Mr Walker to Belfast for a visit in September 1985.' He smirked and tilted his head in my direction. 'Am I right?'

Taken by surprise, I said, 'Maybe.'

'Tell them fuckin nothing!' roared Danny, only to receive a punch to his stomach for his trouble.

Urban halted any further punches or questions from his friend Clive by simply raising his hand. Testily, he told him to take me to his office. We both knew that he had made a mistake by questioning me in Danny's presence.

'Robbie,' called Danny as I reached the doorway, 'about that rotten tooth you were telling me about… these fellas are after fixing it for me. See you later, all right?'

'Later,' I called back hopefully.

The factory was an eerily quiet place at night. Idle machines and their shadows took on intimidating shapes. I led the way through the main workshop, past the washroom with a tap which dripped loudly in the stillness and then past the clock and card racks and up the metal stairs to the office where I had first met Urban. I thought of what was happening to Danny with every clanging footfall.

Clive stood in stony silence after he had made me sit in a chair by the desk until the man with the dented nose entered and told him to go to the loading bay. 'Nothing moves,' he muttered.

I knew it was past nine o'clock but resisted looking at either my watch or the clock on the wall in case I gave any signal that I knew what they were talking about.

'Have you called the cops?' I asked once we were alone.

He pinched the top of his dented nose and looked to the floor while shaking his head. I thought he was laughing at the absurdity of my question when suddenly there was a gun at my head. 'Shut your mouth,' he said, 'and speak when you're spoken to, okay?'

'Okay,' I said.

Like the rest of the men he was jumpy, and consequently very dangerous. I gazed down at my knees while hoping that I had said enough in the boiler-house to sow doubt in Urban's mind about our reasons for being at the factory. They had obviously delayed the lorry's departure but it could not stay in the loading bay until the morning, it would lead to too many questions.

But if there was a possibility that I had put doubt into Urban's mind, what he had said to me had definitely put questions into mine. How had he known of the year I had first met Danny and our trip to Belfast? Who did he think I was talking about when I accused him of killing two of my friends?

I thought I knew the answers.

The office door opened and my heart began to thump. Urban stepped in. His expression was grim, he had a gun in his hand. He saw my alarm and said, 'No need to worry about Mr Maguire. Like you, he is sitting down while we wait for a call. Would you like a drink? Tea or coffee?'

I refused with a shake of the head. The man with the dented nose brought in a polystyrene cup of hot coffee. 'Thanks, Chopper,' said Urban. 'You can wait outside, okay?'

Urban sat down and casually put the pistol onto the desk before he took out a folder stuffed with papers from one of the drawers.

'Are they those forms you wanted me to fill?' I asked.

He scratched the skin under his chin. 'No. But I think you will find them interesting reading.' He took a pack of cigarettes from his pocket. 'Smoke?'

'Nah, I don't.'

'Sign of weakness, smoking,' he said as he pushed the folder my way. When I hesitated he urged me on. 'Go on, take a look. We have plenty of time.'

As soon as I began to sift through the pile of papers I saw that the name of Errol Morgan loomed large in amongst the often badly typed script. Urban rose from his chair and began to circle the room. For a time I was barely conscious of his presence as I read of Errol's activities: times and dates of where he had slept; the places where his Sound had played; the times he had worked out at the gym. I also read names of guys I only half remembered who were in his Sound or who regularly attended the blues parties and the clubs where Errol had played. Some of the sheets were surveillance logs which gave an account of his movements for about the period of one month. The records ceased a week before the two of us had gone looking for a man called the Field Marshal. In amongst the various times and places one address took me by surprise: it was Carmen's.

Errol had stayed with her for four nights running not long before he died.

A curt, contemptuous snort escaped from me. Bitch! How could she have pretended that way with me? She had told me that she hadn't let a man through her door and into her bed since Wesley. She had told me that Tim was a mistake, a result of a teenage hormonal urge and that she had never loved Errol. Crise Almighty, no wonder Tim hated me. Less than two weeks before Errol died the poor kid was probably dreaming of a reconciliation between his mom and dad. I looked at the dates and times again in case I had been mistaken. No, there was no mistake, Errol and Carmen had shared four long nights together shortly before he died. My eyes were smarting as I turned the pages over.

'Ah, yes,' said Urban, looking over my shoulder, 'Gilbert Peters, more commonly known as Hanimal. Never really knew his father. Poor school record, a short spell in borstal. One job since he had left school, lasted five weeks. Unmarried, a dozen or more kids with various women who were invariably losers much like himself. He didn't do anything with his life until he tagged along with Errol Morgan.'

'If you say so.'

'It's not me who says so, it's what the police and Security Service records say. It's all there in black and white. There's also something about Conrad Williams - don't you remember me asking you about him?'

'Nah.'

'Well I did, but as it was shortly after you were fired, I suppose it's understandable that you have no recollection. To refresh your memory: for two years a group of black militants carried out a number of attacks on members of the police service. After the endeavours of the local CID and Special Branch failed to apprehend the gang, the Security Service became involved. After the bomb near the courthouse, the one with the anti-handling device, almost killed an innocent passerby, a certain MI5 officer took it upon himself to eradicate the gang. Because of the repercussions, possible martyrdom, cause célèbre, et cetera, a black terrorist gang could not be allowed to go to trial after so much work had been done to deny its existence. Three men were identified as the gang members: Errol Morgan, Gilbert Peters and Conrad Shaka Williams. I was given the job to find and kill them.'

Urban lit another cigarette and from the corner of my eye I watched blue smoke funnel from his nose. But despite what he had told me and the ominous edge to his voice I felt like laughing out loud with relief. I no longer cared what Carmen had done with Errol or that Danny and I were in immediate and grave danger: I had just been given the answer to the question that had clawed at the frayed edges of my mind for the past two years. I almost felt at peace.

He took his seat and we sat in silence until he finished smoking. I was aware that I was in the presence of an evil intelligence, not unlike Glenroy Campbell but far more intense and calculating. He said, 'That was my job, killing people. I killed my first man when I was twenty-two, almost twenty years ago. And up until very recently I had thought nothing about the men I had killed; every single one of them was a bad man. Now I envy them. I always prided myself on doing a good, tidy job when dispatching people. They had it quick and clean whereas I shall have a much slower, tortuous demise.'

'Errol an' Hanimal didn't have it quick an' clean,' I objected.

He got to his feet again. 'It was a messy job all round,' he said, sounding almost apologetic, 'not one that I'm proud of. But in my defence, I didn't have the access to the information that's sitting in front of you, back then. The plan was not mine. Morgan and Peters were lured to a disused dairy with the promise of a pair of Kalashnikov assault rifles. For some reason Morgan had second thoughts, and after he told a third party to enter the dairy on foot he and Peters drove on. Some short time later he got out of his car and shot and killed a friend of mine who was in a cut-off position at the end of the lane. But Morgan still managed to have a quick death; he had been shooting at our vehicle with a pump-action shotgun when he was thrown out of the car and died instantly. Peters wasn't so fortunate and was trapped in the car as it caught fire. Shaka Williams proved to be quite a resilient fellow. We questioned him about the involvement of any other person for more than four hours. He didn't tell us anything. In the alleyway I took the gag out of his mouth and gave him one final chance to give me a name of any other member of the gang. I lied and told him a name would save his life. He was out of his mind with terror; he couldn't speak or even beg for mercy. And then I killed him.'

I was vaguely aware of what Urban was up to. A few bits of information my way, an attempt at sounding regretful and several pauses and implicit invitations for me to offer the words which would fill in the gaps. I shrugged my shoulders.

While listening to Urban pace the room behind me, I felt the first twinge of regret about Shaka. We had never been friends but he had known of my involvement and yet he hadn't betrayed me. It wasn't what I would have expected from him. From what Tyrone and Urban had told me it seemed as though Errol and Hanimal had been betrayed by an informer.

During all the time Urban walked around the office his gun had remained on the desk, almost within my grasp. I sensed a trap had been set.

He picked up several of the papers, scanned them and, as if it had only then crossed his mind, he retrieved his pistol. 'It is loaded,' he said in response to the derisive curl on my lip. He began to mention dates and places of a number of attacks on police patrols. Occasionally he would look up with a disapproving frown. He turned a page and read out a report which seemed very mundane in comparison. After a short time it became apparent that Urban was reading a report of Errol's movements from someone who had been given the code-name Tarot. A ridiculous name, I thought. The details were, in the main, places, dates and names of people who Errol had talked about in the few weeks before he died.

He tossed the report onto the desk in front of me. 'This Tarot was the person who introduced your friends to the man who offered them the Kalashnikovs. As soon as Morgan expressed an interest in them he as good as signed his own death warrant. He and the rest of the gang were to have driven into the dairy, the man who led them there would have hopped out and we would have shot them to pieces. A small amount of cocaine was to have been sprinkled in the car just to provide the police with a motive for three dead black men in the middle of the English countryside. Their prejudices confirmed, they would have looked no further.'

'Bullshit!' I snapped. 'This is fantasy, man. You been on a creative writin course or somethin?'

'Tyrone Swaby didn't think so when he received the copy I sent him.' He raised the pistol and pointed it at me. 'I know that Conrad Shaka Williams was not a terrorist. When Swaby joined the Brothers of Islam I first suspected that he was the man who had escaped execution. I sent him copies of old press cuttings and then the report. He reacted, but not in the way I had hoped. And then I knew he was not the man I had been looking for. Then my attention turned to you.'

'Bloodclart, you're fuckin crazy, man. Why send this nonsense to us two - 'cause we were the nearest available niggers?'

His face curdled with detestation. 'Niggers? How can you use a word like that? I thought you a bigger man than that, Mr Walker. In many ways I respect you and I've seen too many men opened up with their guts strewn over the ground to let my actions be motivated by the colour of a thin layer of flesh. What brought the pair of you to my attention was the incident which led to Swaby's dismissal. On going through his file I came across his school record, that he himself had supplied, and saw that he attended the same school as Morgan. I knew you two were friends and I then checked your records and discovered that you were also a schoolmate of Errol Morgan.'

'So?'

'So one of you was the man who sometimes kept me awake at night. The anti-handling device was a clever piece of engineering made by someone who had access to machinery. That someone was not Shaka Williams - he possessed neither the intelligence nor the means to produce such a device. Revenge, Mr Walker - that and lust are two of the most potent forces known to man.' Urban paused and looked straight through me. His voice rose to a high pitch. 'And I wanted revenge for the death of a good friend, the man who was killed by Errol Morgan. Don't misunderstand me, I didn't particularly want you dead. I wanted you to kill the MI5 man who had planned the whole affair, whose inept planning meant that my friend was needlessly sacrificed. I thought it would have a nice ironic twist if the person who was permitted to live by a man's gross ineptitude was the one to come back and kill him.'

'Then let me an' Danny go.'

He was staring into space again. 'Too late, it's too late.'

I thought he had offered a slim chance of escape. 'How would I have found this man, know what he looks like an' that?'

Urban smirked as if he had read my mind. 'What does it matter now? It's too late.'

I leant back into my chair. 'Too late for what? Cha, this is all a load of fuckrees. I ain't the mysterious third or fourth or fuckin fifth man you are lookin for.'

A triumphant gleam lit up the deep dark eyes and I immediately knew that he had manoeuvred me into a position where I would find myself in checkmate. 'Then, Mr Walker, if you are not the terrorist I have been looking for, what is the real reason for you being here tonight?'

I didn't reply. There was not anything I could say without incriminating myself: if I hadn't been the terrorist he was searching for then how was it I was now taking part in a scheme using explosives? Either I had been a terrorist who, with the aid of a friend, was now using a knowledge of bombs to exact revenge on a former employer; or I had returned to the factory for another reason, to assist a friend in stopping a lorry travelling to Ireland, perhaps. At that moment I felt outsmarted and vulnerable.

Urban, or the men who worked for him, had obviously watched my house over the weeks and had toyed with me. The confrontation in the washroom with Kyle and the other two men had probably been staged by Urban to test my reactions under stress, to see if I had the stuff to kill the MI5 man he wanted dead. Because of luck, or misfortune, I had unwittingly brought his game to a premature end.

'I'm going to leave you for a while,' he said, his voice barely more than a whisper, 'and while I'm away let's pretend that you were once a terrorist and that you, unlike Tyrone Swaby, can deduce the identity of the person who betrayed your friends. The answer is in the report lying in front of you. I watched you at work in the factory figuring out what was wrong with machines in a sequential and logical fashion. See this as a final puzzle for you to solve.'

28

ALTHOUGH I COULD hear nothing but the gentle hum of the fluorescent strip-light, I could sense the presence of someone standing outside the office door. 'Can I have a drink?' I called. No answer came back.

I returned to the chair and after a time my eyes were drawn; not to the report that Urban had left in front of me but to the other papers that were halfway out of the folder. I pulled the flap of the folder towards me and began to read. The small, insignificant details about Errol's actions and travels moved me; in reading them I felt as though I was reliving a life. I read the short report of Tarot introducing Errol to someone codenamed Viking. The offer of the AK-47s was its main topic and it ended with a claim that Errol said that he would have to consult with 'other members of the organization'.

The term 'organization' made me smile; it was just like Errol to try and sound grand and important. I did recall that he had come to me about the offer of the guns but, not taking him seriously, I had dismissed the idea. Still mindful of our narrow escape from the armed cops who had lain in wait for us in the councillor's home, I had come up with another plan which did not require us to put ourselves at such great risk. A change of tactics was needed, I told Errol as I showed him the four parcel bombs I had constructed. They were to be sent to a Chief Constable, a Divisional Commander whose men had killed two innocent guys, and a pair of local Tory politicians who thought demonizing black men was a legitimate political strategy.

Only the bomb to the Chief Constable which exploded in a sorting office, as Eamon and Kevin would say 'made *News at Ten*' - but it was reported as the work of the IRA. I took that as some sort of compliment.

Of the other bombs which did not receive national publicity, a second one went off while sitting on a Superintendent's desk and slightly wounded the civilian secretary who was walking away from it; the other two devices were destroyed in controlled explosions by an Army bomb squad.

In a period of ten days, between the sending of the bombs and his death, Errol had not only put three bullets into the drug dealer known as the Field Marshal, he had also made a second contact with a Security Service agent called Viking and said that he wanted the Kalashnikovs. My anger at his impetuosity and the rejection of my advice brought me to my feet and I swept the papers to the floor. 'Idyat! We had got away with all of it!' I shouted at his printed name.

What I had read of the papers so far told me that Errol had been looked at by the cops, probably Special Branch, and MI5 but then dismissed as a possible terrorist suspect. Nothing unusual in that; many young black men had been picked up for questioning during that time. Looking at it in print it was so obvious that the offer of the AK-47s was a trap. Errol had possessed a keen sense of self-preservation and was always wary of possible informers, but why did he go back for the Kalashnikovs? *Why?*

The report that Urban had left for me to read had remained on the table. 'Any chance of a cup of tea?' I called out to the unseen sentry. There was no answer and I kicked at the door in frustration. I was uncomfortably warm, my mouth and throat felt dry. A look at the clock on the wall told me it was half-past eleven. It needed a check of my watch before I could believe that I had been alone in the office for so long.

I scratched at my itchy skin. Urban had left me to stew in - if not pick over - the entrails of the past. Each passing second had become a physical weight which pressed down on me; even my teeth began to ache. The paper on the desk he had left for me continued to beckon until I wearily sat down to read.

It was tiresome reading, most of it banal and repetitious. It wasn't until the paragraph in which Errol had hinted to Tarot about his involvement in the attacks on the cops that it became interesting. But I could not see anything which gave away the identity of the informer, except that someone had got close enough to gain Errol's confidence. Yet Tyrone had read the same report and concluded that *I* was the one who had betrayed Errol and Hanimal! I re-read the report from the beginning and then it dawned on me why Tyrone had reached that conclusion: nowhere in the report had my name featured during the period just before Errol died - and yet I was supposed to be his best friend. Tyrone's name was not mentioned either, but that could not have registered with him because he knew that he wasn't the one who had informed on Errol. My stomach heaved and I clamped a hand over my mouth as the acidic taste of vomit touched my tongue. The identity of the informer shone out at me from between every line and forever tainted with treachery the love she had shown me.

The whiteness of the paper became a blur and I puked onto the carpet. As the vomit hit the floor I hoped the thoughts in my mind would be ejected with it. The door opened and Urban stepped in. He looked down to the regurgitated mess and said 'So, you figured it out.'

I wiped my lips. 'Yeah. But it ain't nothin I would-a go kill a man for. I think you will have to kill that MI5 man yourself.'

'What if I had sent you what he had done and said to her?'

'I don't think so.'

'What if I had told you he had threatened to have the body of her baby daughter exhumed and that he would pay her former lover to allege foul-play and press for a second inquest?'

'What's done is done, an' there ain't no undoin, seen?'

'So despite the man ordering the death of your friends, despite the fact that he was prepared to go to any lengths to eradicate the lot of you, you bear him no malice.'

'I wouldn't say that,' I said, teeth clenched. 'I just don't think I would kill him for you, Mr Urban.'

'Would you kill *her?*'

'I'm tired of seein people gettin killed.'

'But not so tired that you would not blow up your former place of work.'

'That's different, I was lookin to damage property. We were plannin to give a warnin so no one got hurt.'

He waved the gun. 'And what was your Irish friend doing with this, about to start a three-legged race?'

'To scare people off in case we got rumbled.'

'But you're an intelligent man, you avoided the best efforts of the police to catch you for almost two years. I was there that time they almost caught you, you know.'

I bristled at his smarmy tone. 'No, I don't know.'

As though weary of my denials, Urban sighed and said, 'Yes, it was that time you and Morgan almost walked straight into a police trap. We had been scanning police communications when we heard of a bomb alert on the other side of the city and I said to Bill, "That's a decoy, the silly buggers are going for the councillor." Surely you should have seen that all his rantings in the local press were bait to lure you to his place.'

'You got me mixed up with someone else.'

'We got there a little late and their trap had been sprung but then we heard that a squad car was following a vehicle carrying black men. I saw the cars had stopped and glanced my van off a parked car. I managed to shake off the patrol cars after a mile or two. I later heard the police went looking for the car they had originally tailed and arrived at the house of a member of the British Legion who had been tucked up in bed that night. Very clever, I thought, you had obviously thought to put the registration number of a similar make and model onto your own car.

'It's the sort of intelligence I can admire: staying close to your enemy but still thwarting their attempts to find you. And yet you are trying to take me for a fool by telling me that you planned it for your Irish friend to plant a bomb while you made a scene at the gate. Hardly the best way to avoid detection. In fact, I would say, from what I know of you, it was an action totally out of character. I don't believe for a moment that what has gone on here tonight was planned by you. I think Maguire and Martin McGrady cajoled you into taking part in their madcap scheme. Come on, Mr Walker, tell me about them and you might get out of this unharmed. Tell me how they knew I was here.'

I remembered the offer he had made to Shaka in the alleyway and saw the redness around his knuckles: Danny had not been persuaded to talk. 'Tell you what, Mr Urban, life has made you into a conspiracy freak. Things are sometimes more simple and stupid than we'd like to think. So, I made a stupid mistake, we all do. I was angry about the way I got fired an' wasn't thinkin straight. Why don't you call the cops an' let me explain to them?'

'Oh, you have definitely made a mistake, Mr Walker. But if you won't tell me the real reason for why you're here with Maguire, tell me why you took it upon yourself to wage war on the police - the same police you now seem so anxious to talk to. I know there was speculation that your actions were linked to the deaths in custody of two black men, but there is no record of you even knowing either man. Were your actions really motivated by the deaths of two total strangers?'

I wanted to explain that any man who has experienced being labelled as 'black' can never view another man who is categorized in the same way as a total stranger - but the urge to deny him the opportunity of having his curiosity satisfied was greater. 'Mr Urban, I don't know what the fuck you are talkin about.'

His face hardened instantly. 'On your feet,' he snarled, 'we're going for a walk.'

We went down the metal stairs and then back along the route I had taken from the boiler-house. In the factory a sadness pressed in on me. I was sad, not angry, that Carmen had been the informer. Looking back, certain little things about her that seemed so inconsequential at the time were now illuminated as acts of a guilty conscience. But even during the times when we were naked and sharing our deepest thoughts she had never once hinted about her act of treachery. I had known several men, robbers mostly, who had spent time in prison because of their inability not to talk about their crimes with the person with whom they were most intimate. I imagined as he lay with her that Errol had talked in a similar way. And as I had always thought: women were strong in a way a man could never be. Carmen had been clever too in the manner in which she had covered her tracks.

I guessed that it was the MI5 man who had wrongly told her of her brother's involvement in the death of the Field Marshal, probably as a means to ensure that she would continue to work for him as an informer. Carmen had sought to protect Tyrone and in not mentioning my name when passing on information about Errol she had also done the same for me.

Once outside, the fog closed in around me and seeped through my skin; its coldness touched my heart. Urban was behind me; the feeling of him watching me with those eyes of his put my insides thrashing against my ribs. The muscles in my neck began to knot with the expectation of a bullet.

My legs were drained of all strength by the time I reached the boiler-house. I opened the door to be greeted by the loud hum of the burners, the smell of fuel oil and the sight of Danny, his head bowed, kneeling in the middle of the floor. There were no uniformed guards about, only four men dressed in similar bomber jackets and denim jeans. And there was Kyle, the bald-headed Ulsterman, pacing to and fro and looking more menacing than ever.

Two of the sturdy-looking guys were standing close behind Danny, each with a hand pressing down on his shoulders. The other pair took me by the arms and roughly forced me down onto my knees beside him. Danny moved his head slightly and made a small smile. 'Sorry about this, Robbie,' he said weakly, 'but I think the shit is about to hit our wee fans.'

My blood ran ice-cold. I knew he was telling me to prepare to die. From the corner of my eye I could see him mouthing silent prayers. On so many occasions I had envisaged my own death and prepared myself for it. There had been times I had imagined that I might blow myself to pieces while putting down a bomb designed to kill a cop but I had never readied myself for anything like this. I had insisted to myself that my death was going to be something heroic and not something so squalid and meaningless. No, I had never pictured this.

The disfigured face of Beresford Samuels flashed in front of my eyes. I swore. What was that piece of shit begging for mercy doing in my mind? To get rid of him I said to God, 'Send me to hell but look after Nathan and don't let me start bawling. Don't let me piss myself, Jesus.'

God wasn't listening. I felt the muscles around my waist begin to loosen and the thought of Nathan put the sting of salty water in my eyes. The door opened and two men stepped in. One of them was in uniform, a chauffeur's uniform, the other in a heavy camel-hair coat. I immediately recognized him as Sir Philip Parkinson. His pink fleshy face looked more flushed than usual. He strode towards Danny and me and pulled a face as if he were surveying two outsize turds. 'Oh, it's you,' he sneered while looking down at me. If my mouth wasn't so dry I would have spat into his face.

Urban said, 'As I said on the phone, Sir Philip, I fear our operation may have been compromised. That one is Daniel Maguire. I executed his father in Belfast two years ago - he was an associate of the PIRA terrorist, Anthony McGrady.'

Parkinson set his jaw grimly. 'I remember it well,' he said. 'It was a job well done.'

An uncontrollable tremor started in my bowels and worked its way down my legs. The fact that he was prepared to speak so openly with Danny and me within earshot could only mean one thing: we would never live to tell anyone what we had heard.

'You fucking murdering bastard!' cried Danny. 'My father was just a poor wee man who happened to be in the same bar!'

Kyle, still prowling bear-like, sprang to deliver a vicious blow to the side of Danny's head. He gripped Danny's throat. 'Shut your fucking bog-face.'

Danny made a low groaning noise as he was struck again.

Instinctively, I made a move to help him but the men at my rear pressed two heavy hands down onto my shoulders. As one of them put a gun to my head the other took hold of a wrist and forced it up my back until I cried out in pain. 'Don't move again,' he snarled.

Parkinson's jowls rippled contemptuously. He said to Urban, 'As regards the concern you voiced to me earlier, I can tell you that I have just received notice of a confirmed sighting of Martin McGrady in

Belfast at eight-thirty this evening. I have yet to receive a report about exactly where he had disappeared to, but I doubt if he was ever near here.'

Urban frowned pensively and then extinguished the faint glimmer of hope I had retained. 'Well,' he said to me, 'it looks as though no cavalry will be arriving for you men after all.'

Parkinson said, 'Nevertheless, we will not take the actions of these two at face-value. That the Irishman traced your whereabouts may indicate that our business may well have been compromised. Dispose of these two and we will discuss measures, including your personal safety and what to do with the consignment, in the morning.'

Urban looked towards Kyle and gave a nod.

'Say your fucking Hail Marys, Taig!' he roared.

No, not now, not so quick, I thought. Give us some time.

Urban held out Danny's gun and said to Kyle, 'Use this one.'

My spine stiffened and my jaws became welded together. I was not prepared. Breath would not stay in my body and I felt everything inside of me begin to quake.

Powerful fingers dug into the flesh on my shoulders, a hand pushed my head towards the floor, my other arm was forced up my back. I felt the blood begin to pulse through every vein, my eyes bulged as I tried to take in Kyle walking towards Danny. Wet wind started to escape from me, I forced my jaws to move. 'Danny! Be brave, man,' I cried out. 'They never beat us!'

He didn't respond to me. He was pulling against the two men who were restraining him. 'Danny!' I screamed. I wanted him to look at me, so the face of a friend would be the last thing he would see. But he was fixed on Kyle, whose eyes were narrow and murderous. The veins on Danny's neck stood out as he shouted, 'Shoot me then, you black-hearted bastard!'

'Danny! Look at me!'

Something - my heightened senses, maybe - made me force my head back to look towards Urban and Parkinson. Their eyes shone with a perverse anticipation.

'Come on ahead and shoot me!' roared Danny.

Their lips made nervous smiles.

'Come on ahead, you Orange bastard! Shoot me and I'll see you in hell, McAllister...'

Kyle growled a sort of laugh as I heard him prepare the gun for firing. Urban and Parkinson tightened their lips.

'...but not before I'll see your wife and kids down there first!'

Their mouths twitched. Urban's eyes instantly betrayed concern: he knew something was wrong.

Shots rang out. I looked for Danny while screaming out his name. Another shot, another flash of flame. I saw smoke. Two more shots. I heard a sound like the dull cracking of a skull. Something like chicken's liver splashed onto the floor in front of me; the weight fell from my shoulders; someone was falling behind me. Danny was on his feet, I couldn't figure out how, but he had a gun in his hand. He levelled the gun at Urban and then swung it at Parkinson. The chauffeur made a charge for him and a shot rang out and the driver crumpled to the floor. Danny blinked. I saw the flame of another shot but I didn't hear the sound. Urban was on the floor, blood spurting from one of his legs. I could see Danny's chest heaving as he took in vast gulps of air. 'McAllister,' he gasped. 'Cover that bastard.'

Still on my knees, I could hardly take it in. Now Kyle was standing over Urban, his head tilted forward, legs bent slightly, his two hands holding a gun trained on Urban's head.

Parkinson was standing frozen with fear; like me, he could hardly comprehend what had just occurred. Danny called out to him, 'Philip Parkinson, you have been tried in your absence and found guilty of war crimes against the nationalist people of Ireland.'

'Quit the Fenian shite!' yelled Kyle.

Danny continued, 'You are hereby sentenced to a roaring death.'

A shot rang out. At first, Parkinson didn't move except to merely look down at the hole in his coat. He looked up to Danny and frowned as if to ask: What have you done? He made a slow silent descent before hitting the floor with a thud. Danny was over him. 'I wanted to hear you roar, you bastard.' Parkinson raised his head before it fell back and twisted in my direction. The blind stare of a dead man fell on me as thick black-red blood spewed from his lips.

'Don't expect me to beg,' called Urban. 'I have no fear of death, you pathetic bastard!'

'Pathetic, am I?' said Danny. He shoved Kyle to one side. 'Well, for a fella who's pathetic I'm not doing so bad. Six of your men dead and I ain't. Funny kind of pathetic, you murdering bastard.'

'Fuck's sake, get on with it,' snarled Kyle, 'or I'll do it for ye.'

'Keep out of this, McAllister.'

'Do the dangerous cunt right now.'

Danny waved his gun and said, 'Go watch the door.' Above the thunder of the boiler's burner he called out, 'Robbie, get you the black bag. Get it and bring it over here.'

Still kneeling, I looked in vain for the black holdall. 'In the corner,' he yelled, before I managed to restore movement to my legs. I stepped over the corpses and took the bag to Danny. 'Set it for fifteen minutes, you know the score,' he said.

Without thinking, I opened the holdall and twisted the timer as far as it would turn and then moved it clockwise until it was at the fifteen minutes setting. Before joining the bare ends of the cables which ran from the battery to the contact arm I removed the protective sleeving and made a final check that the fixed contact was clear of any obstruction and there was no chaffing of the wires' insulation which could result in a premature detonation.

'Come on, Robbie,' hissed Danny.

Everything was fine. I twisted the copper strands together. The bomb was now armed. I straightened up and said, 'It's set.'

I looked down at Urban; he seemed almost serene despite the pool of blood that had appeared around his legs. 'I have no regrets,' he said to me. 'The man who ordered the death of your friends is still using her, he never lets go.' He looked to Danny and said, 'I'm ready.'

'Are we ready to roll?' Danny called out to Kyle.

Kyle came close. 'If you don't finish him now, I will.'

'This is for Hughie Maguire, a decent and much loved man, and for all the lives you have destroyed,' hissed Danny.

Urban made a small nod; whether it was in acknowledgement of what he had done or just a signal to Danny to get on with it, I'll never know. When the shots came a jolt went through me. As if in slow motion, I saw the bullets rip into his torso which twisted and arched before it came to rest with an irrevocable stillness.

Danny lowered the gun. Taking one last look at Urban he said, 'Robbie, lead the way and get us the fuck out.'

Running feet and a barking dog were closing in as we slipped through the hole in the chain-link fence. I was grateful for the cover which the fog provided; although it made finding the car a little harder. 'You drive,' Danny said to me as he sank into the back. The car swayed as Kyle threw himself onto the front seat. With one turn of the key the engine fired up, I put my right foot to the floor and we sped away.

'Lights!' shouted Danny.

Once the headlights hit the wall of fog in front of us I asked Danny where we were going. 'To the motorway and we head north.'

I steered the car through noiseless, misty streets. At first our progress was slow but the fog had thinned by the time we reached the outskirts of the city.

The three of us were content with the silence apart from the even hum of the engine as we travelled. At times I felt numb, as if I had entered a dream-world. Reality only crashed in on me when Danny told me to stop at the next service station so he could buy some petrol and a few cans of soft drink. I watched him enter a shop adjacent to the petrol pumps and for some strange reason Mr Robinson and his joy of life came to mind. I mulled over what experiences he must have endured because as he once said, 'It is only because of death can one truly appreciate life.' Amen to that.

A cold can was thrust into my hand and Danny said, 'Right, let's get a move on!'

For another hour a chain of crazy thoughts flickered through my mind as we chased the stream of orange lights which wound its way into the distance ahead of us.

Kyle growled abruptly, 'Take the next exit.'

I moved onto the slip-road and he told me to make a left turn at the traffic island and then stop at the first telephone box we came to. We headed into the countryside along a road hemmed in by flat fields and sparse trees.

'Will this one do?' I asked.

'I'll check to see if it works first,' he answered.

He walked to the kiosk, lifted the receiver and then came back to the car. A hand rested on the car's roof as he bent down and put his head inside. 'It's fine,' he said to Danny. 'This will do me here.'

'Right,' said Danny.

'Things had better be right by the time I'm home,' said Kyle. He turned his head and glowered in my direction and then slammed the door shut before I could thank him for saving my life.

'Turn the car and head back to the motorway,' said Danny.

I turned the car and drove back the way we had come. 'I didn't get the chance to thank him,' I said regretfully.

'For what? Christ, Robbie, you'll have to travel some way to meet a more evil bastard than that one.'

'But he was on your side all along, wasn't he?'

In the mirror I saw Danny glancing back at the road as the kiosk disappeared from view. 'Take the next turn and stop the car,' he said, 'and then I'll give you the whole story.'

Something in his voice had me gripping the wheel tightly as I said, 'It's all over, though, ain't it, Danny?'

He grimaced and then replied, 'I hope I'm wrong, Robbie, but I think there's a wee bit left to do.'

Epilogue

WHEN I WAS younger, when my body was harder and my energy seemingly inexhaustible, Bubby, my coach, would often urge me on for 'one last round'. I would take in great gulps of air and give him what he had asked for, but on returning to my corner he rarely offered gratitude; more often than not he would start to massage my arms and beseech me to go again for 'just' three more minutes.

My mind told me to refuse him; every sinew in my body was brimming with lactic acid and screaming for mercy. But despite a fatigue that almost made me vomit, when the bell rang my shaking legs never failed to somehow get me to the centre of the ring. Bubby had stretched me mentally and physically, he made me extend the boundaries of what I considered possible, he had helped make the man I had become.

Danny, whose face looked as though he'd been on the wrong end of a one-sided fight with Sonny Liston, had asked me for one more round, possibly another round of killing.

I now understood how soldiers' minds remained intact in the aftermath of war, I understood the resignation Urban had exhibited before he was killed. When death has become so commonplace, it can no longer invoke the same intensity of dread or loathing. I had been numbed by the whole affair in the boiler-house and felt only slightly sickened by it.

For a little longer I would tell my heart to remain like a stone, I would tell my mind to keep out any thought of Nathan and the life we still could have together. From somewhere deep inside I would have to dredge up whatever meagre reserves remained in my body so I could stay strong until Danny finally told me it was over, that the killing was at an end.

We had waited in the car for almost three cold and tortuous hours. If Danny was right about Kyle McAllister, it would not be long before someone would arrive to pick him up. And if Martin McGrady had been correct in his suspicions, that someone would be an MI5 officer.

'So is he, I mean, *was* he ever on your side?' I asked.

'McAllister?' snorted Danny. 'Cut that fucker's throat and he'd bleed orange all over you, swear to God. Didn't you see the second he was after getting a gun in his hand the bad bastard scented Taig and got carried away with hisself? He would've nutted me, no sweat, if I hadn't shouted out that bit about his wife and weans. Still, even then, I wasn't sure that somewhere in his Neanderthal head he didn't think: Fuck it, what's the lives of my family when I have meself the chance to nut a Taig.'

The hateful lilt in Danny's voice offended me. It made me close my ears to him and listen to the faint distant whispers of traffic speeding along the motorway. I wished we were travelling with them. While we waited at the junction of a narrow lane and the road on which we had left Kyle McAllister, fewer than a dozen vehicles had passed by, and most of them were lorries heading towards the motorway. Across the road from us, over a row of tall coniferous trees, the sky began to draw up the first few rays of watery pink light.

My frozen feet prompted me to grumble out loud, 'Why the ras did he have us drop him all the way out here, miles from anywhere?'

'So fellas like us couldn't easily be watching without him seeing.'

'Rakstone! He can't still be in the phone box, it's too cold. We could be sittin here like idyat an' he might have rang a taxi an' pissed off an' garn in the other direction.'

'He might, then again he mightn't. He's probably hid hisself somewhere so he can keep an eye on who's coming down the road.'

'What if the car pickin him up comes from the other way?'

'There's little chance of the man not using the motorway.'

'What if the car we follow back to the phone box is the wrong one? McAllister will see us.'

'I'll take care of him,' he said, patting the Browning 9 mm.

'Whatever happens, the only way that bad fucker is going home is in a box.'

Close to the limit of my endurance, I growled, 'Then why don't we go down to the phone now an' find him, an' then you do what you have to?'

He heard my impatience and said quietly, 'Just a few more minutes, Robbie. A certain man has had a lot of people dancing to his wee tune. But things aren't after turning out as he had planned. There is just a chance that he will come to Kyle in a panic to find out what has happened face to face. We'll know in the next few minutes. I reckon the man won't have been more than three hours away. Stay strong for me for a wee bit longer, eh? When the man comes it will all be over.'

I knew that Danny would stay strong for as long as it took. War had finally claimed my friend, it had hollowed him out and left only a shell of the man I had known. I had once thought of Danny as open-minded, as a man of wide interests and knowledge. But the conflict in Ireland had cut into his spirit, pared down that expansive mind into something more narrow and dark.

Danny had once accused me of being at war with society - and he had been right. I understood his present mind-set: everything and possibly everyone, including himself, was now considered as expendable.

Killing Urban had not healed Danny. Maybe he had lain awake at night imagining the moment he would shoot his father's killer, and believing that at that moment, the anguish which had pierced his heart would instantly vanish. But the more Danny had found out about the machinations which lay behind the slaying in a Belfast bar, the more embittered he became. He probably was not yet aware of it, but killing Urban a thousand times over would not have been enough to heal or satisfy him. Revenge is rarely substantial enough to fill the emptiness for more than a few fleeting seconds.

In order to find some thread of reason for why I had allowed myself to become involved with Danny I said to him, 'I don't wanna hear no more shit. Just tell me why the fuck we're sittin here an' how come you can't be satisfied with killin the guy who killed your old man.'

He again told me of the motives which lay behind the murder of his father. It was part of Danny's bitter mantra, the fuel for his rage, his justification.

'I don't want that shit again!' I snapped. 'Tell me the *real* reason you came back to England.'

He chewed the tip of his thumb for a moment before he began to talk to me in a low, serious tone.

He told me of the men who described themselves as 'Friends of the Union' and how they had decided that a new loyalist paramilitary group should be armed and made ready to kill Irish nationalists, and republicans in particular, should there be any resolution which weakened the Union.

Departing from the original scheme to run drugs to the province was Sir Philip Parkinson's first mistake. Although he had many friends and contacts within British Intelligence, there were those within the Security Service who were not prepared to countenance the formation of any new loyalist organization that was beyond their control.

'So how come MI5 didn't just put a stop to Parkinson?' I asked.

'Because he was a man with powerful contacts who had too much shite on the government and plenty of shite on MI5 about stuff like the guns from South Africa that had already armed loyalist death squads.'

Danny went on to explain that information about the arming of a new terrorist gang had come to him via a leading loyalist paramilitary in Belfast who was alarmed at the prospect that his organization was about to be usurped. In a meeting with republicans he put forward the argument that more guns and a city awash with cheap cocaine would not be in the interests of either community, and a plan to stop Parkinson's scheme would only work with republican involvement. Only a handful of people on his side knew of the threatening developments; one of them was his most trusted comrade Kyle McAllister. His reputation would make it easy for him to infiltrate the new hard-line group.

'Now,' said Danny, 'we were happy to go along with the idea of stopping the arms and drugs over here, once McAllister's family were tucked up in a wee house in Donegal until everyone from our side got home safely.'

I was faintly amused by the grim irony of the two warring factions finally finding common ground in the killing that had taken place in my home town.

'So why kill Kyle, man? Crise Almighty, he saved our lives!'

'He saved nothing but his own hide. Martin had an idea that Kyle, never a deep-thinking man, would go behind the backs of his own comrades to his British Intelligence handler and report back everything that was going on. From very early on, Martin guessed that it was MI5 who wanted the drugs and weapons stopped in a manner that showed Parkinson what could happen if he acted independently of them. Martin was certain he was right when we got to hear that it was Urban and his guys who did the the murders in the bar; it was just another tasty bit of information to ensure his interest. It got him thinking that the steady trickle of information that Kyle was providing was a wee bit too good. He knew MI5 would allow us to dismantle Parkinson's supply line before they moved in and either had us arrested or shot by the cops. So he took advantage of the situation. We gave them what they wanted but in such a way that we would end up getting what *we* wanted.'

'So they were following Martin and the young guys back to Belfast, wonderin what the hell was goin on, while you took care of Parkinson and Urban.'

'That's part of Martin's genius,' Danny grinned. 'See, once Kyle was after telling us that Parkinson was in town to personally oversee his consignment leaving for home, Martin realized this was a chance in a million to rid the world of a very bad man.'

'So *that's* why you came to me.'

'Yeah,' he said contritely. 'Now, the young fellas did not lose anyone belonging to them in the bar, not like me and Martin. Not that they didn't volunteer to go into the factory, mind you, but it was decided that Martin and the boys would play the decoy and I would get the pleasure of killing the murdering scum.'

'But you ain't answerin my question, man. Why are we here now? Why are you waitin to kill Kyle and the MI5 guy?'

'That road ahead of us is the road to Baghdad, Robbie. At the end of it is Saddam and his comrades. It's a lesson that the Gulf War taught me: push on that extra mile and kill them all or live to regret you didn't. Who do you think tipped off the Prods in Belfast about Parkinson's consignment in the first place?'

'MI5,' I answered.

'Right.'

'An' it's funny how they couldn't have done the same when Parkinson had Urban and his men murder your dad an' all those guys in the bar.'

'Dead on, Robbie, dead on.'

Danny paused and took in the reddening sky in front of us and I again asked myself what was this strange bond between men that kept me here.

'Kill them all?' I sneered. 'Jesus Christ, you know how crazy that sounds, Danny? So it was you guys who killed Unadkat?'

'The Asian fella? Ach, no. He was one of the main players on the drugs side but it was Kyle and his buddies who killed him to keep him quiet. Urban's men had been buying cocaine off the Campbells in fairly small amounts over a period of months so as not to attract too much attention. Remember that MI5 have their beady eye on big drug shipments nowadays. Unadkat was a wholesale supplier and his main distributor was the Campbell gang. He got a bit too curious about where the cocaine the Campbells was selling was heading to, and like the cat, it was the death of him.'

'The Cervis?' I asked.

'Yeah, we did shoot the Cervis, it was another job paid for by the Campbells. We looked at it as though we were doing the public a service and that when we stiffed the Campbells the cops would then immediately look to what was left of the Cervi gang. Of course, we didn't reckon on the cops hating the Muslims so much that they would allow prejudice to overcome the good reason we had provided.'

'Then what were you doin when I saw you that time at the back of the Rose an' Crown when Tyrone went in with the bomb?'

'That was a few days before the Cervi business. Martin was making out that he wanted to see the Glenroy fella, pretending he wanted to buy cocaine with the money that was to be paid for doing the Italian crowd. Eamon and Kevin were hanging around the front somewhere.'

'Who recognized Tyrone an' knew he was with the Muslim guys?'

'It must have been someone working for the Campbells who recognized the stupid fucker. I was out covering the back, remember?'

I resented Danny calling Tyrone stupid. Perhaps he had been stupid, maybe the panic in his mind had ensured that the bomb would not have exploded, maybe he had been neither clever or brave but in his despair he had only tried to do what Danny and the others had succeeded in doing: killing members of Glenroy Campbell's gang in defence of a community.

There were plenty more questions that I wanted to ask Danny but I didn't want to hear any more of his answers. He had lied and he may well have been lying to me still. But I understood what it is to be driven to the point when lying to a friend becomes the smallest of misdemeanours. I had once lied to Errol; I had distorted the truth and put him onto that road where he would meet his death. Danny's lies and all their consequences for me were only what I deserved.

I remembered back in the flat Danny and Martin's play-acting so I would agree to help Danny get into the factory.

'Ruthless,' I muttered as a rueful chuckle escaped from my lips.

'What's that?'

'Just somethin Brendan once said to me when I was in Belfast.'

'Oh,' he said and fell silent.

I closed my eyes for a moment, trying to make out if there was any one of them not involved in some sort of double-dealing or exploitation. I doubted if either Eamon or Kevin had been allowed to know everything that Martin and Danny had planned between them. Even Urban had schemed to have me kill the MI5 man he had worked with. And of course there was Carmen; double-dealing, double-crossing, conniving Carmen. She had loved me probably from the time I had begun to admire her, but she knew I could never have loved her while Errol was around. While we were together, we had striven to rid ourselves of our memories of him but had failed miserably because of the parts the two of us had played in his death.

'Robbie!' gasped Danny. My eyes sprang open. He was pointing at a car which had sped past. 'That's him, I'd stake my life on it.'

I turned the ignition and put the car into gear. As Danny had told me, the headlights were left off despite the murkiness. He put the second gun, a Colt 45, on top of the dash. 'The safety's on, Robbie,' he said.

'Crise, man, you don't know it's him.'

'Ach, I've seen that car before, when I followed Kyle from his digs one time. It's the one all right. Not too fast, slow down a wee bit. We want him stopped by the phone box, remember.'

There was a turn in the road ahead before the telephone kiosk came into view. We had to wait until we rounded the bend before we would know what our exact course of action would be: if the car was moving off I would have to overtake and try to stop it.

We rounded the turn. Two bright red lights shone out from the rear of the car ahead; it was still stopped by the telephone box.

'Foot down, Rob, put your foot down!'

In the distance I could see the darkened shape of Kyle McAllister about to manoeuvre himself into the front passenger seat. His head had turned on hearing the roar of the engine. 'Christ's sake, Robbie, don't let them take off!'

My heart's pounding matched the quickening revs of the engine as I pushed the accelerator to the floor. Kyle was in the car as I drew level. I hit the brakes, the car skidded much farther than I had reckoned on. The tyres crackled on the grit. Danny was outside. I heard the first shot while I grabbed the Colt which had slid onto the floor of the car. I was out, safety off, instinctively pointing my gun at the driver who was halfway out - he was in the wedge of space between the car and the open door. Danny was to my right, panicking, shouting: 'Robbie, I'm jammed, shoot him!'

The man's eyes were fixed on Danny. As if in slow motion he produced a gun. My mind was spinning, a centrifugal force froze every conscious thought. 'Robbie! Shoot him!'

I barely touched the trigger. The glass in the car door exploded. The man spun and fell to the ground and out of sight. He was still alive, I could hear him writhing and screaming in agony. I followed Danny to him, hardly believing the amount of blood that was spilling out onto the tarmac.

It was all a blur. Beresford Samuels was on the ground, blood oozing from his chest. 'Yes, Errol, you killed him, man! Now give me the gun.'

But it was a lie: Samuels was already dead when I dragged him from the bath and before Errol put three bullets into his chest. It was a lie that persuaded Errol that he had crossed the line, that he was a killer. It was a lie that had convinced him that he should get the Kalashnikovs. It was the lie that would lead to his death and the deaths of Hanimal and Shaka.

Three shots rang out. I looked along my outstretched arm and saw the whispers of smoke at the end of the gun and a man lying dead in the road.

Danny snatched the gun away from me and put another bullet into Kyle as he lay slumped in the car. A moment of nausea came and went. Danny tossed the two guns onto Kyle's body. 'Right,' he said, pointing at the body in the road, 'let's pull him to the other side of the car before anyone sees him.'

We both took hold of the man under his arms. I felt his warmth, the dead weight. A shudder went through me as I heard his heels scraping over the blood on the ground and the feeling of nausea returned.

'Are you okay to drive?' Danny asked, as we hurried to our car. I simply got behind the wheel.

It was bright and late in the morning before Danny said, 'You can stop anywhere around here.'

I pulled into a supermarket car park. We sat in silence for a while and stared out at the shoppers who were blithely oblivious to our presence. What I wouldn't give to be amongst them - but I never had been. I had always left the safety of the herd to go my own way.

'Robbie,' Danny said, fighting to quell the shaking in his throat, 'thanks for sticking by me, mate. I wouldn't have had the bottle for it if you hadn't have been with me.'

Tears began to stream down his swollen face and along the edges of his misshapen mouth. I turned my face away and let him get on with the weeping he had denied himself for almost two years. Listening to the high-pitched howls which seeped through his fingers I thought about the secret wars that are conducted all over the world. Errol and I had been engaged in such a war once, so intense - so private. And there were millions, if not billions, of casualties of the inner conflicts going on at any one time: people turning in on themselves and fighting a private war within the confines of their own minds. I had experienced that too.

I allowed him to continue with his sobbing; it seemed the right thing to do. When he finally stopped he sighed and said, 'Sorry about that, Robbie, I don't know what came over me. That bastard Urban died too quick.'

'Cha, man, don't lie. There ain't no shame in cryin for your dad. An' somethin Urban told me last night makes me think he didn't die too quick.'

Danny nodded slowly as if he had understood. He said, 'Do you know your way back from here?'

I thought: Was there any way back? 'To the motorway?' I said. 'Yeah, I'll find it, no problem.'

'Right then,' he said, gripping my arm. 'We'll meet again some time.'

I looked into his watery eyes and thought that we never would. 'Make sure it's more of a social call, yeah?'

'No sweat. Thanks again, mate. I'll see you later.'

Danny swivelled and got out, then bent down and looked into the car. 'This thing isn't nicked but if I were you I'd leave it somewhere not too near home and catch the train or something.' He threw two twenty-pound notes onto the passenger seat. 'Will that be enough to get you a ticket?'

'Don't worry about it.'

'Right. So *slán abhaile*, Robbie.'

'Later, Danny.'

I watched him disappear into the crowd of shoppers after he had turned for a last time and raised a hand. I recalled how he had saluted me in a similar way outside the cemetery after Errol's burial. Was it that the circle had been joined, that the cycle was finally completed?

It wasn't difficult to find the motorway even though my mind was preoccupied with seeing Nathan again. In truth, I was scared to go back for him.

I switched on the radio just in time for the midday news bulletin. I shuddered on hearing the first item: an explosion had occurred in a factory boiler-house, six fire appliances were in attendance; there was an unconfirmed number of casualties. I didn't take much notice of the other reports as I waited for the news of the discovery of the bodies of Kyle and the Secret Service man. But it was too soon after the event and they did not receive a mention. I reached over to turn off the radio but the final item stilled my hand and had my foot stamping on the brake.

'The fifth victim of Tuesday night's gangland shooting was named by police this morning. He was Timothy Morgan, a boy aged only twelve...'

I heard nothing more of the report because of the nausea which went from my stomach to the back of my throat. I braked, threw open the car door and tried to take in air. It took the sound of blaring car horns to make me drive on.

I stopped the car in a lay-by just before I reached the motorway. The sky had darkened again before I could decide on which direction I should take.

There seemed little choice and I headed for the north instead of south.

I knew I could never go home again.